HITLER WAS LONG DEAD.
WORLD WAR II WAS LONG OVER.
BUT MORE THAN MEMORIES LIVED ON
—TO CONQUER AND TO KILL...

Two brothers, bound together by a past no human
beings should have to remember, and savagely divided
by every question of morality and mission . . . a beautiful, unscrupulous nymphomaniac, who used every
kind of man to feed her appetite and do her bidding
. . . a bitter and cynical Jew who had returned to
Germany to make his fortune among those who had
almost been his murderers . . . an incredibly erotic
stripper who attracted women even more than she did
men . . . an infallible Indian assassin, who merged
the wisdom of the East with the technical knowledge
of the West . . .

. . . all joined in a spider's web of evil that stretched
from the heart of today's Europe to the ancient hatreds
and contemporary intrigues of the Middle East . . .

Also by Johannes Mario Simmel
and published by Popular Library:

THE CAESAR CODE

THE CAIN CONSPIRACY

SIMMEL

Translated from the German by Rosemarie Mays

(Original Title: CAIN '67)

POPULAR LIBRARY • NEW YORK

POPULAR LIBRARY EDITION
November, 1976

Copyright © 1967 by Droemersche Verlagsanstalt Th. Knaur Nachf
English Translation Copyright © 1971 by McGraw-Hill, Inc.

Library of Congress Catalog Card Number: 79-174627

Published by arrangement with McGraw-Hill, Inc.

ISBN 0-445-08535-5

Original title: *Cain '67*

PRINTED IN THE UNITED STATES OF AMERICA

FIRST MOVEMENT

Allegro ma non troppo, un poco maestoso

MY BROTHER WERNER asked the hired killer how he planned to commit the murder.

"In an honorable manner," replied the Indian. "With a Malayan kris. It is sure and swift. One single slash suffices. Always has, up to now."

"Very good," said my brother. They were speaking English.

"Naturally, I have always dealt with people lying in bed or asleep."

"Naturally," said my brother.

"That is the prerequisite," said his hired murderer. "Sleep. Very deep sleep. Those who are drunk make it easy for me. Also for themselves."

"I shall have plenty of whisky available," promised my brother.

"Whisky is excellent," said the man. He was probably not as old as he looked: hollow-cheeked, emaciated, an enraptured expression in his black eyes. His teeth were almost as black. He spat frequently, his saliva red from betel nuts. His physical deterioration and obvious state of exaltation indicated a steady consumption of hashish, probably a considerable amount. A drug peddler in

Cairo's old section had brought my brother and this man together. That had been yesterday and both had agreed on terms. Tonight, at 11 P.M., this fourteenth of December 1966, they were meeting once more near the old milepost at the southernmost point of the river-island Roda. It was a warm night for December in this region, with its generally extreme differences in temperature from day to night. Both men wore light raincoats.

The Indian's voice was thoughful. "Whisky *and* a sleeping draft would be ideal."

"Where could I get sedatives?" asked Werner. He was forty-eight, five years older than I, but despite the age difference our resemblance was extraordinary. Both of us were tall and well-built; brown hair, brown eyes, wide foreheads, narrow noses, generous lips, and prominent jaws.

"I'll be happy to leave you this box," said the hired killer. "The powder inside these small envelopes dissolves quickly and is without taste. It begins to take effect in about ten minutes."

"Very good."

"There are ten envelopes in the box. Use three of them for one bottle of whisky. We want to be quite sure."

"Quite sure," my brother agreed solemnly.

A dark blue sky. Stars shown brilliantly, as though it were August. The river, Cairo, the sails of the feluccas in the old harbor to one side of the island, the sphinx and the pyramids of Gizeh in the desert were green in the spectral light of the moon. The old nilometer, where my brother and his hired executioner stood, was inside a garden. The fragrance of roses, carnations and oleander filled the air. It was a spot for tourists. At night it was usually deserted. Spotlights, hidden from view underneath bushes, cast a golden-yellow glow: a picturesque sight from afar. A light ground fog diffused the green moonlight to the color of watered Pernod.

From the nilometer one could overlook the garden with

6

its palm trees and acacias. The light of the numerous spotlights and the moon made it easy to see anyone approaching. If one did not want to be seen he could hurry down the steps to the quay five paces away from the nilometer. The quay contained many niches and entrances to subterranean canals which, especially at high tide, protected the island. Canals and passageways prevented a flooding of Roda. Surging waters, thus deflected, discharged into quiet, protected bays. At low tide it was an ideal place to hide or for ready escape. A suitable place to talk about murder.

I stood in a niche of the quay, five meters below my brother and the hired assassin.

I had arrived a half-hour or so ahead of them. They had used the Indian's powerful flashlight to check if anyone was about. I wore rubber-soled shoes. They could not have heard me hurry from the niche where I had been waiting to disappear into one of the canal refuges. I waited until they had ended their search; then I had silently returned to my former waiting place. The waves slapped gently against the quay. The air was calm. I heard every word they spoke.

My brother, breathing hard, demanded, "So tell me. When?"

The Indian chuckled. "You're really in a hurry."

I knew my brother was in a hurry. I was even more so. But he did not know that.

The water gauge was more than eleven hundred years old. In the beginning of the eighth century Caliph Suleiman had had it built to ascertain the Nile's water level. I had been in Cairo twice before and had then visited the island of Roda, its canals and passageways. In ancient times land taxes had been based on the height of the water level since the overflow of this river has always been a main source of economic life for Egypt: its water and the amount of flooding control the yield of agricultural produce. A water level of seven meters was cause for panic. At fifteen meters the irrigation canals were opened and, usually about the middle of August, people celebrated their good fortune and prosperity.

The water gauge—obsolete since modern times—was a very large rectangular well. In its center stood an octagonal column with ancient Arabic measures. One side, that facing the river, had been built higher than the other. Both showed cuneiform writing. My brother and his hired killer were leaning against the wall. From time to time the Indian spat red saliva, either into the well or over the wall. His spittle almost reached my feet.

"So tell me, when?" my brother asked anxiously again.

"Not tonight," came the reply. "First I have to make some arrangements."

"Tomorrow?" Werner urged.

"Tomorrow night. All right."

"What time?" Werner was stammering with agitation. "I have to . . . have to make some arrangements too, I have to . . ."

"I'll be there exactly at one A.M. It's late enough yet not too late. If you start drinking at eleven P.M. I can do my work satisfactorily two hours later."

"How will you get into the hotel? And out of it?"

"That really shouldn't interest you," the Indian said insolently and laughed.

"I still want to know, though," insisted my brother, strangely aggressive.

I'd like to know too, I thought.

"You don't want to tell me?"

"Oh, sure." The Indian spat over the wall. "I'll go through the garage of the Imperial."

The Imperial is on the right bank of Nile Corniche, near the Semiramis Bridge leading to Gezireh, the city's largest and northernmost island: Cairo's most exclusive district. The wide avenue in front of the Imperial, reminiscent of the Croisette in Cannes, is framed by palm trees, jacarandas, flamboyants and lotus trees. From the hotel windows facing this way one could see those tropical trees, the Corniche, the pier for the big, glass-roofed excursion boats near Shepheards and Gezireh. Also in view, the villas and grounds of the wealthy, the Gezireh Sporting Club's pool and other play areas, the racetrack, the beautiful Andalusian gardens, the American Hospital, and a picturesque, small palace. The last, a residence of King Farouk, had housed his overwhelming collection of pornographic movies, books, photographs and art objects.

Standing in the niche of the quay, eavesdropping on my brother and his accomplice, I thought: If the Indian should really come at 1 A.M. and everything goes smoothly I shall be able to meet Lillian near King Farouk's palace at 1:30 A.M. I am positive *she* will be there. I shall also have sufficient time to attend to some necessary details. Naturally, there might be complications. I did not want to think of them. I had decided on a plan, the only one open to me.

"Why through the garage?" asked my brother. The fragrant aroma of a cigarette drifted down to me. Werner usually smoked heavily when he was agitated. "The garage is well guarded even at night! I have seen mechanics working there and men washing cars!"

"I know my way around there," said the Indian. "A spiral staircase leads from the garage to a small elevator. Hotel guests use it after they have left their car in the garage. There is also a small door leading to the street."

"I know," said my brother. "A steel door. It's locked at night."

"It won't be tomorrow night." The Indian giggled. "I know one of the car-washers."

"I'm satisfied," said my brother.

So was I.

"My apartment is number . . ." Werner began.

9

The Indian interrupted him impatiently. "Nine-oh-seven. And you gave me a floor plan of it. Anything else?"

"No. I guess that is all then." My brother sounded disconcerted.

"Except for three thousand pounds," said the hired assassin, giggling again.

Werner laughed. I knew the variations of Werner's laughter. This was a frightened laugh, a short laugh. Then there was silence. Suddenly I was afraid too. Was my brother going to change his mind? Perhaps he no longer wanted to hire this murderer? Supposing he would not pay him? Then my last plan would fail. Then . . .

"Forgive me," I heard my brother say. "I completely forgot. Naturally, in a case such as this one has to pay in advance."

"Where is the money, dear friend?" The Indian was brusque.

"Here," answered my brother.

"Thank you, dear friend."

"But . . ."

"But what?"

"But can I reply . . . I mean, once you have the money you could simply disappear. After all, I can hardly go to the police and say: 'Gentlemen, my hired killer didn't do his job.' "

The response was a gurgling laugh. Something glowing hit the water—my brother's cigarette. He immediately lit another.

"I shall be there," said the assassin. "I give you my word. I can't do any more. I told you yesterday that I always insist on being paid in advance. You agreed to that. As you know, something unexpected might happen."

My brother replied nervously, "I . . . I still do."

"This kind of business has to be based on trust," explained the man. "Put the case over here. Open it. Those are three thousand pounds?"

"Yes."

"In small denominations?"

"That's right."

The Indian had stipulated used Egyptian pound notes, of which no two were to have consecutive serial numbers. It must have been difficult for my brother and his friends to obtain those notes at such short notice. The money was worth 28,000 Deutsche marks or seven·thousand American dollars.

"I'll check the bills later. If any of them should be counterfeit—"

"They are all genuine! All of them!" my brother interrupted hurriedly.

"—then, of course, you cannot count on me."

"I have checked the bills very carefully!" my brother insisted loudly.

The man said, "You leave now. I'll follow in ten minutes."

"Good-by," Werner said. His voice shook. He was obviously very agitated. So was I.

"We shall probably never meet again, my friend," said the Indian, giggling.

My brother walked away in silence.

His hired executioner waited the allotted time, then left.

It was another ten minutes before I also left. The ground fog above the flowerbeds and lawns created the illusion of walking up to my knees in fluorescent green cotton wool. I met no one on the island of the El-Malik-es-Salih Bridge.

It was two kilometers to the mainland, yet it seemed to stretch into twenty. I suddenly felt apprehensive. Then I thought that my brother would be dead in a little over a day, provided everything went as planned. I admonished myself not to think of any problems which might arise but rather of the prospect that my brother definitely would be dead tomorrow night. Soon I felt much better.

When we were children my brother and I had had a

nursemaid. Our parents were divorced. Since our father had been the guilty party, we lived with our mother, who was editor of a morning newspaper—then an unusual profession for a woman. My brother, older and more robust than I, did not need this nursemaid as much as I did. I loved our old Sophie.

Whenever I awakened screaming from a nightmare or had cried frightened during the day, which happened frequently, Sophie had always been there to calm my fears. She had held me, stroked my head with her work-worn hands and, in her hard Silesian dialect, had told me, "Think of something beautiful. Think of angels." Miraculously, my fears had always lessened.

Hurrying through the fog I seemed to hear Sophie's voice again: "Just think of something beautiful and you won't be afraid."

The best thing I could think of this December night was, My brother will have been murdered in twenty-five hours.

One minute after 1 A.M. on December 16, 1966, the doors of suite 907 in the Hotel Imperial opened slowly and almost soundlessly. The heavy linen drapes were drawn in all rooms. I waited behind the opened bathroom door adjoining the bedroom.

The entrance doors closed with a gentle click. I heard giggling and knew that the hired killer had come on time. Quickly and silently he entered the salon. I saw the bright beam of a flashlight reflecting in the bathroom mirror and, a moment later, the Indian in a dark, high-buttoned coat, his face pale, jaws moving from side to side, eyes glittering. He seems to work best when he is high, I thought, but when I saw him trip playfully around the room, flashing his light here and there, I released the safety catch of the .38 Police Special in my gun hand, my left. A ten-inch silencer and six clips of ammunition came with the pistol I had bought the day before in a

12

dirty, narrow street near the Ibn-Tulun-Mosque. The .38 gave me a most welcome reassurance while watching the assassin's antics. After all, I didn't know what an addict might do. Too, it was possible that my brother might awaken, in spite of whisky and sleeping powder. I certainly didn't know if the hired killer would not look around the entire hotel suite—including the bathroom and behind its door. All I did know was that I had to be out of Egypt before daybreak.

The Indian giggled when, in the light of the flashlight, he saw the coffee table in the room: a confusion of ashtrays, empty cigarette packages, glasses, several bottles of whisky and soda, an icebucket.

He made his way to the bedroom. The light beam flashed around the room until it came to rest on my brother in bed. Standing on tiptoe looking in the mirror I could view the scene very clearly. His clothing lay neatly on a chair nearby. I, myself, had undressed him and clad him in yellow pajamas.

The Indian, pleased by what he saw, giggled again. With hands that wore black gloves, he reached into his coat and withdrew the ridged serpentine blade of a Malayan kris. With the flashlight suspended from a button of his coat, he quickly pulled up the bedcover to protect himself and slashed my brother's throat. Blood spurted onto the bed and everything near it. He cackled elatedly, wiped the dagger on the cover and hurried out. A moment later I heard the doors close quietly. I glanced at my watch. It was a few minutes after one o'clock.

I stepped into the bedroom and turned on the light. I switched it off quickly. A quick look at that bloody sight was enough. Werner's face was very pale and wore a satisfied expression. One slash had really been sufficient. The Indian had been worth the money.

In the salon I slipped into my blue camel's-hair coat. The pistol with its silencer was too bulky to fit into my pocket. I separated them, slipped the .38 into a shoulder holster and the silencer into my left trouserpocket.

Two bottles of whisky, one of them unopened, stood on the table. I pulled out the box of sleeping powder the Indian had given to my brother the night before. My brother had already emptied three of the powders into the opened bottle, and I had witnessed the effectiveness of only one drink. I did not want to kill my waiting victim, but insensibility was an immediate requirement.

Time was of the essence. The Lufthansa flight I had booked as soon as I had been sure of the time the hired killer was to come was scheduled to leave at 4:40 A.M. from New-Heliopolis. But it was a twenty-five-kilometer drive to Cairo's International Airport and much remained to be done. It was imperative for me to make that plane since I had a connecting flight in Rome for Zurich.

I had a sizable account at a Swiss bank. To close it suddenly, to have the account—most of it in long-term investments—transferred to Buenos Aires, it was necessary for me to be at the bank to sign various documents. A SwissAir flight left Zurich for Buenos Aires at midday. I was confident I would be able to get a seat since intercontinental flights were rarely filled to capacity. I had valid visas for Egypt and Argentina and two international vaccination certificates. For political offenses such as I might be charged with, Egypt and Argentina did not extradite.

Only this Lufthansa plane left Cairo early enough for me to leave the country. It was my guess that my murdered brother would be discovered at the latest by 9:30 A.M. He was usually called at nine o'clock. The hotel staff would check once he did not answer. The next plane would leave until shortly before noon. Much too late for me.

I opened one of the envelopes containing the sedative. Then, suddenly, I realized the danger of not knowing the exact effect of the drug. Would anyone to whom it was administered with whisky regain consciousness?

No. No. No. I could not risk that. I had to knock a person out quickly, but I could not risk a possible death. That might happen if I used whisky *and* this powder. Instead, I took the unopened bottle of whisky, broke its seal for quick use later on and put it in my coatpocket. I left the suite and locked the door. To get out of the hotel unobserved I planned to use the elevator leading to the garage in the rear. The brightly lit hotel corridors seemed endless as I hurried along. Still, so far everything had gone well; why should anything happen now?

Suddenly I heard voices, laughter, music. A party in one of the suites. A few meters ahead of me a door was flung open and out staggered a young girl in a shimmering silver cocktail dress. The door closed behind her. She was tall, almost as tall as I, auburn hair falling about her shoulders, lavender-blue eyes. Very beautiful, and apparently intoxicated. A night of whisky, I thought. My dear brother full of whisky. Whisky in my coatpocket. This lovely girl drunk on whisky. Yet I smelled only a trace of it on her breath as she suddenly fell against me. She had the fragrance of perfume, youth and vibrant skin.

My blue camel's-hair coat had no buttons, only a wide belt. The coat was open. The girl threw her arms around me, pressing her body hard against me, nearly choking me as she got her tongue deep into my mouth. Then she withdrew her tongue, babbling in English, "Now I've finally caught you. You're not going to get away again. You're going to do it now. You promised. You said you would. Come on, do it now!"

I had never seen this girl before and had no idea who she was. She did not appear to be a common whore. Her jewelry was expensive. "Well, are you going to do it or not?" she asked wildly in a loud voice, rubbing her body against me. She took my hands and pressed them against her breasts. The nipples were large and hard.

"Well?"

"All right," I answered quickly, "sure I'll do it, sweetie, of course!"

Her eyes became hazy. She must have mistaken me for someone else, or else this young lady was terribly drunk. Whatever the reason, I had to get away quickly.

"Come," I said.

"Where to?" She did not move. If someone were to step out of that suite . . .

"My room."

"You just want to fool me and disappear again. You're not going to do that to me twice!" With that she seized the narrow lapels of my coat with drunken strength; she pulled so violently that the right one tore half off. I wanted to hit her.

"Are you crazy?" I hissed, furious.

"I'm sorry, I really am. I'll buy you another coat after you've—"

"Here? In the hallway?"

"Yes. Here in the hallway. You don't want to? You want me to scream?" She opened her mouth but this time I stuck my tongue into it and pressed her to me. She began to moan, suddenly broke a little away from me and grabbed at my trousers.

"Oh," she said, becoming as pale as my brother now was, "oh, God. Oh, darling, darling, darling! It that you?"

"Yes," I said, hoping fervently she would not investigate more thoroughly and discover that it was the silencer of the .38 that had enraptured her.

"Oh, merciful Father in heaven," she cried. "Oh, Mary, Mother of God, is that the truth? Is that really you?"

"Yes," I said, breaking out in a sweat.

"I'm going to faint for sure and right now if you don't—"

"Then let's go," I said forcefully, pulling her along. I held her hand tightly, she staggered and reeled as we almost ran along the corridor. If someone were to see us now I'd have to act drunk too, I thought. We reached the garage elevator unobserved. It was somewhere below. I pressed the button.

"Where are you taking me?" The beautiful girl was leaning against a wall, gasping for breath.

"To my room, naturally."

The elevator door opened. I pushed my unwanted companion ahead of me, the door closed and I pressed the fourth-floor button.

"Your room is on the fourth floor?"

"Yes."

"Show him to me."

"Soon."

"I want to see him now!"

"We'll be in my room in a moment."

"But—" The elevator stopped on the fourth floor. The door opened; I pushed the girl out with such force that she stumbled and fell. The door closed, I pressed the button for the garage and listened but heard nothing. I was fairly certain she had not been hurt. She had probably passed out and was asleep, lying in that hallway.

My watch showed 1:27 A.M.

The elevator stopped. I reached for the .38 before the door opened. I saw no one. From below I heard voices, hammering and the splashing of water. With a quick move I was at the steel door. The key was in the lock.

This night was cool in Cairo. Low black clouds scurried across the sky; there was a hint of rain; the wind was unpleasantly gusty. I stepped out on the square which was at the rear of the hotel. I determined the direction of the wind with moistened fingers. They were chilled. My plane, coming from the east, would have a tail wind and would be on time. Hopefully.

The square, Midan el-Tahrir, so-called because of the "Tahrir," the liberation monument rising in its center, is impressive. Ten avenues converge here. Ministerial buildings, the American University, and the renowned Egyptian Museum ring the square.

I walked quickly toward the museum, keeping close to the hotel to avoid the bright lights of the modern streetlights which shed their glow widely. Flowers grew in profusion, and fan-shaped fronds and leaves of the sycamores, tamarisks and palm trees were rustling in the wind.

Several people and a few occupied cars were still about together with groups of small boys who seem ceaselessly to hang around each hotel in Cairo.

One of them had spotted me leaving the hotel. He came running. The little Arab could not have been more than twelve years old, yet his face was cynical, with coldly calculating eyes. He grinned as, in broken English, he offered to take me to his sister, only ten years old and still a virgin. I pushed the little rascal as he tried to delay me, cursing with the few Arabic words I knew. Not discouraged, he asked in a barely recognizable French if perhaps I would be interested in his twin sisters, also ten and still virgins. I struck at him, but he nimbly evaded my blow and continued to follow me. I had turned the corner of the museum. Through a side road I had reached the Nile Corniche where the Semiramis Bridge leads to the island of Gezireh, now my destination. The façade of the Imperial was brightly lit; people in evening dress stood in the hotel entrance. Cars drove up and left. More small boys were nearby. Not even the police seemed to be able to deal with them.

The boy followed me across the bridge, illuminated by many candelabra. Now, in almost faultless German, he asked me if I would be interested in his eleven-year-old brother. I tried to kick him; again he avoided me and assured me in fluent German that he, too, would be of service to me, should I so desire.

Since attempted blows and cursing seemed to be of no avail I got hold of him, pulled his ear and was just about to curse him again when a big American car on its way from the island came to a halt near me.

The driver put his head out of the window. His eyes were merry; his blond hair crew-cut.

"Having trouble with that little son-of-a-bitch, Mister?" He spoke cordially in English.

I told him the boy had been annoying me; I was now taking him to the police. The American reached over, grinned and opened the door.

"Okay, Mister. Get that little bastard in here. I'll be glad to help you take him to the cops."

That did it.

The boy tore loose and made for the Corniche at top speed.

"Thanks," I said to the American.

Our eyes met, we smiled. Then he noticed something.

"Hey! What happened to your coat? Did that little bastard do that?"

I looked at the lapel the drunken girl at the Imperial had torn. The incident had already slipped my mind.

"The little bastard, yes." I agreed hurriedly.

"Well, you can't go around like that, Mister!"

"It really doesn't matter."

"Sure it does!" He was already rummaging in the glove compartment of the car. "There's always a lot of stuff—wait, we'll try this." He stepped in front of me.

"Really . . ." I began, but futilely.

"It will only take a moment. We'll have it fixed in no time," said the young American. In his hand was a short piece of thin wire. Grinning disarmingly, he pushed the wire through the inside of the lapel and fastened it in place with a few turns.

We stood very close to each other. Americans are truly the most helpful people in all the world, I thought. To hell with all helpful people. Hurry up!

He surveyed his work with great satisfaction. I thanked him.

"Don't mention it. Can I give you a lift?"

"You are driving in the opposite direction."

"So what? I can turn around." That's all I needed.

"I'd really rather walk. Thanks again."

"Okay." He climbed into his car and drove off. I watched him pass the hotel and disappear from view.

Now I walked quickly. Halfway across the long bridge —the east wind gusted strongly here—I threw the hotel key and the box of sleeping powder into the Nile. Once on the island I waited a moment at the entrance to the Andalusian Gardens. No one was following me. I hurried along the romantically lit palm-lined avenue leading to Ex-King Farouk's palace.

1:52 A.M.

I ran, holding the bottle of whisky in my pocket. Random trails crisscrossed the wooded areas on either side of the avenue. The paths were dark. I knew where Lillian was waiting and circled through brush and undergrowth until I saw a black Mercedes, its lights off. I took the .38 from the holster, wound a handkerchief around its butt and crept toward the car. The heavy wind muffled any noise I might make. Once I had reached the left car door I slowly raised my head until I saw Lillian in the right front seat, staring fixedly at the avenue. She was waiting—according to plan. Lillian wore a leopard coat. She had long hair black as her long-lashed eyes, prominent cheekbones, a sensual, wide mouth. I very well knew that she was the only woman I had ever loved— totally and exclusively—and would continue to love. My love for her was more ardent now than ever before as I straightened up and tore open the car door. She turned her head with a startled, suppressed cry. In the darkness I slid behind the wheel. Anxiously she said, "Thank God, dearest. Everything went well then. I was becoming—" I brought the butt of the .38 down on her head, not too hard but hard enough to stop her from screaming or scratching my face. The force of the blow threw her forward. She groaned loudly. I dropped the gun, pulled her head back by her hair and hit her chin with my clenched fist. I pinned her down with my body while I managed to pull out the bottle of whisky and open it. With thumb and index finger I compressed her nostrils. Her body arched and when she gasped for air I forced the mouth of the bottle between her lips, kneeling on the seat between her splayed legs. The leopard coat opened, her green wool dress tore as she writhed and jerked in an effort to free herself. The glass jarred against her teeth, whisky splashed down her throat, spilled down her chin, soaked her clothes and mine. Though she choked and sputtered in her need for air, she gulped the liquor. Suddenly she slumped. Quickly I withdrew the bottle. I watched her gasping greedily, inhaling through open mouth, her face distorted. It recalled that very first time she had been in my arms, panting, her face tortured when she reached her climax. It seemed ages ago. That expression was part of her pattern; each time her ecstasy had brought on a look of exquisite torment.

She straightened up a little. Immediately I pulled back her head and raised the bottle. She coughed and groaned and once again I held her nostrils and thrust the bottle between her lips. She struggled, but her strength was ebbing. I became alarmed. One bottle might not be enough. Suddenly she slumped against the car window. I slid behind the wheel, dropped the now empty bottle and grabbed the .38.

Lillian's eyes were open but I could see only the whites. She babbled. Her makeup was smudged, her hair in disarray, her coat and torn dress stained. Ghostlike, I heard music; violins, drums, a wailing, sad trumpet. I recognized Lillian's and my favorite song. Had the pressure been too great for me? Had I become mad? No, I was not insane. I heard this song because I loved Lillian, only Lillian, loved only her, I told myself—and hit her jaw with the butt of the pistol. She did not stir any more.

No other choice had been open to me without the sleeping powder. In a few hours she, so used to liquor, would awaken. No, no sedatives. This had been the best choice—for her and for me.

I felt her pulse and was reassured. To make her more comfortable I thought I would lay her down, but there was too much baggage in the rear seats to adjust her seat. I strapped on her seatbelt and waited a few minutes just in case she should awaken. The inaudible music, the melancholy voice singing our song, brought back the past. No, no sleeping powder for you, Lillian. You will be all right. I did not kill you. It is said people kill those they love, but I didn't kill you, Lillian.

She did not awaken. Shortly after 2 A.M. I started the car, switched on the lights and drove back to the Semiramis Bridge. If police were to stop us it would be obvious that Lillian was merely drunk. I would say I was taking her home. Her head swayed as I drove. Only drunk. My Lillian was only drunk. The smell of whisky permeated the car, a rental. She had hired it.

The stewardess's voice welcomed us aboard in Italian and English and told us that we would be landing just before 6 P.M. at Rome's Leonardo da Vinci Airport.

The stewardess was a very young, brown-haired, doe-eyed girl. She came from the cockpit, a passenger list in her hand. The entire crew had changed in Cairo.

I was sharing the first-class cabin with two elderly Japanese women in luxurious kimonos and a white-haired Negro minister. I had been the only first-class passenger boarding in Cairo.

The stewardess, bending down slightly, smiled. "Herr Peter Horneck?"

"You guessed right!"

"Oh, that was not difficult. You were the only German boarding at Cairo, you know. You are German, aren't you?"

"Yes, I am."

"Is there anything I can do for you, Herr Horneck?" She was redolent of soap and perfume. "Some coffee? Tea? Milk?"

"Perhaps a little later."

"Would you like something to read?"

"No, thank you," I replied, indicating the newspaper I had placed on a dark-blue grip on the seat adjoining mine. "I have something to read."

She nodded, smiled and walked away. I opened the *Stuttgarter Allgemeine Zeitung* which was to identify me to the man from the international news agency, Associated Press Service. Two days ago I had called its Cairo branch office privately. A woman's voice answered. She had instructed me to buy this particular newspaper, available at the Hotel Imperial.

"Is is impossible for us to accept the material from you in Egypt," the voice told me.

"I see. In the plane?"

"In the plane. Our man will be aboard if you will let us know in advance which plane you will be taking. Our man's identification will be your copy of the score of Beethoven's Ninth Symphony."

"My score?"

"The same you were given by that illustrious party. That's right."

"But . . . but how did *you* get that?" I asked, nonplussed. "I left it with—"

"With your friend Boris Minski in Frankfurt."

"But then—"

"Your friend Minski gave it to Homer Barlow when he heard of your predicament, and he in turn sent it to us. Barlow thought that it would be sufficient identification for our man, who will carry it."

Boris Minski and Homer Barlow!

Hearing their names comforted me. I was not alone— that had been my first thought. *Not alone.*

The telephone conversation had inspired me with courage and I had resolved to fight. And I had fought. Successfully. My copy would be readily recognizable: a rare, leatherbound volume of the first edition of 1824, its title page dedicating the work to His Majesty King Frederick William II of Prussia. It had another characteristic which would confirm that it was the one I had left with Boris Minski: a printer's error. Beethoven had used Schiller's "Ode to Joy," and the final chorus of the fourth movement ran:

> O Joy, thou spark from flame immortal,
> Daughter of Elysium.
> Drunk with fire O heav'n born goddess
> We invade thy halidom.
> Let thy magic bring together
> All whom earthbound laws divide;
> All mankind shall be as brothers
> 'Neath thy tender wings and wide.

When this edition had been printed, in the second verse of the chorale the line "All mankind shall be as brothers" had been omitted. I could easily check when the man from APS contacted me. Once he had taken possession of the blue grip I would have reached my objective. Or at least be very close to it.

The world would then hear what might have remained a secret. It would mean that *I*, for once, was the victor— not my brother. His death alone did not mean I had won. That my accursed brother—not I—had finally lost in our fratricidal struggle would not be established until the news service had reported what had occurred. But I was still waiting for the man from APS. The Japanese women were asleep, heads touching. The Negro minister soundlessly moved his lips as he read his prayer book. I rested my arms on the sides of my chair and began to read my newspaper.

THE CAIN CONSPIRACY

The newly elected German chancellor's address to the nation. CDU, CSU and SPD had formed a coalition government. When the concatenation I'm reporting on here reached its climacteric, Germany had just concluded the provincial elections in Bavaria. Her National Democratic Party, the NPD, had easily exceeded the five percent legal requirement and had won fifteen seats. They already held seats in Hesse. I recalled the early morning hours when Boris Minski and I had discussed the elections. We had been in the "Strip," the Frankfurt nightclub we owned. That had been November 22, 1966, just a short time ago.

I realized that the events which had overtaken my brother, Lillian, Minski and me had all occurred within twenty-four days. I clearly remembered the night in our office at the club, the moment I had answered the telephone—the horror, the pain which had flashed through my mind. In seconds all these had summoned up the memory of my past. In those early hours the snowball had begun to roll, had gathered speed, had become the avalanche which had caused so much harm.

Three weeks and three days: they seemed to enclose my life. In a sense that was true. With luck, what would follow meant a rebirth. Too many terrible things had happened in those twenty-four days.

I read on.

KIESINGER PAINTS PRESENT
FINANCIAL SITUATION IN GLOOMY
COLORS—INCREASE IN TAXES
UNAVOIDABLE—THE GERMAN
PEOPLE WILL HAVE TO MAKE
SACRIFICES . . .

Basically the economic picture was one to inspire

25

gloom and fear. Every branch of industry seemed in a desperate situation.

Was this a deliberate attempt to create panic—to induce readier acceptance of unpopular precautionary measures by the government? Or was this really the end of the "German Economic Miracle"?

The latter possibility seemed the true one.

I read all through the dismal news; the rise in living costs, the demands for payments from our allies, the predictions of economic desolation.

The jet engines were whining their shrill cadence. I mused: If this is all really true and will continue so badly, our part of Germany will soon be grateful if Comrade Ulbricht allows our unemployed into his Germany—which does not officially exist because we don't recognize it—to earn their bread there. Supposing Comrade Ulbricht does not permit that—how soon would it be before our relatives on the other side of the wall would send food packages to us?

The thought came that I cannot return to Germany and with all this in the offing it would be madness even to consider it. All I want is to go to Argentina. With my funds in Switzerland, isn't this the most auspicious time to make oneself and one's money safe? Was luck not with me in this instance too?

I thought: I would have loved to have taken you with me, Lillian. But that is impossible.

The memory of Lillian lingered.

I had driven north without interference to the racetrack on the island of Gezireh. Her head swayed, her spasmodic snoring touched and comforted me. With a heavy heart I realized that the time had come to leave this woman I loved so utterly and completely, had to leave her forever.

I was familiar with the racetrack area. Apart from the stables and the caretaker's small house stood a large

26

barn. The racetrack workers did not live on the island;
the horses were not fed until 6 A.M. I drove the Mercedes
close to the barn, turned off the engine and the lights.
The streetlamps from the wide avenue gave sufficient
light for me to see.

I took a heavy towrope and a blanket from the trunk
compartment. A primitive wooden crossbar secured the
barn door, the warm interior smelled of hay. I threw the
blanket and rope on a heap of straw and returned to Lillian. Carrying her from the Mercedes to the barn exhausted me. I had to rest for a few moments after I had
placed Lillian's inert body on the blanket. Her breathing
came evenly and quietly. She was deep in her alcoholic
sleep.

I bound Lillian's ankles with the rope, turned her
over and tied her wrists behind her back. When she
awakened she would not be able to untie the knots but
she could call for help. The caretaker was bound to find
her soon. I covered her with the blanket, lifted her head,
which showed a bruise but no blood where I had hit her
with the .38, pulled up the large collar of her leopard
coat and gently rested her head on it. For a moment I
listened to her breathing; then I left the barn quickly. I
replaced the crossbar and hurried to the car, then drove
back across the Semiramis Bridge to the Nile Corniche.
I had to get to the railroad station. By now the time
was a quarter to three.

SUIT AGAINST "SPIEGEL" DISMISSED

My eyes were fixed on the headline in the *Stuttgarter
Allgemeine Zeitung*. Slowly I understood its meaning;
gradually the memory of my parting from Lillian faded.
I glanced around the cabin. The Japanese ladies were
fast asleep, the minister still reading.

I had to wait, wait for the man from APS, had to hold
up my paper, had to continue reading.

THE CAIN CONSPIRACY

"SUIT AGAINST 'SPIEGEL' DISMISSED." The National Democratic Party had sued the magazine because it had called the NPD a repository of former Nazis. According to the judgment of the court the *Spiegel* article had been justified.

The newspaper editorial asserted that the NPD had little reason to complain. It listed names of men who had been Nazi party members. The list of names was lengthy.

I began to count the many former National Socialists who had been in important posts in Adenauer's and Ehrhard's administration and were now in the new coalition government. I recalled many well-known names. Then I stopped counting to think better about the errors of all that had been expressed by antifascists or foreigners about National Socialism—as well as by those who believed that they had to explain or excuse its formation and development. They simply had not known. National Socialism had been a genuine internal national movement, the most sweeping that the Germans had experienced. At the time I had not understood that either. Now I knew. It had been to us a true, a pertinent movement, one that persisted despite a lost war, the misery of a divided country, the chaos and hunger of the years after 1945. Any temporary crisis would simply serve to invigorate it.

The world seemed to perceive that too; many were apprehensive—but many others imitated our form of fascism. In many other countries—not only in Germany—prominent German Nazis lived respected, admired, successful. And in Buenos Aires too, where I was now going.

A Jewish banker, born in Holland, had fled from the Germans to Buenos Aires. There, after many years of hardship, he had attained great wealth, annually visited Europe, always came to Frankfurt to transact business. I had been introduced to him at a party. He had been almost rhapsodic about Argentina and Buenos Aires, particularly about the German colony there.

"Charming people," he had told me. "My wife and I have many good and dear German friends. I have heard what you are doing here in Frankfurt. Young man—is that a profession for someone like you? I've heard what you used to do. I know about you. All right, so there is nothing else for you to do here. Then why don't you come to us—come to Buenos Aires. You will find many opportunities there—many!"

Well, now I was on my way. And I was counting strongly on this banker to introduce me to his many friends in the German colony. My countrymen were awaiting me in a foreign land and I would never have to suffer from homesickness. The thought amused me and with glee I remembered Cairo's railroad station. I had parked the black Mercedes there at 3:15.

I hurried through the large hall of the station toward the long row of stacked steel lockers, each large enough to hold a small suitcase. A five-piaster piece would pay for a full day's storage; after that, the owner of the article stored could obtain it from the station baggage department.

My brother had deposited the blue grip in one of the lockers upon his arrival in New-Heliopolis. It had been imperative to ensure the safety of the material. Many things could have happened even between the airport and the railroad station. But nothing happened. I'm certain that my brother breathed a sigh of relief once he heard the lock close.

Here the details of my story become grotesque: my brother, arrogant and boastful, confided its location to me while we were drinking in suite 907 in the Hotel Imperial only an hour before his violent death. Up to then I had not known its whereabouts. I had had to play a game of chance—with my life. And I had involved the

Associated Press Service, as I had already promised them the material, had already told them on which flight I would be to deliver it.

I had adroitly provoked my brother shortly before his murder. He had been quite drunk by then while I had feigned drunkenness. Werner had been so confident. He had even showed me the locker key.

He laughed and scornfully told me how it had amused him to watch my many attempts to find out where the grip was.

"You couldn't find that out, little brother," my brother had bellowed. "Impossible, utterly impossible! I never went back to the station. Friends . . . hic . . . friends of mine put money in the locker. Have to have a good head on your shoulders, you know. Not everybody can have one. Well, don't let it worry you."

One hour later what he had was a head loosely attached to his shoulders. By then I had the locker key.

I had opened the compartment and removed the blue grip. I had hurried back to the Mercedes, left the city, driven about five kilometers along the road to New-Heliopolis, then stopped at a eucalyptus grove. The wind whistled and whined.

The blue bag contained a small, efficient tape recorder of the type used by reporters, and eight four-track tapes in red cassettes. Tihs was my property. I had recorded the events leading to the crime I had been involved in. I opened the tape recorder and quickly checked each tape. I had to know if my brother, to whom I had given the blue bag and its contents before we came to Egypt, had erased the tapes. They were intact. Werner, I thought, must certainly have had plans for them. Whoever possessed these tapes held the key to great power.

I had returned the recorder and tapes to the grip. Then I threw the shoulder holster into the grove of trees and drove away. The road was very dark and deserted. After I had driven about three kilometers, I flung the silencer into a river; a little later I dropped the pistol into a cistern near the roadside. At random, while driving, I had hurled the ammunition clips out of the window into the fields. The locker key had remained in its compartment.

I did not desire power; I wanted to go to Argentina, I wanted safety, a new beginning in a new country—but for once I wanted to prevail over my brother Werner. That was the reason why I had offered the tapes to the Associated Press Service.

Naturally they wanted the material, it would create a sensation. They had suggested a way of getting it through customs. Everything had gone well, for here I was, in a Lufthansa plane, the blue bag in my possession, waiting for the man to whom I was to deliver the tapes. Though I was becoming increasingly nervous, I continued to read my identification, the newspaper.

"Go ahead and laugh. You'll find it's not funny," I read. Fritz Thielen, chairman of the NPD, owner of a cement factory in Bremen, had said that in an interview. His deputy, Adolf von Thadden, had added, "The NPD was founded when the time was ripe."

The NPD, I reflected, had been established in 1964. In only two years the party had experienced extraordinary growth, yet that was but the beginning, Thielen and von Thadden had prophesied. I shared their opinion.

The two Japanese women had awakened. Now the Negro minister was asleep. Both women left for the rear of the plane where the washrooms were. The doe-eyed stewardess hurried to and fro and, passing me, asked, "Coffee now?" and I answered, "Yes, please." She disappeared behind the curtain leading to the tourist class, which she left open. I saw that people there too were beginning to stir, stretch, walk around. The aroma of freshly brewed coffee filled the cabin.

I had reached Cairo's airport just after four o'clock. I left the Mercedes in the parking lot, dropped the car keys through the grating of a street drain, then checked in at the ticket counter. After learning that the plane would leave on time I made my way to the hold-baggage department. A few days ago I had deposited a suitcase with clothing—nothing illegal. The customs inspector nodded, satisfied.

Upon my arrival at the airport I had handed the blue grip to a porter waiting for me outside. He wore the number told me by the APS woman when instructing me by telephone. This man was in the confidential employ of the service.

This porter, whose identity I can hardly reveal, arranged for the grip to be placed on the plane without passing through customs. An inspection would have resulted in the impounding of the material and my arrest. The United Arab Republic and the German Bundes Republic had, in fact, broken off diplomatic relations. Conversely, this was of special benefit to certain national groups.

"There we are, Herr Horneck!" The friendly stewardess placed a breakfast tray before me. I turned for another look at the tourist class. Two stewards and two stewardesses were busily serving breakfast there.

"Thank you," I said. "When will we arrive in Rome?"

"On time, Herr Horneck. In about forty minutes." She poured coffee for me and my seat companions. There was an hour's time difference between Cairo and Rome. I adjusted my watch, which then showed five o'clock. We would soon be in Rome. But where was the APS man?

By now I was very nervous. I drank some of the strong coffee, a little food. As I drank I noticed that my hand shook. If something had happened . . .

Thirty more minutes to Rome.

The stewardess collected my tray. Just then I heard raised voices behind me. I turned.

Two men, speaking English, stood in the aisle between tourist and first class. One was a steward, the other, the tall, blond, crew-cut, merry-eyed American who had helped get rid of the Arab boy on the Semiramis Bridge— the man who had repaired my coat. In his hand was a large leatherbound book. I recognized it immediately. My fast-beating heart was evidence of my relief.

"What's the trouble?" I asked the steward in a loud voice.

"This gentleman insists on entering first class. He says he recognized you and—"

"Of course he recognized me! We do know each other," I said. I raised my arm and called out "Hello."

"Hello!" cried the American, and waved the Beethoven score. The steward seemed embarrassed. Both men came toward me.

"You're on this flight too?"

"That's right. I saw you from back there and thought I'd say hello, but the steward told me I was not allowed in first class. Strict German customs."

The steward told him politely, *"International* rules, sir." He addressed me. "I'm sorry but we really have to—but if you are acquainted . . ."

"Besides, we shall be landing soon," interceded the stewardess.

The young American winked at her. "Then I am allowed to talk with my friend until we land? I'm sorry if I've caused any trouble," he said to the steward. "I'm only going as far as Rome. You'll be rid of me in a little while."

"That's quite all right, sir," said the steward. "I apologize. But the rules . . ."

"Of course," conceded the American. "Where would we be without rules? Well, thank you. Thank you very much."

I placed the grip and the newspaper on my knees. The American sat down next to me.

"At last," I said. The minister had gone; the two Japanese women were talking animatedly.

The APS man handed me the score. "Too many damn Egyptians back there. One never knows. I had to wait this long. And I had to go tourist because first class was so empty."

"You've already watched over me in Cairo. . . ."

"Sure!" He grinned. "But cautiously. No fraternizing! I just had to make sure that you got out of the hotel okay. Everything else went smoothly?"

"Yes," I answered. Comforting warmth spread through me as I thought, Luck! I was in luck again. I opened the old score while thinking that it really wasn't necessary to check. Everything was so settled. The American looked at the newspaper while I studied the score mechanically. Fourth movement. There began the vocal part. I glanced at the second verse, ". . . all whom earthbound laws divide . . ." The line "All mankind shall be as brothers" had been omitted from the chorale.

Yes, this was the copy.

"Okay?" asked the American.

"Okay," I agreed. The captain's voice, through the loudspeaker, asked us to fasten seatbelts and to stop smoking. The APS man and I had anticipated his order. I pushed the blue grip toward him.

"Then that's taken care of too," I said.

He grinned.

"Now you feel better, eh?"

"Much," I said and inhaled deeply. The plane suddenly tilted and the cabin lights flickered.

"Here we go," said the man from APS.

We soared through heavy clouds; lights still flickered; my ears hurt in spite of the gum I chewed.

The weather in Rome was dismal. Heavy rainfall, a biting north wind whipping across the landing fields. Darkest night. The many lights of the airport gleamed.

The bus which was to take us to the terminal had come to a halt outside the Boeing. First-class passengers disembarked through the front, the others through the rear exit. As soon as the plane had stopped, the man from the Associated Press Service had picked up my blue bag, patted my shoulder, nodded and hurried back to the tourist class.

Outside, in spite of my camel's-hair coat I suffered from cold as did my fellow passengers. The Japanese women, even though wrapped in fur coats, were shivering. People quickly boarded the bus. Although first-class passengers were the first to enter, I remained outside. I have always suffered from a mild phobia: I feel uneasy in crowds; whenever possible I avoid them. I try always to be the last on a plane. So, once again, in the rain and cold I waited.

The score protected underneath my coat, collar pulled up, I stood and watched. Transport planes of the Italian, American and German air force were lit by floodlights; trucks waited near the open loading hatches; workers, their clothing glistening in the rain, busied themselves with plane freight. I noticed a red cross on some boxes, probably intended for Florence. That city and the Po Valley had suffered the worst deluge in several hundred years. The people in the disaster area were battling hunger, flood, cold, disease, with many facing death. Irreplaceable art treasures had been destroyed.

A sudden gust of wind almost threw me. A gray-haired man seized my arm and pulled me inside the bus. The passengers—I was the last one—were warming their hands, sneezing and shivering. Slowly the bus started on its way to the terminal.

The man who had forced me into the bus now pushed me to one side. He looked at me, searchingly, through narrowed eyes as he drew something from his pocket. It was an identification card bearing his photograph. I read the name: William S. Carpenter, chief of the APS bureau in Rome. I opened my coat slightly to let him see the Beethoven score. He nodded solemnly, leaned toward me and said, "This is not my bus. As soon as it stops I have to get off and catch another one. I have to take an Alitalia flight to Milan."

I stared at him.

"Or I wouldn't have been able to get to you. They only allow passengers out here, right?" He spoke New York English. "Now I can say I made a mistake in the bus and . . ."

"But why are you here at all?"

"Because everything went wrong," he said, grim-faced. "And because I had to inform you immediately."

"What has—?"

"Not so loud!"

"What went wrong? I turned the bag over to your man as it had been arranged!"

"It had been arranged all right," said Carpenter, "but he was not our man."

I shivered. The bus jerked and bounced.

"Our man was stopped as he drove to New-Heliopolis. The goddamn idiot actually stopped, he probably thought somebody needed help. Well, they beat him half to death. He is in the American Hospital."

Now my teeth were chattering, I couldn't stop shaking. It was not from cold! The bus turned a corner. It could not be much further to the terminal. "They took your score, naturally," said Carpenter. His face had reddened with suppressed fury. "A cretin would have known that that was to be the identification."

I turned and glanced at the people on the bus. There were the two Japanese women. There the Negro minister. The others were strangers to me. The young, blond, crew-cut American was not among them.

"The guy you gave the grip to disappeared right after landing," Carpenter said with bitterness.

I looked at him questioningly.

"Somewhere across the field. Who knows? These guys know their way around. The one thing I don't understand is how he knew by what *you* could be recognized."

36

Slowly I said, "I'd already met this American in Cairo. . . ."

Carpenter started, "American? Where?"

I told him quickly.

Carpenter cursed. "Now it's all clear. You were followed. From the beginning. Probably already in the Imperial. The Arab boy was to delay you on your way to the bridge so that this . . . this American could get a good look at you. Once he could recognize you he didn't need to know your identification. I suppose the bridge was lit?"

"Brightly lit."

"There you are."

"But . . . but how could the *boy* know who I was?"

"Some sign . . ."

"What kind of a sign—oh!"

"What do you mean, oh?"

"My lapel!" I cursed worse than Carpenter had as I showed him the wire on my lapel.

"Enough!" Carpenter interrupted me sharply. "How did that happen? Quickly! Tell me."

I told him about the beautiful young woman in the hotel I had thought to be drunk; how the American had repaired my lapel, which had made it easy for him to study me. While I talked, cold, paralyzing fear gripped me.

"Perfect organization," said Carpenter. "Those guys are still the best."

"What did *your* people in Cairo do?" I asked desperately.

"They tried to contact your plane by radio to inform you—in time. No good. The Egyptians refused. They tried to relay the message via the Italians. They could not make contact. That agent's outfit had done their work well. The Egyptians immediately registered a protest with the American Embassy."

"In the middle of the night?"

"Do you think this business is not important enough?" he growled. "Well, then. An official complaint. Our man, the one they'd beaten to a pulp!—they said he had way-laid an Egyptian courier, also that *several* of our men had helped him rob the courier. The courier managed to subdue *one* of them, the others fled. That's their version. Meanwhile they had arrested all of our bureau staff in Cairo. The embassy there informed the embassy in Rome. They notified me. It's not your fault. It's ours. We should never have let our man go it *alone*. Now all we can do is pray that our people will only be expelled and not—" He broke off.

Shaking with fear I asked, "Why didn't they beat me up instead of your man; why didn't they take the tapes away from me?"

"Wouldn't have been practical. Among other possi-bilities, you might have escaped them. No, once you were aboard the plane, when you couldn't get away; *that's* when they finished it. Naturally, you realize the significance of all this as far as you're concerned?"

Yes, I realized what all this meant. If the American Embassy had been notified, other official agencies had also been informed. They knew my name. They had my description. Finished. Farewell Switzerland, good-by Ar-gentina. So long, safety.

I said, "But you—"

Carpenter interrupted me quickly. "We! We could help you only if we had the material! But that's gone. We can't do anything for you. We can't protect you. No one can . . . now."

Everything began to revolve around me, people, lights, darkness. I dropped into an empty seat when the bus came to a stop.

"I really am very sorry," said Carpenter. One step and he was at the door which opened automatically. Wind gusted through the open door as Carpenter jumped out.

He ran toward another bus already crowded with passengers.

A plane's engines roared. Passengers pushed past me. I could have been the first to leave the bus, but I felt too weak with fear. I glanced out of the window and watched the bus Carpenter had entered pull out.

Finished. I was finished.

Or had Carpenter lied to me? His identification could have been false. How could I be sure he had told me the truth? Perhaps he was one of the others and . . .

No. The man was surely what his identification had shown: Carpenter, chief of the Associated Press Service in Rome. And, further, undisputable proof—the blond young man had disappeared with the grip.

I shivered violently.

If the supposedly drunken girl in the hotel had been working for them, they knew what had taken place there. Most certainly.

It seemed a miracle that I had been able to leave Cairo.

A miracle?

Perhaps they had wanted me to escape—Carpenter had hinted at that. Perhaps they wanted to finish me off in some other place.

Where?

Anywhere. Here, for instance, in the rain, on this storm-whipped, dark, enormous airport. Only the dead were not dangerous. Such as my brother. I was still alive. They now had the tapes I had recorded. But I could still talk. I could tell the story all over again for others. . . . So long as I was alive, so long as I could do that, the tapes were of no value to them.

They had to kill me. It was perfectly clear to me. They had to.

And they would. Most certainly. Without a doubt.

I had no idea who had been given that task. It could be anyone here at the airport, anyone at all. And I had to be killed quickly, now, before I had a chance to talk. Now I realized fully why Carpenter had come to meet me. He had wanted to give me that chance, a ridiculously small one, almost none. How was I to escape from this airport, this bus, if I had to die, momentarily, before I had time to report—?

A hand touched my shoulder.

With a startled cry, I jumped up.

Before me stood a sturdy carabinier. I saw that the bus was deserted. The carabinier's face was as broad as that of a peasant.

"*Prego, signore . . .*"

Was *he* the one? I thought panic-stricken.

Why not? Perhaps he was!

Nonsense. I swayed. The score dropped to the floor. The carabinier picked it up and, with a smile, handed it to me.

I felt exhausted, weak with fear. I wanted to get it over with. Quickly.

But I didn't want to die. . . .

I concentrated on my Italian and asked the man breathlessly, "*Parla tedesco?*"

He shook his head.

"*E . . . e il padrone della polizia del aeroporto?*"

"*Si, signore.*"

"*Devo subito parlarlo,*" I said hurriedly.

I had to talk to the chief of the airport police, talk to him as quickly as possible if I wanted to save my life, my miserable, ruined life.

The man in charge of the airport police was surprisingly young for this responsible position. He had almond-shaped eyes, ebony-colored skin, a well-groomed mustache. His office on the second floor of the control tower was brightly lit by neon strip-lighting. It had an air of modern efficiency in its furnishings. A large window faced the terminal. Lights twinkled outside, shadows moved in the dark Roman night while the wind howled and heavy rain lashed the window.

The carabinier had led me through a door directly opposite the police chief's desk. His name was Major Alfonso Geraldi. I had read it on a framed card on the door. Above it was the notice *"DI SERVICIO."*

Though the major had been on duty through the night now drawing to an end, he appeared bright and rested. Polite and smart in his elegant uniform, he sat behind the desk, I before it.

"What can I do for you, Herr Horneck?" The major spoke accented but fluent German. My passport was in his hand. He had asked for it after I had rushed in with a plea for help.

I answered, "My name is not Horneck. This passport is false. My name is Richard Mark and the Federal Criminal Bureau in Wiesbaden has issued an international search warrant for me. Will you please arrest me now and notify State Prosecutor Dr. Paradin of this fact."

Major Geraldi smoothed his mustache and looked at his desk. On it, near me, was the Beethoven score and before him, face down, a thick book which he had apparently been reading before I had entered. I could see its title and had been astonished that the suave young major had been reading Spinoza's *Tractatus Politicus*—in Latin.

Finally he looked up and asked, "You flew in from Cairo?"

"Yes."

"Is Interpol looking for you?"

"No."

"Then you are wanted for a political crime?"

"Yes."

A low-flying plane made the window rattle and I could not hear what he was saying. He repeated, "No diplomatic relations exist between Egypt and the German Federal Republic. You were in no danger of being extradited. Why, then, did you leave Egypt?"

41

"I had to."

"I see."

"I was on my way to Argentina. Buenos Aires. Via Zurich. A plane for Zurich—"

"—leaves in fifteen minutes," he major said. "Why didn't you take the plane?"

"I'm afraid."

"Of what?" he inquired politely.

"Of being killed."

"Is that so?"

"Please lock me up . . . now . . . until German officials come for me!"

Until German officials come for me. To take me back to Germany. Back to the country I never wanted to return to. Back to . . .

The major was looking at me, in silence, a strange smile on his face. It infuriated me. I cried, "I demand to be taken into protective custody!"

He smiled, still silent.

"If you don't believe me . . . if you think I am a fool or a liar—"

"But I don't, Herr Mark," said Major Geraldi.

"I'm telling the truth!"

"I know you're telling the truth, Herr Mark."

Perspiration was wilting my collar, the palms of my hands were moist.

"You . . . know that?"

"That's right, Herr Mark."

"How? You didn't even check in your criminal search files!"

"I did."

"When?"

"Yesterday," said the major.

"When?"

"Yesterday about seven P.M. when I spoke to Dr. Paradin."

"You talked to Paradin? By telephone?"

42

"No, I spoke to him here, in this office. He sat in the chair you're occupying, Herr Mark."

"Paradin in Rome," I stammered. "Where is he?"

"Right here," answered the State Prosecutor, Dr. Walter Paradin. He had entered through the door between two file cabinets. He was dressed, as always, in a dark suit. Two men in gray suits followed him. I rose, swaying, holding onto the desk for support.

"Good morning, Richie," said Walter Paradin. "Where is your brother Werner?"

I don't know if he intentionally put the question that way, but I assumed so since he was well aware of the relationship between my brother and me. His blunt question had the same effect as if I had been hit below the belt. I could not answer. My mouth was dry, my heart seemed to throb in my throat. I recalled a well-remembered passage from the Bible, known since my early schooldays.

> . . . and the Lord said unto Cain: Where is
> Abel, thy brother? And he said: I know not.
> Am I my brother's keeper?

I had recovered somewhat and answered, "Werner is dead."

Paradin was silent and looked at me. I returned his look and somehow *knew* that we both were thinking of the same passage from Genesis.

Paradin asked, "Was your brother murdered?"

"Yes," I replied.

"I thought so," said Paradin.

"Why?"

"Why else would you have escaped?" asked Paradin. "Why else would you be here now, Richie?"

The Lord and Cain, the dialogue, the Lord's curse kept intruding on my thoughts.

Quickly I said, "Werner was murdered in the Hotel

Imperial. He is lying on his bed in suite nine-oh-seven, his throat cut. At least—he was there a few hours ago when I last saw him. Perhaps he has been found by now. I have no way of knowing that. But why are you here? Who . . . how did you . . . ?"

The white-haired, distinguished-looking Dr. Paradin was of slight stature and wore gold-rimmed glasses which invariably slid down his nose. I knew he was sixty-four years old. I had known him well for many years. Paradin limped. One leg was shorter than the other. Even special shoes could not eliminate the limp entirely.

He said, "We have no embassy in Egypt but we still have a consulate. And many friends. Naturally we could never have persuaded the Egyptians to extradite you, Richie. So a few of our friends watched over you." Paradin smiled. His blue eyes became as merry as those of a laughing child. It occurred to me that quite a few people had watched over me in Cairo. "Our friends didn't get the complete picture, naturally, but they found out enough to know that you had to leave Egypt."

I felt nauseated, dizzy with weakness, and Paradin's voice came to me as through cotton wool.

"As soon as our friends realized that you had to leave immediately they kept a close watch on the international airline ticket offices."

Paradin was speaking in his normal voice. To me it sound muffled. "Our friends took turns. They all had your photograph from the search warrant. Yesterday morning, when you booked your Lufthansa flight, one of them was in luck. He found out when and where you were going and which name you were using." He continued, "Our friends sent a coded telegram. As soon as I received the message I came here . . . with these two gentlemen . . ."

"Detectives?"

Paradin nodded. One of his companions stepped forward and showed his identification. I merely glanced at it.

"Everything has been arranged with the Italian officials," the detective explained. "Here is the document signed by the Roman attorney general; this one is from the Department of Justice . . ."

> *And the Lord said unto Cain, Therefore whosoever slayeth Cain, vengeance shall be taken on him sevenfold. And the Lord set a mark upon Cain lest any finding him should kill him . . .*

"And you're taking me to Germany now?" I asked Paradin.

"Yes, Richie, right away. Don't worry, nothing is going to happen to you." He straightened his dark-blue tie.

"Thank you," I said to Paradin.

"Do you know what to expect once you return to Germany?" asked the other detective.

"I do."

"And still you thank us?"

"Yes," said Paradin before I could answer. "It's all right, Richie. You don't have to explain. *I* know the reason. And it's not only because we will keep you from being killed."

"No," I admitted softly. "Not only because of that."

"You've come to realize that your brother, after all, will not prevail over you even beyond his death."

"I've realized that."

"The tapes you recorded have disappeared. But you will record tapes once more, tell us all we were never supposed to find out." Paradin's glasses had slid down his nose, he pushed them back. "And you will tell us the truth."

"I shall. But the truth is not pretty."

"I know that," said Paradin. "And I also appreciate

how abysmally taxing it will be for you, once you start talking, reliving it, Richie. But I must learn the truth. From you."

"From me! I'm a swine, and I've behaved as one."

Paradin nodded.

"True. But you have not always been one. Don't argue, I've known you for twenty years. No, you have not always been a scoundrel. You became one. You are not the only person to have undergone such a change. Besides"—he laughed—"you had to be a swine."

"Excuse me, why?" asked the Italian major politely.

"One needs swine to find truffles," answered Paradin. "Large truffles. Richie found a very large one."

"Now I understand," said the major. Paradin winked at him, then turned to me. "The major and I, we discovered, share the same admiration for Spinoza." He indicated the book with his chin. "The major can even read him in Latin—how enviable."

"Everybody needs to love something, isn't that so?" asked the major, strangely embarrassed. "I understand that you love music, Herr Mark."

"Others love music too," I said, bitterly. "There's a certain base character I know, Professor Delacorte, who loves music too. I have never been able to understand . . ."

". . . that he too loves the Ninth?" asked Paradin.

"Yes."

"People are complicated, difficult to fathom," said the prosecuting attorney. "While we were waiting for you the major read, or rather translated a passage from the *Tractatus Politicus*. It seems to fit this conversation. Would you please translate once more, Major?"

Bowing slightly, still embarrassed, he picked up the book, leafed through it, found the page and translated with apparent ease, " 'I have tried assiduously neither to ridicule, nor to deplore, nor to detest man's deeds but to understand them.'" He placed the book back on the desk.

"To understand a person's actions one needs to know his past," I said. "To understand how he thinks and is today one needs to know what he thought and was yesterday."

"And you are going to enlighten us," said Paradin. "You know so much—almost all—about those people who were involved in this crime. Your report of their past is an inherent part. You are quite correct, only the past and present together will show us the truth."

Here then is the truth.

I switched on the stereo. As soon as the music—clarinet, piano and strings—of the record came through the loudspeakers, Vanessa began to work.

The first part of her appearance was a common enough act. The girl sheds garment after garment searching for an imaginary flea. The second part was sensational: "Vanessa's Famous Candle Act." The prices were high in the mirror-walled back room with its intimate red light, small black tables and black leather chairs, but our customers felt they got their money's worth.

While the first song was playing Vanessa, with much wriggling and twisting, managed to extricate herself from her black evening gown. In her search for the flea she slipped off her elbow-length black gloves to the music of the second record. Next followed a chemise, and circulating among the tables and with the help of several customers, she began to unhook her bodice.

She winced whenever the imaginary flea bit her; she sat on the laps of a few men and women while they tried to undo her bodice; she sighed, whimpered and moaned. Vanessa, twenty-two years old, a natural blonde, slim and full-bosomed, was our treasure. A first-rate training had made her a past master of chichi. She could affect an enchanting, vapid baby face, pout à la Bardot and wink her big blue eyes.

The Strip was situated in the inner city of Frankfurt am Main. The large club had two bars, many small tables, a dance floor illuminated from below and a small stage for artists and strippers.

They were all excellent, but Vanessa was sensational. Boris Minski, my partner, had signed her to an exclusive contract, its many clauses providing protection for us and penalties for Vanessa should she ever try to leave us.

"She won't leave us," I often said. "After all, you did help her that time and she is grateful to both of us."

"Once you've helped somebody who feels obliged to be grateful you've got to be goddamn cautious," was Boris's invariable answer.

We usually engaged artists and strippers only for a few weeks since we frequently changed the program in the bar out front. The same applied to the combos, too. I say "out front" intentionally since for those with well-filled wallets there was also the other bar, this mirror-walled back room with its soft lighting where Vanessa appeared. We had pushed the small black-lacquered tables and leather chairs close together; the room could hold an unexpectedly large number of people. Friday and Saturday we were always filled to capacity. Today, Monday, the week's poorest day, the mirrored room was three-quarters full. If the country was experiencing an economic crisis it certainly was not evident here. But then Frankfurt with its banks, industry, tourists, fairs and expositions was the ideal location for a club such as ours. Our Strip made us a fortune.

In the back room, to which customers were admitted only by Boris or me, we served only champagne or high-priced drinks. Naturally, we had our regulars, among them a very wealthy lesbian, Petra Schalke. She came twice a week, usually escorted by a bleached-blond dress designer who had had his face lifted, wore gold bracelets on his wrists and affected an intellectual look by wearing black horn-rimmed glasses. Petra Schalke often came with friends, queers or heterosexuals. Most of our customers were quite ordinary and normal.

Another song had started up and Vanessa examined her brassiere and her voluptuous breasts, but the imaginary flea was now apparently in her panties and she began to search for it there.

During the next song a fat man in a tuxedo, sipping Veuve Clicquot 1952, helped to remove her bra and people close by were permitted to see if the flea perhaps could be found on her large white breasts with their pink nipples. She wiggled on the fat man's knees and blinked her big blue eyes. She was a very beautiful girl and she performed with expertise, I thought again as I watched her through the one-way mirror in my office.

We needed that mirror to anticipate any possible trouble during Vanessa's act and, if necessary, call in the bouncers. Since Vanessa's work began at 2 A.M., following the usual show, her audience, after drinking in the other bar, was by then more or less tipsy. We kept a close watch. In our line of work we rarely got to bed before 5 A.M., more often at 7.

"More than twenty-two per cent in Neugablonz," said Minski. Then he began to laugh. He was sitting at his old-fashioned desk, before him a stack of morning newspapers which had been brought about midnight. We usually took care of the paperwork while Vanessa was performing; this night we were reading newspapers.

My desk, as old-fashioned as Boris's, stood next to his, facing the one-way mirror. Behind us was a large safe from the year 1909. There was also a shelf with several bottles and glasses, a shabby couch and chairs, its leather worn and splitting in a few places, an ugly round table and a prewar typewriter on a stand. A threadbare carpet covered the floor. One wall held rickety shelves stuffed with files, folders, books on tax legislation, literature on contemporary history, especially on the Third Reich. Only the stereo, discotheque and the two telephones on our desks were new—the post office had exchanged our old phones for new models.

There was no window in our small office; fresh air was forced in every ten minutes by a powerful fan. The floral wallpaper was peeling. We could have decorated the office, bought some new furniture, but each time I broached the subject Boris had always retorted, "What for?" Actually he was right. The office didn't matter as long as the premises outside were first-class.

"Where in Neugablonz?" I asked as I pulled off my black bowtie and unbuttoned my shirt collar. Our office was very hot—the central heating system needed to be repaired too, but it really was not essential. If one of us became too uncomfortable he simply took off his jacket and opened his collar. Boris had already done so.

"Near Kaufbeuren," he answered. "The town where so many refugees from the Sudetenland live. They manufacture jewelry." Boris Minski, fifty-four, was of medium height. Long lashes, baggy black eyes which never seemed to smile even when his mouth did, glistening black hair, a huge nose dominating a pale face, always the scent of lavender about him.

"In Neugablonz," he read, "two hundred twenty-one of nine hundred seventy-one eligible voters cast their ballots for the NPD. Now they've become scared and could kick themselves."

"Why?"

The fan switched on, rattled loudly. Boris did not seem as bothered by the noise as I was. I resolved to have the damn thing repaired tomorrow and over his objections.

"Because of the way they voted!" Boris yelled above the din of the ventilator. He was a Russian Jew from Kamenets-Podolski northeast of Czernowitz near the Romanian border. He spoke fluent German, though with an accent. "Jewelry is their livelihood, right? Now, I read,

50

a few exporters have told them that they will not buy from them any more—allegedly—and they are panicky. They say that now foreign buyers won't come to Neugablonz because they'll buy in Hong Kong or Japan instead. It's cheaper there. That's what it says here. What do you think of that? Tough luck for the poor people of Neugablonz."

He grunted. "An example of spontaneous zeal. Spontaneity doesn't always work. A little thinking is better ...."

Our office was soundproof. A flick of a switch and, through an intercom, we could hear all that went on in the bar outside. Everything was all right. The record circled on the turntable. Vanessa sat on the lap of Petra Schalke, the lesbian with a mannish haircut, and had slowly taken off her net stockings. This sapphist, a black mink coat draped over her shoulders, had pursued Vanessa for months now—in vain—and was grateful if Vanessa as much as sat on her knees. The silver-blond fashion designer with his frilled shirtcuffs and gold bracelets was studiously examining his fingernails while Vanessa stretched out her bare legs and carried on. Then she permitted her passionate admirer to undo her garter belt.

We had instructed Vanessa always to allow Petra Schalke something like this. She brought us many customers and drank only the most expensive champagne. We simply had to show some human kindness! The forty-five-year-old lesbian—her love unrequited—fussed over Vanessa's garter belt and in her excitement pinched her finger. It hurt. Her escort blew on it, stroking it tenderly. Petra Schalke, her face taut and hungry, whispered something in Vanessa's ear. Vanessa had to giggle and roll her big blue eyes.

"By the way," said Minski, "you owe me a thousand marks."

I pulled out a roll of hundred-mark bills from my hippocket and handed ten to Boris. Now that the newspapers

51

had published the election results I knew that I had lost my bet. Both of us had guessed that the NPD would be very successful in Bavaria. So we had agreed that the one closest in his prediction to the actual results would be the winner. I had predicted no more than ten seats in the Bavarian legislature, he, fifteen. The result was exactly fifteen.

Boris counted the money. "Thank you."

Another record had started and Vanessa jumped and shook herself. It was obvious that the flea had to be in the one garment which she still had on—aside from her shoes. When we had started rehearsing this act I had told Vanessa that she had to be undressed by the end of the first record. After all, two records ran about thirty minutes.

Vanessa had protested. "I need those thirty minutes to get them in the mood for the candle act! Believe me, Richie. No one will be bored. If I can't do very much— *that* I know how to do."

"Yes, darling, yes, but . . ."

"Leave it to her," Boris had said. "I think she has something there."

She had been right. She managed both sides of the record and, during the first part of her act, drinks were still being served by very pretty girls in black miniskirts with tiny white aprons and caps.

The music came to an end. During the few seconds that passed before the next record began, Vanessa slithered snakelike through the room, passing between guests, brushing or touching as many as possible. A superb talent.

The music resumed. Vanessa rolled around on a small carpet in the center of the mirrored room, moaning and wailing because the flea in her panties plagued her. The fourth song had her crawling on all fours, her bottom up high so men, and women too, could try to pull down her black bikini panties. But she was too elusive.

I had gone to Minski's desk. On it were newspapers,

bank statements and a magazine; its front page, in giant letters, proclaimed, "I, EMMY GÖRING, TELL HOW IT REALLY WAS." The series had been running for some time. Frau Göring had related what a devoted father, exemplary husband, friend of the Jews, pacifist and embittered enemy of Hitler the Reich minister-president and marshal had been; how desperately he had opposed the war with Russia; how he and his family often had little to eat; how frequently Frau Göring and her daughter had starved and frozen after the end of the war; how forthright and anti-fascistic her husband had been to the end.

"Don't laugh so stupidly, Richie," Boris had said to me when the series had begun. "Who should know a man better than the woman who loved him and lived with him?"

As mentioned, Minski's election prediction had been uncanny. He drew the slips of paper from his desk on which we had written our guesses.

"I used simple deduction," said Boris who had noticed my fixed stare. "You could have done it too. Very simple. Look." He pulled out a map of Germany, placed on it a piece of tracing paper which, in places, had been shaded in three different colors; cities were marked by different size dots.

In the mirrored room Vanessa, stretching and swaying, took off her tiny black panties.

Not without conceit, Boris said, "I've taken into consideration the election results in Schleswig-Holstein and Hesse. In our beautiful Frankfurt the NPD got ten per cent, right?"

Through the one-way mirror I watched Vanessa begin to fuss with the g-string.

"Then," continued Boris, "I did some reading. Statistics. Poliakov-Wulf, Shirer, Schnabel, Sonneman and so on." He glanced at his political library on the rickety shelves. "I found that the Nazi party during the Weimar parliamentary elections in 1928 received only two-point-six per cent. In 1965, the Bundestag elections, the NPD got two per cent."

"Boris," I said, "the Nazi party was founded in 1920. It had already been in existence eight years. The NPD was only two years old."

"I've taken that into consideration."

"How?"

"I made allowances for the jet age. Time is relative. Today everything is accelerated. Now. Our government is completely . . ."

"The old one. We're getting a new one now."

"Then governments changed continually too. At that time we already had a lot of people out of work. Today that's starting again. Little by little, but it happens quicker, Richie, much faster. Jet age. So, I said to myself, everything will turn out the same as the last time."

Outside Vanessa began slowly, ever so slowly, to take off the g-string which remained all she wore.

Boris was lecturing. "Finally I made this map of West Germany. West Germany will do for now. For the moment. The areas where the Nazis polled ten, twenty or twenty-five per cent in 1930 I shaded differently. The cities—small dot, larger dot, very large dot. You see?"

"Yes."

Something was distracting his attention, he looked out into the mirrored room.

"Who are those two guys?"

"Where?"

"To the left behind Petra Schalke and her gay friend."

"Oh, those." They were "special effects" men of an American movie company shooting near Frankfurt. They were watching Vanessa with detached, professional interest. I told Boris who they were and that I had invited them in the hope that they would love the candle act and give us some free publicity.

"Great," said Boris, "very good thinking, Richie. We'll make as much money here as we can. Where was I? Oh yes. Well, by comparing the maps and statistics I found that the NPD polled as heavily as the Nazis had—in the same areas. Call me computer! You see, where the map is especially heavily shaded the Nazis in 1930 got the most votes in Bavaria. Again they got the most votes there."

"Not the Nazis," I said. "The NPD. That's different altogether, friend."

"Of course," said Boris. "A slip of the tongue. But I must say I'm very pleased with myself. I'm not going to make the same mistake twice."

"Neither will I," I said.

"Just listen to papa," said Boris. He patted my arm and smiled, yet his long-lashed, black eyes remained serious as always. I saw that in the bar Vanessa had shed her g-string. She had finally found the imaginary flea, raised it high and pressed two fingers together.

The red light grew dimmer. The music stopped. A well-rehearsed ceremony followed. Two especially pretty girls in their black, short costumes placed a tigerskin, complete with head, in the center of the room. The beast's glass eyes glittered dark-green. The girls curtsied and escorted Vanessa to the tigerskin, curtsied again and disappeared. Vanessa slowly sank to her knees, rose slightly to a crouch and opened her thighs. There was no music during this last part of her performance. Always a hushed silence—if one discounted the strange sounds Vanessa uttered.

Frankfurt has a lot of hot spots but ours was certainly the most risqué. My friend Boris and I, envied and hated by our competitors, were reputed to be the most cynical and unscrupulous men in our business. We prized that reputation: we had worked hard to earn it. Months ago, just after Vanessa had started, an emissary of the Jewish Culture Association, an old, bent man, his face pale and emaciated, had come to us.

"Herr Minski," this man had said, "you know that

many bars and nightclubs in Germany are owned by Jews."

"Wait a minute," Boris had replied. I had been present during this conversation. "Only fifty per cent of this night-club is owned by a Jew. The other fifty per cent belongs to my partner Richard Mark and he is a hundred per cent Gentile with the Iron Cross First Class, the Close Combat Medal and I don't know what else."

"That's not the point," the dignified old man had said. "Your partner will have to bear his own responsibility as a Christian."

"I'll do just that," I had said.

"That's your business. I wouldn't have come at all if your newest entertainment had not been so scandalous."

"If it's scandalous why don't you make an official complaint?" Boris had asked, grinning, his eyes sad.

"You know why as well as I," the man had said.

"You could ruin my business if you wanted to!"

"That's right and the entire country would be gloating. Jew against Jew!"

"I knew I could rely on you," Minski had replied. "All right. What I'm doing is scandalous. But it is not against the law, is it?"

"Unfortunately not," our visitor had said.

An act such as Vanessa's can only be prohibited if it is termed an offense against public morals. Someone would have to go to the police and state that he found the performance obscene. The act could be stopped; those involved could end up in jail. Vanessa had been working for eleven months now and not a single guest had taken offense. The police could do nothing.

"What do you mean: unfortunately not?" Minski asked the protesting emissary. "Why don't you leave me in peace. Am I hurting anyone?"

"Herr Minski, you know that there are about thirty thousand Jews in Germany. Twenty thousand of them are foreigners, as you are. Not even you can convince me that we are loved here."

"I don't need love, I need money. A lot of money. How can one make so much money this easy? Well, then!"

"Herr Minski, you must realize that there are a lot of decent people in this country who are saddened by what you, and Jews like you, do. It creates animosity, a new anti-Semitism."

"I keep hearing 'new,' " Boris said.

"You understand me perfectly. You've heard of the NPD. They say that the Federal Republic is suffocating in a morass of moral turpitude, that youth has no ideals or examples to pattern themselves after, that the people are systematically demoralized and corrupted by an appeal to their basest instincts. You can see how successful the NPD and such slogans are. Your impropriety is immeasurably damaging to the Jewish cause."

My friend countered, "How terrible. I can only hope then that the Frankfurt prostitutes do not cause immeasurable damage to the Catholic cause."

"What do you mean?"

"Because ninety per cent of them are Catholics," answered Minski.

On the twenty-first of June 1942, the rural police sergeant Fritz Jacob wrote a letter to Lieutenant General Querner: "Naturally we're sorting things out here; especially as far as the Jews are concerned. We're not sleeping on the job. Every week three to four raids. Sometimes Gypsies, another time Jews, partisans or other such riffraff. . . . Well, only a small percentage remains of the twenty-four thousand yids living here in Kamenets-Podolski. Those Jews living in the area surrounding the town are also within our jurisdiction. We're paving the way ruthlessly and then '. . . the waves close, the world is calm.' "

I don't know what the future had held for those two

gentlemen. I had found this excerpt from an original letter in a book *The Yellow Star* by Gerhard Schoenberger and had shown it to Minski.

"Yes," Boris had said after he had read it. "In June 1942 they were almost finished in our district. By then I had already spent four months in Maidaneck. I had no idea where my wife was or even if she was still alive. We had been separated at our arrest."

His wife, Rachel Minski, at that time had spent four months in the Kolomyya concentration camp. In 1942 she had been twenty-four years old and very beautiful. Minski, then thirty years old, had been teaching biology at a high school in Kamenets-Podolski where his father and grandfather had been teachers before him. The Minskis had moved there in the early nineteen-hundreds from Vinnitsa after an extremely violent pogrom. It was Boris Minski's dream to become so financially independent as to enable him to devote his life to the study of butterflies. There are more than one hundred thousand species of the Lepidoptera. Very little was known of the majority of this insect order; therefore, he could contribute something of value to the area of entomology.

Maidaneck was a so-called extermination camp in which, somehow, Minski survived. When the Red Army liberated the camps in July 1944 he had been en route to Auschwitz-Birkenau. At that time half a million Hungarian Jews had been rushed to that camp and murdered. Haste was thought to be essential as the Western Allies had landed in France and German lines were crumbling rapidly. For six weeks the ovens in Auschwitz were in continual use.

"The bastards worked like cart horses," Boris once told me. "They worked until they were ready to drop. But they couldn't kill us all. Why? Because we were too many."

Himmler then ordered inmates to be deported to Germany. Camps in the east were evacuated. In the bitterly cold February of 1945 Minski, who still did not know his wife's fate, and other prisoners tightly packed in open freight cars, without coats or blankets, were shuttled along the bombed, partially repaired railroad system of a devastated country. They slept standing up, relieved themselves standing up, died standing up. It would have been easy to escape; hardly anyone did. They were too weak from hunger, too exhausted. The train that carried Minski and many other such trains moved from one camp to another. Refused entry, the diverted trains went elsewhere. Minski's journey took him from Auschwitz to Buchenwald, to Dachau, to Flossenbürg.

Trains rolled for many days without a stop. Whenever they did the side doors were slid open. Many cars held only frozen corpses.

The rapid advance of the Allies forced the SS to evacuate remaining camps in extreme haste. Now the prisoners were driven along the highways. Those unable to go on were shot on the spot or burned alive. Young people in various parts of Germany told me after the war that they vividly remembered the endless columns of pitiful, wretched people staggering along the highways. Minski was sent to Bergen-Belsen. Typhus there had reached epidemic proportions. All the Minskis were tough as wild animals and difficult to kill, he once said.

The survivors of Bergen-Belsen were liberated by the British. Minski, near death, was removed to a hospital. He recovered quickly, then went to a displaced persons camp for half a year. Still no news of his wife. It was by chance that he was released: among the camp administration were members of a Polish division who, allied with the British, had advanced through Germany. One of them was a first lieutenant whose ancestors had come from Kamenets-Podolski. From him Minski received new papers, money, food-ration cards and—a special privilege—permission to move freely in the three western zones.

The officer helped Minski however he could. He wrote

useful letters to the Allied occupation troops and referred Minski to the Red Cross tracing service.

The first clue led to Hamburg. Minski had been told that his wife had been in Ravensbrück and that those prisoners had been transferred to Hamburg. The winter in 1945 was very severe. On foot, or when he was lucky in an army truck, through snowstorms and bitter cold, Minski began his search. The information proved wrong.

He went from one office to another. He learned that some inmates had been sent to Hamburg. Most of these, however, especially prisoners from the eastern provinces, had been sent to Bavaria where they had been liberated by the Americans—sometimes while still in cattle cars. He discovered that Rachel had been taken to Kolomyya. Now, presumably, if still alive, she would be in a Bavarian DP camp. Boris went south. He tried camp after camp, one Red Cross office after another—in vain. Some of the camps had been dissolved—it was now spring 1946. Minski tried the registration offices and mayors' offices too.

For seventeen months he searched for his wife, until April 1947. An official of the mayor's office in Hof informed him that a Rachel Minski had died on November 11, 1945, in a camp near the town and had been buried in the Jewish cemetery. Minski found the cemetery, found a weatherworn, overturned wooden board with a burnt-in star of David, its inscription still recognizable:

RACHEL MINSKY née LITMAN
5.1.1918 — 11.11.1945

The names and dates were correct. Minski stood motionless before the grave. He had told me, "As I stood there I resolved to kill myself. Suddenly five butterflies were fluttering around the grave and me. They were a faint yellow with black markings. *Papilio podalirius* they're called. A beautiful, sunny day, not yet twelve noon. You understand?"

I didn't understand. He explained that, since time immemorial, many regarded the butterfly as a symbol of man's immortal soul and they believed that, according to color and the time of day, they were an omen of good or evil. Light-colored butterflies seen before noon on a sunlit day promised especial good fortune.

"Superstition, of course," Boris had said. "But I'm a bad Jew—always superstitious—I told myself I mustn't kill myself when butterflies fluttered around me, five of them, on a sunlit day before noon. So, I pondered, if I don't kill myself I have to make a living and then I remembered that a distant cousin had a business in Munich, in Möhlstrasse. A Yank gave me a lift in his truck to Munich and my cousin gave me a job in his business."

The Möhlstrasse, after the war, had been the center of vast black-market activity. Nine months in his cousin's business—a wooden shack—and the gentle teacher Boris Minski, whose dream it had been to search into the mysterious world of butterflies, had become calculating, unscrupulous, extremely successful as a black-market racketeer. As such, he was sought out by shrewd profiteers for advice or, perhaps, for friendly association with a resourceful man. By the spring of 1948 Minski had become independently wealthy.

Having learned the imminent monetary reform he skillfully manipulated his fortune through the currency changeover. As soon as he could afford it he began visits to his wife's grave in Hof every two weeks. Once a granite headstone had been set and fresh flowers regularly placed on Rachel's grave, he had bought a small bench on which he often sat, silently communicating with his wife. His effort to have her remains transferred to the Jewish cemetery in Munich had been thwarted. That exhumation was not possible as Rachel's coffin had been but a paper sack. Minski, by then a dealer in scrap metal, lived in a three-room apartment in Bogenhausen, a fashionable district in Munich, not far from the place of his first, assiduous post-war operations. In August 1948 he received a letter from the Sanatorium Hornstein near Frankfurt am Main. He was informed that his wife, Rachel Minski, née Litman, had been under care there since December 1945. The letter was signed by the director of the sanatorium, Professor Dr. Peter Mohn.

A black-haired girl, dressed as a maid, tripped through the mirrored room to Vanessa, who was crouching on the tigerskin, curtsied and offered her a black, silken cushion, holding a red candle. The girl curtsied again and slipped away. Vanessa deposited cushion and candle alongside.

Through the one-way mirror in our office I watched our star performer half-close her eyes and begin to caress her nipples. I turned up the loudspeaker which brought in the sound from the bar and heard Vanessa softly sighing. In a little while her right hand moved down and the soft sighs became more audible moans.

"What's the matter with her? She sounds hoarse. Does she have another—"

"That's right," said Minski. "Another cold. Quite a bad one this time."

"It's really not surprising," I said. "In there it's hot while those damned corridors outside are cold and drafty enough to blow one down. Every day the girl runs around there half-naked. It's amazing she doesn't have a chronic cold. Or, with this crazy weather, pneumonia."

The weather this fall had been capricious. Sunshine and mildness one day, snowstorms and chilling cold the next.

"I called Dr. Fellner right away. The girl is costing me a fortune but it has to be. God forbid she gets the flu. Fellner says no."

"No, what?"

"No flu. She is supposed to sleep in her dressing room tonight, she's not to go outside, he's coming again tomorrow. Gave injections of antibiotics and some other stuff, as usual. She costs me a fortune," Boris repeated. "But what can I do? Aren't we remodeling all the time? That corridor just can't be fixed! We'd have to move and Dr. Fellner is cheaper than that."

The old house which held our Strip was one of the few in the Taunusstrasse which had been spared by the bombs. Spared, but the violent shocks had caused some damage. We were always repairing, for we did not want to move. The Taunusstrasse was an ideal location for us. Minski, stingy with money, knew where it had to be spent: for instance—a priority—the expensive treatment of Vanessa's frequent colds by an excellent physician.

"Well, she won't do it for ever," I said. "Only until she reaches her goal."

"I hope that won't be for a long time yet!" Minski murmured, wistfully knocking on wood.

I saw that Vanessa's breathing had become irregular; her full breasts rose and sank. The audience sat spellbound. Petra Schalke of the mannish haircut held her hands pressed to her mouth, biting her knuckles. The two special-effects men were whispering excitedly.

The telephone on Minski's desk began to ring.

The caller was Minski's New York stockbroker. It was eight o'clock in the evening in New York, the usual time Boris and his broker spoke to each other. Our telephone bill was outrageous. ("I need a broker, I have to talk with him," Minski had declared when I had protested about the telephone bill. "Besides, I take care of your business as well as mine." He was right. He was always so goddamn right.)

Since the Americans had committed themselves in Vietnam we had bought stocks of American manufacturers of war materials. Recalling the Korean war, Boris had calculated the risks and acquired shares while still low-priced. We had even borrowed to buy as many as possible.

In the mirrored room Vanessa on her tigerskin became very restless. Her hips swayed, her fingers moved softly. Someone tipped over a glass. Minski was still talking.

I remembered what he had said when we bought the American stocks, "The Vietnam war is going to make the richest country on earth even richer, that's simple deduction, Richie. Then there'll be another stockmarket crash against which the Black Friday will be a mere trifle. But, meanwhile, there's money to be made."

He had been correct in his predictions. The Vietnam war was costing the Americans a lot of money but the war industry was getting richer. There were "Vietnam millionaires," not only among the armament manufacturers but also those who had bought the right stocks. We had not become millionaires but we—Minski, that is—had bought the right stocks.

We had an American brochure which statistically proved that the war in Southeast Asia was by far the most expensive America had ever fought: "The cost of each enemy soldier killed—$52,500," the leaflet stated.

I looked through the mirror. Vanessa was grinding her teeth. She had rehearsed that thoroughly. It was most effective. I lowered the volume of the loudspeaker so that Boris could continue his telephone conversation undisturbed, then watched Vanessa reach for the red candle on the silk cushion, pull her hand back as though ashamed, reach out again, bite her lower lip, sigh and go on with her performance. . . .

"The economic results of the Vietnam escalation are, for us, the whipped cream on top of the cake!"

A prominent California industrialist had said this to a reporter of *Newsweek*, which had published the quote, and Minski had read it to me, triumphantly.

The profits of a firm which delivered fifty thousand 2.75-inch rockets and forty thousand bombs to Vietnam each month had risen 155 per cent during the last six months. One aircraft firm had had a 70 per cent increase in profits in 1965; another, with government armament orders totaling 1.7 billion dollars, was by far the Pentagon's most important business partner. The firms' shares had rocketed.

Someone would have to be crazy to sell such profitable shares now, even at those fantastic prices, I mused, since the Vietnam war could certainly continue for some time. It was then that I heard Boris say, "Don't give me any lectures, Goldstein! I said *sell*. Everything, that's right. Of course, at the highest price! But *quickly*. Everything has to be sold by the end of the year. Have the money transferred to Zurich right away."

"Boris," I said, aghast, "are you meshugge?"

"Be quiet!" Minski gestured nervously. He huffed and puffed while he hurriedly instructed his broker.

Vanessa suddenly, with resolute determination, reached for the red candle, pushed it into herself and groaned loudly. Loudly and hoarsely. If only she didn't come down with the flu!

The fan switched itself on and rattled. Boris, yelling above the noise, told Goldstein not to ask stupid questions but to do the job for which Minski was paying.

"I wish you'd stop contradicting me. You live in the States, I live here. I know what I'm doing! Enough. Good night, Goldstein." He replaced the receiver and said, "If there's anything more exasperating than a stupid Christian it's a stupid Jew. I need a new broker!"

"I'm a stupid Christian," I said. "I don't understand a thing. You're going to sell, now, when our Yankee shares are doing so well?"

"That's right, now," said Boris and rose. He carefully tied his bowtie since it was customary for both of us to go to the mirrored bar following Vanessa's act. I rose too and, while we talked, we made ourselves socially presentable again.

"The Federal Republic's budget is short a few billion marks, right, Richie?"

I nodded.

"A cretin could guess what is going to happen now."

"Tax increases . . ." I started.

He waved, deprecatingly. "That in any case. Other measures. Measures which could hurt us. What could affect us the most?"

"What?"

Through the loudspeaker, although I had turned it down, we could hear Vanessa. She acted so convincingly that one simply had to believe she was nearing climax. She uttered short, high screams. Her hand moved rapidly. I hope she doesn't have to sneeze now, I thought.

"Currency control regulations would prove the most dangerous for us," Minski enlightened me. "Sweeping new regulations. And they come quick as lightning! Pretty soon you won't be able to transfer marks to other countries, and if you have foreign money they'll exchange that for German marks."

"How will they know that I have money in another country?"

"They'll find out. The Americans will help them. Their budget is going to be shot too. They'll also have tax increases and monetary control regulations and only—"

"But we have a lot of money in the States!"

"—and only, if you'll let me finish, only those people will be unaffected who can *prove* that they have put their money into international investment funds. Why? Those funds are investing their monies in Western industries. Now, do you understand?"

Vanessa outside, screamed, "Yes! Yes! Yes!" and yelped like a puppy dog.

Boris applied the finishing touch to my bowtie and continued, "There's going to be a rude awakening, Richie! And then everybody will try to save all they can. But I don't want to wait that long. Once before I waited until people realized the situation. The next elections are due in 1969."

"So we have almost three years."

"Almost three years!" Boris warmed to the subject. "We have to be gone by then! Long gone! We must be in Switzerland long before that!"

"We" meant four people: his wife Rachel and himself, I, and Professor Dr. Peter Mohn, director of the Sanatorium Hornstein north of Frankfurt.

In his large, bright office the psychiatrist Professor Dr. Mohn, born in 1898 in Leipzig, director of the Hornstein Sanatorium, was quoting from the Hippocratic oath to two physicians in SS uniforms who had come from Berlin. "That you will exercise your art solely for the cure of your patients and will give no drug, perform no operation for a criminal purpose, even if solicited, far less suggest it."

The two SS physicians exchanged glances. Then the older asked, "You are a member of the party, Professor?"

"I am," Mohn, tall and slim, answered calmly. He had a narrow face with exceptionally large brown eyes.

"Since when?" asked the other SS doctor.

"Since 1933."

"You are also the youngest director of an institution and you were one of the youngest professors in Germany, is that not so?" asked the older one.

Mohn nodded.

"Am I correct in my assumption that your rapid promotion is not in the least due to the fact of your having been a party member of long standing and your connections with influential party officials?"

"You are correct in your assumptions."

"Then you joined the party only for the sake of your career?"

"By no means *only!* My father—he died two years ago—became a party member in 1930. I too was convinced that the Führer would be Germany's salvation. Well, once I had joined the party I naturally availed myself of the advantages and the patronage of my father's friends to advance as quickly as possible," Dr. Mohn declared. "Wouldn't you have done the same in my place?"

The older SS doctor said grimly, "And after all that you have the audacity to defy the Führer's order. That is what you are doing. We did understand you correctly, did we not?"

"You understood perfectly," answered Dr. Mohn. "Permit me to read you another passage from the Hippocratic oath . . . which you seem to have forgotten, gentlemen. 'That into whatsoever house you shall enter, it shall be for the good of the sick to the utmost of your power, you holding yourself far aloof from wrong, from corruption, from the tempting of others to vice; that you will exercise your art solely for the cure of your patients.'" Mohn paused and repeated with emphasis, "'For the cure of your patients.'"

"Then you refuse to fill in the questionnaires?"

"Not only that. I shall not permit even a single one of my patients to be examined or transferred by you or members of your organization," Dr. Mohn answered.

The organization he had mentioned had come into existence as a result of a proxy issued by Hitler to two men and went as follows:

> Reichsleiter Bouhler and Dr. Brandt, M.D., are herewith charged with developing the responsibilities of physicians, to be specifically named, in guaranteeing that those judged incurably ill after careful critical evaluation may be granted a merciful death.
>
> (Signed) Adolf Hitler

This order, given at the outbreak of war, applied generally to the hopeless cases. The authorized representatives, however, concerned themselves chiefly with the mentally ill who were usually housed in institutions off the beaten track. This situation meant that the euthanasia order would not attract undue attenion.

Thereupon there came into being the Reichs-Study Group of Sanatoria and Related Institutions, whose members decided the life or death of its patients; the Charitable Foundation for Institutional Care, which provided funds for the liquidation; the Charitable Ambulance Service, Inc., which transported those to be killed. A decree of the Reichs-Ministry of the Interior ordered all directors of institutions to complete questionnaires of their patients "in view of the necessity of economic planning."

Those questionnaires inquired about the type of mental illness, the form of treatment and its duration, the prospect of cure, as well as data on the criminally insane, on noncitizen patients and about those who were not of German or related stock.

The members of the organization were sworn to secrecy. The headquarters was in 4 Tiergartenstrasse, Berlin. The address of the small villa provided the code *T4*, for the liquidation program.

Dr. Bouhler, his superior and the man in charge of the Reichs-Public Health program, Dr. Conti, chose carbon monoxide as the most appropriate expedient. At the first test in the Brandenburg-Havel penitentiary, a Dr. August Becker, chemist for the Reichs-Department of Criminal Investigation, caused death to four inmates within 22 seconds. February 1940 saw the beginning of the large-scale enterprise in the gas chambers of Hademar (Hesse), and in several other installations.

The doctors working in institutions, given very limited time, could not possibly enter proper medical diagnoses on the questionnaires. But then, the assessors did not even read them. For instance the Bavarian public health officer Dr. Prannmüller dispatched 2,090 in a two-week period; 258 and 300 in two days each.

The assessors marked either a red plus sign or a blue minus mark on a rectangle provided for that purpose on the questionnaire. The red plus denoted the death of the patient; the blue minus, that the patient was allowed to live. By means of the questionnaire secretaries in Berlin compiled transportation lists and the Charitable Ambulance Service, Inc., took the patients to the stations. Usually they were disposed of immediately. Gassing took place in the disinfection chambers; cremation, according to facilities, three to six corpses per oven.

Many doctors in charge of institutions tried to fill in the questionnaires advantageously to their patients. As soon as that became obvious the so-called Flying Commissions were sent. They were most effective. In the institution of Neuendettelsau under the leadership of a Dr. Steinmeyer 1,800 forms were completed within a few days. Not a single patient had been examined; most of them received not even a routine checkup.

Until August 1941 German doctors murdered more than 100,000 patients by simply marking their questionnaires plus or minus. Hitler discontinued action T4 when rumors began to circulate: soldiers at the front talked about the possibility of being gassed in the event they should sustain a head injury. This did not exactly boost troop morale. The program labeled *14 f 13,* concerned with concentration camp inmates, Poles, Gypsies, and Jews, replaced T4.

Most institutional directors complied with Hitler's orders. Many did not. One of them had been that Professor Mohn who had quoted part of the Hippocratic oath to the SS inspectors and who had refused compliance.

His wife Anna and his colleagues were concerned about his work and his safety.

"Naturally, I did not feel too good about it," Mohn said during his denazification trial after the war.

"Did you ask for help from any of your acquaintances among party officials?"

"I did not ask anyone for help," Mohn answered. "I did not want to involve anyone."

"What was done to you?"

"Nothing," said Mohn.

"You were not arrested?"

"No. Not arrested, not questioned, not suspended from my position, not reprimanded. My doctors and I were left undisturbed—and all my patients."

"Do you know of similar instances where orders were defied?"

"I do," answered the slim, tall professor. "Perhaps a dozen or so. Those men, also directors of institutions, who acted as I did, were not harmed. At the worst they were transferred to other institutions where they had to work in subordinate positions. Their original hospitals were not visited by Flying Commissions, but . . ."

"Yes?"

Mohn said softly, "But sometimes it was all in vain anyway. In Bukenow, for example. A colleague there defended his patients and yet in 1946, just one year, 2,006 patients died. That was during the chaos of the few months following the end of the war. The supply of food to institutions had broken down. So many patients had survived the Nazis yet they died after the war. But we had started the war."

The denazification board classified Dr. Mohn as not guilty. He was permitted to continue his work in the Sanatorium Hornstein. On August 14, 1948, the now fifty-year-old, still youthful, professor was seated in his bright office across from thirty-six-year-old Boris Minski, whom he had notified that his wife Rachel had been undergoing treatment in the sanatorium. Eight years earlier, in the same room, Dr. Mohn's unwelcome visitors had been two renegades to their profession—the SS physicians. The elder of these was now, and had been, since 1948, director of an exclusive private clinic on the outskirts of Cairo.

"Your wife was picked up by the police in Frankfurt

on the seventeenth of December 1945, Herr Minski,"
Professor Mohn said. "She was wearing only thin, ragged
clothes, although it was bitter cold and snowing heavily."
Mohn's voice was pleasant, his movements deliberate
and his brown eyes invariably held the attention of his
visitors. On his desk stood a photograph of his wife with
an earthenware vase of tulips.

"What was Rachel doing in Frankfurt?" Minski asked.

"Begging. For food."

The sun shone brightly through the open windows of
the large room and Minski could hear women's voices
raised in song. The windows faced a garden. Minski
noticed many patients working there. Several paintings
done by patients decorated the walls.

"For food," Minsky repeated, dully.

"An American soldier took her to the nearest German police station. Your wife had a concentration camp
identity card in the name of Ludmilla Szydlowski, a Russian, but the photograph showed a completely different
face. When she was asked as to who she really was—she
speaks excellent German, Herr Minski . . ."

"That's right," he replied. "Rachel comes from a
wealthy family, Professor. She'd had a tutor for German
and tutor for French. Very rich people . . . all dead now,
I think. The fuss when Rachel said she was going to marry
a poor devil like me . . ." Minski's voice subsided.

Mohn continued quietly, ". . . as soon as she had been
asked she became very upset because she did not know."

"She . . . what?"

"She didn't know who she was." Mohn offered a cigarette case to Minski, lit his own when Minski refused.

"Your wife was very agitated. She was brought here
the following day." Mohn rose and began to walk up
and down. "The only thing we found out concerning her
identity was a number tattooed above her wrist which did
not help us much."

"Of course not," Minski agreed.

"We've had several such cases here. Refugees too. As a means of identifying we call them by the consecutive letters of the alphabet. Up to two weeks ago your wife was Mrs. E."

"Mrs. E," repeated Minski. "Mrs. E . . . up to two weeks ago . . . for three years I heard nothing . . . why all of a sudden—"

Mohn interrupted his pacing to look at Minski.

"I have spent a lot of time with your wife. It was professional interest at first. After intensive therapy your wife began to remember her name, where she came from, her marriage and your name. The Red Cross did the rest. The fast progress was due to the fact that you had made inquiries at so many Red Cross offices."

"But . . . then who was buried near Hof?" Minski stammered.

"The Russian woman, Ludmilla Szydlowski. We have ascertained that too. Both women were confined to the hospital station of a DP camp in November of 1945. You know what went on in 1945: not enough medical doctors, not enough nursing staff, few drugs available, very little space—but an abundance of ill people! Files were not kept up to date. Doctors were overworked; many of them, former concentration camp inmates themselves, still too weak, collapsed. Your wife, we found out, was suffering from acute rheumatism in the fall of 1945. She and Ludmilla Szydlowski shared a room, if you could call it that, actually only a partitioned-off compartment in a wooden hut with two American army cots. Their clothes hung from nails driven into the wooden walls. Her roommate died of heart failure on the night of November eleventh."

"How did you know that?"

"The Red Cross found a death certificate. Heart failure was given as the cause of death. As for the rest we have to rely upon conjecture," Mohn continued. "It could be— and I think it probable—that your wife was already at

73

that time mentally ill and panicked when her roommate died. In the darkness she mistakenly took the dead woman's clothes which also held her concentration camp identity card, climbed through the window and ran away.

"I am merely guessing," the professor went on, "but I imagine it is pretty close to what actually took place. The doctors and staff of the morning shift who found the dead woman and the vacant bed probably assumed that the missing patient had been discharged the previous night. After all, the clothes were missing too. The ones still there contained the identity card of the former concentration camp inmate Rachel Minski."

"But the photograph!"

"Unfortunately not all identity cards had photographs," Professor Mohn explained. "This identification card was still in the registry office in Hof. Your wife's paper had no photograph. And so the other woman was buried under your wife's name. So many people died then, Herr Minski. You remember the chaotic times. . . ."

"Yes, I remember," Boris murmured. He stared at the photograph on the desk. "And how did my wife get to Frankfurt?"

"She does not remember. When she was questioned by the police she was not even aware of being in Frankfurt. She thought the uniformed men were the guards at the concentration camp Kolomyya."

"Good God in heaven!" Minski exclaimed, "Will she ever—"

Mohn answered gently, "She is still very ill, Herr Minski."

"What exactly is wrong with my wife?"

"It is difficult to explain but it is not an incurable illness, Herr Minski!"

Tears welled in Minski's eyes.

Mohn fell silent and smoked his cigarette. Minski dried his eyes and mumbled, "Excuse me."

Mohn placed a hand on his shoulder, "Your wife is always pleasant and calm. She lives in an open unit. She . . . she . . . well, she doesn't really know where she is and she is confused as far as people's identities are concerned. I am the only exception. She always thinks I am the same person."

Minski said softly, "She must have had terrible experiences."

"Without a doubt. Recovery is a very gradual progress. It might take a long time. You must have faith and patience. Do you think you will be strong enough?"

"What would I do if I weren't, Professor?" He remembered something. "You are the only person my wife always recognizes as the same one?"

Mohn nodded.

"Who does she think you are?"

"I look younger than I really am. She thinks I am an SS file-leader by the name of Kleppke," Mohn said.

Minski started.

"This Kleppke," Mohn explained in a gentle voice, "had been in Kolomyya. He never mistreated your wife. On the contrary he was good to her even though it could have proved dangerous for him if one of his comrades had seen it and denounced him."

"How do you know that he was good to my wife?"

"She still thanks him, that is, she thanks me," Mohn said.

"What does she thank you for?"

"For some bread," Mohn replied. "The SS guards used to think it amusing to throw food to the dogs while the hungry prisoners were watching. Your wife once said, 'If I could have one wish I would wish to be a dog because the guards like dogs.' Well, apparently this Kleppke had heard her and quickly and cautiously slipped her some bread. He must have been just as afraid of his superiors as his prisoners were of him. Shall we go now?" Mohn said. He stepped to the desk, opened a drawer, took out something—Minski could not see what it was—and slipped it into a pocket of his white coat. Minski rose, glancing once more at the photograph on the desk. "We shall have to be careful not to upset your wife," Mohn said. He instructed Minski how to conduct himself while they walked along the bright corridors of the hospital.

"Professor . . ."

"Yes?"

"I'm afraid . . ."

"Don't be afraid. She is your wife. And you love her, don't you?"

"Yes," Minski said. "Very much." He hesitated. "On your desk . . . is it a picture of your wife?"

"Yes."

"Does she live here at the hospital with you?"

"She did live here. She loved the country. And tulips were her favorite flowers," Mohn said. "She died in 1945, in December. Pneumonia. Times were difficult . . . she had grown very weak during the last few years of the war. She died a few days before your wife was brought here."

Rachel Minski, accompanied by a nurse, was walking along a gravel path through the garden where flowers, vegetables and fruit trees grew. She was walking directly toward Minski and Mohn. The doctor had stepped out into the garden, into the sunshine. At his suggestion, Minski had remained in the shadow of the doorway.

The garden was large, its high enclosing walls visible in the distance. Many women were working here, some were singing. The garden was aglow with color; it was deep summer.

Minski saw butterflies—*Gonepteryx rhamni* and *Apatura iris,* he thought subconsciously, a little astonished that he could still remember their Latin names. Rachel was close now. He was greatly shocked.

She had a ghostly appearance: emaciated, smaller than Minski remembered her, with sparse white hair framing a prematurely aged face. Not yet thirty years old, and

76

she had been one of the prettiest girls in Kamenets-Podolski . . .

Minski noticed that several of Rachel's teeth were missing. She was wearing striped institutional clothing. Minski was suddenly drenched with perspiration. He was about to run to his wife when Mohn blocked his way. He signaled the nurse to leave.

Minski's heart began to beat faster when he saw a smile come to his wife's face. A second later he realized that the smile was meant for the doctor. She appeared to see no one else.

Rachel stopped, raised her right arm and said, "Heil Hitler, corporal."

"Good afternoon, Frau Minski," Professor Mohn answered quietly. "How are we feeling today?"

Minski, with unbearable sorrow, saw his once-beautiful wife snap to attention and reply, "Very well, corporal." She laughed, gurglingly. "Aren't I lucky, corporal? I'm transferred from Kolomyya to this camp and when I get sick whom do I meet again in the infirmary ward?"

Mohn nodded, beaming.

"You, corporal! You, too, were transferred and they even made you a medic! I'm very lucky! I'm always thinking how very fortunate I am." An expression of extreme desire showed in her lackluster eyes as she stared hard at the doctor. She whispered. "Today, too?"

"Today, too," answered Mohn. "But why are you whispering, Frau Minski?"

"If your fellow guards should hear us . . ."

"They won't tell. I have told you so often they are all decent men here. Not like those in Kolomyya. We don't have to whisper here." He reached into his pocket and took out a roll which he offered to Rachel. That's what he had taken from the desk drawer, Minski thought fleetingly. His heart quivered when he saw his wife's face light with happiness as she kissed Mohn's hand.

"Don't do that!" Mohn spoke severely. "How many

times must I tell you that you are not to kiss my hand, Frau Minski?"

"I shall kiss your hand every time you give me food," Rachel answered. "And since you always give me bread when you're on duty I shall kiss your hand until I die."

The clear voices of women working in the lovely garden came as an accompaniment in the soft, perfumed air.

Rachel hastily ate the roll, crumbs spilling through the gaps in her teeth.

"Eat slowly, Frau Minski," admonished the doctor.

Rachel shook her head.

"Have to eat quickly," she declared. "Somebody might take it away from me or someone might see it and I'll end up in the oven and God only knows what will happen to you, corporal. It is against the rules. If something were to happen to you, I would be all alone, without a friend, here in this new camp."

"I brought a friend along today," Mohn said cautiously. "A very nice man. My best friend. You can trust him, Frau Minski. I wanted to introduce him to you so that you know that you have two friends, since my friend is also your friend."

Mohn pulled the trembling Minski from the shadow of the doorway into the bright sunshine close to Rachel.

She looked at her husband out of fixed dull eyes with pupils no larger than pinpoints. Still chewing the roll, she swallowed, once again raised her arm, mumbled, "Heil Hitler!"

Minski, shaking uncontrollably, whispered to Mohn, "Do I have to say Heil Hitler too?"

The doctor shook his head. "My friend will come often from now on," he said quickly.

"It's a pity," said Rachel.

"A pity? Why?"

"A pity that you're not the only one on duty here in the infirmary ward."

"I'm always on duty, Frau Minski! But my friend will come anyway. Don't you like him?"

"Oh, of course," Rachel said quickly, anxiously. "Will he bring me food, too?"

"Yes, I'm sure he will."

"Oh, good! I like him, really I do!" Rachel said. "But now I have to return to work or I'll be punished."

The doctor nodded.

She again raised her arm in salute, smiled at Mohn and Minski, then hurried back to one of the vegetable patches.

"Shall we go? I'm very glad it went so well," said Mohn.

"*Well?* You call that well?"

"It could have been much worse," the professor said softly and took Minski's arm. Minski allowed himself to be led a few steps along the corridor when he stopped.

"My wife is in a ward . . ."

"Yes, naturally—she was without funds. All this here costs money . . . and we . . . you must understand . . . If it were up to me . . ."

Minski interrupted, "In a ward with many other patients . . ."

"With about twenty other women, yes."

"I'd like my wife to have a private room," Minski said. "Or would that be inadvisable? Would that be bad for her? To be alone, I mean?"

"It would not be good for her to be alone—even though she is no longer ill," said Mohn. "She spends the day with the other patients; sometimes, she told me, she would like to be alone, especially at night. Naturally the ward reminds her of—"

"Exactly. Then provide a room!"

"It is quite expensive, Herr Minski."

"That's all right. I have some money. And if it takes a long time I shall have much more money. You don't have to tell me, professor, I've seen for myself. It will take a long time."

Mohn was silent.

"I can work," Minski said. "And I shall. For my Rachel. Only for her. So she will be comfortable here—no matter what it costs."

"The administration will be pleased," Mohn said. "We desperately need money. There is just not enough. But it could . . . it really could take years, you must realize that."

"I do realize," said Boris. "Don't worry. Minski pays. On the dot. Minski moves to Frankfurt. Minski already knows what he's going to do in Frankfurt."

With the money he already possessed, with the proceeds from the sale of his apartment in Munich, and the legal essentials of Displaced Persons papers, a residence permit and a liquor license—all obtained through helpful friends—Minski channeled his inexhaustible drive into a practical investment. He opened a bar in Frankfurt, for American soldiers. It was a place for GIs who wanted to get away from the restricted atmosphere of official clubs, their superiors and their superiors' wives. Minski named the club "GI Joe." He hired a band and several girls who performed what were then called "aesthetic dances." He dealt in script dollars, cigarettes, gasoline and chocolate. Within a short time he had acquired a reputation—of a special kind. The members of the Jewish Cultural Society groaned if they as much as heard the name Minski.

GI Joe, which later was to become our Strip, was repeatedly posted "Off Limits" to soldiers. Minski's friends, members of the military government with whom he dealt and who dealt with him on the black market, saw to it that the restrictions were promptly rescinded.

Punctually Minski paid for his wife's stay in the Hornstein Sanatorium.

I met Minski for the first time when I came with a military police patrol to check the GI Joe. At that time

I was working for the Americans as an interpreter. MP patrols frequently came to Minski's and similar establishments to check the papers of soldiers and "Fräuleins." Nonfraternization was a thing of the past, although German girls were still called "Veronica Dankeschön," a euphemism for "V.D." or venereal disease. By order of the provost marshal, Minski had had to display large photographs, mounted on wood, of diseased genitals on the wall, accompanied by printed warnings such as "DON'T BE A SAP AND CATCH THE CLAP" or "DON'T GET A DRIP AND MISS YOUR SHIP."

Minski and I became friendly. I knew nothing of his or his wife's life. By 1958, when I became his partner and the enlarged GI Joe was converted into the Strip, I knew everything. Much had happened to me in the ten years following 1948 of which I shall have to report later. . . .

The Strip proved to be a gold mine from the beginning. Soldiers came rarely. Now they could not afford to be our patrons. The majority of our guests were Germans and foreign visitors. The economic miracle was in full bloom. Yet, years ago Minski had predicted the end of that miracle, years before Ludwig Erhard had asked for restraint, and Minski had taken excellent precautions. . . .

Under the care of Professor Mohn—I had met him through Minski who venerated him—Rachel had grown stronger and healthier. Her mind had become more lucid; Minski had become her trusted friend. Then, four years after the fateful day on which Minski had again seen his wife, she recognized him, calmly, without undue excitement.

Soon thereafter, however, she suffered a setback which completely wiped out the progress she had made. Dr. Mohn and his staff renewed their intensive treatment. Finally, after four years, in 1956, Rachel again recognized her husband. A cure seemed to have been effected. Rachel left the clinic, but soon it became apparent that she was unable to withstand the stresses and strains of a fast-moving, changing world. She needed rest, a quiet life, tranquillity.

Professor Mohn had aged suddenly, his hair had turned white, he trembled slightly. His work at the clinic did not suffer; on the contrary, he was indefatigable.

Rachel Minski, cured but in need of continual care, could have gone to the most exclusive nursing homes. Minski was well able to afford it now. But, "I want to stay with the professor in Hornstein!" Rachel had insisted. She stayed. Through the years a bond had formed between the Russian Jewess and the former Nazi party member. Professor Mohn was due for retirement in 1968 when he would be seventy years old.

Minski, just as convinced as Rachel that his wife needed "her professor," had learned that Dr. Mohn owned a modest home inherited from his parents on Lake Maggiore. There, he and his wife Anne had intended to spend their declining years. Now the doctor regularly spent his vacations there alone. As soon as Minski had discovered that he began to prepare for a permanent move to Switzerland. He invested his money there and it was there that he wanted to invest Professor Mohn's modest savings.

"But I can't leave here just like that, Herr Minski!" the professor had protested when Minski had first mentioned it. "A doctor cannot desert his patients just like that."

"You're not deserting your patients, professor. But when you're seventy, when you're retiring, then you'll have to leave here. Then you can go to Switzerland. You've always wanted to go there, haven't you?"

"Of course, Herr Minski, but not until—"

"Until you're seventy. I understand perfectly. I've thought about it and taken everything into account. There will be enough time."

"Time?"

"It will be close but I think it will be all right. What I mean is Rachel and I won't have to leave here before 1968." He knocked on wood. "The political situation will probably hold until then. How wonderful that you're old enough to retire! And now you'll permit me to attend to your money . . ."

Mohn agreed. He knew how Minski made his money—he merely shrugged his shoulders when the subject came up. This doctor knew about me too—a great deal. He knew that I too wanted to follow Minski, with his unerring instinct, to Switzerland before political history repeated itself—in a slightly different form perhaps. Possibly the pattern would not change that much.

I had many reasons for leaving: my life since 1945, my past which Minski had called my "future" after he had once remarked, "Richie, you're a man with a promising future behind him."

Vanessa on her tigerskin was approaching her finale.

Her audience in the dim red lighting sat spellbound, eyes bulging, silent. We heard Vanessa's hoarse sounds through the loudspeaker. Once she almost sneezed. While Minski was brushing off my tuxedo I glanced at the newspaper on the desk.

"Emergency measures," I said.

"Hm?"

"The new government will institute them, it says here—in the spirit of democracy naturally. Just in case an emergency will occur."

"It's already here," said Minski. "You want some lavender? No? The most dangerous emergency in our democracy is already here, I said."

"I heard. What do you mean?"

"The dire lack of democrats in our democracy," Minski said. "It's a joke. You know, something to laugh at!"

"Oh, yeah," I said. "You realize, of course, Boris, that once they've made just a little headway with their new laws, they're going to close down our joint. At least the mirrored section. Right?"

"Sure, I know," answered Minski. "They'll have to prohibit performances such as ours. Why? They're a danger to the state. The most important laws in any dictatorship or a democracy about to become one are the death penalty and those based on absolute moral rectitude. It was never as moral and clean as under the Hitler regime. For a while, I think, they'll permit us to put on some tame shows—because they'll need the taxes. They're sure to increase those taxes to such an extent that we'll be forced to close by 1968. Well, did I guess right? That is what I've prepared for! Our money is in the fund— whatever we make now we'll save for taxes so they'll let us go." He splashed lavender on his face.

Vanessa on the tigerskin opened and closed her thighs; her head lowered, her blond hair cascaded over her face, she whimpered in a high monotone. Her body arched, her free hand alternately pounded the rug or drummed on her flat abdomen. The fan switched on again; I thought of our saving grace, the IIO.

The International Investors' Organization was one of the world's largest, representing almost two hundred investment funds. Licensed in Panama, its administration was in Geneva; stocks and shares were with Bankers' United in London. The Swiss Finanzbank in Zurich handled the ready cash and payments.

Minski, on January 1, 1955, had paid in $25,000, and withdrawn $2,500 each year, which was then transferred to an open account. During the last generation IIO deposits had quadrupled every ten years. That meant in effect that the $25,000 Minski had invested on January 1955 was worth $97,352 at the end of 1964. Yet, in the interim years, Minski had received a full return of his original investment through the distribution of capital gains and dividends.

We continued to invest. I, too, deposited $25,000 in

January 1959 and the same amount in 1960. Minski also invested Professor Mohn's modest fortune. Naturally, no one could predict with any degree of certainty that the deposits would again quadruple over the following ten years. They might increase five- or sixfold in the event that other wars, such as Vietnam, were to break out.

Deposits were not likely to decrease in value since there had been a number of wars within the last generation and there was no evidence to suggest that there would not be any more. Were an atomic war to erupt the IIO would be defunct too. But then, as Minski remarked, "In that case one probably would not need any money, even in Switzerland." A small pause. "Presumably."

Through the loudspeaker came sounds as international as the IIO, understood by people all over the globe: Vanessa acted out the climax. She cried out loud, her voice died down to a murmur, she gasped for air and sank down on the tigerskin, her body twitched.

"How do I look?" Minski asked and stepped before me.

"Great," I answered.

"And I'm fifty-four," he remarked. "Eleven years older than you! You ought to look much better! But you don't take care of yourself."

"But you do."

"I have to—if I'm to think for all of you. Have to watch my health, eat a lot of fruit, mustn't smoke, no alcohol . . ."

Vanessa was still motionless. It was part of her act. At last she rose. The two girls dressed as ladies' maids brought a knee-length ermine cape which they draped about her shoulders and disappeared with candle, cushion and tigerskin. The light became brighter now and Vanessa walked from table to table, her big blue eyes opened wide. From time to time she played with herself and amorously displayed her fingers to the guests.

It was *ne plus ultra!*

Guests were speechless as always, except for the two special-effects men, who were whispering animatedly.

"Just look how happy we've made them again," Minski remarked.

"And when you consider—just an act."

"It's almost as easy to make people happy as it is to make them unhappy," said Minski, the man who had once dreamed of devoting his life to butterfly research.

Just as we were entering the mirrored room Vanessa was leaving, her bearing queenly in her "ermine" cape— actually dyed rabbit. In the dim light the fake was indiscernible. The audience had come out of its trance. They applauded enthusiastically.

"Few actors get so much applause," Minski said.

We devoted ourselves to our guests. I went to talk to the two special-effects men.

"Well, gentlemen?" I asked. They were so engrossed in their conversation that they did not notice me. As usual, following the act, the guests were chattering noisily. Our costumed girls hurried to and fro, drinks were ordered and served. I tried once more.

"Well, gentlemen, what do you say?"

They still ignored me.

The tall blond man was trying to convince the short, dark-haired man. "No, Charlie, no! Believe you me. It's the only solution. She's got to have one! I couldn't do it any other way for any chick if they offered me a million dollars!"

The short man became aware of me.

"Fantastic gimmick," he said to me. "Congratulations, Mr. Mark."

"Thank you."

"Absolutely fantastic," the other one said. "And now do tell us. We'll keep it a professional secret. She uses a sponge, eh?"

"No," I answered, serious.

The blond man, who appeared to be quite drunk, murmured, visibly shaken, "You swear to God that's the holy truth?"

"Sure," I said. It was no risk. I had been damned a long time ago and I was sure to burn in hell, if there was a hell in which one burned.

Solemnly and drunkenly the tall one declared, "If she doesn't use a sponge it's a miracle."

"It is," I said just as solemnly, "it is a miracle." I excused myself and promised to come back to have a drink with them in a little while. My usual excuse. I never, or rarely ever, returned to a table. There was too much to do.

Naturally, Vanessa used a sponge but I would never have admitted it. My questioner knew his business. But when I swore to God, he believed me and thought it a miracle. It's easy to lie to drunks.

I stopped at a few more tables, engaging in polite conversation, gratified that our girls were busily serving magnums of champagne and expensive Scotch. As I was leaving the room to congratulate Vanessa in her dressing room I heard Minski's voice, "What would you have me do? Lie to you? Yes, that's right, each and every time she gets carried away like that. A phenomenon, Herr Direktor! What do you think that girl is costing me?"

The corridor leading to the dressing rooms of the artists and strippers was drafty and dangerously cold. I wondered why this old, ugly, badly built house had been spared by the bombs. I was just about to knock on Vanessa's dressing-room door when I heard voices from within. I did not knock but listened instead.

"Honestly, Madame, it distresses me to have to tell you this so many times—but it is impossible! I have . . . I . . . I am in love with—" Vanessa's voice was high-pitched now—we had taught her well, it was part of her act.

"In love!" That was Petra Schalke's deep voice. "With this Greek! Then where is he, this Greek?"

"In Paris, you know that."

"And you're here. And he doesn't come here."

"He can't. He has to—"

"What can be that important! If he really loved you, my child, he would be here and not in Paris!"

"He really does love me," I heard Vanessa say. Her voice shook.

Poor Vanessa, I thought.

This Greek, Panos Mitsotakis, actually existed, he really was in Paris and he never came to Frankfurt. Vanessa would have been very happy had he loved her. In a way he had been instrumental in presenting us with Vanessa.

Poor Vanessa.

Even if Panos did not love her she could at least say that he did—in his absence that couldn't be refuted—and that usually served to rid herself of any irksome admirer. Love still stirred people's emotions, I thought, even if it only existed in one's imagination or hope.

Yet it did not seem to have any effect on Petra Schalke.

"That Greek!" Her voice was contemptuous. "That marvelous Greek who is never here. That wonderful, splendid man. Stop telling me about men! What can a man really do for a girl?"

"He can love her and be tender and make her happy. . . ." Vanessa's babylike voice trembled.

"I can make a girl much happier and love her much more and be more tender than any man," she countered.

I was freezing and rubbed my hands together, but I continued to eavesdrop. Petra Schalke owned one of the largest brassiere factories in Germany. She had inherited it in 1960 from a girl friend of long association. This friend had owned a Bonanza. She had employed a pilot even though she was an excellent pilot and preferred to fly the plane herself. On her way across the airfield in Frankfurt she had slipped, struck the back of her head in falling and died two days later. Her will had made Petra Schalke her sole heir. There were no relatives so there had been no problems. Petra had inherited the factory and real estate apart from a fortune in cash, the private plane, the pilot, jewelry, furs, and a seagoing yacht.

For six years the lesbian had enjoyed a life of luxury —globe-trotting with girl friends. The business was managed by employees. Then the heiress had seen our Vanessa. Now she was suffering.

"Madame," squeaked Vanessa, whom we had instructed to be as polite as possible to our free-spending guest, "I believe you . . . it distresses me to have to keep refusing you . . . but I . . . I don't only need tenderness, I also need that which no woman has, I—"

"I have that too."

"You have—"

"An assortment, my child. We shall find the one you enjoy the most and I shall be your loving man, your wild, gentle man . . . and your wishes—whatever you want—I shall fulfill them, but don't let me beg you like this. Look, I'm kneeling before you . . ."

"Please! Don't! Please get up!"

"Let me—"

"No!"

"Just one time . . ."

"No!" Vanessa's sudden loud scream made me jump. Her cold. Perhaps she was running a temperature. "Leave me alone! Get up! And don't touch me! Get your hands . . . if you don't get your hands off me I'm going to scream so loud everybody in the building will come running!" Vanessa's voice was not high-pitched any more. She was yelling loudly, obviously very upset. It couldn't have been the cold, I thought. I remembered Rambouillet and Vanessa's experience there. It must have been an emotional shock.

Petra Schalke was wailing, "Darling . . . dearest . . .

we'll go wherever you want . . . we'll take a trip around the world . . . we'll make a cruise . . ."

"Get out!"

"My God, how can a young girl be so cruel," I heard the woman sob. "All right, I'm leaving . . . and there is no hope . . ."

"No! No! No!"

I had just had enough time to hide in a corner in the dark before the dressing-room door was flung open and the lesbian, intoxicated and blinded by tears, stumbled out. The door slammed shut behind her and she staggered along the corridor in the direction of the mirrored room.

As I watched her disappear I had the strange feeling that this despondent woman would someday play an important part in my life. I brushed it off as absurd. Two weeks later my premonition had become a fact.

When I entered, Vanessa in a blue terry robe was sitting before a dressing table removing her makeup. A convertible had already been made up for the night. Vanessa was to spend the night in her dressing room because of her cold.

This dressing room was the largest and relatively the nicest. Frosted glass windows, their upper part louvered, barred on the outside, led to a courtyard. Vanessa had decorated the walls with a medley of whatever struck her momentary fancy—chiefly posters and photographs from books or magazines. Above the bed hung a page from a note pad, on it several words in Greek.

"Hello, Richie," Vanessa greeted me. Her voice was normal now, and her face no longer had the vapid, wide-eyed baby-doll expression. She was not performing now —a young, beautiful girl, cultured and sad as always.

"Am I glad to see you," Vanessa said.

I kissed her forehead, congratulated her on her performance and told her that the audience had been thrilled, simply ecstatic. I must have said the same thing to her at least hundreds of times before and each time her melancholy, off-duty face had brightened for a moment and she had breathlessly inquired, "Really, Richie? Really?"

People have called me Richie ever since I worked for the Americans in 1946, who had nicknamed me. The name stuck.

"As a matter of fact," I answered, "they can't seem to stop talking about you."

"Did you and Boris watch too?"

"Yes," I lied. "Boris told me to ask you if you'd recognized someone from Hamburg among the guests because you were so great tonight."

Her face became gloomy.

"No, no one. You?"

"No." I added quickly, "But then, whom do we know in Hamburg? It's quite possible that people from Hamburg were here tonight."

"It's been two weeks now that I haven't seen anyone I know," Vanessa said and stared at a used tissue before she discarded it.

"But what about November? Five men on two different evenings! And all of them knew your family! One day, Vanessa, one day you'll make it, definitely!"

"Yes," she said and her face became a grimace of hatred. "One day I'll succeed. I'll fix him." She laughed, shrill and malicious. "I've already come a long way, haven't I?"

"I should say. What we've heard so far . . . your father seems pretty vexed with what you're doing."

"One day he'll be finished, Richie," Vanessa said. She smiled now and her face was beautiful again. "Then I'll have reached my goal!"

"I hope she won't succeed for a long time to come." Minski had said that, I recalled, but I nodded and assured her, "Sure, Vanessa. You will."

"Then I'll throw a party! Will we celebrate!" Her smile

vanished. "That Schalke woman was here again," she murmured.

"I know. I was outside the door."

"I really do everything you tell me! But this is becoming intolerable! This woman is . . . horrible!"

Rambouillet, I thought. The shock she received at Rambouillet. Hatred toward women. Hatred toward her father.

"You really gave it to her," I remarked when she suddenly sneezed three times.

"Gesundheit!"

"During the act I almost sneezed. I just managed to . . ."

"I noticed. Good girl. Another one or two injections and by tomorrow night it'll be all over."

"What did you say a moment ago?"

"Gesundheit."

"Before that."

"Before that? Oh yes. That you really gave it to Petra Schalke!"

"And how many times have I done that before?"

Many times, as I well knew.

"She'll come back," Vanessa said ruefully. "She always does. She seems to like this kind of treatment! Actually I ought to reverse . . . but I can't. I really can't do that, Richie!"

"It's all right. Be calm. When it gets too difficult *we'll* have a talk with her." I did not feel that confident that we would or could ever talk to this wealthy woman—a woman of her type was likely to stir up trouble for us by going to the police.

I felt uncomfortable under Vanessa's glance, so I began to move around the dressing room. That's when I noticed the book on a table by the made-up bed. There were also foreign and local newspapers, news magazines, contemporary books on physics—and this book.

Stan' Still, Jordan.

I clenched my teeth when I read the title in thick black letters on the white, well-thumbed cover.

Vanessa had risen. She came to me.

"What's the matter?"

"That book."

"I was going to read in bed."

"Why?" I demanded, suddenly filled with rage.

"You know! Because it's my favorite book."

"Favorite book? Trash, that's what it is!" I said. Blood was shooting to my head.

"Oh, Richie . . ." She sneezed again.

"Stop saying 'oh, Richie!' " I said, roughly. "It's a god-damn mendacious book. How did it get here anyway?"

Vanessa answered, helplessly, "I have all your books."

"At home, yes!"

"When . . . when I heard I was to stay here overnight because of my cold I took it with me. When I feel bad I often read in it."

"It can only make you feel worse! Goddamn, why don't you get rid of my books. How many more times do I have to tell you to do that. It makes me sick just to see them!"

"And when you wrote them?" Vanessa inquired timidly. "When you wrote *Stan' Still, Jordan* did it make you sick then, too?"

"Things were different," I said, my hands clenched. "Times have changed. Nothing ever comes back."

"What kind of world would this be without beauty?" Vanessa asked softly.

The unexpected encounter with the book I had written shortly after the war had upset me; I could only think of myself.

"The world we live in!" I raged. "Nothing lasts. Every-thing changes. Times, people. And not to the good. From day to day the world is growing worse. Nothing will ever be the way it's been."

I did not notice Vanessa's pleading eyes; I stared at that damn first book I had written.

I had taken the title from a Negro spiritual, *Stan' Still, Jordan:* its story, one of brotherliness, peace and the victory of reason. But there was also another line in the song, one which was repeated often, one I had tried to ignore, one I had tried to show as absurd in my book.

". . . but I cannot stan' still!"

It was that line which had been proven right, not I.

Stan' Still, Jordan—shit!

I grabbed the old book and hurled it against the wall, when I noticed that I was gasping.

"Richie . . ."

"Yes?" I looked at Vanessa. She was pale, her lips quivered, she looked helpless and lost, and I—who had just begun to bathe in a sea of self-pity—realized how I had hurt her.

Vanessa said, "You . . . you're unhappy, that's why you say these things."

"I? I'm not at all unhappy!"

How the devil could I get off this subject?

If anybody was unhappy it was Vanessa—because of her life, her father, this Greek boy, even because of me. As beautiful as she was—she had had little luck with men.

She was too intelligent to delude herself. She knew Panos would not return to her, had known it for some time. Perhaps because she had been unhappy, or grateful to me, or just out of her natural need for love—to be close to someone else, we had become intimate; slept together a few times; played at being in love. At that time I had also gone through a period where I too had felt that I could no longer bear to be alone.

It had been a mistake for both of us. How could one lost sheep lead another back into a sound world which did not exist? It reminded me of the story defining the differences between philosophy, communism and religion.

In it philosophy was defined as the activity of persons searching for a black cat in a dark room; communism as the activity of those looking for a nonexistent black cat in a dark room; religion as the activity of others searching for a nonexistent black cat in a nonexistent dark room—and then insisting that each had already found the cat. A joke that I found not at all amusing.

Vanessa and I, as was probably true of a great many of us, accepted that definition of religion.

I was touched by her sadness and said quickly, "I'm talking nonsense. Of course there will be beauty. And lovely happenings. Especially for lovers! Your Panos will—"

"That's right," Vanessa's voice was bitter as she interrupted me, "my Panos will come to me and he'll take me to Athens as his wife and we'll have many children and live happily ever after, I know."

"Vanessa, you'll see . . ."

"If," she interrupted me again, her voice becoming even more cynical, "if you don't steal a march on him and ask me to marry you. After all, we loved one another too, only something came up—principles I guess; one does not have an affair with one's employees, right?—but love will prove stronger, for you too, Richie. One day you just won't be able to contain yourself, then what am I going to do? Panos and you! So much love, so much desire, I . . ."

"Stop it."

". . . won't know how . . ."

"I said, stop it!"

". . . to cope with so much happiness, how to decide between you. I think I'll decide in your favor, Richie . . ." She sneezed several times. I offered her my handkerchief and she noisily blew her nose. She continued, ". . . because you're so smart, Richie, much smarter than Panos. What you said a moment ago—"

"—was utter nonsense!"

95

Poor Vanessa. We had always studiously avoided talking about Panos and us. Now this damn book had caused this irritating conversation.

"I'll be all right," Vanessa whispered, hoarsely, and placed a hand on my shoulder. "Don't worry. I know that what you said is true. The world is the way you say it is. Why don't you write about that? Why don't you write a new novel about that, at long last?"

In trying to help me, to console me, she who needed comforting herself in her helplessness had once more touched on the reason which had provoked this debate. I began to rage once more.

"Now you can stop all this trickery!"

"Trickery?"

"Stan' Still, Jordan—I bet you just happened to place that book on the table quite inadvertently? Quite accidentally I keep finding my old books here again and again!" My nails were dug into the inside of my clenched hands. I felt nauseated. "You know why I don't write. Why I never will write again!"

"I just know that that's what you're telling yourself. But it's not true, Richie!"

"It is true," I shouted and kicked at the book. "I cannot write any more!"

"You're wrong," she said, picked up my book and clasped it protectively to her breast.

"If there's one thing true in this wonderful world it is this: I cannot write any more and I won't ever be able to write again!"

The door behind us was flung open and we turned quickly. Minski stood in the doorway, very pale, breathless, nervous.

"What's the matter?" I asked angrily.

"Telephone. For you. In the office. Come on! Something's happened there!"

"Where?"

"I don't know where . . ." He pulled me toward the door.

Vanessa, her voice hoarse and heavy with cold called, "Who would call Richie now, at this hour?"

Troubled, Minski answered, "Lillian Lombard."

I stood there like an idiot. I couldn't utter one word, and I heard Vanessa hiss, "What, his Lillian?"

"She's not my Lillian," I yelled as if I'd suddenly lost my senses.

"Oy. Oy. Oy," Minski said, "when he yells like that she's still his Lillian."

"The devil she is." I was still yelling and pushed him away from me. "She is not my Lillian! Not any more! Go and tell her that I'm not interested in whatever has happened this time! I don't want to know! There's always something happening to her. What is it this time?"

"She took her own life," Minski answered. Vanessa sneezed again.

"Perhaps you'd be good enough to close that door?" I yelled. "Vanessa hasn't got enough of a cold? Took her life, eh?"

Minski's foot shot backwards. The door slammed shut.

"Don't yell at me!" Boris screamed.

"Lillian's already tried that once before!" I shouted.

"Twice!" Vanessa screamed.

True. She had tried twice to kill herself. Vanessa knew a great deal about Lillian and me. I also knew a lot about Vanessa.

"Twice, nebbish," Minski said, suddenly calm. "But now the third time it seems it's going to work."

"That's why she's telephoning, eh?" With exasperation I noticed my hands shaking.

"She can't talk," Minski said. "Just mumbles—'swallowed something . . . poison'—I could hardly understand. She's in mortal fear, and that's why she called you."

"Me, of all people!"

"It seems that despite everything you're the only man who—"

"Shut your mouth!"

I was in a rage. In a flash I recalled my past with Lillian. Go to the devil, Lillian, I wished. Die, then I'll have some peace! The moment I had formulated that thought I realized that Minski—as usual—was right. Cold fear for Lillian's life gripped me. I ran to the door, flung it open and stormed along the corridor, hurrying toward a telephone—and my destruction.

"No, no, don't go, Richie! Boris, stop him!" Vanessa screamed. "Richie! Please, please, Richie, come back. This woman has always brought you only bad luck."

I hastened along the corridor without looking back. I heard quick steps behind me and Minski's angry voice, "You stay here! Do you want to catch your death of cold?"

"Richie," Vanessa screamed. "Please, don't! Think of what this woman has done to you!"

"You can see what the matter is with him." Minski's urgent voice grew calmer. "Be sensible, Vanessa! Use your head!" The dressing-room door banged shut.

The long corridor led to our office on the other side of this poorly designed old house. I took the shortcut through the cloakroom and mirrored room, pushing through the closely placed tables, brusquely shoving people aside, cursing loudly. The rage I felt, the curses I uttered as I forced my way through the crowded room were aimed at Lillian: at her and my life with her, the years I had wasted, my own miserable life.

Some guests looked at me shocked, amazed. I must have appeared frightening.

Lillian. Lillian. Miserable, deceitful, dishonest, beloved Lillian.

Most guests were intoxicated and excited, pawing and kissing, laughing loudly, talking animatedly, drinking, still drinking. Two couples danced closely entwined, illuminated by the red light. Music swelled through the loudspeaker. The scene was usual at this hour.

I squeezed past Petra Schalke, her head resting on her hands, crying into her champagne glass. One arm of the platinum-blond fashion designer was around her shoulder. I saw the frilled cuffs, the gold bracelet around his wrist, I heard him comfort her, "Don't cry, dearest, that's how women are, nothing but trouble. I know that, my poor little Manny, I know it well."

So that's what she's called, *Manny,* I thought. Lillian, I prayed, please, don't die.

"Excuse me . . ." I pushed the designer aside. He didn't even notice my rudeness.

"My God," he said, "if only you could love men, my poor, poor Manny."

I hurriedly opened the door to the office which had been built into the same mirrored wall which also concealed the one-way mirror, slithered to the desk where Minski had placed the receiver. I held it to my ear. "Lillian!"

There was no answer.

"Lillian!"

Just then the fan began to operate with its usual noise. I swore obscenely and senselessly and yelled loudly, "Lillian! This is Richie! Lillian!"

Through the receiver I heard only the hum of an open line.

"Say something! Where are you?"

Suddenly I heard groans. I had known Lillian as well as one can ever know anyone and I was afraid: This groaning was no hysteria, not an act; these groans had the sound of imminent death.

"Lillian!"

Now I heard an agonizing, throaty rattle, then a dull bump. I knew: the receiver had slipped from her hand. The ventilator stopped.

Fervently I hoped that she did not have the strength to hang up the telephone. I hastily picked up Minski's phone from his desk and placed it next to mine. I listened again to my receiver. The moans had become weaker. If only she didn't hang up—dear God, please. I'll do anything, I'll start a new life, but please don't let her hang up, God, and don't let her die.

Only something as desperate as this made me pray.

Meanwhile I had dialed information on Minski's phone.

A woman's recorded voice answered, "Information, one moment, please. Information, one moment, please . . ."

My watch showed ten minutes past three.

Few girls would be working in information at this hour, I thought. I held the other receiver to my other ear. Lillian's soft, irregular moans filled me with gladness.

Thank you, dear God. She didn't hang up. She is too weak. She—

". . . moment, please . . ." The recording stopped and a girlish voice answered, "Information, operator eighteen, good morning."

The voice sounded very tired.

"Morning! Operator, my number is 57 64 32. I also have a second telephone, 43 12 61. I received a call on this line. The line is still open but the party does not answer. I'm afraid something has happened there. Can you find out who is calling me and from where?"

"The number is 43 12 62?" the tired voice asked.

"Not 62! 61! The number is 43 12 61!" I yelled.

"I can understand you better if you don't shout, sir."

"I'm sorry."

Moans.

Go to hell, Lillian!

Please, help me, dear God, let her live.

Lillian, Lillian, how happy we'd been . . .

"Is this call domestic or from a foreign country?"

100

"I don't know! These days one can dial foreign countries direct!"

"You can only dial direct to Italy, Austria, Switzerland, France or—"

"Miss! Operator, can you tell me who's calling me?"

"If the connection is still—"

Sighing came through the other receiver.

"I'm still connected!"

"Please wait, sir."

Moaning. Silence. Groans. Silence.

I glanced through the one-way mirror. They were still there, in the bar with the red lighting, necking, dancing to music I could not hear; Petra Schalke still grieving. I saw opened mouths, laughing, screaming; flushed, perspiring faces. I saw this soundless scene and thought that if there was a hell there was no need for burning—just spend eternity in this fashion. (Situations such as this made me philosophical.) I no longer saw the two special-effects men.

"Hello!" I cried. "Hello, Operator!"

No answer. I knew this was going to take time. Yet I wondered who was tracing the call, where and how.

Moans came through the other receiver. . . .

The office door leading to the corridor was pushed open. Vanessa, sneezing, wearing her blue robe and high-heeled slippers burst in, Minski right behind her.

"She ran away from me!" he shouted.

"I don't want this woman to make Richie unhappy again!" Vanessa rushed at me and tried to wrest the receivers from me.

"Boris!" I roared.

He threw himself at Vanessa, trying to pull her away from me. Vanessa scratched, kicked, sneezed, screamed at me to hang up the phones, all the while cursing Lillian.

I heard the operator through Minski's telephone. "Hello, are you still there?"

"Yes—"

"Put down that phone!" Vanessa screamed and threw herself at me again.

"Is anything wrong?" the telephone voice asked.

"No, nothing . . . what were you going to say?"

"Your number 43 12 61 is connected with 66 33 in Treuwall."

"What's the name of the place?" I stuffed the other receiver into my tuxedo pocket and reached for a pencil.

"Oh, Richie, Richie, I . . . I . . ." Vanessa suddenly swayed and before Minski could catch her she sank down on the worn old carpet, sneezed, swallowed hard, gagged, retched and vomited. She gasped for air, sneezed, gasped and vomited again.

"Excitement," Minski said. He was ministering to Vanessa, holding her head, supporting her. "She's terribly upset. There, just look at that—green. Pure bile. Because she loves you."

Vanessa was still retching.

"Hello, hello, what's going on there?"

"It's all right, operator. Please give me that name again."

Her voice sounded undecided. "I think I had better call the police."

"There's no need for that. Someone here just feels sick. My name is Richard Mark. I'm calling from my club, the Strip."

"Oh," said the operator. It seemed to have allayed her doubts. She giggled. We must have had some reputation in Frankfurt.

"The name, please . . ."

"Treuwall."

I wrote it down.

"Where is that?"

"In the Lüneburg Heath."

I made a note of it.

"I'll give you the area code," said the operator, still

giggling. Her voice no longer sounded tired, it was bold and curious.

"You must have quite a club there! Naturally, someone like me never gets to go——"

"The area code, miss. Please!"

She gave it to me.

"The address is 24 Waldpromenade. The name of the party is——"

"Lillian Lombard. That I know. Thank you, Miss."

"You're welcome. Good——"

"Just a minute!"

"Yes?"

"In Treuwall . . . is there a hospital?"

"Why do you need——? Oh, I understand! I don't know. Treuwall is a county seat. There should be. Just a moment, please."

I pulled the other telephone receiver from my pocket and held it to my ear.

Agonized moans could still be heard but now at longer intervals.

I looked at Vanessa. She was a sorry sight sitting on the carpet. Minski was holding her. Her face was gray, her lips blue. She said, "Idiot. You stupid idiot."

"Sh . . . sh . . ." Minski comforted her.

"An idiotic idiot who can only talk nonsense and think nonsense and who lies to himself and others and who is beyond help," Vanessa said before she collapsed into Minski's arms. His tuxedo was a mess.

"Great," Minski said grimly. "Just marvelous. A cold. All those injections. And now this! Do you know what this means to us financially if, God forbid, she can't go on tomorrow? Or maybe even for several days? I knew why I was so shaken. I knew how this Lillian would affect you. Simple deduction." Carefully he lifted up Vanessa. It was difficult for him since she was taller than he. He carried her to the shabby, leather-covered couch, laid her on it and placed a cushion under her head. Vanessa, weak with exhaustion, was murmuring softly.

"Yes," Minski said gently. "Yes, my little one, just calm down, be still, very still, do it for me . . ."

"Take that cushion away," I said.

"What?"

"Take the cushion away. Just in case she starts again. And put her flat on her side. Watch out she doesn't swallow her tongue."

He looked at me sorrowfully, then carried out my instructions. Vanessa was still mumbling.

How long did this oaf from information need to find out if there was a hospital in Treuwall? Through my telephone receiver came faint moans.

"Operator!" I yelled.

But there was no answer.

Minski was kneeling beside Vanessa, stroking her hair, saying something in Yiddish.

"What did you say?"

"Das arme, kleine Menschele," Boris said.

On the night of October 1, 1965, a nude, blonde girl ran screaming through the park of a small castle of the town of Rambouillet. This exclusive refuge of particularly wealthy persons is situated about thirty-five kilometers southwest of Paris. The park through which the screaming girl ran was outside the town on a road leading to the main road. It was enclosed by a high wall interspersed by equally high, thick, connected wrought-iron pointed staves—an array of menacing lances.

A Paris-born taxi driver caught sight of the girl through the staves. He turned the steering wheel sharply so that the headlights of his cab now shone into the park, stopped and jumped out. He noticed several people near the pale-yellow castle, among them two women, who hurriedly withdrew. One of the women held a torn piece of cloth.

"Help me! Please, help me!" The naked girl screamed. "I can't get out of here!"

"Over here!" The young driver ran ahead a little way, scaled the ancient, moss-covered wall from which stones had crumbled in places. The girl already on the opposite side, toes and fingers pressed into holes and crevices in the stone wall. The driver, dressed in corduroy trousers, turtleneck sweater, a short leather coat and a visored cap, was now lying flat atop the wall.

"Slowly," he admonished. "Careful you don't hurt yourself. Give me your hand." With great care he pulled the girl up and helped her down to the ground.

The girl had sustained several abrasions on her thighs and chest. One scratch was bleeding. The young driver ran for the first-aid box in his trunk.

"No, don't."

"It could become infected. Better it's done. . . ." He painted the scratches with the brown liquid.

"Ouch!" exclaimed the girl.

"Almost finished . . . or would you rather get blood poisoning?"

"Sure," said the girl who stood naked in the light of the headlights. "What do you think?"

The young man took off his leather coat and handed it to the girl. She slipped it on.

"Now what?" he asked.

"Away . . . just let's get away from here."

"To the police?"

"No, not the police. I'm a foreigner here, and the Avignolles are a very influential family."

The young man looked toward the castle.

"Yes," said the girl. "Those people."

It was cold. It was late. "Then what else?" asked the chauffeur.

"I don't know . . . I really don't know."

"Well, I don't mind giving you a lift, and you can tell me what happened and then we'll consider what can be done," said the man. "But I'm a foreigner too, Greek. I'm not going to have any difficulties because of you, am I? Did you do something wrong?"

"No," said the girl.

The driver looked at her, brooding. He had dark eyes, dark hair and a classic Hellenic nose.

"Don't you believe me?" asked the girl.

"Foreigner . . . from where?"

"I'm German."

The young man grimaced.

"You don't like Germans, do you?"

"Nonsense. What makes you think that?"

"You're Greek. I can understand that a great many people don't like us Germans. It's understandable after what has happened."

"Understandable and dumb," said the driver. "How can one dislike an entire nation? What do I know of each German? And what fault is it of yours that you are German?"

"I see you love Germans. Your face is bright with joy."

"Now stop it! I . . . I have nothing against Germans!"

"Especially when they're young girls . . ."

"Ah, the devil," said the driver. "Get in!" He thought how really stupid it had been of him to make that grimace and he also thought of what he had seen, all that now hidden by his leather coat. "I'm sorry," he said, and helped the girl into the car.

Once they were driving he offered cigarettes. The almost leafless trees lining the road seemed to fly past in the light of the headlights.

"How fortunate for me that you happened to be passing by," said the girl. Although both of them were foreigners they spoke an almost accentless French.

"I had a fare," said the young driver. "Son of some wealthy oil man. Has a castle near here too. He got so loaded in Paris that he couldn't even start his Jaguar. Were they going to rape you?"

"Yes," she answered. "Two women. Madame Avig-nolle and her girl friend. They were both drunk."

"High society."

"In my room."

"Excuse me?"

"Both of them came to my room. I was fast asleep. Suddenly I felt someone next to me and—"

"Do you usually talk like this?"

"Like what?"

"Haphazardly?"

"No, not really."

"The excitement then," said the chauffeur. "After all rape is not an everyday occurrence."

"It was Madame Avignolle."

"I see."

"Who was lying next to me, I mean."

"Aha."

"Her friend was just about to . . . I really couldn't help it!"

"Help what?"

"That my knee hit her in the teeth. When I awoke and felt what was going on I pulled up my knees and one of them hit her. That, by the way, was when I jumped up and ran away, those women right behind me. I managed to get out of the house, but without your help I would never have been able to escape from the park."

"A pleasure," said the young Greek. He drove fast. They were some distance from the little Le Toucan hotel, where he had rented a room: a shabby room in a cheap hotel in a poor neighborhood near the Gare du Nord. It was noisy and smelled of poverty. But it was inexpensive.

"Madame caught up with me in the park," the young girl declared. "That's when I lost my nightgown. She tore it off. Is this the new Citroën?"

"Yes."

"You know, I'm not a virgin. But women! I have never . . . and tonight . . . it really was horrible!"

"I can imagine," the young Greek commiserated. "It stands to reason that there are as many decent people in Germany as there are in other countries."

"You talk pretty haphazardly yourself!"

"I am . . . I'm a bit confused too," he explained.

"And so insidious," the girl continued. "While I was sleeping! They had drunk at least three bottles of champagne. They would have had me in the park if it hadn't been for the gardener and the cook. My screams had roused them. The butler wasn't there. He doubles as chauffeur."

"Aha."

"I mean, he didn't come because he had to drive Monsieur Avignolle to Marseilles. They left yesterday. Today is Saturday, isn't it?"

"That's right. How do you feel now?"

"Oh, much better, thank you. Naturally I cannot ever go back there again."

"I'll pick up your things tomorrow."

"Would you? You really are nice!"

"You're nice too."

"Yes," agreed the girl, "aren't I? I'm a nice German."

"I wish you'd stop that! Please! Tell me, how did you come to the Avignolles?"

"I came to perfect my French." The girl laughed. "You know how girls nowadays take positions in foreign countries to learn a language. I came for that reason. Isn't that odd?"

"And you came to Rambouillet, that's odd too."

"Why?"

"During the first half of the seventeenth century a Marquise de Rambouillet lived in a palace in Paris. Hôtel de Rambouillet." The young man quickly overtook three produce-laden trucks probably on their way to Les Halles. "For many years she gave her famous parties for the most elegant and sophisticated people in France. Among them were an extraordinary number of women."

"How do you know that?"

"It's part of one's education," the young Greek said, grinning. "The marchioness encouraged French culture in the spirit of preciosity. They were called 'Les Précieuses.' Molière wrote a comedy about them." The driver laughed. "And three hundred years later in Rambouillet . . . voilà, immortal France!"

"Where did you learn all this? You're really not a taxi driver?"

"No. Or yes. But only at night."

"And during the day?"

"I study physics at the Sorbonne," answered Panos Mitsotakis.

Panos Mitsotakis, born in Athens in 1939, had had a very happy childhood. It lasted three years.

His father, a cheerful man, was a tailor; his mother, a pretty woman who loved to sing, helped her husband with his work. They were an affectionate family.

Panos's father never concerned himself with politics. Near the end of June 1942, he left to deliver a pair of trousers and was trapped in a battle between monarchist and communist resistance groups. Italian and German soldiers were also engaged. They, together with Bulgarians, had invaded and occupied Greece.

Greece had suffered severe political unrest since 1936. That had not been resolved either by General Metaxas' dictatorship nor King George II's trip to London before the arrival of German troops and their allies. The Italian military government originally in control could not cope with the civil strife.

Achilles Mitsotakis, hit by bullets from all sides when he attempted to deliver the trousers to a house behind which monarchists were taking cover, died instantly.

Such incidents were commonplace during that time. Within a year the incompetent Italian government had been replaced by a German military government. Then there was more order, more dead, and a famine.

From this the young widow Aglaya Mitsotakis saved her young son and herself by befriending a German corporal working at the army supply depot. This corporal, twenty-one years old, came to see her whenever he could, surreptitiously and cautiously. A relationship with a Greek woman was fraught with danger. He never came without food. He played with Panos, who quickly learned to speak German.

King George II, who had formed a new government in London, regularly broadcast speeches via the BBC. He predicted the destruction of the aggressors, assured of his return from exile and threatened severe punishment to those who had collaborated with the enemy. The king was very comfortable in London.

Between August and October 1944 the Germans were forced to leave Greece. The young corporal left Panos and his mother in the beginning of September. He died four days later in an ambush by partisans.

King George II finally did return to his country in September 1946, still torn by civil strife a year and a half after war's end. The king kept the promises he had made in London. He decorated or promoted many of his subjects—others were jailed or killed.

Immediately after the Germans' withdrawal Aglaya Mitsotakis had had her hair shorn by patriots and had been forced to walk through the streets of Athens, a large sign hanging from her neck. She was cursed, spat upon and beaten. The placard said:

I, Aglaya Mitsotakis
was a whore of the
German murderers.

Her small son watched helplessly as his mother was being mistreated. Although he could read he did not understand what "whore" meant. He knew Germans but until now had not known that they were murderers. He saw that the Germans were hated. Now Panos hated them too. They were the cause of his mother's suffering. A German murderer had come as a friend; from a German murderer they had accepted food and eaten it! He thought about it; he dreamed about it.

Panos never spoke to his mother of his thoughts or dreams so as not to add to her obvious suffering. By keeping his troubled thoughts a secret his hatred for the Germans was aggravated excessively.

Six months after his return King George II abdicated; King Paul I succeeded him. The civil war continued. In the mountains in the north it was not to end until 1949. Meanwhile, the struggle brought as much misery and hunger as during the German occupation.

The hair of the still-pretty Greek woman had grown again and she had moved to another part of the city where no one knew that she had been intimate with a German. She worked behind the counter of a bar frequented by reporters of international press agencies who had been sent to Athens to report on the civil war.

Once more Aglaya saved herself from starvation by becoming the bed-companion of an *Agence France Presse* correspondent. Once Panos learned that no one thought of the French as murderers he began to like the journalist as much as he had liked the young German corporal. His mother had not been happy for a long time; now she sang songs again.

The reporter stayed two-and-a-half years in Greece, during which time Panos learned the French language.

While attending school his teachers thought him so exceptional that they urged his mother to send the gifted boy to high school. She had no means to continue his education.

Then someone remembered that her husband had been killed during the German occupation. Aglaya received a document honoring her husband, a small pension and a scholarship to a high school for her son. Panos graduated with honors and attended the University of Athens on another scholarship. He planned to be a physicist.

The country had not resolved its disrupting problems. Frequently changing governments closed the university on numerous occasions. Panos found his studies interrupted. A change of school was essential. Although he knew that not all Germans could be murderers, his memories of events were still too painful to consider a German university.

His mother's former lover, the French correspondent, wrote to encourage Panos to try for the Sorbonne. He promised to look after him. When Panos arrived in Paris he showed an affectionate interest. That lasted only a few months, however, for his paper sent him to Africa. There, during a revolt in the Congo, he was accidentally killed.

By then, Panos's professors at the Sorbonne were so favorably impressed with him they offered a scholarship.

He took a job as a taxi driver to enable him to live and study, since he could not become a burden on his mother's small pension. He lived frugally, studying by day and driving at night. He was young; it mattered little to him that he worked hard and slept little, so long as he could complete his studies. When he met Britt Rending so unexpectedly on that first night of October 1965, he was twenty-six years old.

Britt's mother Elsbeth was the granddaughter of the founder of the Petersen Fish Canneries near the harbor in Hamburg. His son modernized and enlarged the factory and Petersen delicacies were soon in great demand. Elsbeth's father, a wealthy man when she was born, had a villa in Blankenese. She was a nervous, homely child, later a nervous, plain girl with dull blond hair, a pallid complexion, large blue eyes showing constant astonishment, and an uninteresting body. Her father's fortune made her attractive to a certain type of man.

One of them was Thomas Francis Rending, some of

whose ancestors had come from England, an extremely handsome member of one of Hamburg's oldest patrician families. The Rendings had been millionaires while the emperor reigned but had lost almost everything during the inflation and economic crisis.

Thomas Rending, trained to luxury, played golf, tennis, cricket with equal skill and rode superbly. He had never been a worker nor did he intend to be.

Unattractive Elsbeth met the charming Rending at a reception at the Overseas Club and promptly fell in love. Rending's common sense overcame his cultivated taste for women and he adopted the unaccustomed role of suitor. The war had begun and Rending (who had connections) became an army captain stationed in Hamburg. Though ten years younger than Elsbeth, once they had declared their love, he assured her that this would never make the slightest difference. Elsbeth was only too willing to believe that.

Their wedding in Hamburg's Michaelis Church was an aristocratic affair. Despite his influential friends Captain Rending was transferred to the eastern front. He had often expressed a desire to participate in the heroic fight of the German people, rifle in hand, but he was unhappy in his new career.

During the dreadful air raids by the British on Hamburg in July and August 1943 almost half of the city and well over half of the harbor installations were destroyed. That situation resulted in a special leave for Rending in September 1943. He found the villa in Blankenese untouched by bombs, the factories not too badly damaged. His family—following an invitation by Elsbeth's mother —were at the Petersen retreat in the Black Forest. Elsbeth had remained in Hamburg with her father. Rending was astonished to find that his wife had changed. Now energetic and efficient, she had ably assisted her father to return the business to full productivity.

Quite naturally, Rending was gratified over the condi-

113

tion of the factories; he did not particularly like the change in his wife. Yet a certain concern for himself made him especially loving. Once again at the eastern front he received a letter from Elsbeth. She was pregnant. Captain Rending thought that it had been right for him to show his concern and affection.

Her father now insisted that she too move to the relative safety of the Black Forest, Elsbeth wrote, to give birth to her baby there.

Britt Rending was born the twenty-eighth of May 1944 in a private clinic near Baden-Baden. (At that time Boris Minski was on his way from the concentration camp Maidaneck to Auschwitz; nine days later the allies were to invade Normandy.)

Elsbeth returned to Hamburg just before the end of the war; she had left her child in the Black Forest. A telegram had informed her of the death of her father, who had been killed during a bombing raid. Elsbeth's mother collapsed. She died six months later.

Elsbeth lived the next three years in the basement of her villa in Blankenese which, miraculously, had remained undamaged. British officers lived upstairs. During those years the frail, delicate Elsbeth and her employees worked under the most difficult conditions to rebuild the factories. Production started again in the spring of 1948.

Petersen's delicacies were again in great demand after the war. Through skillful manipulation Elsbeth managed to save the firm's capital during the monetary reform. She was absorbed in her work. Her husband was a POW in Russia; her little daughter remained in the Black Forest. Britt saw her mother on the rare occasions when she came for a short visit. She was taken to Hamburg only after ex-Captain Rending had returned in 1949. Their first meeting was distressing. She saw him as a strange, disquieting man and shrank from him. In her confusion she gave all her love and affection to her mother.

Thomas Rending alternately considered his daughter's

behavior as annoying or as an attitude to be ignored. Now *he* took over the business, now *he* was the boss, a situation which he emphasized. During the five years he had been a POW the Russians had shown him the meaning of authority. They had regarded him as a parasitic playboy and probably a coward.

He knew it—but those he dealt with did not. Vitality and ruthlessness in business always inspire admiration. Rending had soon become a respected and envied member of the magical circle of masterminds who gave Germany what was usually described as the "miracle."

In 1955 Rending, one of Germany's first new millionaires, was awarded the Federal Order of Merit.

Elsbeth had aged suddenly. Specialists confirmed a heart ailment.

"There is no cause for alarm," the doctor had advised her. "If you live sensibly and avoid undue excitement and overexertion you could live to be a hundred, madame."

"I already feel that old," Elsbeth Rending said. "Especially when I think of my husband. He is so healthy, a young man—and stuck with an old woman. . . ."

The doctor's efforts to change her attitude were in vain. He was aware that it was a subconscious sense of self-preservation. He prepared himself for the prolonged treatment of an extremely wealthy patient.

Admired by men, adored by women, Thomas Rending was well aware of the advantages his wife's illness held for him. The belief that her husband had never loved her, had married her only for her money, became a certainty to Elsbeth. She decided to "punish" him by exaggerating her illness.

He soon understood her scheme and became more cautious in his ventures. Her attempts to make matters difficult did not disturb him. Subtly, he appeared sincere whenever he comforted Elsbeth, assured her of his love and commiserated that she was not able to be by his side to discharge those duties required by society. He should forgive her, Elsbeth begged slyly, and do whatever he thought necessary.

Rending forgave her. He did whatever he thought necessary. His daughter, Britt, irritated him, since he understood that she thought him an enemy. He decided to send the child, then ten years old, to one of the most exclusive and expensive boarding schools in the French-speaking part of Switzerland.

"It is customary for people of our standing," he said curtly when Britt, tearfully, had begged him to be allowed to stay with her beloved mother.

Elsbeth remained silent.

Excerpt from a textbook for youth-welfare counselors:

> According to international statistics 85 per cent of children under the age of twelve who are sent away from home because of unhappy marriages and are left without guidance by child-welfare counselors develop serious emotional disorders. Moreover, it is immaterial if the parents are poor or wealthy. Disorders are numerous. A child may develop antisocial tendencies, commit criminal acts, engage in open or covert prostitution, alcoholism, sexual deviation. The prognosis for recovery is poor.

In the Swiss boarding school Britt Rending met a group of girls from wealthy families. Each hated or despised one or both of her parents or, in some instances, loved both desperately. These girls, deprived of parental care, gave vent to their grievances through cynicism, snobbishness—and a veritable drive to accumulate sexual experiences.

When Britt was thirteen she was seduced by a sixteen-year-old boy. At fourteen she seduced one sixteen years old and by fifteen had had two more experiences: a tele-

116

gram messenger and a married lawyer. She could have passed for eighteen when only fifteen. Though she had her mother's large blue eyes, her hair was golden, her lips pouting, her body alluring. In walk, conversational manner, lazy smile, she seemed flamboyantly erotic.

The obvious desire she created in men titillated her extremely sensual nature. Despite her success in the carnal sphere she remained melancholy and despondent.

This condition persisted even when, during vacations, she returned to her beloved mother in Hamburg. Elsbeth had retreated further into her illness, unable to face even slight exertion or excitement.

Britt's father had meanwhile been appointed consul to a South American state. He continued to be successful and had lost none of his vivacity. Despite his sophisticated discretion his amatory adventures were talked about, guardedly yet without reproach. What, after all, should a man do who was married to an invalid wife so much older?

Britt soon heard of her father's private life. Her hatred increased. She would not upset her mother by broaching this subject and was, therefore, astonished when her mother unexpectedly told her that she was fully informed about her husband's escapades.

The conversation took place in the garden of the villa in Blankenese. The mother was resting in a chaise longue. Britt, sitting on the lawn next to her, stared unbelieving.

"Oh, certainly, I've known for a long time," Elsbeth Rending said and studied the Elbe River. She spoke softly, a method in the role she had chosen to play.

"You have?" Britt asked, aghast.

"Just now there's only one girl, a little actress. Yvonne Horn." She mentioned the address to impress her daughter with how much she knew. "He visits her often, he is always very cautious—but not careful enough to evade a good private detective."

"But . . . but why—" Britt's voice broke.

The mother smiled.

"Why I put up with this? That's what you were going to ask me, weren't you?"

Britt nodded.

"I *can* put up with it because I decided to ignore it. Your father is convinced that I know nothing and you must swear that you'll never tell him of this conversation. Swear it!"

Britt swore.

"Good," her mother said, satisfied. "You see, your father is polite and considerate, and I want things to remain the way they are."

"Remain the way they are?"

"Please. Not so loud!" The mother grimaced. "I can't stand loud voices."

"I'm sorry," Britt said and through a veil of sudden tears looked across the garden down to the glittering river, the red, blue and white ships, large and small, going upstream to the harbor or down to the sea.

"You know, I dare not allow myself to become upset, and a talk with your father about this would upset me. It would not change what he does. And I do love your father—in spite of everything—and I love you, my sweet . . . I love you very much." Self-pity overwhelmed her, made her voice tremble. "That's why I say nothing. I have to consider my heart. . . ."

How I hate him, Britt thought, oh how I hate him!

"We've had happy times too," the mother continued. It was a beautiful day. She felt better than she had for some time. "Nothing lasts. But I am content. As long as he doesn't leave me I am satisfied."

Britt's life might have been different had she been aware of the meaning of the exultation in her mother's voice.

"But he won't ever leave me . . . never! Our factories, my child, they were built up by my father and grandfather and me. I rebuilt them with my hands. My father had had the good sense to insist on a marriage contract. Your father has *no claim* on those factories or anything else should he divorce me or is proven guilty of adultery. You see, as long as I live he is going to remain my husband, mine. No one is going to get him before my death. Now you can understand, can't you?"

Britt nodded. She was trembling with suppressed anger, hatred for her father, hurt and pity for her mother.

And the water of the river shimmered and the ships were bright in the sunlight on this summer afternoon in 1962.

Elsbeth Rending died on just such a summer's day in 1963.

Britt had graduated with honors in July and had returned home from Switzerland a week before her mother's death.

At her casket, lying in state at the villa, Britt told her father, "She's on your conscience!"

The very attractive actress Yvonne Horn became Britt's father's second wife exactly a year later. The widower married the brunette, green-eyed Yvonne, her face faintly reminiscent of a cat, in the old and venerable Michaelis Church, attended by members of Hamburg's patrician families.

Britt had not gone to the church—because of illness it was said. When the wedding party returned to the villa they were greeted by a very pale, very beautiful and perfectly healthy Britt Rending. It was the beginning of an open war between Britt and her father's wife.

Britt snubbed her whenever possible and created difficult and embarrassing situations for her.

Thomas Rending, fifty years old, loved his twenty-nine-year-old wife with jealous passion. Yvonne was secure in her knowledge that she completely dominated him. She demanded that he buy an apartment for his daughter.

Britt studied French at a language institute; she intended to become an interpreter.

"Either your daughter leaves this house or I will," Yvonne said.

Rending did not argue. He informed Britt bluntly that, through her own fault, it had now become necessary for her to leave the house they had shared. Naturally, her lawful claims to family possessions were not in any way affected by this.

Britt made no protest. It was clear that, once more, she had lost a contest. She moved into a comfortable apartment and completed her studies with excellent grades. On the day of her graduation she heard that Yvonne had given birth to a boy.

Now her stepmother's position was more secure than ever. Britt's hatred for her and her father remained undiminished.

The language school arranged for its students to live and work for reputable families in foreign countries to enable their students to perfect their chosen language.

Britt, not quite twenty-one, wrote her father for permission to go to France for one year, to stay with a Monsieur and Madame Avignolle.

Monsieur Hercule Avignolle, she wrote, was reputed to be one of Paris's most prominent art dealers, with an apartment in Paris and a castle in nearby Rambouillet. Her father was happy to give his consent. Britt went to Paris.

It was 3:30 in the morning of October 2, 1965, when Britt and Panos entered his room in the hotel Le Toucan. She felt cold, took off the leather coat she had worn on the drive from Rambouillet and quickly slipped into an old brass bed.

The young Greek had returned the cab to the garage and had asked to be relieved for the remainder of the night. He lied, saying he did not feel well.

Panos apologized to Britt for the shabbiness of his room.

"Not at all! I think it's romantic and very cozy!" Britt declared.

"Nonsense . . ."

"Word of honor! What does that mean in German?" She pointed to a slip of paper hanging from a nail on the wall above a book-laden table by the window.

Panos, still embarrassed, answered, "It says, 'Man has little luck.' Einstein once said that."

"Einstein was a great man."

"Oh, yeah." Panos said.

On the nearby Gare du Nord locomotives and trains were shunting, clanking, puffing, screeching. Once in a while a siren wailed. It was even noisier during the day. The white paint of the room had faded. A dirty drape hid a sink and bidet. A board over the sink held a small gas burner. Three chairs, a shabby plush sofa, and a large, patchy mirror on the outside of a wardrobe facing the bed completed the furnishings.

Panos switched off the dreary single light after he had turned on a green-shaded bedside lamp.

"Now it's simply luxurious," Britt declared. The cover had slipped and, though partially exposed, she did not move. Panos stared at the large breasts, one of which was smudged with iodine. He coughed, turned, lit a cigarette, extinguished it and disappeared behind the drape. Soon he returned wearing a faded pair of pajamas. Panos picked up the leather coat and went to the sofa. He was conscious of Britt's burning eyes. During their drive he had told her of his life and she of hers.

Panos knew much of this girl he had met only such a short time ago and who was now in his bed. He was embarrassed. Had he known nothing he would not have hesitated. Self-consciously he sat down on the sofa. Their eyes met. She smiled and said in German, "Don't be silly."

121

He rose.

"Take off your pajamas."

He took them off.

"You are beautiful, Panos," Britt Rending said as the bedcover slipped from her. "Come to me."

The din of the train from the railroad station continued, trucks noisily rolled through the still deserted streets and it began to rain softly.

Panos jumped up. A cheap white alarm clock on the bedside table showed a few minutes past nine. Dim, gray light came through the window, rain beat against the window panes. Panos stared at Britt next to him. Her eyes were open. "The alarm . . . I forgot to set it," Panos said. "I . . . I have to—the first lecture . . ." He jumped out of bed.

"There's no lecture today," Britt said. She looked at him, her glance traveled downward. He blushed when he felt his body react.

"Today is Saturday," she explained.

"Saturday—"

"All day. Come to me."

"Shouldn't we . . . oughtn't I . . . I have coffee here and I could get a few brioches . . ."

"Later," Britt said.

They breakfasted at eleven o'clock.

They were happy and gay and spoke German and French alternately. Both of them thought it was excruciatingly comical that Britt could not leave the room since she had not one piece of clothing—a virtual prisoner, Panos said.

"The happiest prisoner in the world!"

Panos glanced at her, inquiringly.

"You are happy?"

"Yes. And you?"

"I am too," Panos answered, seriously. "I am very happy too."

"With a German girl."

He blushed deeply. "Don't," he said. "Please, don't say that. I . . . I'm an idiot, but I told you how it was in Athens and—"

She placed a hand over his mouth.

He kissed her palm.

"What are you going to do now?"

"Whatever I want to!" Britt said. "I'm twenty-one. No one can tell me what to do. Now I need a lawyer."

"Why?"

"You forgot that I'm rich. A goldfish! Now we'll see how much of my father's money belongs to me. And then, who knews, I could study too—here in Paris—or I'll find something else here in Paris."

"Why in Paris?" he asked, softly.

"Idiot," Britt said affectionately. "Or do you intend to stop studying at the Sorbonne and continue in Boston? All right, let's go to Boston! Or how about Princeton? That's where you really ought to go. Einstein was in Princeton . . ."

"You're crazy."

"Of course!" Britt laughed. "Aren't you? All that's been happening to us—isn't that crazy too?"

They spoke one sentence in German and one in French and they were still laughing.

"It certainly is," Panos agreed. "Absolutely crazy."

"And today is Saturday."

"Right. And I'm going to the garage and see if they'll lend me a car," Panos said. "I'm going to drive to Rambouillet to get your clothes. Meanwhile you can cook something. Can you cook?"

"I don't know. They taught me in an exclusive Swiss boarding school."

"I'll be back in two hours at the latest. And then . . ."

"Yes," Britt said. "And then."

"But I have to work tonight again." Panos fretted.

"Tomorrow is Sunday," Britt consoled him.

"I shall be late tonight," Panos continued. "Very late. There's this man, you see. He doesn't speak French as I do—only German. He comes regularly every eight weeks for a weekend and always asks me to be at his disposal. He stays at the Scribe. I interpret for him too."

"What kind of a man is he?"

"He's nice. Owns a bar in Frankfurt. He comes to look at the newest acts in some clubs here."

"Striptease?"

"Yes. He says he needs international performers. He offers them engagements or he steals their acts. He's pleasant, though. Gives generous tips. His name is Minski."

"Those three suitcases contain Mademoiselle Rending's possessions. If you had come half an hour later I would have turned them over to the police. I've been waiting since eleven."

The speaker, an elegantly dressed gray-haired man of dwarfish stature with the florid complexion common to heavy drinkers, wore horn-rimmed glasses. He spoke rapidly and sharply. He stood stiffly in the library on the ground floor of the castle of Rambouillet. A fire crackled in the fireplace. Panos had been admitted by a bland-faced maid who had led him to the library. The waiting man had pounced on him before Panos had uttered a word.

"My name is Tissot. Jules Tissot. Attorney-at-law." He held a card for Panos to read.

Tissot . . .

It suddenly came to Panos where he had seen this gnomish face before: in newspapers! Tissot—a lawyer whose court trials could best be compared to sensational theater premières.

The light was dim in the library heavily lined with bookcases. The wind was beating rain and leaves against the high windows.

"Monsieur Tissot . . . but why . . . and what do you mean by police?"

Jules Tissot had already formed his course of action. He understood character and, therefore, despised most persons. In this instance he knew that timing was important. Threats and an aggressive attitude would panic this young, unsophisticated man. Roughly, he prodded Panos's chest with his finger.

"*I'm* talking. You've seen my card. Where's yours?" He pursued, "Well? Perhaps you'd be good enough . . . or perhaps you don't even possess an identification card?"

Confused, Panos pulled out his passport.

Humans, thought Tissot. Then he remembered his fee. He opened the passport and grunted derisively.

"Foreigner, I see. Limited residence permit. What are you doing in Paris?"

"I'm studying at the Sorbonne. Now will you please . . ."

"I'm certain you know where this"—Tissot gestured deprecatingly—"this young woman is."

"I passed by her in my taxi and saw—"

"Taxi? You drive a taxi?"

"Yes."

"Naturally you have permission to do that."

"Look here, monsieur, I—"

"Be silent. You can thank God when this business does not result in bad consequences for you."

Panos stammered, "Consequences? If there are any consequences as a result of what took place here they will be Madame Avignolle's!"

The lawyer took off his glasses and polished them while he narrowed his red, inflamed eyes. This young man was resisting—but only feebly, Tissot thought.

"Please, repeat that!" Tissot said gently.

"You heard. Where is Madame Avignolle?"

"Away on a trip."

"That's not true!"

125

"Young man, I'm warning you. This little German tart—"

Panos clenched his hands.

"You shouldn't have said that. I'm going to swear out a complaint."

"I've already done that," Tissot said calmly and put on his glasses. The wood in the fireplace crackled loudly. Panos shivered.

The attorney noticed it with satisfaction.

"You've done what?"

"Last night I swore out a complaint against this . . . against Mademoiselle Rending. On behalf of my client Madame Avignolle. The young woman has certainly rewarded my client's hospitality with ingratitude . . . well, pathological, she can't help herself, but we don't have to have it in France." The lawyer again prodded Panos with his finger. "You keep out of this or I'll see to it that you, too, will have to leave France within forty-eight hours. I don't know how you would explain that to the Sorbonne—or any other university for that matter."

"You've asked for Mademoiselle Rending's deportation?"

"My request has already been granted. In cases such as this our police work very quickly. You're going to tell me where the young woman is at present and your address. The gendarme who is waiting in the kitchen is going to accompany you to the Quai des Orfèvres. A detective will then see to it that the Fräulein will be served her expulsion order. She has forty-eight hours to leave France. If she has not left by then a warrant for her arrest will be issued and she will be deported by force." The little man inhaled. Before Panos could speak, Tissot continued his staccato talk. "I have nothing against you, Monsieur. I'm even willing to give you the benefit of the doubt. But I'm advising you: keep away from this, this—"

"Now see here, Mademoiselle Rending's father is one

of the wealthiest and most prominent men in Germany!"

"What does that mean?" Tissot barked. "A threat?"

"No . . . I . . . of course not. But—"

"I'm sorry for the father. Unfortunately one cannot choose one's children. But the spectacle his daughter has made of herself here last night in her drunken condition was disgusting. Even the gendarme I called following Madame Avignolle's telephone call said—"

"Britt was not drunk!" Panos shouted. "She had not had anything to drink. And the disgusting—"

Tissot's index finger jabbed so forcefully that Panos stumbled backwards. Tissot said sharply, "You're not going to shout here again, do you understand me? The Fräulein *was* drunk. And in this condition she molested Madame Avignolle, who was already in bed, in a way that can only be described as—"

"But that's not true!"

"Not true? Madame's screams for help roused the entire staff and a friend of Madame, the Comtesse de la Tournière. Their statements to the police coincide with Madame Avignolle's. They are statements made by French nationals . . . hm. . ."

"These people can't possibly say that . . ."

Tissot went to a telephone.

"I've had enough of you now. Two foreigners trying a little blackmail, eh? I think it would be best if I gave your name to the police too."

Panos's thoughts were in turmoil.

Statements to the police. A successful lawyer. All French nationals. My studies. Britt's expulsion ordered. I'll be next. It must not happen. I need time. Perhaps something can be done later. Not the police.

Tissot was already dialing.

"Put the phone down," Panos said quietly.

Tissot turned and looked at the young Greek, his eyebrows raised.

127

"Then you're going to be sensible. I suppose you've remembered the influential position of the Avignolles."

Panos sat down on one of the three suitcases.

"What's the matter with you?"

"I feel sick."

"I can well imagine," the lawyer said, as though furious.

"Call the gendarme who is to go to Paris with me."

"That's sound thinking, my friend." The attorney placed a hand on Panos's shoulder.

"I'm not your friend," the Greek said. "And take your hand off me."

Jules Tissot complied, smiling.

Fiat justitia, he thought. Justice reigns supreme indeed.

Minski was not a pathological miser, merely a utilitarian one. He lived in two rooms he had rented from a widow who believed he was a waiter in a nightclub.

I lived on the first floor of a lovely old house in the Humperdinckstrasse near the Park Luisa. A few years ago the second floor of the villa became vacant and I asked Minski to rent it. He merely said, "What for?"

He had no car but three tuxedos and an excellent wardrobe. He had his hair cut by an expensive barber, took care of his business in the bar of one of Frankfurt's best hotels and whenever he traveled it was first-class only. His expenses were astronomical.

"One has to make a good impression," Minski told me when I questioned his expense account. "It's part of business. An investment. It all comes back."

Whenever Minski went to Paris to find new attractions for our club he was a generous tipper and well-liked wherever he went. He was in Paris for the weekend of October 2, 1965.

Britt Rending, elegantly dressed and with the assurance of those born to wealth, signed in at the Scribe at nine in the morning. At about eleven she called Minski's room, identified herself and said that it was important for her to speak with him. Would he come to her room?

"I'll be there in ten minutes," Minski said.

He wore a dark-gray suit, a white silk shirt, a silver-gray striped necktie with a pearl exactly on a gray stripe. Britt wore a flaming-red peignoir of crêpe georgette with red lace over a red brassiere and panties, and high-heeled, red silk slippers trimmed with red marabou feathers. She was heavily made up.

Minski said, "You're the Fräulein Rending my taxi driver told me . . ."

"Yes," Britt said. "Please sit down, Herr Minski."

"Does Panos know?"

"No." Her voice sounded hard and determined.

Minski rose quickly.

"Please wait! Panos is sleeping. He was with you all night and he was very tired this morning."

"So am I," Minski said. "Panos told me what has happened to you."

"I must leave France today."

"Panos wants to swear out a complaint against this woman in . . . in . . . you know where. He wants you to stay with him. He wants to—"

"I know what he wants," Britt said. "That's why I left when he was sleeping. Cognac?" She took a bottle from the partially unpacked suitcase.

"I don't drink, thank you."

"I do. Now, for instance." She opened the bottle and half-filled a glass. Minski watched her with curiosity.

"Skol," he said.

"Thank you." She drank. "I bought the bottle yesterday. I thought I might need it today. The clothes too."

"Which clothes?"

"The ones I'm wearing. There are stores where one can buy the craziest things. I waited until Panos had left and then I went shopping. Pretty, aren't they?"

"Very pretty," Minski bowed without rising.

Matter-of-fact Britt said, "I'm giving up against those Avignolles and the Tournières and this high-powered lawyer."

"Wouldn't do that," Minski said. "There's a German consulate. The police ought to hear your version. It's not as simple as you seem to think."

"It's simple against people such as Panos and me, for instance. The lawyer saw that right away. In any case I have no intention to create problems for Panos. He must continue his studies."

"In love?" Minski asked.

"What's that?" Britt asked. She drank again. "So you have not found anything for your club."

"No." Minski was still watching her, becoming increasingly more interested. "Only an American in the Chat Noir."

"The one who does it with the long cigarette holder," Britt said. "Panos told me about it but she is booked until '68, isn't she?"

"Unfortunately."

"I'm twenty-one. Would you engage me?"

"I've been thinking about it," Minski said, serious. "If it's possible for me to do that."

"You *assumed* that I would ask?"

"Naturally, after this reception. And considering all Panos had told me about you and your father?"

"Of course. And?"

"There's one problem. Your father. Suppose he makes trouble, goes to the police?"

"He won't," Britt said. "If I weren't certain of that I wouldn't have asked you to come."

Minski nodded in agreement. "I know about your mother's marriage contract and that your father would have no claim to your mother's estate were he proven guilty of adultery. But that alone is not enough. There has to be something else too."

Britt looked at Minski with interest. "There is. The

130

most important paragraph stipulates that this clause would have effect if proof of adultery were to be uncovered after the death of my mother."

"I see. Before her death your mother must have given you the reports and photographs and names of witnesses the detective had handed over to her and——"

"How do you know?"

"If you didn't have proof you wouldn't be sitting here. Where are the papers now?"

"In a safety deposit box in Hamburg. My father knows nothing of their existence."

"Naturally not."

"Why do you say that?"

"If he had known he wouldn't have treated you the way he did. I think a court would decide in your favor."

"I know that," Britt said. "I've made exhaustive inquiries. You can rest assured."

"I won't until *my* lawyer says so too," declared Minski. "Now, why haven't you gone to court before now? You could have had your revenge a long time ago!"

Britt's voice sounded hoarse "A court action would not ruin him! His fine friends knew what he had been doing. Did they do anything? Did they cut him? They would help him!" Britt's cheeks flushed. "He belongs to Hamburg's society, to those noble families. But once word gets around what his daughter is doing and what he is condoning by his silence, then society will not be able to ignore it. Then no one will help him any more, they will . . ."

"You're drinking too much," Minski said.

". . . avoid him. Then I will go to court and he *will* be ruined. I had thought how to embarrass my father but yesterday when I heard about you I thought of a way to finish him completely."

Britt's blue eyes were almost black now. Her breath came quickly. "People come to the club from all over, don't they?"

Minski nodded, sad, yet fascinated.

"From Hamburg too?"

"Naturally."

"They'll see me. And talk! My father will be forced to keep silent. I can show you the papers as soon as we get back to Germany. *I* am going to tell him what I'm doing and where I am and the proof I have against him. Why are you looking at me like that?"

"I think I've never realized what hatred can really be," Minski said.

"Now you know," Britt said. "I've known since I was a child! I am beautiful—don't you think? I'm sure I can do whatever this girl in the Chat Noir can do. Do you have a cigarette holder?"

"I . . . I don't smoke."

Britt took a candle from the candelabra. Then she undressed.

"The door—"

"I locked it when you came. Where . . . where should I . . ."

"On the carpet," Minski rubbed his chin.

Fifteen minutes later Britt, once more in her negligee, sat across from him.

"Well?"

"Well," Minski said, "firstly: my attorney will have to assure me that your father would lose this court action. I have to be reasonably certain that he is going to keep quiet. Until then I can't promise you anything."

"I have to leave here! I hope you don't have any scruples about—"

"Scruples? Now that the idea occurred to you, you would do something like this in any case—if not for me then for the competition!"

"Definitely!"

"Then I'd rather you work for me. Secondly: you were not bad—hm, not bad at all, but there is still a great deal more to learn."

"With pleasure."

"Thirdly: will you be able to perform with many people watching you?"

"I shall always think of my dear father and stepmother and I'll be able to perform before an audience. Now, how much are you going to pay me? I don't suppose I can expect any checks from my father and I do have to live."

"Which brings us to the fourth point," Minski said. "I shall have to see how we can build you up, advertise you."

"Who is we?"

"My partner, Richie Mark, and I."

"Richard Mark? There's a writer by that name."

"That's Werner," Minski said quickly. "He is Richie's brother."

"I don't mean Werner! I've read his books too, but I'm thinking of *Stan' Still, Jordan* and that book was written by Richard Mark. Your Richie!"

Minski nodded, embarrassed.

"My mother gave me the book—a long time ago."

"It's been a long time since Richie has written a book," Minski pulled at his collar.

"What's the matter? Why are you so nervous?"

"I'm not nervous."

"All right." Britt frowned. "Why doesn't Richard Mark write any more?"

"Why do you want to perform at my club?"

"I see," Britt said. "He has a reason too. I think I will get along splendidly with your partner."

Minski held up his hand. "Not so quick! First I have to see my lawyer. When he gives me the go-ahead then we shall talk about a contract. Meanwhile I'll pay you something to keep you going. Of course you're going to live in a guest house and not in the Frankfurter Hof—"

"I don't care."

"I shall also pay for your training. What do you say?"

"Yes, naturally."

133

Boris rose.

"I'm leaving tomorrow. When do you want to leave?"

"As quickly as possible."

"Good." Minski walked to the door.

"What's the matter?" Britt asked surprised.

"What do you mean?"

Britt glanced at the bed and then at Minski.

"I thought it was customary . . ."

"Not with me," he said. He was in a hurry to leave. "I'll book a seat for you to Frankfurt and call Richie to meet you at the airport at the information counter. Wait until he has you paged."

"Thank you, Herr Minski," Britt said. "You've helped me a lot."

"How can you be so sure?"

"I know. Thank you."

Minski asked, "And what about Panos?"

"I've left a letter for him," Britt answered. She looked out at the autumnal rain and the Boulevard de la Madeleine.

My Dearest,
Now you are asleep. I shall go now. To see Herr Minski. Don't be angry at him. It is not his fault.

I shall work for him. He knows nothing of this yet but I'm certain he will accept me. I shall write you from Frankfurt. Immediately. I would have had to leave in any event. And you must continue your studies. I shall probably never have another such opportunity to ruin my father. You won't understand this. You can say I'm a crazy boche. We cannot see each other now but you could write to me. Please, Panos! I shall write often. We could have been very happy together, couldn't we?

My address will be in my first letter. Do

write. Sometimes. It won't compromise you. And it would make me very happy. I thank you—I don't know for what—for everything.

Become a good, successful man, Panos. I have never prayed for anyone else except my mother. Now I shall pray for you. I embrace you.

Britt

P.S. *I took the paper with Einstein's quote. You can write it again, you know Greek. And Greek writing looks so pretty.*

Panos dropped the letter. It was almost four o'clock. He sat before the book-laden table on which he had found the letter. He sat motionless. His thoughts were in turmoil. She shouldn't have done that. It hurts. Strange, I've never felt this way before. The devil with Minski. I'm not going to drive him after this! I won't be able to reach her now, she's probably in Germany by now.

He made some coffee, sipped the hot bitter liquid and twenty minutes later could think of no good reason why he shouldn't drive Minski. He was generous. And it was not his doing. German women. I knew Britt two hours and we were in bed together. Her story? Perhaps just that, a story. Possibly that lawyer was right—and Britt had lied. A whore. A blessing that things turned out this way. And I was beginning to fall in love. Really wanted to help her. Go to court for her.

I might have been suspended from the Sorbonne! My poor mother! I have to write to her, before I pick up Minski. It's Sunday. Britt? I'll be damned if I write even one single letter, or even read one of hers. She probably won't write anyway . . . a nymphomaniac—perhaps she's frigid, that would explain it—but she is beautiful. So beautiful. I really thought at first . . . I'll forget her, this rich tart, if she is rich. What did I say, I will forget her? I've already forgotten her. I can't even remember how she looks.

He placed his head down on his arms. If only it didn't hurt so much, he thought.

Britt Rending took her papers from the safety deposit box and Minski's lawyer examined them. He agreed with Britt that her father would lose any court litigation.

She wrote her father—in great detail.

In a letter he begged her not to ruin him, to please leave him in peace.

The letter convinced us and the lawyer that Rending would do nothing to prevent his daughter from appearing in our club.

Two experienced strippers now undertook Britt's instruction. They worked hard with a very ambitious Britt. She had written five letters to Panos during the first four weeks of her stay in Frankfurt. When each was returned stamped "REFUSED" she stopped writing. Though unhappy, she tried not to show it. Both she and I were lonely at that time. We drifted together. She had my sympathy. I found her a small apartment and was her frequent escort in private social entertainments. It was natural that we became lovers, though casual ones. Rather we developed a friendship. Poor Britt, she had little luck with men.

She began to admire me as an author. Now I know that this admiration made her jealous of any woman I knew, but chiefly of Lillian Lombard. She, Britt said, was the cause of everything that had happened to me. She hated Lillian. Poor Britt, so full of hatred.

Britt's success was instant. She became the focal point of the Strip. Guests crowded in every night. Among them people from Hamburg.

Rending did nothing. (The Cultural Society did more!) Months passed and we heard gossip that Rending and his wife were frequently ignored—at the theater, in restaurants, at parties. Apparently they had not been invited to some especially exclusive parties. Rumors only, but they made Britt very happy.

"You see," she would say. "You see . . ."

She had given her act its name: the "Candle Act." Minski had provided her artist's name from one of his favorite butterflies, *Vanessa atalanta.*

"We'll call her Vanessa, *das arme, kleine Menschele,*" he had said to me.

Now, on this November night as I waited for the operator to tell me if Treuwall, this town in the Lüneburg Heath, had a hospital and Minski was ministering to Vanessa lying on the office couch—now Minski again said those Yiddish words.

Through the receiver of my telephone I still heard intermittent moans. Lillian Lombard was still alive.

"Hello," the information operator on Minski's telephone said. "Can you hear me?"

"Yes?"

"There is a hospital. The number is 2222."

"Thank you," I said. "Thank you so much."

"I hope you're in time," the girl said. Then the connection was broken.

As soon as I dialed the number a man's voice answered. I asked for emergency. Once connected I spoke hurriedly to a Doctor Hess and informed him of what had taken place.

"The address?"

"Lillian Lombard," I began and heard the doctor inhale quickly.

"What is it?"

"Nothing."

"Do you know the lady?"

"No . . . that is . . . 24 Waldpromenade, right?"

Now I caught my breath. "How do you know?"

"No time for explanations. We're leaving immediately. Thank you for calling."

"One moment!" I cried. "I'm leaving too!"

"It's quite a way from Frankfurt. Wouldn't you rather wait until I call back?"

"No! I'll call you from a restaurant on the autobahn."

"All right. Good-by."

The line went dead. I listened to the other receiver and still heard Lillian's barely audible moans before I hung up. As I passed by Vanessa her eyes glittered, his face wore the same expression which it had whenever she spoke of her father. I knew it was useless to say anything. Boris was bending over a map.

"There," he said and indicated a spot on the map.

My heart sank when I saw the distance from Frankfurt to Treuwall.

Minski's finger indicated the best route for me to take.

"Autobahn to Braunschweig. Then take the B-4. It's the shortest route."

"Shortest route," Vanessa grumbled. "Four, five hundred kilometers. Stupid ass!"

"My car easily does one hundred and eighty kilometers an hour," I said. "It won't take long."

"Won't take long?" asked Minski. "It's pouring outside and there's bound to be fog, but it won't take long."

Minski was still looking at the map.

"Look," he said. "It's beautiful country. A national preservation area. They'll have their county elections in June 1967. In 1930 the Nazis polled more than twenty per cent in the heath. There, take the map." He folded it. "In Treuwall they even had twenty-five per cent," he added.

I looked at him.

"Go on," Minski said. "I'll stay here overnight. Have to look after Vanessa. Call me. From the autobahn. I'll be here."

He helped me into my camel's-hair coat.

"Thanks," I said. *"Wiedersehen,* Boris, *Wiedersehen,* Vanessa."

138

"You . . . you . . ." she started, but Minski stopped her.

"Never mind, Vanessa. He can't help himself. The spirit is willing but the flesh is weak. Go on, Richie, go on!"

Vanessa sneezed, then she screamed, "That's right, you idiot! Go on, run, as fast as you can! Run to your destruction! Run!"

I ran.

Near Kassel the rain stopped, but fog was heavy until Göttingen. After that a strong north wind pounded the car. Whenever possible I drove one hundred and sixty kilometers an hour. My back ached. I was cold.

Twice I called the hospital. Lillian was alive but in critical condition.

Twice I called Minski to inform him. Vanessa answered the second time. Minski had fallen asleep.

When I reached the B-4 and drove though the heath it began to snow—small, hard flakes which remained on the ground.

It was just after seven in the morning. Signs informed me that troop training grounds on either side of the road were restricted areas.

Trucks were passing me from the opposite direction. One side of the road was a forest, the other heavy thicket, behind it reeds and bogs. I smelled its pervasive odor. The road was hilly, which surprised me. I had imagined the Lüneburg Heath to be flat, sandy, with few trees or houses. I saw forests and many houses in small villages. I recalled that the heath had cairns and large boulders but I had not seen any. I wondered about Lillian. Had she died?

I approached Treuwall from the south. It was snowing heavily. The town was larger than I had expected. Forty to fifty thousand inhabitants, I guessed. Soon I saw the first sign: KREISKRANKENHAUS. I drove past ugly houses,

139

dirty factories, across an old bridge over a swollen river, into the more prosperous part of town. Parks, ancient trees, beautiful framework houses, two large churches with towering steeples, an enormous town hall—Gothic architecture in brick—but also many modern buildings, among them a theater.

Old villas nestling in gardens, new houses, wide, quiet streets. I drove along a tree-lined road, when it suddenly became very bright. Before me was a brightly lit parking area, beyond it a six-story building, its wings connected by glass-enclosed bridges to the main building. This was a supermodern and obviously very expensive hospital.

I parked my dirt-covered car and made my way through the icy wind and snow to the main entrance of the building. In the spacious neon-lit foyer hung the usual directory. The hospital had been built 1957–1960. The head of the large board read:

KREISKRANKENHAUS TREUWALL
DIRECTOR: PROFESSOR DR. CLEMENS KAMPLOH

An elderly nurse was seated behind a desk in the emergency department. She asked me to wait in the waiting room; she would inform Dr. Hess that I had arrived but ignored my urgent questions as to Lillian's condition. I walked nervously in the green waiting room. Had Lillian died? Why hadn't the nurse given me any information? I was certain Lillian was dead.

Above the door hung a crucifix. I tried to pray but could not. The air in the room was foul. I tried in vain to open the window, lit a cigarette, then crushed it in an ashtray. The smoke made me nauseated. My head ached. I looked out at the whirling snow over the parking area when a door opened.

I turned to talk to Dr. Hess.

It was not Dr. Hess.

It was my brother Werner.

140

SECOND MOVEMENT

Molto vivace

MY BROTHER LOOKED at me, suspiciously. "What do you want?"

"Help me on the chair."

"Why?"

"Because I want to stand on it."

My brother shrugged his shoulders and helped me up.

"Thank you," I said. Then with all the strength I could muster I punched his face. Blood spurted from his nose. I was much shorter than he: I could only reach his face if I stood on a chair.

Werner had been born in 1918, the same year as Rachel Minski, and was five years older than I. Both of us had brown eyes.

My brother yelled with pain, stumbled backward, regained his balance. His face set. He punched me in the stomach. I fell off the chair, rolled on the floor, hands pressed to my body. Now I yelled.

"You underhanded bastard," Werner said and kicked me. That is my first memory.

My yelling brought our old Sophie, followed by mother. Sophie cradled me in her arms, comforted and questioned me at the same time.

My mother was in her robe. It must have been a Sunday morning, since that was the only day when she did not have to go to her office. She was, understandably, embittered by the disturbance which had disrupted her sleep.

The complaining Werner, a handkerchief pressed to his bleeding nose, was sent to the bathroom with Sophie. My mother angrily pulled me upright and shouted, "Why did you do that, you nasty child?" I looked at my mother whom I loved so much yet could never tell her so. There she stood, her face pasty, swollen from sleep, her short-sighted eyes dull and lackluster as herself.

Answer me!" she shouted.

Instead of an answer I asked two questions. "You don't like me, mommy, do you? You hate me, don't you?"

I'd given anything had she protested. Perhaps she was upset by the constant fighting of her sons, drained by her work at the newspaper, by the responsibility of raising two sons after her husband had left her for a younger woman three months before I was born. Six months later he had obtained a divorce and remarried. Today I know that my mother had grown up without love. She became bitter and hardhearted to hide her sensitivity.

How well I remembered her maxims.

One does not become ill. If one does, one must not talk about it. One must do one's duty. One must not complain. Nonachievement is an affront to God. One must not talk about one's failures. One must make oneself indispensable.

One must, one does not.

On that Sunday morning my mother snapped at me, "Hate you? You hysterical brat! I don't hate you but if you go on behaving this way one day I shall——" She interrupted herself but I had heard enough.

"Then it's true." Suppressed tears made me aggressive.

"You're insolent, too?" My mother's pale cheeks reddened. "You will tell me this instant why you hit your brother in such a malicious manner!"

I was silent. My heart ached. I wanted to hug her, kiss her, cry on her shoulder, tell her I loved her, and she threatened me. My brother had been right, I despaired.

I would not answer and a moment later my face stung from two slaps. She had never done that before. I clenched my teeth and looked at her. In spite of the pain I would rather have died than burst into tears.

"You nasty, obstinate lout," my mother cried and burst into tears. "Go to your room. You'll stay there until tomorrow. Do you understand? *Answer me!*"

But I would not.

I slammed the door of my room shut as hard as I could and I remember that I thought: Just wait. One day . . . one day . . .

I had no idea what I would do that one day. I just knew it would be something terrible. As had Shakespeare's Richard III, I, too, resolved definitely to become a villain.

Sophie brought my lunch and urged me to eat. I found out that my mother had returned to bed after taking a sedative. Werner had gone to a children's movie.

"That was a nasty thing you did, Richard. Wicked. You ask Werner to help you on the chair and then you hit him. His nose bled terribly, all over the bathroom."

"It did?" My lunch suddenly tasted delicious.

Sophie shook her head. "You shouldn't have done that. You're a good boy. And I love you."

"Yes, you do!"

"Your mother loves you too."

"She hates me! She hated me even before I was born! She wanted to get rid of me!"

"What do you mean?"

"She wanted to kill me! Werner said so!"

"Werner . . . that's why you hit him?"

"Yes! And mother hit me. And Werner is allowed to go to the movies. And I have to stay in my room. And he said she loves only him."

"But that's nonsense."

"It is not! Mommy told him. I've heard her. You know, too, that she says that!"

Sophie had been with us since Werner had been an infant, our housekeeper and my mother's confidante. Now she said, "It's difficult for your mother, Richard. Alone with two children."

"Perhaps daddy left because she was mean to him too. I'm going to leave too when I'm bigger. Werner, Werner, always Werner. She loves him. She wanted to kill me!"

"No!"

"Then swear that she didn't! You're so good, you talk about God and the angels and all! Swear it!"

"You'll have to believe me when I tell you it's not true."

"It's true," I said. "Or you would swear."

Poor Sophie. She tried her best to convince me.

"I'm going to be a musician when I grow up. You know why? Because the last time daddy was here mommy yelled at him—they always yelled at each other—'Musicians! They're the worst!' I want to be the worst. I want to make everybody unhappy."

Father was a professional violinist with the Bavarian State Opera in Munich. His visitation rights called for two days every other month, but he could not always come to Frankfurt. His work, a chronic shortage of money, and frequent tours of the orchestra made regular visits impossible. Still each visit was a catastrophe. Mother expended her bitter resentment by shaming father before us children.

She was pleased that my brother refused to go with father. I did—I had noticed that it upset my mother. Also, I shyly admired this strange man.

Father was a gentle, impractical person, charming, polite, and at times even merry. We were in harmony with each other. It was he who introduced me to the world of music. He took me to operas and concerts which I re-lived in my dreams, wonderful dreams filled with harmony and beauty.

On my seventh birthday he gave me a violin. I only had it for one day. That night I heard my mother come into my room and rummage in the dark. I feigned sleep and switched on the light to look around only after she had left. The violin was gone. Then I heard the splinter-ing of wood. I was too afraid of my mother, who had wanted to kill me even before I had been born, to leave my bed. So afraid that I did not even mention the violin to her. I told father that I had lost his present in the park. He looked at me with sadness and nodded.

"I understand," he said, softly.

This happened in 1930, the year in which Professor Mohn and his father joined the Nazi party, convinced that only Hitler could stabilize the crisis tearing Germany.

My father took no interest in politics.

He used to say politics were not for poor people.

My brother stood underneath the crucifix above the door of the waiting room. He looked ill. In the harsh fluorescent light of the hospital his unshaven, sallow face showed an almost greenish tint; his cheeks were hollow; black circles ringed his eyes; his mouth twitched ner-vously. He wore a short, fur-lined raincoat.

"You . . ." I said hoarsely. I had expected the doctor, certainly not my brother. The last time we had met purely by chance. That had been two years ago. Then he had been healthy, successful, self-assured, an *homme aux femmes*. He had had two books published, both bestsell-ers. What could possibly account for the way he looked now? I was nonplussed.

"Hi, Richie," Werner said.

"Werner . . . how did you get here?"

145

"By car," he said with a wry smile.

"Don't be funny," I said, irritated. "How did you know that Lillian—"

Werner's voice was deep, pleasant, his speech usually dignified, modulated in the manner that he gave his lectures. Now he spoke fast, not at all sedate.

"I received a telephone call. From your club. A girl. Va—Va—"

"Vanessa?"

"Yes, that was her name."

"Vanessa called you in Bremen?"

"Can't you understand what I'm saying?"

"But . . . but how—" I broke off. Vanessa. Goddamn, I thought. That bitch! That lousy bitch! She had seen to it that there would be trouble here. There always had been whenever Werner and I had met during the last ten years. Vanessa had known that.

"I'm very grateful to the girl," Werner said. He lit a cigarette and I noticed that his hand shook. Again the smoke filled me with nausea.

"When did she call you?"

"About five."

Right after I had called. When Minski had been asleep. That lousy bitch!

"She informed me that Lillian had called you, that she had tried to . . ." He broke off, shook the ash off his cigarette, cleared his throat at great length. He was obviously very agitated. Well, so was I. "She told me everything," he closed.

"And it upset you so much that you jumped into your car and came here."

"And why not?" His voice rose, belligerent.

"How touching."

"No more touching than your sympathy. After all, perhaps you can recall, I was once married to Lillian."

If he had punched me with all his strength, as he had when we had been children, it could not have been more painful. Yes, my brother had been married to my Lillian. *My* Lillian? She had loved me. Yes, but she had also loved *him!* Because of him she had . . .

The door opened. A man in a white coat stood there. Round-headed, bald, pale, about fifty years old, with black horn-rimmed glasses, he seemed fatigued.

On a note of surprise he said, "Oh! Two visitors? Which of you is Herr Mark?"

My brother and I turned.

"I am." Werner and I answered simultaneously.

"I am Dr. Hess," he said. "But why——? Oh, you are brothers!"

"How is Frau Lombard, Doctor?" I asked, walking toward him.

"With whom, with whom did I talk?" Dr. Hess seemed distressed. No, not distressed but rather intimidated. Intimidation that he tried to hide. Obviously extreme physical or psychological stress. Perhaps both. Perspiration beaded his upper lip.

I said, "You talked to me on the telephone."

"Mark . . . Mark . . ." he began, rubbing his forehead. "You're the writer, aren't you?"

"No. My brother is the writer," I said.

"But didn't you also write——"

I interrupted him rudely, "I asked you how Frau Lombard is doing, Doctor!"

He jumped. What was the matter with this man? And with my brother? Why were they so nervous? What was going on here?

"She is alive," Hess answered.

"Would you please be a little more explicit?"

"No."

I stared at the bald-headed man.

"What?"

"Would you please follow me?" the doctor said. He avoided our eyes.

"To Frau Lombard?"

147

"No one is allowed to see her," he said quickly. "To my office."

"What are we supposed to do there!" My brother was indignant. "Why all this secretiveness about a suicide attempt?"

"It wasn't a suicide attempt," the doctor said.

"No suicide?" My brother's voice broke.

"What then?"

"Herr Eilers will tell you. He's waiting in my office."

"Who is Herr Eilers?" I asked.

"Police inspector," Dr. Hess explained. "Now will you please come along."

The house we lived in when we were children had a flat roof enclosed by a wall. On this roof grew a birch. The wind must have deposited a seed into a crack in the wall. The roof belonged to our apartment and was our favorite place during the summer. The tender green shoot growing from the crack was a sensation.

We carefully enlarged the crack, filled it with earth, watered it. It grew quickly and to our surprise we found it was not just a plant or bush but a birch tree. Within two years it had grown to a height of a meter, its graceful trunk L-shaped with several branches and leaves. One day a chimney sweep who knew nothing of our tree tore it out and threw it into the yard.

We were saddened. Sophie even cried.

Autumn came, winter, and the coming spring saw a small miracle. I discovered it when, one day in March, I climbed to the roof. Another seed had germinated in the crack. We once again had a birch on our roof.

At that time my brother and I were attending a nearby high school, my mother had become editor of the newspaper's art department, and my father had been dead of a heart attack almost two years.

Mother had refused to attend the funeral. So had Wer-

ner. My mother, at long last, gave in to my defiant behavior and passionate demand to be allowed to go to my
father's funeral. I was twelve years old and the journey
for me was a daring adventure.

Father was buried in Munich's Forest Cemetery. I stood
next to his widow who was crying softly beneath her
black veil. I was grieving but tears eluded me. Father
had loved Beethoven's Ninth Symphony and it had been
his wish that a string quartet play the third movement at
his grave. Friends from the orchestra now fulfilled this
wish and played the *Adagio molto e cantabile*.

"For me the third movement is the . . . the transfigura-
tion," he had once said. He spoke the word shyly as if he
had been ashamed. "The exulting, glorifying song of man
released from suffering . . . perhaps then it is the song
of the dead. . . ."

Now father had been released. Even today I think of
him with love mingled with sadness. My mother also has
been dead for many years. I had loved her too, though I
can no longer visualize her. But I can still see my father's
face clearly.

The music drifted across the otherwise silent cemetery.
The young widow took my hand. She did not speak to me,
not now, never. Someone handed me a shovel and I
threw some earth down into the grave, turned and walked
away. In the white, wispy clouds high in a sultry sky I
thought I recognized my father. Walking toward the exit
past rows of graves, my eyes raised to heaven, I said,
"I'm going to become a musician too, I promise. . . ."

Music was inconceivably wonderful. Surely father had
also been wonderful no matter what mother said. Equally
unimportant was what she would say to *this:* I would
study music, just as he had.

I bought a Munich newspaper to read on the train. I
leafed through it absentmindedly until a name suddenly
caught my attention.

OUR BIRCH
BY
WERNER MARK

It was a short story. A very poetic story of beginning and end, of life continuing and unending, a moving, symbolic story without a trace of sentimentality. Werner's modern, factual style was most effective. His favorite author, not without reason, had been Hemingway, whose books, at that time already banned in Germany, were on the shelves of our library.

Werner had written a story! And it had been published, not by my mother's newspaper, but by another paper! I was elated.

"You've read it, then," my mother said when I returned home, the paper in my pocket.

"Yes," I answered, "and I think it's a marvelous story!" My brother's face was pointedly indifferent. "Congratulations, Werner! A lovely story."

"Isn't it?" My mother was beside herself with pride and joy. About a dozen of the Munich newspapers were on a table near the window. "What a surprise! Werner has made me very happy and imagine, Richard, he sent the story to the paper without saying anything to me! And today we had a letter. They asked for other stories, they want to meet him. Oh, God, I'm so happy!"

And father is dead, I thought suddenly, and neither of them asked even one single question.

"Werner is only seventeen!" Mother, who had had to work so hard to raise us, radiated joy. "He's going to be a writer, a famous author. . . ."

"It was a very beautiful funeral," I began.

"Your brother is a good boy. Now I'm rewarded for all the care and worry."

"They played the Ninth, the third movement. . . ."

"Werner is going to write his first book soon, and he is going to make a lot of money and I won't have to work any more—although that's not the most important: important is that your brother is going to be a writer."

I said, "I'm going to study music and then I'll compose."

"Shut up!" Werner said quickly.

Mother's face fell. For a moment I thought she was going to cry. She had not forgiven my father, not even after his death.

"You're tired from your journey," she said, her voice flat. "Go to your room, lie down for a while."

My brother smiled.

A few minutes later, in my room, I thought, furious with rage, that this morning my father had been buried. The pastor had read from the Gospel of St. John. "In the world ye shall have tribulation: but be of good cheer; I have overcome the world."

I was going to look up the exact words in my Bible. I missed my dead father and I felt heartsick longing for him.

But I did not read St. John. I opened the Bible where a silken band marked the pages—had for some time.

". . . and the Lord had respect unto Abel and to his offering. But unto Cain and to his offering he had no respect. And Cain was very wroth, and his countenance fell."

I read it out loud.

And my face was very dark and I was very angry.

On this November 22, 1966, it did not become light. Earlier on it had been snowing heavily. Now, an hour later, it was pouring rain. Black, low clouds whipped by gusty winds were scurrying across the sky. In Dr. Hess's office a fluorescent light was burning too. The storm rattled the windows.

Chief inspector Ernst Eilers, to whom Dr. Hess had led us, was a tall, slim man—narrow face, blue eyes, brown hair brushed back. He seemed very young at first glance but soon I noticed gray temples and lines in his face which had not been immediately noticeable in the glaring, ugly light. He was about my brother's age, I guessed. His hands were delicate with long, tapered fingers stained yellow at the tips. He probably smoked too much. While he listened to our explanation of why and how we had come, he lit one cigarette from the butt of another. A cautious, intelligent man. I liked him. At times he seemed to be overcome by fatigue or resignation; his face took on a hapless expression.

We had taken off our coats. I was in my tuxedo; Werner wore an elegant blue suit. I felt dirty. My hands were shaking too. Werner had interlaced his fingers and dully, repeatedly I sensed something inexplicably strange in his behavior even though my frame of mind was not much different.

"Inspector," I said when Eilers had interrupted his questioning for a moment and I tried to remain calm and polite, "I think we have informed you thoroughly. Would you now tell us what has occurred here?"

Outside, in the rain, the wailing of an ambulance siren came closer and stopped with a squeal.

"Naturally, your statements will be checked," Eilers said. He too, seemed oddly nervous; his eyes repeatedly searched out those of the round-headed doctor.

"I've had about enough of this," my brother said vehemently. "What do you mean: statements will be checked? Why are you questioning us? We are not criminals! We would like to find out—"

The doctor's telephone rang. He answered it. His face became grayer, his thick lower lip began to twitch.

"No," he said. "No . . . no . . . it's impossible right now. There are . . . two gentlemen arrived . . . no, friends of Frau Lombard, Richard and Werner Mark . . ." He suddenly yelled, "I'm telling you, I can't right now!" He threw the receiver down and mumbled a curse.

Eilers looked at him pensively. To my brother he said,

"You want to know what's going on here. Perfectly understandable. But you must also understand me. Murder is a nasty business."

I jumped up.

"Murder? Who has been murdered?"

"Sit down, Herr Mark. No one has been murdered—if the doctors can save Frau Lombard. Then it is attempted murder. Otherwise . . ."

Wind rattled the windows, rain poured against the panes. My brother said softly, "Attempted murder."

Just as softly Inspector Eilers said, "That's why I'm here."

"Someone . . ." I pulled at my bow tie and opened my collar. "Someone tried to murder Frau Lombard?"

"That is correct," said the doctor. He continued to avoid meeting my eyes and searched out those of the inspector.

"How? With what?"

"With E 605," the inspector answered.

Dr. Hess's office was quite large. In addition to the office furniture it was partly furnished as a bedroom. My attention was particularly directed to a large, colorful Spanish poster advertising the traditional bullfights in Pamplona and one of those leather pouches which, in Spain, are used for wine. The poster called to mind those in Vanessa's dressing room and I thought how different persons do the same things. But then, how different are people actually?

News of the attempt on Lillian's life had stunned me. I was numb with horror. My brother looked as if he had died sitting in the chair. He did not move.

"If you would give a short report of this matter, Dr. Hess?" said Eilers.

Hess rose, chewed at his thumbnail and seemed very annoyed that the inspector had asked him to speak.

"Well, hm, yes, well . . ." the doctor began, pushing up his dark-rimmed glasses.

"Well!" I said.

"So . . ." Hess shot a furious look at Eilers, who turned aside and smoked. "So, after you called I immediately went to 24 Waldpromenade, the address you gave me, and there—"

"Just a moment," I interrupted. "When I called you I mentioned no address, only the name Lombard. You knew where she lived. How come you did, by the way?"

"What is it?" asked Eilers frowning at the doctor.

"I knew nothing—*he* gave me the address!" Hess cried and his face became very red.

"I only told you the name, *you* mentioned the address. I remember it surprised me at the time. You also told me you had no time for explanation!"

"Is that true?" asked Eilers. He rose and stepped closer to the doctor, who was leaning against the desk. Beads of perspiration on Hess' upper lip formed small rivulets.

"Did you say that?"

"Not a word, Inspector! Herr Mark is mistaken."

"I am not," I said gently and looked into Hess's eyes. He looked at the Spanish poster.

"You were very upset then, Herr Mark—extraordinarily excited. Perhaps it merely slipped your mind. Either you or Dr. Hess must be mistaken."

"I'm not!"

"Neither am I," cried the doctor.

The telephone rang again. Hess grimaced, picked up the receiver and yelled, "Good God in heaven, don't you understand me? It's impossible right now. I am not . . . What? I don't care! Say that . . . oh, just leave me alone!" He threw down the receiver, brushed his hand across his forehead and said weakly, "Excuse me, gentlemen, but they seem to think I'm a magician."

"Who thinks that, Doctor?" Eilers asked, pleasantly.

"These . . . the . . . oh, those people, confused about a

gall bladder colic. I already sent two colleagues. But they still want me to come. As if I . . ."

"I thought you were in emergency."

"I am. So?"

"You also work in surgery?"

"The man came . . . I mean the woman first came to emergency by ambulance and then . . ."

"Oh, I see," said Eilers. His face looked tired and disgusted. He turned to me. "I'm sure you were very agitated, Herr Mark. You must have misunderstood."

His sorrowful eyes looked at me steadily.

"And if I have not?"

"Then the doctor misunderstood."

"I see," I said. "All right. I was mistaken. Forgive me, Doctor. Go on."

Hess wiped his face and began again. "So we arrived at 24 Waldpromenade. We had to break open the door. The key was in the lock, on the inside."

"Was there no one in the house?" my brother asked.

The doctor looked at him, almost imploringly.

"No," he answered. "Frau Lombard was alone. We found her in bed. On a bedside table was a telephone. The receiver dangled. I observed dyspnea, perspiration, cyanosis, convulsions, white foam flowing from her mouth. A penetrating odor of garlic. I immediately thought of E 605."

"Typical symptoms?" my brother asked without raising his head.

"In the advanced stages of poisoning, yes. A lung edema had already developed. Frau Lombard must have taken the poison two or three hours before our arrival, presumably before she had gone to bed. She fell asleep and awakened already suffering cramps. What did she say to you on the telephone?"

"She could not speak, she only groaned."

"But you told me of an attempted suicide with sedatives!" he cried, triumphant.

"Yes—I—that's right. . . ." I stammered. "I . . . I thought of . . . of suicide. . . ."

"Why?" Eilers interjected sharply.

"Because Frau Lombard had tried twice before to kill herself." *Minski!* He had mentioned suicide. Had Lillian still been able to tell him something?

"Your explanation convinces me," Eilers said. I looked at him quickly. His smile was thin-lipped. "E 605. Do you know what that is?"

"A plant protective."

"Yes. Phosphoric acid. Has been used in quite a few murders. Extremely dangerous poison. I immediately injected atropine." Hess cleaned his glasses. "The antidote in this case. Intravenously. We'll probably have to use about 200 ampules before the pupils dilate again."

"How long will that take?" I asked anxiously.

"A day, several days," answered Hess, walking to and fro, avoiding my eyes. "If there are no complications."

"Complications?"

"Stop it, Richie!" my brother said, loudly. He rose and addressed Eilers. "Did Frau Lombard call the police?"

"No."

"The hospital?" Werner whirled to face Hess.

"No. The first I heard was when your brother—"

"Isn't that strange?" Werner asked. "I mean: if someone takes poison or is poisoned and still manages to make a call, one would presume that the police or hospital would be the logical choice, right?"

"I agree," said Eilers.

"Frau Lombard, however, called my brother. She had to know the area code and dial this plus the regular telephone number."

"You're not the only one racking his brains about this, Herr Mark," said the inspector. His look became insidious. "What do *you* make of this?" he asked me.

"I—I can't understand it either."

"You say you haven't seen Frau Lombard for years?"

"That is correct," I insisted.

"It's all right, don't be upset. Then how did Frau Lombard know your telephone number?"

"We . . . she called me . . . sometimes."

"When was the last time?"

"I've no idea . . . it must be seven, eight months ago."

"From where did she call?"

"From Paris. She was on vacation. She called to say hello. . . ."

"Just to say hello?"

"Yes."

"Was this customary with you? I mean, was it common practice for Frau Lombard to call just to say hello?"

Blood rushed to my head. Lillian. Lillian. Our love, our peculiar kind of love. What would these people understand even if I tried to explain? Nothing.

"Yes," I agreed. "It was not unusual. We've been friends for many years."

"But *you* never called her, did you?"

"I had no idea where she lived."

"You did not know that she had been living *here* for the last two years?"

"No."

"And you?" Eilers looked at Werner.

"I knew," he said.

"You knew that . . ." I began.

"Bremen is not very far from here. I could have told you, little brother." Werner's voice became malicious. "I never had an opportunity to tell you. You must know, gentlemen, that my brother and I, for personal reasons, were out of touch with each other."

"I see. Well, I assume you will be staying here at least until Frau Lombard is out of danger?"

"Definitely," I said.

"You and Frau Lombard were never married?"

"No, but . . ."

"Yes?"

157

"We had lived together for a long time. We . . . we . . ."

"Were in love," the inspector said, quite matter-of-fact. I nodded.

"But this love has been . . ."

"Yes," I said softly. "For many years."

"Strange," he said and pulled a locket on a thin gold necklace from his pocket. The locket was about an inch in diameter. I knew it well. I had given it to Lillian.

"Open it!"

I opened it. When I had given her the locket it had contained photographs of Lillian and me. Now I looked at the photo of a man in his fifties, with rimless glasses, a light-colored mustache, thinning hair and a long dueling scar.

Eilers instructed me to remove the photo and turn it over. On the reverse side of it were both telephone numbers of the Strip, the area codes and my private number.

"Frau Lombard wore the locket when we found her," Dr. Hess explained. "This photo was next to the telephone."

"Very strange," the inspector mused. "Isn't it strange, Herr Mark?"

But he looked at my brother, not at me. There was panic, a look of abject fear on my brother's pale, ravaged face. Was this fear related to Lillian?

My brother's first book was published in 1937—when he was nineteen years old. *The Bridge* was acclaimed by critics, became a bestseller, made my brother famous. The book related the lives and experiences of a group of people during the construction of an autobahn bridge.

I have promised the State Prosecutor, Dr. Paradin, to tell the truth so that the crime which has been perpetrated may be fully understood. That is why I am not saying that my brother's book was a success merely because its topic was acceptable to the Nazis. Most good writers had by then left Germany, been imprisoned or murdered, and only a few were allowed to write without interference. No, whatever else my brother was, he was always an excellent writer.

My mother's dream had come true when Werner's book received the Kleist Award. Six months later Werner was invited to write for the SS journal in Berlin. He was required to join the SS. He was offered a generous salary, the opportunity to travel and freedom to write. He accepted.

"The *Black Corps* is the journal of the elite," he said when he returned to Frankfurt. "It's above the bourgeois narrow-mindedness. A great honor for me. And you, mother, you don't have to work any more now. You can enjoy a rest at last!"

Mother hugged and kissed him. To me, she said, "Then there is such a thing as justice. You've given me so little joy, Richard—I'm not angry with you, it's not your fault that you take after your father—but my good Werner is giving me the joy I need."

Some months later—I was still attending school (a poor student except for German and English)—my brother appeared in his smart black uniform with the silver skull on the black cap.

This happened in August 1939, at the time when Panos Mitsotakis was born in Athens.

Inspector Eilers took the thin gold necklace with the locket from me and asked us to accompany him to Lillian's apartment.

My brother looked up abruptly. "Why?" he demanded, hostile.

Eilers pondered. "An attempt to shed some light on this case. Perhaps you or your brother, since you've known Frau Lombard well and for some time, would recognize or find something which might help me."

"I can't imagine what—" my brother began but was

interrupted by the inspector. "Herr Mark, would you prefer that this case not be cleared up?"

My brother jumped up, furious.

"I won't have you talk to me in this manner! I'm going to complain to your superior!"

"Werner," I said, amazed by his outburst, "have you gone crazy? *I* want this cleared up—as quickly as possible. Whatever is the matter with you?"

My brother seemed to be awakening from a bad dream. He became very embarrassed.

"Excuse me," he looked from me to Eilers. "The excitement . . . after all, Frau Lombard and I have been . . ."

"Married, we know." Eilers remained calm. "Then, I think, you ought to be all the more interested in having this matter cleared up."

"I am, of course. I'm just so upset, naturally I'll come with you to the apartment, if that's what you think necessary. Please forgive my outburst."

Eilers nodded, annoyed.

We said good-by to Dr. Hess and stepped out to the corridor. Nurses and patients were walking about. I stopped short.

"What's wrong?" Eilers asked.

"Forgot my scarf." With that I hurried back to Dr. Hess's office. As I reached the door I heard his voice, snatches of his conversation. ". . . with Eilers. They're driving to the apartment. . . . No, that won't work now— something has to be done. *You* have to do it, quickly. . . . You or . . ." The voice became silent as I approached and flung open the door. Dr. Hess's face was ashen. He said, "What do you want?"

"My scarf," I answered. "I left it behind. There, on the bed, you see." I entered the room. He followed. A voice could still be heard through the receiver on the desk.

"Your call," I said.

His eyes were uncertain. He hung up the phone.

"What did you hear?"

"I'm sure you remember what you've said." I picked up the scarf and walked to the door, where I turned. "I hope you're going to look after Frau Lombard. I have friends, you know. If something were to happen to her it would have serious consequences for you and for the person you've just talked with."

I had no idea what Dr. Hess's part in this affair was. I had no idea what was going on here. Yet my empty threat was effective. Hess sank into his chair behind the desk and stared at me, his mouth hanging open. He had the appearance of an ugly fish.

"Well, did you find your scarf?" Werner stood outside the door; I collided with him as I left the room. Behind him was Eilers. What had they overheard?

An icy wind whipped across the parking lot as we left the hospital. The sky was lead-colored. The streetlamps were still burning. The wind was swirling around wet leaves, large branches had broken off trees. Melted snow had collected in dirty puddles. I looked up at the hospital façade. Almost all the windows were illuminated. Which room was Lillian's? Had she regained consciousness? Lillian. My heart was heavy.

The inspector said promptly, "Second floor, left. The sixth window from the end of the building."

I glanced at him. He smiled.

"Thank you," I said.

My brother had also looked up and I was shaken by jealousy and anger. It was absurd of me.

I had met Lillian in 1946. A different time, a different world; a time of hunger, cold, misery, when we had been very poor. Yet very happy for we had had strength then, faith, courage, and laughter came easily, quickly, often.

There had been reason, friendliness, insight, even honesty. We will experience all that only when the world is in ruins again. Perhaps. If, the next time, there still is life in those ruins.

"Where is your car?" I asked my brother.

He indicated a new, black one parked near mine.

"We're taking the official car," Eilers headed toward a green auto. A young man in a trench coat was behind the wheel, reading a newspaper. Eilers introduced us to the young blond detective by the name of Robert Lansing.

The roads were busier now than at my arrival. A few people, bent forward, fought against the wind. Cars drove with dipping headlights, their taillights glowing red. I again saw the beautiful villas and large gardens, many of which adjoined a forest. Bare trees, shiny from rain, were buffeted by the storm. Rotting leaves covered the roads.

"Perhaps the storm will reach here too," Lansing, at the wheel, said. "There have been storm warnings for the north coast for tonight. Nine o'clock. News." He switched on the radio.

The news was concerned almost exclusively with the gain of fifteen seats in the Munich Parliament by the right-wing National Democratic Party as a result of the Bavarian elections.

"Soviet and American newspapers voice concern for the alarming symptoms of the rise and influence of the neofascists in the Federal Republic," the newscaster reported.

"And whom do we have to thank for that?" asked Lansing. "Our dear government, that's who. They've done all that could be done to help the neofascists."

I glanced at Werner. His face was blank.

"They've taken good care of the old Nazis, watched that nothing untoward happened to them. . . ."

"We're on duty. It's against the rules to talk politics," Eilers murmured sleepily.

Lansing did not apear to hear. "Adenauer! Where would the Nazis be without his fatherly care? Didn't he take all the old bigwigs into his party so he would assure his election?" Lansing shifted awkwardly. The transmission screeched. "Twenty years! Man, our government did a good job!"

Since I knew it was against regulations to voice political views it seemed obvious that Eilers had instructed Lansing to deliver this monologue. Why? To see if we would applaud? Or protest? Whether we were Nazis or anti-Nazis? What had I stumbled into? I seemed to hear Minski's voice, ". . . In 1930 the Nazis polled more than twenty per cent . . . in Treuwall, even twenty-five!"

Was Eilers a Nazi? Lansing?

Were both of them antifascist? One of them? Then a thought shook me: Was this possibly not just a criminal case? Was politics involved? Lillian! Blood throbbed in my temples. Lillian was still in danger, enmeshed in some dark, sinister business.

Lansing began again. My brother's lips were thin. "How old are you, Herr Lansing?" He was sitting behind him; I was behind Eilers, whose eyes were half-closed. Was my brother taking the bait?

"Twenty-eight. You probably think I'm too young to feel the way I do, right?"

"I'm not thinking anything." No, Werner was not that simple. "I was just interested in your age."

"You know," the driver said, "some people are older than their birth certificates say. Me, for instance."

"And why?"

"My father was hanged by the Poles. SS war criminal. That's why. I was ten years old then. Too bad my father was extradited. He could have been in Bonn today too. That's a certainty."

Eilers was studying his fingernails. He began to clean them with a match.

"The *Daily Telegraph's* headline says 'Neo-Nazi Success in Bavaria' and the *Evening Standard* 'Nazi Spirit on the March,'" the newscaster continued.

"Sure it's on the march," Lansing said. "Who else? The Communist party perhaps? Those bastards have been ruled unconstitutional. Can't be done with the National Democratic party, the government says. Or those SS reunions! Or the soldier reunions! Those people have to be assured that they had not been part of an enormous crime, no, they had only discharged their duty to the fatherland."

"Now that's enough." Eilers's voice was exaggeratedly loud. "After all, we do live in a democracy."

"Democracy?"

"Isn't it?" Eilers dramatically indicated the radio. "There! Foreign opinions. Nothing is censored! If that isn't democratic! Now I don't want to hear any more!"

"Yes, chief!" Lansing sat at attention. I thought that this, perhaps, had not been a provocation but genuine; that Lansing's father had indeed been hanged by the Poles and that his son hated Nazis. Damn, if I could only tell fact from fiction. I rolled down the window to breathe some fresh air. Was I dreaming all this? No, it was true enough.

"Shut that window!" my brother said angrily. "Are you crazy? I'm getting completely soaked!" I looked at him. He seemed even more distressed and looked ill. His lips twitched. I wondered: How much of what had happened to Lillian are you guilty of? If only a minute part of it is your fault I'll kill you, I'll . . .

I pulled myself together, closed the window and saw Lansing watching me in the rearview mirror. Then it had been a calculated plan after all? To see who would lose his self-control—my brother or I?

I inhaled deeply, leaned back into the seat so that Lansing could no longer see me in the mirror.

"We're here," the driver said and switched off the radio. We had stopped outside a villa surrounded by a very large garden. The Waldpromenade was a quiet street with few houses spaced wide apart. Two cars were parked in front of us—presumably also police cars.

We left the car. Beyond the villa I again saw the forest,

storm-whipped. Icy-cold rain hit me. A gate stood open in the high iron fence surrounding the property. Next to it a wide, locked gate. A driveway. All windows of the villa were lit. Where did Lillian live? If there was more than one apartment—the house was two-storied—why then had Lillian been alone last night? Where were the other tenants? Who were they? One of the cement supports on either side of the gate held an intercom. Below the bell button I saw a brass plate. I leaned down to read the name: PROFESSOR DR. CLEMENS KAMPLOH.

"Kamploh?" I straightened up and looked at the inspector, whose face was expressionless. "Kamploh? Who is . . . I've heard that name." Then it came to me. "The director of the hospital!"

My brother, standing next to Eilers, was watching me, his face blank. Behind him Lansing was watching all of us—also expressionless.

"I thought we were going to Frau Lombard's apartment!"

"Frau Lombard lives here." Eilers did not take his eyes from me.

A gust of wind hit me so suddenly I had to hold on to the cement post for support.

"What do you mean, lives here?"

"Professor Kamploh has rented her the second floor."

"Then why isn't her name here? Why is there no second bell?"

"This is a small town, relatively," Eilers said. "People talked . . . the difference in age alone . . . but they've calmed down. Frau Lombard and Professor Kamploh wish to be left in peace, so she has been registered as a tenant with the police, she has her own private telephone number." Eilers was walking through the gate. "It's fortunate that she has! The professor is away."

I grabbed the inspector's shoulder. "Do you mean that Frau Lombard and Professor Kamploh are lovers?"

Eilers nodded.

"Since when?"

"Oh, it must be two years now." He stopped and looked at me, searching. "You actually knew nothing of this?"

"No!" I looked at Werner. "And you?" I asked. "Did you know?"

"Certainly, Richie," my brother answered.

My brother became one of the most successful and renowned SS war correspondents, a protégé of Dr. Goebbels, a man admirably suited to his profession. In 1940 Werner was promoted to SS Sturmführer. His reports, published by the majority of German newspapers, were widely propagated by the Great German Radio. Werner Mark. In the first year of the war that name had become a national institution.

He intuitively knew a great deal about psychology. In his reports he invariably created a gripping, authentic mood of adventure, of a fight for right and justice—without ever mentioning such proper words. His remarkable success, I think, came largely from his ability to view events through the eyes of the common people—never the intellectuals—and always with deference to the sentiments of women.

Eminent men have mentioned my brother in their memoirs, praising his work. His worst enemy had to admit that Werner was an exceptionally talented correspondent and writer.

How proud mother was! Werner will surely meet a criterion of God: He looks with kindness on those who honor their mothers. No son could have made his mother happier than Werner did.

I had always caused her much worry by my indecisiveness, my inability to become enthusiastic about the war—this "great fight" for freedom, the *Neue Zeit* and its representatives—and my stubborn, nostalgic yearning for music through my secret study. This did not remain secret when my teacher, who assumed that mother knew, asked her to dissuade me from further study since, as he said, I was hopelessly untalented. At mother's insistence he repeated his remarks before me.

A year later I too had become a war correspondent. This career I owe to the sinking of the British battle cruiser *Hood,* a mad physical education teacher, my brother Werner and the poet Hermann Löns, who, as coincidence would have it, had lived in the small town of Müden, a half-hour drive from Treuwall.

The German battleship *Bismarck* had sunk the *Hood* in the Denmark Strait on May 24, 1941. The following day Armin Knäblein, our physical education teacher, a fanatic Nazi, conducted a victory celebration. He had us doing exercises while we were singing the march on England with lyrics by the sensitive poet from the heath, Hermann Löns.

We were on our backs treading air, roaring the words of the song, Knäblein walking up and down, directing.

". . . don't cry for me, my love, remember that for the fatherland I gave my blood."

That's when I began to laugh.

The boy opposite me, a very fat boy exercising too violently, had sung the words—with gusto—about the fatherland for which Hermann Löns had shed his poet's blood, when his rectal muscle let him down. The ridiculous victory celebration combined with that inappropriate flatus was too much for me. The class became silent. Knäblein was furious. He ordered me to stop. I could not.

"You criminal!" Knäblein ranted. "You Communist pig! You're an enemy of the people! I'm going to take you to court! To jail!"

A quarter of an hour later I was in the director's office; half an hour later I had been thrown out of the school; two days later a man from our local Nazi party office informed my mother.

Our family doctor was called. Mother had suffered a collapse. Our old Sophie had informed the doctor of the events which had been the cause of mother's breakdown. After he had given mother an injection he had a talk with me. He made me realize the precarious situation I was in and advised me to appeal to my brother for help even though he knew of my feelings toward him.

I called Werner in Berlin and told him what had occurred. He was enraged at my conduct, but when I begged him and told him that only he could help me now he relented.

"I'll take the first available plane," he said. "I'll take care of the matter—for mother's sake, of course. Not yours."

"Of course not for mine," I said.

Werner did straighten out the matter. Later he explained, "I told them that you had been annoyed by this stupid teacher's idiotic idea to have you sing in this fashion. You laughed in protest! *Hood.* Löns! England! And this simpleton makes you tread air and bellow! Well, he's in for it now. I also told the director and the party officials that I would be taking you in hand just as soon as you had graduated. That, ostensibly, is an order from above."

"Taking me—what does that mean?" I asked with trepidation.

"You'll join the press corps. I love my mother. I don't want you to cause her any more worry. From now on I'm going to keep my eye on you."

And, by God, he did! Once I had been drafted he seemed to follow my every step. He appeared wherever I was and protected me by simply being there. The devil ought to roast my brother in little pieces over a small fire. He was a wicked man—but more than likely he saved my life. Without him I probably would have gone to jail, into a penal company or, as one unworthy to serve in the military forces, into a concentration camp.

My cursed brother taught me the rudiments of writing, edited my first work as a new member of the press corps. He wrote the first two articles for me. Needless to say, both were excellent and I was made.

"I'm so glad that your good brother put you on the right track," my mother wrote to me at the battlefront. But good old Sophie wrote, "I go to church every day and pray that no harm may come to the young master."

I never attained my brother's prominence. I am no hero. I never felt the need to be one. This war was not my war. With millions of others who would have preferred to remain at home, who had no desire to conquer strange lands for the Führer's and fatherland's honor, I had to put on a uniform and take up a rifle. Just as those millions who did not voluntarily and enthusiastically set out to commit war atrocities, to kill and to conquer, who were, as was I, too young, too naïve, too indolent or too cowardly to prevent Hitler's rise to power—just as those millions, I had little luck.

I received my baptism of fire as a war correspondent during the capture of Sevastopol. My report found favor in Berlin. Now I nurtured the hope that I might be recalled from the battlefront as my brother had been. I knew that many frontline reports were fabricated—in rear echelons, in Berlin—far removed from the actual battles. I knew that many of the most striking battle scenes seen in newsreels were shot somewhere on the Polish steppes, on troop training grounds in Pomerania or Mecklenburg, even on the lot of the Wien-Film studio. I hoped to be given such an assignment.

That was not to be my lot.

I was sent wherever the fighting was the fiercest—east or west, in Africa or in the Arctic Circle. I was wounded, was awarded the Iron Cross First Class and the Close Combat Medal. My mother wrote to me at the hospital. She congratulated me and said how proud she was of me. Poor mamma! I realized for the first time, with a feeling of uneasiness, that all these years I had mistakenly thought her to have been intelligent.

Sophie also congratulated me, yet added the peculiar request, "Always speak the truth, since in the Holy Scriptures it says, 'For what is a man profited, if he shall gain the whole world, and lose his own soul?' "

I was sent to France. There I remained as a war correspondent until the Allied invasion, when I was taken prisoner near Saint Lô.

I had asked Sophie to stay with mother, who was in poor health. That dear protector and comforter of my childhood agreed to do so. She and mother died on August 12, 1944, when a bomb scored a direct hit on our house during an American air raid on Frankfurt.

I did not hear of their death until after the war. In August of that year I was in Camp Alva, Oklahoma. POWs of the former Africa Corps were in command of the camp. The Americans were pleased with the strict discipline maintained. That several antifascists, sentenced by kangaroo courts, were found strangled with telephone wire did not bother the Americans. The officers' administration merely declared that those executed had been Communist criminals. During my four months in Camp Alva four men were murdered. Once—in a case of mistaken identity—an American asleep in a barrack was garroted.

Those of us who had not belonged to the elite of the Africa Corps were now moved to Camp Dermott, Arkansas. There we picked cotton. In Camp Rupert, Idaho, we harvested sugar beets and potatoes. I was shipped to Le Havre in 1946; there followed a short stay in another camp, and in May of that year I stood before the bombed ruin of our house in Frankfurt. Mother, Sophie and the other tenants had been buried in a mass grave.

Armin Knäblein, my former physical education teacher, turned up one day at the Strip, a champagne salesman. He did not know me; I recognized him immediately. Minski prevented me from throwing him out. He said, "Are you going to start now to sit in judgment over all the poor, little *Menschele?*"

"Little *Menschele!* That bastard nearly ruined my life," I yelled. "I told you how—"

"How many people nearly ruined my life?" Minski asked. "The champagne he sells is good. I'll try to get his price down a little more. If you can't stand to see him then let me talk with him."

So even in 1966 we were still buying some of our champagne from my former teacher, now an elderly gentleman who had survived a war in which my mother and Sophie had died.

Officials gave me the number of the mass grave where mother and Sophie had been buried, also a bag which mother had clutched when she had died. It contained a number of newspaper clippings—articles by Werner, some by me—and mother's glasses.

The well-thumbed, yellow paper had become brittle, but parts of articles were still readable. On a warm day in May I sat near the muddy waters of the Main and, with utter amazement, read my brother's reports: this gifted writer, this demagogue who had described defeats as though they were victories. Werner had reported up to the end of the war; he had written for the *Panzerbär* in surrounded Berlin exhorting fifteen- and seventy-year-olds to resist the Red Army a little longer until a secret, a miracle weapon, could be utilized.

I learned later that he had written then, "Victory is really imminent." I also learned that millions of people who had read or heard Werner's reports during the last few months were once more inspired with courage and hope. What a magnificent writer! During those concluding months more people died than in all the previous war years. My brother had had a small but significant share in their deaths.

The Russians pulled Werner from a shelter near the

Reichskanzlei in Berlin. They were well aware of his work, had heard his reports on the radio, had read reports such as the yellowed selection that, together with an old bag and a pair of steel-rimmed glasses, I threw into the muddy waters of the Main on a warm day in May 1946.

The Russians placed Werner in a POW camp. They have always appreciated true talent and ordered him to write a camp newspaper. Werner, too, knew how to use his talent: he turned out first-class Communist propaganda, written with the same subtle, applied psychology which had made his Nazi reports so effective. The Russians were delighted—and he was not released for some time.

He did come home eventually. His return brought suffering and misfortune for me and others—but not for Werner! He was a man who had not been unduly affected by a murderous war; a bitter, severe defeat; POW camps; lies, treason. He was a callous, ruthless man who had always arranged his life the way he saw fit and who even arranger what became his own death—for a December night in the Hotel Imperial in Cairo.

Professor Kamploh's villa had a large hall from which wide stairs led up to the first floor. There were thick Persian carpets on the marble floor, original paintings by French impressionists, East Asian works of art, sculptures, wood carvings, statues. Men were walking about, some taking photographs, some questioning a resolute, plump woman of about fifty. Next to her stood a young officer holding a shorthand pad, and a thick-set, bull-necked, older man.

"How many more times do I have to tell you?" the woman said, annoyed. "I don't live here. Only the professor and Frau Lombard live here. I come every day at nine—with the exception of Saturday—and I leave at six.

Saturday at two. I live nearby—2 Kurvenalstrasse. I don't know anything."

"When did Professor Kamploh leave?" asked the bull-necked man. His voice was rasping.

"Yesterday morning. To a symposium in Munich."

"By car?"

"Only as far as Hanover. Then by train. He doesn't like to drive. The lecture was last night."

"Why didn't he take a plane?"

"He doesn't care for planes either. Whenever possible he takes a sleeping car."

"When is he returning?"

"Tomorrow. Wednesday."

"Where does he stay in Munich?"

The housekeeper must have just arrived. She was still wearing her coat. It was just after 9 A.M.

"Hotel Vier Jahreszeiten."

Inspector Eilers cleared his throat. The thick-necked man turned. His hair was gray and thin; beneath sly, narrowed eyes bulged heavy, purple bags suggesting grapes. Not a pleasant face. He was Inspector Fegesack. Eilers introduced us. Then came the routine misconception I had borne for years.

"Mark? The writer?" Fegesack looked at me.

"Yes," said Eilers.

"No, that's my brother."

"Eilers, then why do you say—" Confusion did not make the inspector any more appealing. His crafty eyes were mere slits.

"I used to write," I said. This was usual. It didn't even hurt any more.

"You wrote too? I know several of your brother's books. Werner Mark . . . One is just now on the *Spiegel's* bestseller list, isn't it? I read the *Spiegel* regularly."

So that's what *Spiegel* readers looked like too.

My brother nodded.

"Yes, my latest book has just been published."

173

"And you?" Fegesack looked at me again.

"I haven't been writing for years."

"What did you write?"

"Novels. Nothing special."

Eilers spoke to his superior in a low voice. He nodded.

"All right then, shall we have a look at the house?" said Eilers. His hand motioned for us to come. Lansing gave me an ingratiating smile. The four of us climbed the stairs to the second floor. Standing before the empty open fireplace in the hall Fegesack continued to question the housekeeper.

"When did you leave here yesterday?"

"At the usual time, at six. What has happened here? Now will you please tell me what?"

The second floor had half-a-dozen rooms. All these had large windows, some had balconies. I saw the storm-whipped trees, the dance of rain-laden leaves, the dark, surging forest at the end of the property. The heating system was working at full pressure, and so the expensively furnished rooms were stifling hot.

"Professor Kamploh must be a wealthy man," I said.

My brother was silent. His face was gloomy as he walked beside me.

"His position at the hospital is well-paid. He also has a flourishing private office in town," Eilers explained. "People come from afar. Great physician."

"Since when has he been director of the hospital?"

"The old one since 1955. The new one since 1960."

"How old a man is he?"

"Fifty-nine."

And Lillian is thirty-nine, I thought. Lillian and a man of almost sixty years are lovers. My brother seemed to know what I was thinking. He said, "Lillian always did have a great need for security. Don't you remember?"

I shot him a furious glance.

"Isn't that true, Richie?" Werner pursued, spiteful. "Of course it is."

174

We followed Eilers once more into the library. Here stood a grand piano; near it an expensive stereo system had been built into the book shelves. The stereo, oddly, was open, one record still on the turntable, another resting against the upper half of the record player.

One wall of shelves contained an extensive music library. Hundreds of records in mahogany compartments with narrow cards in brass frames contained references. Kamploh had apparently collected all of Beethoven's works, including the same pieces played by different orchestras, various conductors and soloists.

There was an impressive collection of books in several languages, as well as medical reports and evaluations and interpretations of Beethoven's music. The bottom shelf held large, leatherbound full scores.

"A music devotee," Lansing smiled. "Beethoven forever." Nearby stood an old rocking chair. On the piano were two dust jackets. They probably belonged to the two records on the stereo. I liked this comfortable library redolent of fragrant pipe tobacco and leather. A cultured man, Professor Kamploh . . .

On the grand was a worn leatherbound full score.

"You can touch it," said Lansing, still watching me. Eilers was watching my brother, who was staring straight ahead. "The men have finished photographing in here."

The score was opened to the second movement. I turned the pages. This was one of the oldest printed scores of the music my father had loved so much, Beethoven's Ninth Symphony, printed in 1824, dedicated by Beethoven to His Majesty, King of Prussia, Frederick William II.

The pages were thin and yellowed. First, second, third movement. The third had been played at my father's funeral.

The fourth movement, with the words of Schiller's "Ode to Joy" set to music. I read—and stopped short.

There was a fault in printing the ode. The words "All mankind shall be as brothers" were missing.

The detective I had seen in the hall showed his notes to the inspector. Eilers whistled through his teeth, handed the pad to the blond Lansing who quickly skimmed over several pages, then looked at Eilers, eyebrows raised. Lansing returned the pad to the young detective who left. Brows still raised, Lansing looked at me and at Werner who had angrily sat down in the rocking chair. Lansing pursed his lips and whistled the *Marseillaise*.

"Do you usually conduct your inquiries in this manner?" Werner asked. "What was the purpose of this stupid visit?"

"I've already explained that to you," Eilers replied, patiently. "I hoped that you might find something here which would help us. You've not noticed anything unusual?"

"No," my brother said.

"And you?" Eilers lit a cigarette.

"There is a line missing in the vocal part of the fourth movement in the score of the Ninth on the grand over there."

Eilers looked at me, thoughtful.

He went to the piano, leafed through the score until he had found the particular place. He and Lansing checked. Finally Eilers said, "Indeed. Anything else?"

I shrugged my shoulders. "If I were as passionate a music lover as Professor Kamploh seems to be I would have taken the time to close the stereo and slip the records back into their dustjackets before I left. I would have put away the score too. It is very valuable."

"Bravo," said Eilers. "You see?" He addressed Werner. "Your brother discovered something. You don't seem to be very interested. But you will be."

"Look here . . ." Werner began, but Eilers motioned him to silence.

"Looks as if Kamploh listened to the Ninth before he left, doesn't it?" Lansing asked.

"It does," I said.

"And that he didn't have time to put away the records, et cetera, right?"

"Perhaps he forgot," my brother volunteered.

"I wonder why?" Eilers looked around. "He seems to be a very orderly sort of man."

"How should I know why?"

"Would you like to know why? We just found out."

"Found out what?" I asked.

"Why the professor left things like this. He had listened to the Ninth on the night before last, Saturday night. About eleven. Then he received the telephone call from the Munich University to come immediately."

"I don't understand a word," Werner said. He seemed nervous again, rocking the chair impetuously. Lansing and Eilers spoke quickly, alternately.

"Kamploh was to lecture there."

"But he was not to lecture last night but the coming Friday."

"Then another lecturer fell ill and plans were revised. Kamploh had to leave hurriedly last night. He had to pack, prepare the lecture and so on. The reason why the score and records were left out."

"How do you know?" I asked.

"The housekeeper just told us."

"Oh, that's what you read."

"On the shorthand pad, yes," said Eilers. "We had noticed the records too. Now we have the explanation."

"Kamploh had called the housekeeper after eleven on Sunday night and informed her that he had to leave Monday morning. When she arrived at nine he had already left."

"Why didn't she straighten out here?" I asked.

"She was afraid to touch anything, she said."

177

"Well, and Lillian—I mean Frau Lombard?" my brother asked.

"She arrived only last night."

"Arrived?"

"From Tenerife."

"Tenerife?" I blurted, surprised.

"Tenerife. Kamploh has a house there. You didn't know of course."

"No."

"And you?"

My brother's lips twitched again.

"Well!"

"I knew about the house—I didn't know that Frau Lombard was there."

"She has been there for the past three weeks," Lansing explained. "She returned about seven. Also telephoned the housekeeper. Told her that she was back. She regretted not seeing the professor. Was supposed to be a surprise."

"Surprise?"

"Today is Kamploh's birthday. He's fifty-nine. Frau Lombard was to have stayed on in Tenerife. Kamploh had planned to fly down there to spend the holidays with her. He has to take a plane there. In spite of his aversion to flying. Too far."

"She was supposed to stay there until after New Year's, the housekeeper said."

"But Frau Lombard returned. The housekeeper said that she told her not to bother to come, she would fix herself something to eat, which she did. Used dishes still in the kitchen. There was ample food in the house," Eilers explained. He went to a corner of the library and opened a door built in to the shelves. Light in a bar fell on glasses, a shiny cocktail shaker, bottles on glass shelves. "Mostly hard liquor, hardly any liqueurs."

"There's also a well-stocked wine cellar," Lansing said.

"Wines from all over Europe. The best." Eilers looked at my brother. "Even Armagnac."

"So?" Werner asked.

The inspector took a bottle from the bar which contained only the dregs.

"Especially old Armagnac," he said reading the black and gold label, "1875. Very difficult to obtain. Comes from the Gascony district, it says here. The German importer is Feddersen, Bremen. You live in Bremen too, Herr Mark, don't you?"

"Yes. So?" Werner asked, fiercely.

Eilers's voice was gentle. "Have you ever heard anything of this firm Feddersen?"

"No! Never," my brother cried.

"I see. That's what I thought," the inspector said. He replaced the bottle. "Now we'll go to Miss Lombard's apartment."

Lillian's apartment on the third floor was almost a duplicate of the one below except for the furnishings. They were modern, predominantly black and white: white carpets, black wallpapers. After the antique furnishings of Kamploh's part of the house Lillian's apartment was a startling surprise. The atmosphere was decidedly feminine—and somewhat untidy. Magazines, newspapers, clothing, shoes were lying around. The fragrance of Lillian's perfume lingered. It brought back memories of those wonderful postwar years when I had bought that same perfume for her on the black market, of those years when we had known happiness, laughter, hope.

"The professor has never been married?" I asked while we were walking through the apartment. Men were busily taking photographs, dusting for fingerprints, searching through closets. They did not pay any attention to us. The windows, blurry with rain, could not be seen through. Lights were burning in every room.

"His wife died many years ago." The inspector's voice seemed to come from a great distance.

There was one of Lillian's shoes, there a stocking. I felt ill. We were in the drawing room.

"Look," the inspector said. "Here is a jack for the telephone. To judge by the imprint on the felt here it seems to have been mostly by the window. But we found it in the bedroom. Come with me, please." He was already walking ahead.

Lillian's bedroom showed utter confusion. The bed rumpled and soiled, overturned chairs, the contents of drawers strewn around the floor, nightgown, robe, bedroom slippers scattered around.

The inspector was apologetic. "Our people, and those from the ambulance . . . so sorry . . ."

I stared at the soiled bed. Lillian had been there, a few hours ago, suffering, groaning, when she had called me, afraid for her life. There was the white telephone next to the bed.

"That's a little puzzle too," Eilers said when he noticed me looking at the bed. "Why is the telephone here and not in the next room?"

My brother answered, "Why shouldn't it be here? There's a connection for it. Without a doubt Frau Lombard often had the telephone in her bedroom. Or she wouldn't have had the connection installed."

"Right. Whenever she did have it in her bedroom she probably meant to make some calls or because she expected one, don't you think? From whom? In any case we assume that she moved the telephone before she fell ill. Why?"

"No idea," said Werner.

"Too bad," said Eilers. Once again I had the feeling that he was trying to provoke Werner. He was certainly succeeding.

"What do you mean, too bad?" Werner bristled.

"I thought that perhaps you might have an idea."

"Why me? Why not my brother?"

"Your brother said that he had not spoken with Frau Lombard in months. You, on the other hand, said that you telephoned with her occasionally. It seems natural to assume that perhaps you intended to call or did call her . . ."

"I will not tolerate such insinuations! I did not call and did not intend to call her!"

". . . or that Frau Lombard called or intended to call you!"

"She did not!"

"Why are you shouting?" I asked my brother. He didn't appear to hear me. He was very agitated.

"It's also strange that she did not call you," Lansing said.

"Why?"

"You lived so much closer to her than your brother, and you were still in contact with her. But she called your brother. Can you find an explanation for that?"

My brother was furious. "She did not call the police or hospital or a doctor either. Can you find an explanation for that?"

Eilers shook his head and smiled.

"Then we'll have to assume that Frau Lombard was panic-stricken and acted irrationally."

"For all that she still managed to take the photograph from the locket to read and dial the telephone numbers on the reverse side."

That's when I saw the photograph in a silver frame on the dressing table. It was the man from the photograph in the locket; the same photograph enlarged. I stepped closer.

"Is this Kamploh?" I asked.

"Yes."

A narrow head, high, wide forehead. He had looked directly into the camera, smiling. The light-colored eyes behind rimless glasses were unsmiling. Like Minski's, yet

181

the expression in the professor's eyes was different. Bushy, fair eyebrows, thin fair hair, a well-groomed mustache, a thick dueling scar on his left cheek which ran from the chin close to the corner of the mouth to the cheekbone.

The handwriting across the lower corner of the photograph was strong and pleasant.

FOR MY LILLIAN WITH LOVE

CLEMENS

I could not take my eyes from the photo. When I had seen it first in miniature in the locket I had been too confused, too excited to ask the man's identity, although even then I had had the peculiar feeling that I had seen him somewhere before. Now this feeling became very strong. I had seen this man! Where? When? I could not remember. Those pale eyes, especially that thick scar . . .

"You still haven't told us how Frau Lombard . . . had her accident." That was my brother's voice. I looked up.

"Another little puzzle," the inspector said. "The professor always ordered his Armagnac from Feddersen in Bremen. Always two cases of twelve bottles each."

"How do you know?"

"It came by railway express. The local firm delivered last night about eight. We've checked. The driver carried them into the basement. Frau Lombard signed a receipt. When we found the cases one bottle had been removed. Presumably Frau Lombard took the bottle upstairs. She drank a small glass of it, probably after she had eaten."

"She always liked Armagnac," I suddenly remembered.

"You're very helpful," Eilers said.

"Always your brother," Lansing provoked Werner. "Never you. Unfortunately."

"As we've seen, the bottle of Armagnac in the library had little left. So Frau Lombard opened a new bottle. It was this newly arrived Armagnac that contained the poison," the inspector said.

While there had been conversation I had not noticed

the storm. Now the rain beat furiously against the window panes.

"E 605," after a moment Eilers said. "A powder. Dissolved. In all twenty-four bottles. Enormous amounts. Had Frau Lombard had more than a small glass of it she could not have been saved. We have checked with Feddersen in Bremen. It seems that the firm did not send the shipment."

"You just said—" my brother began.

"I said the professor always ordered from Feddersen. I did not say that they had shipped the last two cases. You must have misunderstood, Herr Mark."

The inspector scrutinized Werner.

"But then who—" he began.

"Do you have any ideas, any suspicions?"

Werner and I shook our heads.

"How could we? We don't even know the professor. At least *I* don't," I added.

"I don't either," my brother said.

"The taste of the Armagnac concealed the smell and taste of the poison," the inspector lectured. "E 605 does not show its deadly effect until two to three hours later. According to the police examiner she must have taken the poison between eleven and twelve P.M."

"That would be right. She called me about three A.M. . . ."

Eilers said, "There! When she awakened she was already suffering the advanced symptoms of the poisoning—"

"Just a moment!" I interjected.

"Yes?" Eilers looked at me, curious.

Again I stared at the photograph on the dressing table. Where had I seen this man? I would remember. Soon. Slowly I said, "Frau Lombard accepts the shipment and drinks of its poisoned contents. But . . ."

"Yes?" Eilers said very softly. "Go on . . ."

"But . . ." This photograph. This man. I did know

him. ". . . but actually she was not supposed to be here! She was supposed to have stayed in Tenerife!" I raised my eyes. They were all watching me. "She arrived here unexpectedly . . . and Professor Kamploh had to leave unexpectedly for Munich. . . . So if a murder was planned . . ."

"Yes?" Eilers prompted. "Yes? Go on!"

". . . it means that someone planned to murder the professor and not Frau Lombard!"

Werner's face was ashen. He sat down on a chair.

"We were curious to find out when you would come to this conclusion." Lansing said. "And who would conclude it, you or your brother. Your deduction is perfectly right."

The telephone rang. Eilers answered.

"Yes," he said, "yes, he's here. . . ." He listened.

My brother, his back turned, stared at the floor. Lansing and Eilers also had their backs to me. I looked at Kamploh's photograph again, deeply puzzled. Who? Who was this man? Suddenly the realization came to me: When I had seen this man his name had not been Kamploh! His name was . . . was . . .

Nothing. I could not remember.

What I did now was madness. I acted as if hypnotized. I could not even say why I was doing what I was doing.

Through the dressing table mirror I could see that the three men behind me still had their backs toward me. I picked up the photograph.

At that the door opened and the bullnecked inspector, Fegesack, entered. I saw him observe me in the mirror; he saw me slip the photograph into my coatpocket. His eyes became mere slits. Finished, I thought. I thought I saw his thick lips contorted in an amused smile. I turned and faced him. The grin had disappeared. He was not looking at me then but at Eilers, who had just replaced the receiver. His gravel voice asked, "The hospital?"

"Right," Eilers answered.

"I told Hess to call here. He called downstairs first."

"Hess? Hospital?" My heart pounded. "What is the matter? Lillian?"

"She wants to talk with you, urgently."

"Is she . . . is she . . ."

"No! She's better. Very upset. Asked if you had arrived. Wants to see you immediately."

"But it's impossible that she can already . . ." Werner began. I looked at him and noticed that I had narrowed my eyes as Inspector Fegesack had narrowed his. You live in Bremen, I thought. Where the Armagnac comes from. The poisoned Armagnac. You still spoke with Lillian from time to time. Your behavior is very peculiar, open to question.

"Hess thinks that in view of her extreme agitation it would be best for her to see your brother. He is accepting complete responsibility. She has a strong heart. She will become calmer once she has seen him," Eilers explained.

"Why should you object to him seeing her?" Lansing asked Werner.

"I don't object, I'm just concerned . . ."

"I have a feeling that your concern may be justified," Eilers said, brusque.

"What do you mean?"

"I'll explain it to you. You're coming with us."

"To the hospital?"

"Yes. We'll have a talk there. Just the three of us," Eilers said. Lansing was walking to the door. He looked at the dressing table, quickly at me and then at Eilers. When the inspector passed by the dressing table he too saw the photograph was missing. They looked at each other, smiled quickly, as had Fegesack, a knowing smile. I was baffled, puzzled.

"Shall we go," Eilers said to me.

The photograph seemed heavy in my pocket. In the door I turned. Fegesack had remained in the room. Again he was smiling, his eyes narrowed.

I felt cold in spite of my warm coat.

She was lying in bed. Her face waxen, blue-black hair disheveled and damp, cheeks sunken, sensuous lips purple, eyes closed: Lillian Lombard, one of the most beautiful women I had ever known. She was receiving a transfusion. The drapes were closed; a covered lamp provided a dim light.

"Lillian," I began, breathless, as soon as I had entered the room together with Dr. Hess. He immediately placed a finger on his lips, motioned to the intern and nurse standing by the bed. They left. Dr. Hess did not. His bald head had a green tinge in the dim light. There was a strong smell of medication and the garlic odor of E 605.

I pulled up a chair, bent my face over Lillian's. I whispered her name.

The bloodless lips, in a contorted smile, bared her beautiful teeth. Now that she had begun to talk they chattered from time to time.

"So glad . . . you came . . ."

I placed my hand over hers. It felt small, delicate and very cold.

"You came at once."

"Of course."

"You are . . . you are . . ."

Dr. Hess had stepped so close his white coat was touching me. I glared at him, furious. He looked at me, his eyes expressionless, and did not move.

"Richie . . ."

"Yes?"

"I . . . I must . . . tell you . . ." She moved her head. The blue-black hair was damp with perspiration. She strained to open her eyes but closed them again immediately, groaning.

"Keep your eyes closed," I said quickly.

Lillian's eyes!

They were as dark as her hair. I have never seen eyes

186

so large, so beautiful. I had fallen in love with them, these beloved, damned eyes. Damned because I had not been able to forget them and knew that I never could.

"We . . . are . . . not . . . alone?"

"Dr. Hess is here."

"Tell him . . . go away. . . ."

Hess did not move.

"Didn't you hear?" I asked him.

He answered, cold, "I can't leave; Frau Lombard's condition is still critical."

"That's why you permitted me to see her, eh? That's why you told the inspector there was no risk, I should just come right away!"

"I am responsible . . ."

As I rose my coat opened and Hess caught a glimpse of the silver frame protruding from the inside pocket, the frame of Kamploh's photograph I had stolen. He must have seen it—glancing down quickly, I saw it too. He did not even blink. My face was close to his.

"Get out!"

"Just a minute!"

"I want you to get out of here!"

"I'm the doctor! If anyone is going to get out of here it will be you!"

"That's what you think! Inspector Eilers and my brother are waiting in your office. You throw me out of here I'm going to tell them about that telephone call I've overheard." I had heard very little, but he didn't know that. He paled.

"Telephone call? What are you talking about?"

"Don't let's start that now," I said.

"You're crazy!"

"Perhaps. It would be interesting to see the inspector's reaction."

"It's your word against mine."

"You dirty liar!" I said, loud. If he doesn't throw me

out now he's deeply involved in this business, I thought. He didn't throw me out.

"Five minutes. In five minutes you must . . ."

"Out!" I said almost soothingly.

He left, quickly.

I sat down. The silver frame dug into my chest. I took Lillian's right hand in mine.

"We're alone now," I said. "What's the matter with your eyes?"

"They hurt. I can't open them." When she spoke the smell of garlic became stronger. "Richie . . ."

"Yes."

"I . . . I'm bad . . . I'm no good . . . I'm worth nothing . . . a whore . . ." She coughed. I could see that it hurt her. Her breathing was irregular. Soon she began again, "But I . . . I can't say it . . . it sounds so ridiculous after all that has happened. . . ."

"Tell me!"

"I . . ." She was searching for words. "A woman, no matter how many men she has known, a tramp or not . . . there will always be one man . . . one she truly loves . . . one man she longs for. She couldn't bear it . . . if she lost him . . . to another woman."

The impudence of a whore, I thought. But also the truth. I was a fool. I should have released her hand and run away, as far away from her as possible. But I stayed. I was happy. I was crazy. I was in love.

"You telephoned me," I said. "Me . . ."

"You're all I have left. He wanted to kill me, Richie . . ."

I froze. If my brother . . .

". . . because I said I was leaving him. . . ."

The room began to revolve around me.

"To whom did you say that?"

She whispered, "Come closer . . . must be careful . . . Clemens . . . I'm afraid . . ."

"Of Kamploh?"

188

She nodded, swallowed hard.

"I'm afraid, terrified . . . the poison . . . he'll try again. . . . He's very clever . . . he'll kill me . . . he said so. . . ."

"Kamploh threatened you?"

"Often."

"When the last time?"

"Last Friday . . . he telephoned . . . I was in Tenerife. . . . He said he knew that I had a lover there. . . . It's not true, Richie, not true, I swear."

"Calm yourself. You musn't become so excited. Go on."

"He said to come back—right away. If I didn't return he would come and kill me. . . . I flew back then."

"Why are you so afraid of him?"

"He's sinister. He knows something. So many people are afraid of him here—politicians, the police, his doctors, so many people. He . . . he could kill me here in this town and get away with it. He has a lot of power. . . "

Perspiration beaded Lillian's forehead. She was out of breath. I sat motionless.

"Lillian, do you know what you're saying? You're not imagining things?"

"I'm . . . I'm perfectly sane. . . . I came back because I could no longer stand the fear. I was going to collect my things to leave him. I took the risk to be killed by him. He was not there when I arrived. Can you imagine how relieved I felt?"

"But the housekeeper said . . ."

"Naturally I lied to her."

"Then it's not his birthday today?"

"Yes, it is, he left a letter for me . . . that he would call me, late, after his lecture . . . because it was his birthday. I was going to tell him then that I wouldn't be there when he returned."

"That's why the telephone was by the bed."

"Yes. But he didn't call . . . or perhaps I didn't hear the telephone ring. I took a sedative, I was so upset."

"Where were you going to go?"

"To you."

"To Frankfurt?"

"I . . . I didn't know what to do. I would have come to you, Richie. You wouldn't have sent me away, would you?"

I asked, "What about Werner?"

She opened her huge eyes: the pupils were pinpoints, the lids fluttered, but she kept them open in spite of the pain.

"Werner . . . he tried and tried to see me those last months."

"He wants you to come back to him?"

"Yes, but I don't want to. . . . He says he still loves me. I don't believe him—he had other reasons to bother me. I'm not lying, Richie. Really, I'm not!"

"Who says you are? Close your eyes."

She closed them and sighed.

"If anyone has lied as much as I have . . . lied to you especially. . . ."

"I believe you," I said. I did—at this moment. I was always like that. Doubts, disbelief always came later, always had come later. Too late.

"Why do you think Werner wanted to see you again?"

"Because of Clemens. I told you, he is awesome. He is . . . he's a devil—he blackmails and threatens and tortures people."

"How?"

"He knows something . . ."

"What?"

She shook her head. "I've no idea."

"Does he know something about Werner too?"

"No—on the contrary, Werner knows something about him."

"What?"

190

"He won't tell me but I have this feeling, intuition. I couldn't stand it any longer, Richie . . . I know what you're thinking."

"What's that?"

"How I could . . . with a man so much older."

"I was not thinking that." But I was. Exactly that.

"I . . . I was . . . I had reached the end of my rope when I met him. I didn't dare ask for your help again. I was destitute, worn out. Then he came . . . I was past caring so I took him, as a whore would, just a whore."

"Stop it!" I said, very loud, startling her. "So, he's threatened you for months."

"Many months—I've been living in panic for months. . . . I fled to Tenerife . . . even there I was not safe from his jealousy, his threats, and when I returned he wasn't there, but the Armagnac, I like Armagnac. . . ."

"I know."

"He certainly planned carefully, didn't he?"

"Not well enough—you're alive."

She gripped my hand suddenly, strongly; her nails dug into my skin.

I'm still alive. What will he do when he returns? Now that the first attempt has failed . . ."

It was a nightmare. I had to allay Lillian's fear. As long as she was here she would be safe. How safe? I must speak to Eilers. Lillian must have police protection. Could the police be trusted if I were to believe Lillian? Whom could one trust here? In this town where, apparently, there is much to hide, much that Kamploh knows.

"Where is Werner?"

"He's here too," I said. "In a bit of a predicament . . ."

"Why?"

"The police suspect him . . ." I could have bitten my tongue. It was too late. Lillian's eyes opened wide.

"They believe he tried to murder me? Oh, God!" She gasped.

"Don't! Please! Calm yourself! I'm sure he has an alibi. When Kamploh returns it'll all be cleared up. We'll find out the truth. Now I'm here. . ."

"You . . . you're not going to leave me?"

"No, Lillian, no. Please, calm yourself."

"You swear you won't leave me?"

"I swear," I said. I suddenly remembered Vanessa's predictions, Minski's misgivings, my experience with Lillian during the last twenty years, the suffering she had caused me. Now she took my hand and placed it between her breasts. I forgot everything, remembered nothing.

"I . . . Richie . . . I've really always loved only you, only you. Do you believe me?"

"Yes," I said, hoarse.

She whispered, "I want to be with you, always. Do you still want me now, despite everything?"

I felt the warmth of her breasts. I thought, you've lied, cheated, deceived, used me, made me look ridiculous, driven me to despair—it did not matter now.

"I do," I said.

"I only want to be with you . . . I'm afraid of people. They are bad, and they can do bad things. Not you, Richie, you still love me, don't you?"

Why else would I have driven here as soon as she had telephoned me? Why else would I be here now? And she? Perhaps she did not love me? Why shouldn't I believe her?

"Richie . . . do you still . . . love me?"

"Yes," I said.

A jubilant smile lit up her haggard face.

"We'll be together," I said. "We'll go away, far away." I meant it. Switzerland. Safety. Peace. Happiness.

"Kiss me," she whispered.

I touched my lips to hers.

"Everything will be all right," I said, raising my head.

"Yes, Richie, yes . . ."

Behind me the door opened.

"I'm sorry, you must leave now." Dr. Hess's voice.

I kissed Lillian's cold hand. "I'll be close by. I'll be back. Now," I raised my voice, "now I'll look after you. Don't worry."

"I'll try," she whispered.

Her eyelids fluttered, her face contorted in pain. I gently brushed my hand across her forehead, cold and damp with perspiration. I turned and saw Dr. Hess silhouetted in the open door against the brightly lit corridor.

"Well? Are you coming or do I have to have someone to fetch you?" the doctor growled.

"Fetch me?" One more glance at Lillian now resting motionless, then I walked toward Hess. That's when I saw the attendant in a white jacket and faded blue trousers next to the doctor. The man was huge with a broad, once-fractured nose, thick lips, black curly hair, a cruel expression on his face, large powerful hands.

He grinned. I quickly scanned the corridor. It was deserted. The door of a service elevator opposite Lillian's room stood open. Everything happened so fast I did not even have a chance to cry out. The orderly grabbed me and, although I'm quite tall and heavy, effortlessly lifted me into the elevator. Hess followed, pushed a button, the elevator began to descend.

"His arms," Hess said. The giant behind me twisted my arms back and up. I groaned.

"One move and I'll break your arms," the man said, giggling.

Hess was about to reach into my pocket where he had seen the silver-framed photograph I had stolen when I saw the syringe in his other hand. Instinctively I picked up my knee and jabbed him in the groin. He cried out, fell back against the elevator. The attendant pushed my arms up. Excruciating pain brought tears to my eyes.

Hess, obviously in pain but still holding the syringe,

came toward me again. He was afraid, I could see that—but surely not as frightened as I was of the syringe.

"Once more and this needle will be in your arm." Hess's bulging eyes behind his strong glasses now had a crazed expression as he pulled the frame from my coat pocket. He gasped for air and suddenly paled.

"What's up?" asked his helper who still held me in an iron grip.

Hess shoved him the frame. The photograph of the man known as Kamploh was not there. I may be naïve, but I'm not stupid.

The elevator stopped abruptly.

"Out!" Hess ordered.

The attendant pushed me out into a brightly lit, white-tiled basement. It stank of disinfectant. There were an unusual number of water faucets, one wall with closed metal doors, refrigeration pipes white with frost above and below them. Angled marble slabs with drains made me realize immediately where I was.

The powerful orderly pulled off my coat, threw it to Hess, who quickly searched it. The ruffian threw me to the ground, pinned me down. Hess dropped my coat, kneeled down beside me and systematically, thoroughly, began to search me. I struggled. I kicked and caught Hess at the neck. He began to bleed. Blood dripped onto my shirt and suit. Now I too reeked of disinfectant from the damp floor.

"Where is the photo?" Hess demanded.

I did not answer.

"Okay!" he said.

His helper grinned, pulled back his fist and hit me in the stomach. I choked, gasped for air. The man's thick lips grinned, exposing strong white teeth so close to me— just then it came to me where I had seen Kamploh. Not once but often. On a photograph which belonged to my old friend Homer Barlow. His was the older photograph.

The mustache had confused me. Kamploh had grown it later. For a very good reason.

"Where is the picture, you bastard?" the attendant demanded.

I remained silent; he hit me again and before I lost consciousness I thought of Barlow.

He was a baritone at the Berlin Opera. Rigoletto, Yago, Papageno: his first three roles had propelled him to fame.

Homer Luther Barlow had had a happy childhood. It was happy for the first three years of his life.

Homer had been born in 1924 in Birmingham, Alabama, of poor but devoted and pious parents.

In September 1930 a bomb exploded during the Sunday morning service at the well-filled Baptist church where Homer's father was employed as a sexton. Thirty-six Negroes were killed, among them eleven children; eighty-seven other Negroes were seriously injured.

The bomb killed the minister and Homer's parents. Homer had been ill and had not been taken to church that morning.

An investigation disclosed that the bomb had been planted by the Ku Klux Klan.

Homer was placed in a state orphanage. Over the years he grew into a tall, healthy, strong, young man. He was hard-working, gentle, polite and pious. He had a beautiful voice and loved to sing.

Someone affectionately called him Tiny (by now he was six feet four) and the nickname stayed with him. It stayed with him when he joined the Army, when his unit was sent to England, through the invasion of Normandy, France, Germany. At the Elbe river he made friends with the Russians during the time when the Americans and Russians, united in their fight against fascism, were still good friends—at least those who had fought in the field. They drank together, played together, sang together. The war had come to an end. Immeasurable misery prevailed in Europe; a promising spring became a beautiful summer; hundreds of thousands died of starvation; millions hopefully awaited a new era just before the first two atom bombs were dropped on Hiroshima and Nagasaki.

Tiny's unit was ordered to withdraw. Following the agreements of their politicians, the Americans withdrew their troops from large German territories they had conquered and ceded them to the Russians.

When Tiny's unit was disbanded he was attached to a Military Police battalion in Frankfurt. The MP station was near to the completely destroyed main railroad station where I began to work as an interpreter after my release from an American POW camp in May 1946.

"He's coming out of it," a voice said.

I felt nauseated, my head hurt. Cautiously I opened my eyes. The odor of the disinfectant made me gag. I was still on the floor of the mortuary. The brute still held my arms; Hess straddled my legs. The blood on his neck glistened in the harsh, bright light.

"The photograph," Hess said. "Where is it?"

I was silent.

"All right. We can't stay here forever," the doctor said. "If you think that's going to help you, forget it. I'll give you a little injection now. When you awaken we'll have another little talk. At a very quiet little place. Hold him," he instructed the gorilla and proceeded to get up. I spat all the saliva I had collected in my mouth while he had been talking, directly between his eyes. His hands went up reflexively to protect his face. I kicked Hess in the abdomen with both feet and all the strength I could muster. He was thrown backward against one of the marble slabs; his glasses fell off, broke on the floor. The attendant, surprised, grunted, relaxing his grip on me for just a moment. On a nearby table were a mallet, a chisel, two autopsy scalpels. Probably used for opening skulls, I thought as I grabbed the mallet and brought it down on the orderly's head.

He made a whistling sound, sat down and passed out. Hess, meanwhile, was back on his feet but at a disadvantage without his glasses. I hit him in the jaw; he fell against the tiled wall. This time he stayed down.

A bell rang, a light flashed above the elevator. It was needed upstairs. I had to get out of here fast. I quickly straightened my clothes, grabbed my coat, hurried to a door marked EXIT. I left the empty photo frame. My entire body ached. I ran doubled over; my abdomen hurt.

I flung open the door. Another service elevator. Probably for transporting the plain coffins stored in this roughly cemented part of the basement. I knew that coffins were usually picked up at night and from a remote part of a hospital. I hoped that this would be the case here too. I closed the elevator doors behind me, pushed the "up" button. The elevator stopped on the ground floor. I stumbled down a short, dusty corridor. A door led out into a yard in the rear of the hospital. Leafless trees, garbage cans, crates with empty bottles, cans. It was raining heavily.

I ran across the grounds to the front of the hospital. My feet sank into the rain-sodden earth, my trousers became muddy. Unshaven, with my dirty, disheveled clothes reeking of disinfectant, I must have been a disreputable sight. I was grateful for the exceedingly bad weather. In the continuing darkness of this day—it was now after 10 A.M.—in the heavy rain visibility was poor.

There was the parking lot.

There the green police car.

Before we had left Kamploh's villa, with Eilers's permission I had gone to the bathroom and there removed the photograph from the silver frame and folded it twice. Finding no suitable hiding place for the frame I had returned it to my inside coat pocket. On our drive to the hospital I had unobtrusively slipped the folded photo between the upholstered seat and backrest. It wasn't wise, I thought, to take the picture into the hospital. I was suspicious of Dr. Hess, Fegesack, too, since he had derisively watched me steal the picture in Lillian's bedroom. Hess had spoken to Fegesack on the telephone. Had Fegesack informed him that I had Kamploh's picture? Probably. But Eilers and Lansing had also known that I had the picture. Somehow they seemed more trustworthy than Fegesack, especially Lansing. Why hadn't they taken the photo from me? But then, neither had Fegesack. All of them probably wanted to see what I would do with it or, conversely, what would happen to me and it.

"People are bad. They can hurt others."

Lillian had said something like that.

I had been caught in the cross fire of conflicting interests. It didn't take any heavy thinking to know that something rotten was going on.

I opened the car door—I had made certain it would remain unlocked—extracted the photograph and hid it under my shirt. I glanced at the hospital. People were entering, leaving. It looked very peaceful. For how much longer? Eilers, his assistant, my brother were in Dr. Hess's office. Soon I would be missed. I remembered that the doctor's office faced the parking lot and I hurried.

The police car was parked between Werner's black Mercedes and my silver-gray Thunderbird. I had seen a suitcase on the rear seats and suits hanging in my brother's car. I had been puzzled. Werner must have expected a prolonged stay. Or had he intended to take a trip? I was in luck. His car door opened. I took the suitcase, two suits, hurried to my car, threw them and my coat into the rear seat, slipped behind the wheel, started the car. The tires screamed.

The wall was spattered with blood to a height of two

meters. Innumerable bullet holes made the wall appear a lunar landscape. In time the blood had become brown, black, gray, rust-red, green. It had splashed over the wall more than twenty years ago. The bullet holes also dated from that time.

The wall was one of four in Tiny's bar in the basement of his villa in the Grunewald.

He had bought the house in 1956 at the beginning of his promising career as an operatic baritone. Tiny had fallen in love with Berlin, with the Grunewald, this villa near the Hagenplatz. It had been in poor condition. Repairs had been made only sporadically.

The villa had once been the exclusive residence of a Jewish banker. Several Nazi notables followed, someone prominent in the organization for total war, a Gestapo squad, a Russian commandant, a British MI-5 man; then the house reverted back to the German Jews.

The Jewish banker had shot himself in Rio de Janeiro in 1943. Tiny bought the villa from his sons, naturalized Brazilians, who were determined never to set foot in Germany again. The house remained unoccupied until Tiny's success brought him the means to renovate it. Everything was changed except for that blood-stained, bullet-riddled wall.

Guests entering the otherwise comfortably appointed bar for the first time were taken unawares by the wall which so brutally confronted them with the past. Some thought the wall a hoax; others fell silent, distressed. Some became loud, aggressive, began discussions of the crimes of the Nazis, the Russians, the Poles, the French, the Americans, the Jews—the number of accused was limitless. Tiny chose his friends on the basis of their behavior when confronted with the wall.

Facing that wall, on a large wooden board, were about two hundred photographs: men, women, children, in civilian clothes or uniforms, people Tiny had met during the time he had been a member of the Military Police.

Near the center of the board was the photograph of a man who now called himself Kamploh.

I remembered the photo and its exact location on the board. I had seen it often since I visited with Tiny each time I came to Berlin. He had once recounted the story connected with the man. It had been a fantastic one but that was all I could recall about it. I had seen the photograph only three months ago when Minski and I had been in Berlin to engage a new girl who performed with a python.

Right now it was imperative that I call Tiny to ascertain Kamploh's true identity. I could not risk telephoning from Treuwall. I could not stay here now that I was carrying the photograph.

From a safe distance a fat, gray rabbit, crouching in a hollow under a dense juniper shrub, was watching me change clothes. Its long ears were folded back, black-button eyes shiny. I had pulled off the main road and followed a muddy path into the woods.

I rid myself of my soiled clothing, reeking of disinfectant, throwing it from the car window. Werner's gray suit and white shirt fitted me well, as did his shoes. The suitcase was well filled. How long had Werner expected to stay in Treuwall? Or had he intended to disappear? Lillian had not thought him involved in the attempt on her life. Once I had heard about Kamploh I was inclined to believe that too. I believed Lillian once again. Surely she was too ill and weak right now to fabricate complicated lies.

And yet!

In any case she was not the *only* one involved here. Primarily, that seemed to be Kamploh. Why else would I have been attacked? Why else would Dr. Hess have behaved as he had, which now left only one way out for him—to disappear? Yet, suppose Kamploh had not tried to poison Lillian, his threats against her notwithstanding,

200

but had himself been marked for murder. Lillian may have unwittingly become implicated.

According to Lillian many people in Treuwall would have liked to have seen Kamploh dead. As she expressed it, he had blackmailed, tortured, threatened them. But why, how, with what?

I had to call Tiny. Right away.

The sudden rattling of a machine gun made me jump. A second, third joined. The first of a series of shells exploded. Instinctively I ducked. A helicopter rumbled overhead. I glanced at the rabbit. It had not moved.

Then I remembered the large warning signs along the road I had seen on my drive to Treuwall. Troop training grounds. Today I know that half of the state-protected area of Lüneburg Heath is an enormous training ground with secret, heavily guarded nuclear warheads, landing strips and starfighter bases. Near Müden the Europe Missile is being perfected. Here a continual war game with bombers, supersonic fighters, tanks, rockets and conventional weapons was being played.

The innocence of the heath . . .

That had been a myth for the past quarter of a century. Hitler had had Europe's largest airport built near Fassberg. On the heath's idyllic paths the V-1 had been tested.

Right now I was assured by the fat rabbit. It was obviously used to the infernal noise. I fastened the last cufflink, liberally rubbed some of Werner's eau de toilette on my face and hands, sprinkled a little on my coat. That still smelled a little of disinfectant even through the scent of eau de toilette.

Here it seems necessary that I clarify one point: no heroic or idealistic ideas motivated me when I began my search to ascertain Professor Kamploh's true identity, but only love and concern for Lillian. I wanted to protect her against a man I believed to be a potential murderer. There was also fear—considering the experience

I had had in the hospital mortuary. Love and fear, only those. I need hardly pose as a hero since my intention is to record only the truth.

I drove south to the Autobahn Helmstedt-Hanover as fast as I dared on the slippery road. I intended to call Tiny from a restaurant on the autobahn.

The military police station near the almost completely destroyed Frankfurt Hauptbahnhof had been established in the requisitioned furniture store of a house two-thirds destroyed. Only the main and first floors remained. The MP battalion quickly made the station serviceable. The new store windows were painted green, man-high, to conceal the interior from the curious. Everything was painted green including the sign above the entrance door, lit at night, which proclaimed this a military police station.

Each shift had a staff of four. We worked in three shifts around the clock. We interpreters were permitted to arrange our own tours of duty. There were three of us: Eugene Reck, Dr. Walter Paradin and I.

Reck had held an executive position in a German-American private bank. In 1942, with the bank closed by the Nazis, Reck was forced to work as a laborer in the armament industry. The traveled, cultured man was now hoping for the reopening of the old bank by the Americans. In 1946 he was fifty-two years old.

Paradin was a former public prosecutor. In 1946 he was forty-four years old, prematurely white, a slight man with a limp. Even in those difficult postwar years he was always neat in his dark suits.

I did not even own a suit then. I still wore my uniform with the prominent white POW printed on it when I entered the MP station to inquire about an interpreter's position.

It was Homer Barlow who obtained for me American uniforms, dyed dark-blue. He also found a room for me—as he had for Paradin—in the house of a then-fugitive Nazi official. We lived there together with about a dozen displaced persons, Poles and Germans, and a number of boisterous children.

Tiny, a driver, as were many Negroes in the Army, came to visit often. He never came empty-handed. He brought food, candy, cigarettes, soap, liquor, even coal which, so it was rumored, he had stolen from a nearby Army pool in the bitter-cold winter of 1945. We all loved Tiny and Tiny loved us. He was happy in Germany.

"People are friendly here," he often said as though he found that incredible. "No one calls me a goddamned nigger here. Certainly there must have been a lot of evil people in Germany. But as individuals you are not evil. You've been tyrannized and forced to wage war. Children come to me, I can amuse them. Boy, oh, boy, if I'd done that in Birmingham!" Tiny liked children. Soon aware of that, they exploited him. He accepted the situation amiably.

Tiny said, "I don't want to return to the States. I want to stay here where I'm not treated as a second-class human being."

He fell in love with Ellen Herbst, then twenty-two. She had lost both parents, her fiancé had died at the front, leaving her with a daughter, Michaela, now four years old, whom Tiny nicknamed Mickey.

Loving them both, he was determined to marry blonde, blue-eyed Ellen as soon as legally possible. The law imposed by the Allies did not permit fraternizing, but this was generally ignored.

Despite his unusually large stature, Tiny moved with the grace of a dancer. He could imitate Mickey Mouse, speaking falsetto, and invariably showed delight when his audience seemed surprised.

About a month after I had started as an interpreter we were sent to arrest a wanted Nazi. It was a routine assignment—even the strangest occurrences soon became routine. Fights; accidents, shootings; raids on bars known for black-market dealings; supervision of women who had contracted VD (an overwhelming group) and enforcing their regular medical examinations; mediating discord between Germans, arguments between Americans, or between nationals; patrolling "Off Limits" bars; the rescue of cats from rooftops; the picking up of frauleins from a general's villa when his wife arrived unexpectedly. It was a mad life—yet to us, routine.

The Nazi's arrest on sight was mandatory. We surprised him in his apartment, delivered him to a prison under the jurisdiction of the military government. At the station Tiny pulled me into the back room. On the table stood a typewriter.

"For you," Tiny beamed.

"Where did you get that?"

"From the Nazi's apartment. He won't need it any more. You do." He pushed his helmet back, delighted with himself.

"Why?"

"Well, you're a writer. Writers need typewriters. Or are you going to write only by hand?" He laughed. "I've watched you write whenever there was nothing to do here. What is it going to be? A book?"

I shrugged my shoulders, embarrassed that Tiny had observed me. I had no idea if the twenty or thirty pages I had written so far would ever become a book. I wanted to write, yet I felt uncertain, often inclined to tear it all up and abandon the attempt.

"A book!" Tiny was overcome with awe. "Jesus! Who'd have ever thought I'd meet a genuine writer!"

"I'm not really a writer, Tiny!"

"Shut up! Of course you are! And you're going to write here. Every night. I'll watch out for you. What are you writing about?"

"Oh, I don't know—about the war . . . the times now . . . all that."

204

"Great! It's going to be a bestseller. I know it will. And I gave you the typewriter!"

The following night he had brought me supplies: white paper, pencils, erasers, carbon paper, pencil sharpeners. Tiny had told his friends that I was working on a book. They were all most impressed.

It was a quiet night. I was sitting in the little room in back of the station, typing all I had written so far when Tiny entered. His voice was normal but I noticed tears in his eyes.

"Tiny!"

He brushed his large hand across his eyes.

"Just heard some story," he said. "A teacher gave his class an assignment. Eight-year-olds. Here in Frankfurt. They were to write a composition: 'The Luckiest Day of My Life.'"

"Well?"

"A little girl wrote, 'The luckiest day of my life was February 12, 1945. My brother Karl died and I was given his coat and shoes.'" Tiny looked at me, sadly. "Children, Richie! Goddamn, what a shit world this is where children write such things! What fault is it of theirs?" He poured himself a drink, gulped it and said, "Write that down too, Richie. Write it all down! All of it!"

I wrote it.

I worked on my manuscript summer, winter, the following spring, at night, whenever possible.

I recounted my experiences, past and present, sad and humorous. In my position as an interpreter I saw and heard much. My first book thus became a tragicomedy.

Slowly my doubts, uncertainties, fits of despair lessened. I began to believe in my work. Tiny, who was feverishly learning German, thought it "Great! Just great!"

The little girl's composition was the motto of my first book. For its title I chose *Stan' Still, Jordan,* a line from a Negro spiritual Tiny often sang, one of many his mother had sung to him.

There was also a dedication.

FOR TINY, WHO KNOWS WHY

In the fall of 1946 an influenza epidemic raged, killing many. During the winter thousands more died of cold and starvation. The beautiful spring which came upon our land of ruins brought a recurrence of the epidemic! Exhausted, undernourished, spent people died in great numbers.

In the late afternoon of a lovely day in April 1947 the sun, still bright and golden, streamed diagonally into the MP station when I heard a bell as a bicycle was placed against the house. Tiny, looking out above the green paint of the window, whistled appreciatively through his teeth.

"What's the matter?" I asked.

"You'll see in a moment," he answered.

The door opened.

A young woman of medium height entered. She was fashionably dressed. Blue tunic dress, its white skirt pleated, white shoes with clunky cork heels, white costume jewelry. Her long hair, falling in soft waves to her shoulders, was as blue-black as her very large, long-lashed eyes. Lips full and sensuous. Wide cheekbones gave her face a Slavic look. Beautiful teeth, long legs, firm breasts partially exposed by the low-necked dress.

The desk sergeant put down the book he had been reading and rose, straightening his tie. The assistant desk sergeant rose and stared. I forgot about the report I had been working on and got up too. Tiny bowed solemnly and, in his strongly accented German, said, "Beautiful Fräulein!" He pointed to me. "Interpreter there," he said, and to me, "You lucky dog, you." Unobtrusively he began to work his way toward her back to startle her with his trick voice.

The young woman turned to me. "I'm Lillian Lombard."

I drove almost twenty kilometers along the autobahn before I came to a restaurant. It was near Meerburg. The land was hilly, wooded, snow-covered, bleak and depressing in the whirling snow and the dreary light of this dark day. From the south, the Mittellandcanal, came the muted, sad sounds of tugboat horns, the hoarse hooting of sirens.

A Mercedes and four trailer-trucks were parked outside the restaurant. When I entered the truck drivers in turtleneck sweaters, leather jackets and corduroy trousers looked up briefly. At another table two men, probably businessmen, in conservative clothes, their backs toward me, did not turn around.

"Yes?" the young, plump waitress asked.

"A cognac," I ordered. "And a beer."

The girl sniffed. I had left my coat in the car. I must have still smelled of the eau de toilette. She probably thought I was gay. "And I'd like to make a telephone call. Long distance."

I stood quite close to the two men who had the appearance of businessmen. One of them wore dark-rimmed glasses, the other smoked a cigar. Papers and coffee were on their table. They still did not look at me, but at the papers before them. They did not talk.

"The telephone booth is over there," the buxom waitress said. "You can dial direct. I'll set the clock."

She stepped behind the counter to the automatic telephone timer, set the hand to zero, pushed a button, nodded to me.

The telephone booth was on a corridor redolent with the odor of cooking. I looked up Tiny's telephone number in my address book and dialed. I heard a repeated ring, while worrying that no one would answer. At last I heard a woman's voice.

"Barlow!"

It was Tiny's wife, the former Ellen Herbst. Tiny had married her, adopted her daughter. Mickey had become a pretty young lady of twenty-four. She was studying German philology at the Free University in Berlin.

"Ellen, this is Richie Mark."

"Richie!" Ellen's voice was low, husky, unexpected in such a tiny, blue-eyed, blond-haired woman. "Where are you?"

I explained.

I watched for anyone approaching the telephone booth. The businessmen were now engaged in an animated conversation. Two more truck drivers entered, one of whom deposited a coin in the juke box and selected a record. I wondered if there was any way in which my call could be monitored and if the plump waitress was doing just that. I did not see her then.

"Is Tiny in Berlin?"

"No. In London. He's doing some recordings. He is supposed to be back the day after tomorrow. Is there anything I can do for you?"

The waitress had returned. She took the two drivers' order. One of them patted her behind. She slapped his hand, but amiably. I said quickly, "It sounds a bit crazy, I'll explain later, but right now . . ." I described Kamploh and asked her to find his photograph on the board in the bar, hoping it would have his name on it.

"All right, Richie, hold on." The two men, presumably owners of the car outside, had turned and were looking toward the telephone booth. Their faces were ordinary, of the kind easily forgotten. The one smoking the cigar said something to the other who nodded. I was beginning to feel warm in the booth. There was a strong smell of onions and fat. I wished I could have opened the door. How long was Ellen going to be? I looked at the walls of the booth covered with telephone numbers, graffiti, names. Someone had carved a swastika into the wood paneling next to the telephone. Underneath it in crooked letters was the inscription "GERMANY AWAKE!" Below that some other artist had added "SHIT!"

"Richie?" Ellen's voice sounded breathless.

"Did you find it? Was there a name?"

"Yes. But I could have told you who—"

"Who is it, Ellen? Who?"

"Well, this Victor Delacorte. I'm sure you remember Professor Dr. Delacorte, don't you? In 1946 near Darmstadt, Tiny . . ." Ellen's voice suddenly began to fade until I could no longer hear it. I was perspiring profusely.

Yes, I remembered Professor Dr. Victor Delacorte.

From the summer of 1940 to the end of 1941 he had been one of the psychiatrists responsible for the planning and execution of the euthanasia action T4.

He had originated the questionnaires sent to the mental institutions, had worked as an assessor, had "trained" a number of doctors, had inspected hospitals, gas chambers, concentration camps.

Professor Delacorte, alias Clemens Kamploh, director of the hospital in Treuwall, Lillian's lover, was one of the most infamous war criminals of the Third Reich.

On February 12, 1946, a weapons carrier of the American Army was driving north on the Autobahn Mannheim-Frankfurt. Two soldiers with machine guns were guarding a fair-haired man with a prominent scar on his left cheek. He was clad in a creased double-breasted suit too large for his emaciated body, a frayed shirt and well-worn tie. An army coat was thrown around his shoulders. It was a bitter-cold winter's day. Both soldiers wore heavy winter clothing.

The civilian was shivering with cold. His hands were

red. He was handcuffed. The truck bounced, swayed, hitting potholes, sliding across the icy road.

Homer Barlow, the driver, had a problem in driving safely on the slippery surface. Beside him sat another Negro who held two machine guns. The soldiers, members of the 765th Military Police Battalion, had taken the handcuffed German from Frankfurt jail to Nürnberg for two days to be witness against the war criminal Ernst Kaltenbrunner. The witness was Delacorte, who had conveniently become affected with an almost complete lapse of memory.

Now he was being returned to Frankfurt after having been in jail for some time. He had been evacuated to Denmark with an entire hospital staff who treated only brain-damaged soldiers. At the end of the war he had been arrested and interned there until his transfer to the county court in Frankfurt. Delacorte was awaiting a trial scheduled for 1947 in Nürnberg against him and other Nazi physicians.

During the first two years following the end of the war the autobahn was used almost exclusively by military vehicles. Groups of children loitered alongside it in all kinds of weather, summer or winter, hoping for coal, wood or potatoes to fall off a truck; hoping for the soldiers driving past to throw them some food, candy, cigarettes. Entire hijacking bands had formed which on occasion had unloaded a truck in record time. The spoils were quickly disposed of by accomplices hiding behind bushes and trees.

Homer Barlow had already exhausted his supply of candy and fruit when, near Darmstadt, a little girl in pigtails suddenly darted across the icy road. Tiny grappled desperately with the wheel. The truck went into a skid, turned around, slid off the road and overturned not far from the terror-stricken child.

Then everything happened very quickly. Before Tiny and his co-driver could climb out of the driver's cab they heard curses, yells, shots. The prisoner Delacorte had been the first to regain consciousness. One soldier was still unconscious. Delacorte kicked the other one's face, then quickly slid underneath the partially closed tarpaulin in the rear of the truck. He fell, rose, and keeping well down, zigzagged across the frozen earth toward a cluster of trees.

The soldier, bleeding profusely, followed him, cursing and shooting. Tiny and the other man joined the pursuit. Their shots missed Delacorte, who had disappeared among the bare, dark trees of the grove. Dusk, resembling amber-colored fog, was shadowing the land. The sky was dark and heavy with snow.

Tiny immediately notified headquarters in Frankfurt via radio. Within a short time hundreds of soldiers, jeeps, dogs, helicopters were engaged in the search for Delacorte. A large area surrounding the place where he had escaped was closed off and systematically searched. The escaped prisoner could not be found. Three days later the search was discontinued, although his arrest warrant issued by the court in Frankfurt was regularly renewed.

Tiny and the other three soldiers were court-martialed but subsequently acquitted. All this took place shortly before I began to work as an interpreter. Tiny had told me about Delacorte, who had escaped on his way to the prison in Frankfurt where I am now writing these lines.

March 13, 1967. The prison guard brought cleaning materials and stayed with me until I had finished cleaning my cell.

Officer Stalling, in his twenty-sixth year at the prison, is fifty-two years old, gray-haired, thickset. Although he worries about his chronically ill wife and their two difficult teen-age children he is always polite, patient and in good spirits.

I was brought here December 16, 1966, more than three months ago. In the beginning there were daily interrogations, conferences with the examining magistrate,

Dr. Heinz Hellweg, the public prosecutor, Dr. Paradin, and my lawyer, Dr. Wilhelm Hill. It soon became apparent that my case was but one part of this affair. They could not predict how it would develop or even when my case would come to trial. It had been Paradin's idea for me to write this report in those weeks, maybe months, preceding my trial. It is not difficult for me. I am competent in shorthand.

The pads of shorthand notes are typed for Dr. Paradin's, the magistrate's and my lawyer's study.

My daily writing sustains me, convinces me that I have won my first real victory over my cursed brother who even in death had seemed to prevail over me. Paradin had told me, "By giving us a truthful account you will be helping us . . . and yourself, Richie."

I am recording the facts, every day, regularly. I have already filled many pages.

I am not allowed visitors, only newspapers. My cell is large, reasonably comfortable. I can look outside, since the window faces a courtyard, but I can see only other barred windows.

During the first few weeks following my arrest newspapers were prohibited to me as my case was too well-publicized. Now, three months later, I am no longer newsworthy. Only rarely is an article cut out by the censor.

Everything in the published news, of which I had been so long deprived, interested me: Germany's slow recovery from economic crisis; the final conversion of the private Krupp firm to a joint-stock company and its borrowing of a million marks to save 200,000 workers from unemployment; the possible salvation of the National Democratic party through a change of leadership—a change Minski had predicted months earlier, while assuring me that the NPD with its many Nazi members would not be eliminated. (Such silly items as the comments of a beauteous columnist, whose photo decorated her articles, were not to be missed, at least not by me.) The heavy death toll in South Vietnam, civilians included, shocked the Pope, the UN secretary-general, and me. I read it all eagerly.

Officer Stalling worries about his wife, who has a heart condition. Five years ago she had been an attractive woman (Stalling had shown me photographs); now, at 42, she looks as if she had died. Distressingly thin; skin waxen; dull, sunken eyes.

"She's upset and worried about the children. We've worked hard to give them a better chance than we had. They're better off than we were, but do you think they have any ambition? On the contrary. They're lazy, sloppy. Jochen, he's eighteen, just lies around all day on the couch and listens to records. We'll be glad when he has to go into the army! I hope they'll drill him until he doesn't know his front from his arse. Excuse me, but you don't know . . ."

Stalling's monologues don't change but they are a break in my solitary, daily monotony. I am grateful just to hear a human voice.

"Do you think Monika would ever clean the apartment? No, she spends hours in the bathtub, in front of the mirror. With all that makeup she looks like a whore. Proud of her bosom as if she were the only one who had one. Plastic earrings, bangles, sunglasses, patent-leather coats—all essentials. What a generation! You can be glad you have no children. By God, I was no Nazi, just a member, but we never had this going on when we had the Führer. Sure, some dreadful crimes were committed then—but we still had *ideals,* right? Especially the youth. The Führer intended only the best for the youth, right? And today? The Beatles. James Bond. Juvenile delinquents. Hippies. They have no ideals. Am I right? I often talk with Herr Karger and Herr Jakowski about this. They, too, agree."

Those two gentlemen have been in this prison since 1963. Both of them, for their crimes against humanity, were sentenced to life imprisonment at the 1965 Auschwitz trials. Their appeals are not expected to be heard until 1967. They have been—and will be for some time to come—living a comparatively pleasant life here.

Both of them have volunteered for work, cleaning, giving out meals, in the prison. They are conscientious workers, polite, untiring, well-liked by guards and inmates.

Stalling repeated, "I'm not a Nazi, never was. But I see what I see. I don't mean to offend you, Herr Mark. One cannot compare what they've done with what you've done. But you are here for political reasons *too*—I mean the *same* political reasons, right? You know, in all those years here I've come to know people. It's a question of character. Either one has discipline and orderliness or one has not. Don't you think I'm right?"

Karger and Jakowski treat me with deference since they found out the reason for my being here. Before me on the table is a small souvenir—a present from Jakowski. I'll never know how he came to save it through all the searches and inspections. Paradin permitted me to keep it. He didn't even ask who had given it to me. Once, when we had been in the prison yard for exercise, Jakowski had surreptitiously pressed it into my hand: a small, silver skull, the insignia each SS man had worn on his black cap.

Officer Stalling admired the emblem occasionally. He well remembers Professor Dr. Delacorte.

"I'd been a guard here for only four years when the Americans transferred him to this prison. I hadn't been in the army because of my kidney ailment. Was allowed to work right after 'forty-five though. As I said, I've never been a Nazi, only nominally. Anyway, they arrested the professor in Denmark, right in the hospital there. And of course they impounded his belongings. Do you know

214

that there was a shrunken head among his things? Complete with skin and hair! Needless to say it disappeared. I'd like to know who took the professor's good-luck charm and where it is today! One of the Americans, a Jew who understood German, told me about that head when the professor was brought here. Every time I see your silver skull I'm reminded of the professor's shrunken head. It's strange that you of all people and the professor . . . and that both of you end up here with me . . . very strange, don't you think?"

The odor of onions and fat pervaded the telephone booth in the autobahn restaurant.

"Richie . . . are you still there?" It was Ellen's voice.

"Yes . . ."

"What's the matter with Delacorte? I wish you'd tell me! I'm afraid . . ."

I am too, I thought. The two men were still watching me. One said something, the other nodded. "No reason to be alarmed," I told her, clearing my throat. "But do me one favor. Call Tiny and tell him that I think I've found Delacorte."

"You've what?" I heard her catch her breath.

"Tell Tiny to call Dr. Paradin at the Frankfurt County Court. He can get the number from information. Will you do that?"

"Of course. What's the name again?"

"Paradin. Tiny knows him. He used to be an interpreter at the MP station. Paradin will tell Tiny what to do. We need witnesses."

"I'll call right away. I wish there was something else I could do."

"It's all right. Must go now. Thanks, Ellen. So long." I depressed the telephone but continued to hold the receiver to my ear as if I was still talking. The waitress was writing on her pad, the two men were paying their check.

I hoped fervently that they would leave, that perhaps they were not interested in me at all.

The men rose. The waitress helped them into heavy winter coats. They walked toward the exit. I stepped out of the telephone booth. At the bar I finished my cognac and drank some beer.

"Check, please."

The waitress looked at the telephone timer.

"Have a good trip," she said sullenly, despite the generous tip I had given her. She did not say thank you. She looked pale. Perhaps she did not feel well.

The snowstorm hit me with such force I almost fell when I stepped through the door. Bent forward, I fought my way to my car. Visibility was only about ten meters. The car was covered with snow. I brushed off the windshield. When I climbed into my car I was freezing. I had put the key into the ignition when I suddenly heard a man's voice.

"Where is the photograph?"

I looked up. One of the two men who had left the restaurant before me looked at me through the open window on my side. The man wearing glasses stood in front of the car. Very close to it. His coat collar was turned up, hat pulled down over his face, his hands in his pockets.

"Well!" The man closest to me smelled of stale cigar smoke. "Well, where is the photograph?" he demanded.

I said nothing, just gripped the steering wheel tightly. The man motioned to the one with glasses, then reached into the car, opened the rear door and got in next to me. He slammed the door and grinned.

"Hell, Herr Mark," he said.

The beautiful young woman in the blue dress said, "My name is Lillian Lombard."

The desk sergeant and the assistant desk sergeant had risen, staring admiringly. Tiny was sneaking up on her to use his falsetto gag on her.

216

"My name is Mark," I introduced myself. "What can I do for you, Fräulein Lombard?"

"Frau Lombard," she corrected me. She jumped, startled, as Tiny behind her squealed, "Frau, not Fräulein? What a shame, what a shame!"

"What's the matter with his voice?" Lillian Lombard was bewildered. Her glance alternated between Tiny and me. Tiny's face was blank.

"I always speak like this!" he squeaked.

"It's a joke," I explained. "A gag."

Lillian Lombard laughed, confused.

"Wow!" Tiny's voice, now normal, held admiration. "Oh, boy, ain't she beautiful when she laughs?"

Lillian Lombard turned to me. In the sunlight her exceptionally large black eyes seemed luminescent.

"I'm a secretary," she said. "I work for an architect. Master. Perhaps you've heard of him."

"Yes, I have," I replied. Master had designed mess halls, clubs, movie houses, snack bars for the Americans.

"The office is just around the corner," she continued. "I meant to come before but somehow . . ."

We were still looking at each other. She was beautiful. I had never seen a more beautiful woman.

". . . in any case," she continued, "I don't even know if you'll be able to help me. I have tried so many different places."

"What did you try?" I asked. The Americans were still staring at the young woman. It irritated me even though I was staring at her myself.

"I have been trying to find my husband," Lillian Lombard said.

"What's that? She's got a husband?" Tiny squeaked.

I nodded.

"Too bad," Tiny remarked.

I stood and stared at her. I felt as if I could have stood there an eternity just looking at her.

"Soldier?" I asked, hoarsely.

"Yes," she answered. "Missing. Can you help me?"

"We can try," I said and reached for a pad, twice before I found it. We usually forwarded such requests to a special Army branch, but on occasion we had been able to help find husbands, brothers, sons. "Your husband's name. Rank. Date of birth. Last communication."

There was a very sad expression in Lillian Lombard's eyes. No, not sad, rather helpless, bewildered, discouraged.

"Kurt Lombard. Born October 12, 1922. Sergeant." She stepped very close to me. "Fieldpost number 58753. His last letter was dated June 2, 1944. It had been written in Gacé, a little village near Falaise in Normandy."

Her eyes. Unforgettably beautiful eyes. I think that no one who has ever looked into those eyes could ever forget them.

I said, "I know where Gacé is."

"Me too!" Tiny squeaked.

"You do?" Lillian Lombard asked.

"Yes. I was taken prisoner in Normandy."

"Brave Kraut," Tiny chattered. "Bad Americans bang, bang, Richie POW! But Richie nix kaput. Richie-boy go to United States, return, write book!"

"For Christ's sake, shut up!" I said.

"You're writing a book?" Lillian asked.

I nodded, embarrassed.

The desk sergeant brought a chair. "Take a seat, ma'am."

"Oh, thank you!" Lillian smiled at him, sat down.

"A novel?"

"And that was the last you heard from your husband?" I asked. I would dream of those eyes.

A car horn honked. I heard steps and voices from the street outside, a plane above, whistling of a locomotive, so many sounds, yet I felt that Lillian and I were alone, the only people. Later, much later, when I held her in my arms, she was to ask me, "Do you remember our first meeting . . . in the MP station? I felt as if we were alone, the only people, only you and I."

"So answer my question, a novel?"

"Yeah, a novel! In the back room. At night," Tiny interjected.

"Perhaps it will become a novel," I said. "You never received any notification that he had been killed? Or presumed missing?"

"No."

"The Red Cross . . ."

"I've already been there."

"Would you give me your maiden name, please? I shall also need your date of birth, the date of your marriage."

"Elsner. June 21, 1927."

"Then you're only . . ."

"Twenty, that's right."

"When were you married?"

"In 1944. January 7." She looked at me, uncertain. "We married because I was afraid I might be pregnant. I wasn't."

"Or you wouldn't have married?"

"Never," Lillian said, matter-of-factly. "I was seventeen! My first . . . first experience. I was young and dumb. We went to school together. Then, when Kurt came home on furlough . . ."

"I understand."

"No, I wouldn't have married him if I hadn't been afraid of having a baby . . . and, after all, he had to return to the front. But now I'm married," she continued. "As long as I'm not sure what happened to my husband I cannot remarry."

Suddenly the street noises seemed to swell.

"You want to . . ."

"Yes. A young architect. He, too, works for Master. We would like to marry soon. As soon as possible. How long will it be before you will know anything?"

"I can only hope we'll be able to help you. You told

219

me yourself that you'd tried many other offices—without success."

"Yes, unfortunately."

Her callousness, her haste to marry again made me feel resentful.

"It's difficult to say how long it might take."

"Oh yeah!" Tiny was enthusiastic.

"If you'll leave your address I'll notify you." I was annoyed.

She gave me a strange look.

"156 Stresemannstrasse," she finally said. "The house belonged to my parents. They're dead. American officers live there now. I'm permitted to live in the basement." There was no rancor in her voice. She was still matter-of-fact. A woman who accepts reality. I made a note of the address.

"You'll hear from me," I said. She was very beautiful, yet I did not like her any more. I have to modify that: I still liked her looks but not her manner.

"Thank you," said Lillian. She left the station quickly without looking at anyone. The door closed behind her. I heard her take her bicycle from the wall. The bell jingled.

The two men who had climbed into my car were grinning at me. The man with glasses next to me tried to open the glove compartment. It was locked.

"In there, eh?"

I said nothing.

The jack was underneath my seat. If only I could get at it. But there were two against one. Hopeless. Now they had me.

The man wearing glasses reached into his jacket and pulled out an identification card.

"Detective Sergeant Geyer," he introduced himself. "Criminal investigation department. We are part of Inspector Eilers's group. My colleague Ericksen too. Show

Herr Mark your identification, Paul." The man sitting behind me passed it to me. Both IDs showed photographs
of their owners and, as far as I could determine, seemed
to be genuine.

"How did you get here?" I asked.

"Inspector Eilers sent us to keep an eye on you,"
Ericksen explained. "So that the photograph will really
reach Dr. Paradin."

"What do you know of Paradin?"

"Well, the inspector and Lansing questioned your
brother in the hospital. Your brother mentioned that
you've known Dr. Paradin for quite some time. Met him
right after the war, right?"

I nodded.

"Simple deduction that you were going to take the
photograph to him, right?" Geyer asked. He was still
wearing his hat.

"Is that what Inspector Eilers wants? Why?"

"Difficult question," Geyer said, scratching the back of
his neck. "You know there are a lot of people in Treuwall
who know that there is something wrong with this Professor Kamploh. But no one talks. We've tried to find out
the reasons. Without success."

"I find that hard to believe. It shouldn't be difficult for
the police to find out."

"It is, though. We're not the top brass. Eilers isn't
either."

"Does that mean . . ." I began.

"It means that we were never instructed to investigate
Kamploh," Ericksen, behind me, said. He lit a cigar and
opened the window a little. Icy air surged in. The storm
whistled louder. "We're only detectives. We cannot start
investigations which may turn out to be far-reaching without the nod from upstairs. Even if we wanted to . . . Naturally, investigation of an attempted murder cannot be
forbidden. Well, perhaps something will develop."

"You understand, of course, that we would deny this

221

conversation had ever taken place should you ever think of mentioning it," Geyer said. "It would be our word against yours. Now, what are your plans?"

"I'm going to Hanover."

"Where in Hanover?"

"To the airport."

"To do what?"

"To telephone and something else."

"Telephone Dr. Paradin?"

"That's right."

"All right. We'll accompany you to Hanover. You can also call Dr. Paradin. You are not suspected of having committed a crime . . . according to our superiors. Should Dr. Paradin give us any instructions we shall carry them out. The criminal investigation department must furnish support to the public prosecutor. That's the law."

I nodded.

"You know sometimes it seems as if certain people are invisible," Geyer continued. "Until someone makes a mistake, as for instance with the E 605: the wrong person drinks Armagnac, another steals a photograph and knows a public prosecutor, his brother arouses suspicion and is arrested. . . ."

"You've arrested my brother?"

"Uh-huh," Geyer uttered. "In the hospital."

"Why? On what charge?"

"So far there isn't one. We can hold him for twenty-four hours without charging him. We'd like to hold him incommunicado for that long. Especially now that everything is rolling nicely and Dr. Hess has disappeared too."

"He's disappeared?"

"We've searched for him everywhere."

"Who is 'we'?"

"Eilers, Lansing, Ericksen and I and several others."

"You were in the hospital? Where?"

"Professor Kamploh's office. Questioned his secretaries and doctors. To no avail."

"In the basement," I said. "Did you search the mortuary?"

The two men looked at me, silent.

"Well, did you?"

"No," Geyer said.

"You should have," I said. "Perhaps he is there. Three quarters of an hour ago he was."

"Perhaps you'd better tell us about all this," Geyer said.

I did.

Geyer whistled through his teeth.

"I must call Eilers right away."

"Just a moment," I said. "Lillian—Frau Lombard— she is in danger."

"She's under guard. Eilers's orders. You don't have to worry. Who is Kamploh?"

I remained silent.

"You don't want to tell us?"

"I do. But you're going to call Treuwall now. Suppose someone listens in?"

"That could be." Geyer chewed his nail.

"Do you have a Special Register in your car?"

"Yes."

"Well, have a look under D. Delacorte. Victor. Professor."

"Delacorte?"

"Yes. He's a wanted war criminal. You could give Eilers the page number where he's listed. Unobtrusively in a sentence. I'm sure you can do that. I see it on the TV all the time."

"Smart," Geyer cackled. "I like that. Delacorte, eh? I like that name, too. Well, we'll see." He climbed out of the car and I watched him disappear into the driving snowstorm.

"How did you find me?" I asked Ericksen.

"When we couldn't find you or Dr. Hess, we were given your description, that of your car and license number."

"Who gave you my license number?"

"Lansing. He also gave us the tip about notifying Dr. Paradin. We saw you drive off just as we were leaving the hospital. You didn't notice us."

"No."

"We followed you. You got some gas near Bienrode, right? And asked how much farther the next autobahn restaurant was, right? We questioned the gas attendant. We overtook you on the autobahn."

"I didn't notice you."

"Very unobservant," Ericksen said. "You're too preoccupied and inattentive. You must pull yourself together or something might happen to you."

Exit Peine. Exit Vöhrum. We were driving toward Hanover. I was behind the wheel of my car, Geyer next to me, Ericksen driving the blue Mercedes behind us. Following a short conversation between them after Geyer's return from the restaurant Ericksen had gone to their car and had left Geyer with me.

The snow diminished, I could drive faster. We were now driving through the Hämeler forest. Tree trunks, dark and close together, clung to the curb, diminishing the light. I switched on my headlights. No oncoming cars. No car overtook us.

"Up ahead is a rest area where you can park," Geyer said suddenly. "Pull up there. I've got to take a leak."

I pulled into the rest area. Here the snow was light, the trees grew very close. It was semidark. Before I had come to a halt I saw the lights of Ericksen's car behind us. Geyer got out, walked a few steps away from the car. Ericksen climbed out of the Mercedes.

"What's the . . ." he began when both of us saw the gun in Geyer's hand. His face pale, his eyes behind his glasses, huge and bulging, he seemed to have gone mad.

"Get out!" he told me. "Get out or this will go off," indicating the gun. "And reach for the sky, both of you!"

Confused, I climbed out.

"Leave the keys," Geyer instructed me. "Walk around the car. Keep your hands up. You too, Paul. Over here."

"You've gone crazy," Ericksen was bewildered. "You've lost your mind, man. What does this mean?"

"It means you're stupid assholes, all of you!" Geyer cackled, listened for a moment and, when everything was quiet, fired the gun at the four tires of the Mercedes. He had hit three of them. "Right. That's that," he said, satisfied. "No brute force unless necessary. You'll stay here for a while. I need a head start. And the photograph." He held his gun on us, bent sideways, opened the car door, pulled the keys from the ignition and tried to open the glove compartment. The second key fitted. The compartment opened. The photo was inside.

The moment Geyer reached for it two shots rang out. In a split second Ericksen had put his hand in his coat pocket and shot through it. Geyer was hit in the thigh. He gave an animal howl before sinking onto the snow-covered ground. Blood began to seep through his trouser legs.

"You goddamn louse," Ericksen said, pulling his gun from his pocket. "Since when have you been working for—"

He couldn't finish the sentence. Geyer, from the ground, had shot two more times, hitting Ericksen in the chest. The force of the shots turned him around before he crashed to the ground, face down. The snow around him became red. The stain grew rapidly. With all my strength I stepped on Geyer's hand. He howled and dropped the gun, which I quickly pocketed. I ran to the other man and turned him over. His eyes were fixed, already glassy. Ericksen was dead. Only a half-hour ago he had warned me to be more cautious. Now he was dead.

I put Ericksen's gun into my pocket too and returned to Geyer.

"I didn't want to do it," he moaned, sitting up, holding his knees. I kicked his shoulder, he screamed, fell back onto the snow. His legs were at an odd angle.

"No, you didn't want to," I said. "But you did."

"Listen, listen to me . . ."

I took the car keys from him and went to the car.

"I had to work for them, I had no choice. They blackmailed me."

"Yeah, yeah," I said.

"There was this boy, he was under age. . . ." Geyer's glasses had fallen off. He looked strangely blind and naked. I thought for a moment, went back to him and stepped hard on his glasses. Frame and lenses completely broke.

"I'll admit everything! Even if I have to go to jail!"

"Don't talk nonsense," I said. "You don't have to admit anything. You'll go to jail for murder in any case."

"Good Lord, he fired first! I didn't want to . . ."

"Of course not," I agreed and got into my car.

"You can't leave me here! In this cold!"

"I can try," I said.

"I'm going to die!"

I put the key in the ignition, started the car.

He yelled, "They'll get you, you bastard! They'll get you too!" Then he burst into tears. A moment later I had reached the autobahn. I took the photograph from the open glove compartment and pushed it underneath my shirt. That's when I noticed that my teeth were chattering, that the car was winding in and out. My hands were shaking uncontrollably. I had never known such fear.

I passed several restaurants and highway telephones but did not stop to telephone. I was afraid. Ericksen was dead. No one could help him. I did not think Geyer would bleed to death in a short time. If he did, that was just too bad. Right now I had had enough. I realized that now my life was in jeopardy.

"Richie? What's happened? Where are you?"

I breathed a sign of relief. I'd been in luck. Dr. Paradin had been in his office in Frankfurt when I made my call from a telephone booth in the post office of the airport building in Hanover. I hoped that Dr. Paradin's telephone had not been bugged. Many telephones in Germany are "to protect our young democracy."

Quickly and precisely I informed Paradin of what had occurred, and especially where Geyer and Ericksen could be found. While I talked I heard him give instructions from time to time. I dispelled his doubts when I assured him of the striking resemblance of Tiny's photo and my photograph of Clemens Kamploh.

Paradin told me that a search warrant for Delacorte had already been issued. "By the way, he left his hotel in Munich two hours ago."

"Damn! He must have been warned!"

"Naturally," Paradin agreed, his voice calm as always.

"By whom?"

"Take your choice. According to your report there are any number of suspects."

"Where did he go? Did he say anything in the hotel?"

"That he was going home, naturally. With a bit of luck he's already in Austria or even further . . . by plane."

"He doesn't like to fly," I said idiotically.

"Perhaps he overcame his dislike," Paradin said. "Perhaps he's still in the country. Then he won't be able to get out. His description and photograph have already been sent to frontier stations, airports, harbors. Naturally, he could shave off his mustache, dye his hair, disappear. Even if he is still in Germany we can't be certain that we will catch him. We're doing all we can. You know that he is one of the last of those gentlemen."

I did know. Three others who had been responsible for the euthanasia action T4 were no longer alive. One had been discovered in Argentina. Following his arrest he had swallowed poison in his cell. It appeared that he had been forced to take it.

227

The second man—a popular gynecologist—had shot himself in 1959 just before he was to have been arrested in Hamburg. Circumstances here were also peculiar.

The third man, arrested in 1961 in Bavaria, was sent to the Frankfurt prison where, accompanied by two court officials, he had hurled himself through a fourth-floor window. The two court officials had disappeared. The dead man's jacket had been found in a toilet on the fifth floor. An autopsy established that the dead man had been drugged, and was only semiconscious at the time he went through the window. Oh, yes, Paradin had reason to be greatly interested in Delacorte's whereabouts.

"When will Tiny call?" he asked me.

"As soon as his wife talks to him. What should I do with the photograph?"

"I need it. As quickly as possible." His voice was calm, restrained. "When is the next flight to Frankfurt?"

From the telephone booth I could see the large board which listed plane departures and arrivals. Above the board was a large clock.

"It's 12:20 now," I said. "The next plane to Frankfurt leaves at 1:10 P.M. Another at 1:30 P.M."

"Good. Call me back in a little while. Right now you should go to a newsstand and buy a manila envelope. . . ."

I followed Paradin's instructions and felt very much relieved when I finally saw the envelope being thrown into a sack of express airfreight, which in turn was loaded onto a cart and taken out to the plane. I was assured it would be on the plane leaving at 1:10 P.M.

Back at the post office I made another call to Dr. Paradin.

"All taken care of?"

"Yes."

"I've some news for you, Richie. The police have been checking all the rest areas in the Hämeler forest. They have not found either Geyer or Ericksen."

228

"But I've told you the truth!"

"Don't shout. We believe you."

"It's impossible! They must be there!"

"Why must they be there?" Paradin's calm voice asked. "You know that many people are involved in this. The two detectives will have been . . . ah . . . taken to safety. Especially Geyer. He was still alive, wasn't he?"

"Yes. But listen—they must have found blood on the ground of the rest area—footprints, tire marks, and the Mercedes with the punctured tires!"

"One would think so," Paradin said. "Nothing has been found. So far the police have not even found a spent cartridge. We are dealing with some very sharp operators. They work quickly, efficiently."

"But . . . but how could they have moved the car?"

"A moving truck."

"But that's impossible in such a short time."

"They had time from the moment you left the rest area. I'm sure they were following you—and probably still are."

I suddenly felt cold.

"That's why I want you to come to Frankfurt as quickly as possible. I must talk to you before deciding what to do next. Take the plane at 1:30 P.M."

"I can still make the earlier one."

"No! Two planes. I need you or the photograph. It's the only recent picture we have. Ours are twenty years old. That's why I must insist on your taking the later plane."

"Very thoughtful of you."

"Merely logical. I shall arrange to have you met at the Frankfurt airport." His voice suddenly sounded strained.

"What's the matter?"

Immediately his voice was calm, as always. "Nothing. I need you here, now, Richie, for . . . for several reasons. Do you have the two detectives' pistols?"

"Yes, I do. Geyer's is empty. There are four bullets in the clip of the other one."

"Good. Now, I don't want to have a member of the airport police accompany you so as not to arouse . . ."

"I've had enough of police protection to last me for some time, thank you!" I exclaimed. "I can manage."

"Richie, we made this call a conference call. Inspector Eilers has heard all you've just said. He wants to talk to you now."

Eilers's voice. "I'm sorry about what happened to you, Herr Mark. I had thought Geyer and Ericksen to be two of my most trustworthy men."

"Well, Ericksen was."

Eilers said, his voice hoarse, "But Geyer . . . one cannot trust anyone any more . . . no one here."

"Is it true that my brother has been arrested?"

"Yes."

"And that Frau Lombard is being guarded?"

"That's true too. Did those two tell you that?"

"Yes. Did Geyer call you?"

"When?"

"After he had found me—from a restaurant."

"He did not call me."

"But he left to telephone!"

"Sure," Paradin interjected. "But not to Eilers."

Eilers said, "We have a good idea whom he called. *If* he made a call."

"He probably did," Paradin's voice again. "And Delacorte's prospects look very good."

"Why was Geyer supposed to call me?" Eilers asked.

"Because of Dr. Hess. I told him of my experience with him—didn't Paradin tell you of that?"

"Yes, he did."

"Did you search the mortuary? Did you find him?"

"We found Dr. Hess. But not the attendant you described."

"And what did the doctor say?"

"Nothing," Eilers answered. "He's dead."

"*What?*"

"Stabbed through the heart. With one of the autopsy knives. Exacting work."

I held on to the telephone.

"What's the matter? Hey, Mark, what's wrong?"

"I'm all right."

Fiery wheels were whirling before my eyes. Ericksen shot. Hess stabbed. The attendant disappeared as had Ericksen and Geyer. Why hadn't Hess disappeared too?

"The attendant!" I finally said. "I described him to you. Is there no one in the hospital of his description?"

"No one," Eilers answered. "A search warrant has been issued for him. The hospital has never employed anyone fitting your description of him. Besides, all employees are accounted for. I doubt that he even was an attendant."

"But I told you . . ."

"Don't upset yourself!"

"Do you believe that I . . ."

"No, I don't believe that you invented the attendant and stabbed Dr. Hess," Eilers explained. "Your fingerprints were not found on the murder weapon."

"My fingerprints? Where did you get . . ."

"From the dust covers of the Ninth which you handled in Kamploh's . . . ah, Delacorte's library. No, we did not find your fingerprints on the autopsy knife. Neither were they your brother's."

I began to shout. "Now look here! I've just about had enough! I don't like your tone of voice!"

"I'm sorry," Eilers apologized. "I really am."

"Forgive me. I'm a little . . . a little nervous."

"We all are," Paradin's calm voice reassured me. "Have a drink, Richie, after you've booked your flight. Once you're in Frankfurt we shall discuss all this in detail. And don't worry about Frau Lombard. She is under guard."

231

"She's protected by my best men," Eilers said.

"You thought Geyer was one of your best men too," I said bitterly.

"Yes," he said. "Unfortunately. No one regrets that more than I. I . . . I shall take turns with Lansing and we will stay with her in the hospital. Does that set your mind at rest?"

"Yes. And please excuse my shouting."

"It's okay. It's perfectly understandable," Eilers said. "I would like to thank you, Herr Mark, for everything you have done and are still doing."

"I'd like to do that too, Richie," Paradin added. "We thank you. You're a good fellow."

That's what he called me.

Writing this I recall the dreadful deeds I was yet to commit and I despise myself.

As the world knows only too well the Nazis came to power at the end of January 1933. With only three ministerial seats and without a majority of the electorate they quickly established a dictatorship under Hitler. Their control became complete with the dissolution or prohibition of other political parties: the propagation of the so-called "Unity of Party and State."

The thirty-one-year-old Dr. Walter Paradin had been arrested at the beginning of February 1933. At the county court of Frankfurt am Main he had prosecuted numerous cases of national-socialistic crimes. Well aware of what to expect, he had sent his young wife Claire—his parents were dead—to Paris only a few days before his arrest. He had remained to wait for his forged passport since he could no longer cross the frontier on his own passport. The forger, arrested, soon disclosed his client's names.

Paradin was sent to Buchenwald, then still under the control of the SA. Here Attila Hanselmeyr, butcher of Tutzing, Upper Bavaria, smashed his lower leg with a spade. Hanselmeyr was known for his bad temper. He suffered from cirrhosis as a result of alcoholism. One day he had taken exception to Paradin's manner of digging one of those pits which had to be leveled as soon as it had been completed. He tore the spade from Paradin's hands and hit him. Paradin left the hospital ten weeks later. The badly knit bone had shortened his leg and left him with a limp. The SA man was merely reprimanded.

Paradin limped through Buchenwald until 1935, often narrowly escaping death. He and four other prisoners escaped in August 1935. The other men were caught and hanged. He escaped into Switzerland, then France.

Paradin and his wife were united again in France. Together they fled to Spain, then Portugal, where they obtained United States visas. Before he was permitted to pursue his profession in America, his wife worked for two years in a factory while he prepared for his bar examinations. He passed with honors. Shortly thereafter his wife died of a stroke. Paradin never remarried.

Paradin worked diligently. He joined a law firm. Soon colleagues and judges alike respected and admired him.

He declined to become an American citizen. "I'll return to Germany as soon as the war is over," he often said. In the winter of 1945 he had already returned to Frankfurt, the city where he had been born.

A few months later I met him in the MP station where we were interpreters. Tiny had found us rooms. There I learned what I have just written down.

Since he had refused American citizenship, he lived as did other displaced persons—food coupons, clothing coupons, occasional CARE packages, Tiny's presents. He was not able to transfer his money from New York and so was as poor as all of us were at the time.

I still vividly remember our talks in his spotlessly clean room.

"Why did you come back?" I had asked him.

"Because I belong here," he had answered simply. He

233

laughed, his eyes happy as those of a child. "This is my country. I love it. The land and its people."

"People of this country have . . ."

"You know," he said, "you cannot condemn an entire people for what some of them have done. We have always been susceptible to . . . well, to the Hitlers. Have been and still are. I have come to realize that since I returned. I must try to understand why things happened, how they happened, and why everything seems in such jeopardy . . . and the future so foreboding."

"Is it?"

"I'm afraid so," Paradin said. "If something is done soon to avert the evil perhaps then it can be prevented."

"That's the reason for your return?"

He nodded.

"But what can you do, as an interpreter? Why aren't you active in politics, in the administration of the law?"

"Soon I will be. My application for reinstatement as a German national is being processed."

I stared at him. "Reinstatement?"

"That's right. After all, the Nazis took away my citizenship. Have to obtain it again. I hope it won't take much longer."

I was incredulous. "But the Third Reich doesn't exist any more! And your loss of citizenship does? After all, you didn't apply to lose it!"

Paradin smiled and continued to press a pair of trousers. He was rarely inactive.

"The German government holds the view that one cannot force an emigrant to become a German national again, which an automatic reinstatement of citizenship would amount to."

"Damn it all, then it would be up to each emigrant to decide whether or not he wanted to become a German citizen again!" I was outraged. I was very young, full of enthusiasm; justice for me was spelled with a capital *J*.

234

"An automatic reinstatement might make amends for the humiliation, the outrageous . . ."

Paradin grimaced.

"Make amends. I think that will soon become a word no one in Germany will want to hear any longer," Paradin said, carefully pressing his trousers.

"In any case, citizenship ought to be offered immediately. As far as I know there are no plans of depriving our war criminals of their citizenship."

"It is not likely," Paradin said. "Which is another reason why I've come back to Germany. I wanted to be here, from the very beginning, to try and find out—right now I can't think of a better way of putting it—what makes people tick."

I had liked Walter Paradin immediately. Soon a deep friendship developed. Later I met a man, a minister, who had known Paradin in Buchenwald. He told me of Paradin's concern and help for his fellow prisoners.

"He was also greatly interested in the actions and reactions of the SA guards. He studied victims and oppressors alike, just as a young boy might take apart a watch to find out what makes it tick."

It was shortly after 3 P.M. when the detective who had met me at the Frankfurt airport and I entered the brightly lit courthouse. It was not snowing but the sky was dark and forbidding. Shop windows were illuminated; streetlights were lit; cars and trams had their lights on.

An elevator took us to the fifth floor. We walked down a seemingly endless corridor until we reached Dr. Paradin's office.

Three secretaries were busy in the large, wood-paneled anteroom, one of whom announced us. Paradin appeared a moment later, limping, smiling, his arms stretched out.

"Hello, Richie!" He shook my hand, patted my shoulder. I thanked the detective, who left. Paradin told me that the photograph, picked up from the airport by one of his staff, had already been sent to the criminal investigation department for processing. At this moment he was in conference with detectives, examining magistrates, attorneys.

"You'll have to be patient for a few minutes, Richie. Please, go in there. I'm also awaiting another guest. It won't take long," Paradin said as he hurriedly limped toward his office.

I had not seen him for about three years. He had not seemed to age. He certainly did not look sixty-four years old. The door closed behind him.

I opened the door to the waiting room he had indicated. Minski was inside.

"Good day, Boris," I said, surprised.

"Like to know what's good about this damned day, you stupid ass," Minski growled.

I had never seen Boris so upset. His face was pale; purple bags under his eyes reminded me of Inspector Fegesack's. Minski probably had accidentally poured as much lavender on himself as I had intentionally used of after-shave. Together we were redolent as a beauty parlor.

"Have you gone crazy?" I asked, annoyed. "Why do you speak to me like this?"

Minski threw up his arms.

"Have *I* gone crazy, he asks me, the meshuggana!" I was about to say something, but he continued, "Be quiet, I know everything. Your friend, the prosecutor, told me."

"Told you what? I mean, why are you here anyway?"

"Because he called me and asked me to come."

"Paradin called you?"

"Don't you understand me? Yes, he called me! Since I am your partner. He has some plan, he said, and he needs to talk to you and me. Now we're involved with the public prosecutor's office!"

"Well, don't wet your pants."

"But you don't know what's happened! Oh, God, oh,

236

God, it's incredible. As if we didn't have enough troubles. My friend, my best friend! An intelligent man—at least I thought so. Doing this to me. To me and to himself. Intelligent! I could strangle you!"

"Just a minute," I was angry now. "You think it was crazy for me to inform Paradin about Delacorte?"

"Crazy? Suicide, that's what it was, you . . . you . . ."

"What do you mean, suicide? Calm down or you're likely to have a stroke."

"I'll have that anyway! But you'll regret it, mark my words! We were going to work another one or two years. Quietly, without attracting any undue attention. We were going to Switzerland. But how do we get there? Only if we're not involved in scandal, in any court actions, without our names in the newspapers. What do you do? You ruin everything!"

"But how . . ."

"Today, at lunch," Minski lamented, "I was in my office, alone. The telephone rings. I answer. A disguised voice, obviously a handkerchief placed over the mouthpiece. 'Herr Minski?' Yes, I say. He says, 'You dirty little yid, we'll fix you and your partner. You won't have your lousy business even for one more week. You and your partner will wish you were dead, if you aren't by then.'"

"That was a telephone call—"

"One call? Five calls! Different voices, various threats. They're going to set fire to our club. Plant a bomb when we have a lot of guests. Kill us. Throw acid into Vanessa's face. At one o'clock they threw the first incendiary bomb. Through the door into the bar. I was alone. I was lucky to have been able to extinguish the fire."

"*Boris!*"

"I'm still shaking. I put out the fire. Then I told the police it was just a prank. Made light of it just to avoid making a complaint."

"You didn't swear out a complaint?"

"I'm not meshugge! Those hoods told me they'll kill us if I say anything to the police."

"Ah, shit!"

"Bravo, superman! Don't believe that, eh? They haven't killed anybody, I suppose?" Minski was right there. "How could we keep the club open if I made a complaint? Police attending each performance? A candle act for the gentlemen of the police? So they'll close us up? I'm not crazy."

"The pigs," I said, "Those dirty pigs."

"We're not debating what they are," Minski said. "You're not supposed to marry them. You're supposed to keep out of this business. You must! If I have to kill you, you will keep out of this!"

"Don't yell at me! I will not keep out! I cannot! It's too late for that anyway. . . ."

"Why too late?"

"Lillian is in danger. I can't desert her now!"

"No, only she can do that, the lousy bitch!"

"Shut up, Boris!"

"Now, who's yelling?"

I had indeed been shouting. I pulled myself together.

"I'm sorry to have involved us in this business."

"Sorry, hah!" Minski said bitterly.

"Does Vanessa know?"

"No one knows. Only you and I. And those . . . those who telephoned me. You'll keep out of it, won't you. Richie? *Please*."

"No."

His face turned dark red. "You won't? You can't? Which?"

"I can't."

"I see. A hero! A stupid hero! Has to pursue a Nazi murderer, the lover of his former—"

"Shut your mouth or I'll—"

"Go ahead! Hit me, you idiot!"

I sat down, trying to compose myself. Yelling at each

238

other served no purpose. Finally I asked, "Then you would not have denounced Delacorte? Not even considering Lillian. You wouldn't have done it?"

"No! Even if I had stumbled into this mess the way you did with Lillian. I'd have disappeared as quickly as possible, I would have heard nothing, seen nothing. The only sensible thing to do!"

"Sensible? This Delacorte is one of the most notorious war criminals!"

"So? Is that something unusual? Is he the only war criminal still at large? You stupid ass! Thousands are still at liberty! The statute of limitations lapses in 1969. You can see how sensible our government is. But you? You have to denounce a war criminal! If you'd made your discovery in 1969 Delacorte would have sued you for defamation of character."

"It's not yet 1969."

"True. Delacorte's guilt has shrunk since the end of the war. Year by year. In 1969 it will be wiped out altogether. And because of that you're endangering our lives? Do you realize what you're doing?"

I said wildly, "I realize that Lillian was almost killed because of this man, that two men were killed, that this man is sought by Paradin! And that he can still be punished to the full extent of the law!"

"Full extent! Ha!" Minski had risen to his full height. He was moving up and down on his toes, his face almost purple and damp with perspiration. He was in a furious rage. "How long a prison sentence do murderers such as Delacorte receive? Seven years? Nine? Once in a while one might even get fifteen. Then he appeals, naturally. Two years later the sentence is reduced. Seven years. Meanwhile the poor man has become a diabetic or has a bad heart and is disabled and back at home. That's how it is. Not even Paradin is going to be able to change that!" He inhaled deeply. "No one wants to have anything to do with this any more! No one! No judge, no

239

member of a jury—only a few lunatics! Look at Austria! Twice someone like Delacorte was put on trial and judged not guilty! Twice! And that's no isolated phenomenon. The people have had enough! And it is enough! Let it be enough. But no, you, the idiot that you are, you must—"

"Boris! Delacorte's complicity in the death of a hundred thousand people . . ."

"So? Suppose Paradin does catch up with him: does that bring those hundred thousand back to life?"

"What kind of an answer is that? Aren't you ashamed?"

"Why should I be ashamed of something that's perfectly reasonable? Will even one of those hundred thousand come back to life?" He threw up his hands. "It's the mass of people, the enormous number of them which makes it difficult to pronounce a judgment. Can you imagine one hundred thousand murdered people? *I* can't. *One* person, yes. For instance the young child whose mother was sentenced to fifteen years a couple of weeks ago. *That* was disturbing; the verdict was universally applauded. Why? Because people could picture it in their minds—the bestial mother who murders her own child. But one hundred thousand? That defies the imagination! And no one wants to visualize that; it is . . . it is revolting, that's what it is!"

I said, "Forgive me, Boris. I'm not a Jew. I see things from a different point of view. But I had to do what I did."

He replied fiercely, "The fact that I am a Jew has nothing to do with it!"

"Oh, yes, it has."

"No. Vanessa shares my opinion!"

"Because of Lillian!"

"No. Because she is afraid for you. As afraid as I am for you, for all of us!"

"There you are: it's fear after all!"

Softly Boris asked, "Aren't you afraid, Richie?"

"I?" I asked. "I'm more frightened than both of you together."

"And in spite of that . . ."

"Yes," I said. "In spite of that. What about Vanessa? Did she believe your story about that bomb?"

"I really don't know. She seems to. She's very upset. Because of you and Lillian, naturally. She's so over-wrought, her period came a week earlier. . . ." He mopped his damp forehead. "Instinct! Right after Paradin called. The poor girl has more sense between her legs than you in your head!"

For a moment business considerations came to the fore. "Then she can't perform. Have you . . ."

". . . . informed Corabelle? Yes. Her python is ill."

"Damn! Now what do wo do?"

"Ah, now you're beginning to worry? That's nothing! She borrowed a colleague's python. She's practicing now. Because they don't know each other. Thanks, Richie, thanks a lot."

"Don't be an idiot!" I cried. "Just because of this shit-snake you can't—"

"It's not because of the snake," Boris said, serious. "You know what I mean. I'm frantic with worry, Richie. You know that I am not on good terms with the Jewish Cultural Association. But I do know several Jews who work there and they've told me that occasionally some down-and-out-characters turn up there. They say they've been in the SS and for fifty or a hundred or five hundred marks they would divulge the whereabouts of a wanted Nazi criminal. What does the rabbi do? He throws them out—all of them, without exception. Even though some of them probably do have some knowledge. The rabbi is the smartest man I know! This is what behooves us, not only us Jews, all of us who were not murderers: hands off! But I'm wasting my time on you. And you have Lillian to consider as well. I knew she was going to bring us

241

bad luck when she telephoned. Now we're already right in the middle of it."

The door opened.

A man wearing an overcoat entered. Very tall, slim, narrow face, unusually large eyes, white hair disheveled. He looked tired.

Boris inhaled sharply.

"Professor!"

Professor Dr. Peter Mohn from the Hornstein Sanatorium said, "Dr. Paradin asked me to come here. Your wife sends her love to you, Herr Minski. Hello, Herr Mark."

"I asked Professor Mohn to come since he and Professor Delacorte were students together and well acquainted," Dr. Paradin said, limping to and fro before the large desk in his office. "It is important that he tell us about Delacorte, important for me and you, gentlemen." He looked at Boris. "I can understand that you are extremely annoyed with Richie, Herr Minski."

"Annoyed? Why?"

"Well, after the bombing attempt at your club . . ."

"That was no bombing attempt, Dr. Paradin!" Minski exclaimed. "Just a prank! That's what I told the police!"

"You know and I know that it was not a mere prank, Herr Minski. That's why I have asked you to come here."

"Why?" Minski snorted.

Paradin was amiable. "Very soon I shall need you and Richie. Your help, your cooperation. To gain that I must convince you that Richie did the right thing." Paradin's glance encompassed us all. "Also I want us all to gain a clear picture of Professor Delacorte. An objective, undistorted picture."

Ten minutes had passed since Professor Mohn had arrived. Paradin's carpeted office with its wood-paneled ceiling and walls was lined with books. Traffic sounds were muffled, though not the frequent roar of a plane landing or taking off. The office was warm. Opposite the desk hung a plaque with brass lettering:

> The dignity of man is inviolable. To respect and protect it shall be the duty of our state authorities.
>
> The German people affirm the principle of human rights as inviolable and inalienable, the moral obligation of every community, for world peace and world justice.
>
> Article 1, Basic Rights
> Federal Republic of Germany

Paradin, limping past the plaque and small table on which stood a vase with yellow mimosa, said, "To inform you very quickly, gentlemen: Delacorte's new photograph has been distributed to all airports, frontiers, harbors. Tiny—I mean, Mr. Barlow—called from London. He will be available for identification purposes any time after tomorrow. The fingerprints from the dust jacket of the Ninth in Delacorte's villa have been identified. There is no doubt. Richie has discovered the right man." He paused before me. "Frau Lombard is feeling much better, Eilers asked me to tell you. He looks out for her personally. She sends her regards."

Minski said something in Yiddish which did not sound very friendly.

"Your brother is still under arrest. It turned out that he had already been in Treuwall yesterday morning."

"What?"

"He was seen and recognized by two witnesses."

"Where was he?"

"In the Waldpromenade. So far it does not mean anything. It seems suspicious that your brother refuses to give an explanation for his presence there. He even denies having been there. He says the witnesses were mistaken.

243

Well, perhaps the developments of the next hours will change his attitude."

Lillian . . .

Did my brother have something to do with the poisoned Armagnac after all? Or with Delacorte? What did he really want from Lillian? He had begged her to return to him. Had Lillian told me the truth? My brother's behavior this morning seemed to indicate that.

During the following half-hour my thoughts persistently returned to Lillian. Yet I heard every word Dr. Mohn said. Not unlike the flare of a shooting star, the flicker of a glowworm, these memories lasted but seconds, yet seconds rich with long memories of happiness.

"Delacorte was, without a doubt, one of the most gifted and progressive psychiatrists among his contemporaries." Dr. Mohn's voice was deep, slow. "I was already a resident at the Freiburg University Hospital when Delacorte was still attending Professor Dr. Alfred Erich Hoche's lectures. Delacorte was taking his degree in Freiburg and was working at the hospital with me. He came from a Huguenot family. As far as I can remember his father owned a factory in Duisburg."

"Correct," Paradin said. "They manufactured machinery for the mining industry."

"That Delacorte happened to have attended Professor Hoche's lectures seems to me to have been of decisive importance. Hoche, one of the handful of German scholars who had resigned their teaching positions as a protest against the new rulers, had been a vehement antifascist. Yet his thoughts on 'life–unworthy life' had actually prepared the ground in German medicine and law for the euthanasia murders. You know," Mohn continued, "it seems incongruous that Hoche, a man of undisputed integrity, was to be the man who provided Delacorte with the mental equipment for the crimes he was to commit later."

*Rationale for the Extermination of Indefensible Lives.
Its Extent and Usage* had been a paper published in 1920
by the professor of psychiatry Alfred Erich Hoche and
the renowned Leipzig lawyer Karl Binding. Both were
men of high repute and moral worth, inspired by the
best intentions. Nevertheless their paper influenced the
thoughts of an entire generation.

They were favorably disposed toward mercy-killings in
certain cases, yet insisting on the most legal control.

Terminal or severely injured patients no longer able to
articulate their wishes—for instance, an unconscious, piti-
fully disfigured person—would thus be spared an agonizing awakening; also idiots, the lowest form of human life,
in whose nature, as the authors stated, there could neither
be the desire to live nor to die.

Professor Hoche advocated these opinions after Binding's death—Binding died the same year the paper was
published—and continued to impose ever new safeguards
and limitations.

Yes, that was how it began: with a dedicated scientist
expressing his well-considered views—and an unusually
gifted student by the name of Delacorte who enthusiastically made those theses his own. . . .

"Hoche's views," Mohn continued, "actually were not
far removed from those of Martin Luther. In the sixteenth century in his 'Table Talks' Luther had said that
a twelve-year-old idiot ought to be drowned since he was
'mere flesh, *massa carnis*, created by the devil since there
is no soul within. . . .'" Mohn pushed the piece of paper
from which he had read the quotation back into his
pocket. "Four hundred years before the action T4," he
said slowly. While I heard every word of the conversation, my thoughts were with Lillian and the memory of a
December night. . . .

The night before Christmas Eve, 1947. For days now,
steadily, seemingly inexhaustible the snow had been fall-

ing, blanketing the ruins of Frankfurt. We were on duty, huddling around the glowing pot-bellied iron stove of the MP station, sipping hot chocolate, when Tiny began to tease me.

"Do you know that you always talk about your sweetie when you're drunk?"

"Sweetie?"

"Come now! The one with those huge eyes! The one who came here last spring. In the blue dress. It was love at first sight. Don't lie. I saw it."

"Oh," I said. "I know who you mean. Love. Ridiculous."

Tiny rolled his eyes, his teeth bared in a wide grin. He winked at the desk sergeant and his assistant.

"She was something, wasn't she?"

"Hm."

"Say that she was exciting!"

"Hm."

"Can't you talk any more?"

"She was exciting."

"Why don't you go and see her sometimes? You have her address."

"Why should I? She never came here again."

"Pride and prejudice," Tiny said. "You ought to be ashamed of yourself."

"I am ashamed," I said. "I'm just too proud to show it." We didn't drink only chocolate that night. We were all high.

It had been a busy year for me, filled with turmoil and longing. I had finished my novel in the summer. It was accepted by the first publisher I had approached. (One thousand marks advance and another thousand at publication. A thousand marks at that time bought one hundred American cigarettes on the black market.)

In October Tiny and I celebrated the arrival of the galleys, printed on the poor-quality paper of the postwar period. I had completely changed the heroine of the book.

Now she closely resembled Lillian Lombard. I had not been able to forget Lillian. Wide awake or dreaming—I saw her before me. On several occasions I had even mistaken other women for her on the street. She never returned to the station.

With each month that passed my restlessness increased. I often considered going to the Stresemannstrasse but lost courage each time. I remember that the one girl I had that year left me, furious, after I had repeatedly called her "Lillian." She, too, had had dark hair and brown eyes.

"You're right, Richie," Tiny said, his long leg stretched out toward the red-glowing stove. "The lady did not return. The lady doesn't want anything to do with us. Besides, she's probably remarried by now."

"She can't be!" I cried. "She's still married. There's been no notification! As long as it has not been established that her husband died she has to wait—that will be May 8, 1950! That's the law! That's—" I broke off when I saw that the three Americans were grinning. Tiny had tricked me.

"You son of a bitch," I said to him.

"A young man's unrequited love is a sad thing," Tiny said. He rose. The other two rose also. "Follow me into the back room," he said. There he removed a cover from a large box filled to overflowing with canned foods, cigarettes, several bottles of whisky.

"We've decided to give these things to your girl for Christmas," Tiny said.

"My girl—ha!"

"Shut up! The desk sergeant, you and I are going on an area patrol. The assistant desk sergeant is going to hold the fort here," Tiny squeaked in his gag voice. We were all good friends by then, forgetting that they were the victors and I one of the vanquished.

I protested, but they declared that it was my duty as an interpreter to accompany them on the area patrol. At last we left, dressed in heavy, fur-lined, hooded coats, the box on the floor of the jeep.

It was late. We drove through the deserted streets of Frankfurt to the quiet Stresemannstrasse. A few houses had remained there, spared by bombs, between ruins and burned trees which seemed to be reaching toward the sky like black, gigantic fingers.

Number 156 was a three-storied villa built in the style popular about the turn of the century. A small Christmas tree, its lights twinkling, stood in the tiny front yard. Laughter and voices came from behind the brightly lit windows. The basement winds were dark.

Tiny stopped. We dragged the heavy box through the snow to the locked door. In the light of Tiny's flashlight we saw three American names next to the top bell buttons; below them was the name Lombard. Tiny rang. I turned to leave but he held my arm.

"Trying to skip, eh? Remember you're a member of the master race! You're going to stay and interpret for us! We wish her a merry Christmas."

Lights were switched on, steps approached. Before I realized what was happening, Tiny and the desk sergeant raced back to the jeep and jumped in. Tiny started the engine.

"So long, Richie-boy," he yelled. The jeep slithered away. I saw its taillights sparkling. My heart began to beat furiously when I heard Lillian's voice on the other side of the small, barred window in the door. "Yes? Who is there?"

"Richard Mark," I said, embarrassed. "You probably don't remember me. I'm the interpreter in the MP station in the Baselerstrasse. In April . . ."

The little window was opened. In the light of the decorated Christmas tree I saw her. A flower-printed robe, black hair disheveled, eyes large and luminous— those eyes I had not been able to forget.

"Did something happen? Any news of my husband?" Lillian's voice sounded cold, brusque.

"No. Nothing, unfortunately. You must not lose courage. Sometimes these things take a long time. . . ."

"And to tell me that you wake me in the middle of the night?"

"I'm sorry if I awakened you. My friends played a joke on me."

"Your friends? Where are they?"

"They left. That's the joke. You know?"

"I think I understand." Her voice now was flat.

"No, no! For Christmas we wanted to—I mean Tiny wanted—"

"Who?"

"The big Negro, I'm sure you remember him! He meant well. He . . . we . . . we brought some presents. After all, it is Christmas, a sad Christmas for us Germans. Perhaps this would help make it a little more pleasant for you . . . and your fiancé. . . ." The last few words stuck in my throat. "Would you open the door for a moment so I could give you this box?"

"I no longer have a fiancé."

"But you told me . . ."

"Yes, I did. But that was in April." She laughed derisively. "Then I did have a fiancé. We were as good as married. We both worked for the same firm."

"Yes, I remember."

She said, hoarsely, "Herr Master has a daughter. Two years younger than I. My . . . my fiancé told me in May that he intended to marry her. They married eight weeks later. Now he is her father's business partner. Good night, Herr Mark."

"Just a moment!" I pushed against the small window she was trying to close. "The box . . ."

"Take it with you."

"But I can't carry it! It's too heavy!"

"Please go," Lillian said, her eyes narrowed.

"Really, Frau Lombard, I . . ."

"Go away," she repeated. "It was an interesting premise. Under certain circumstances I might have found it amusing. As things are I don't." She closed the window. The lights went out.

I stood in the snow, freezing. I kicked at the box and cursed. Finally I rang one of the other bells and roused one of the Americans. I told him that I had brought something for Frau Lombard but apparently she was already asleep. Could he help me?

"Sure, bud, sure. Just a minute."

He helped me carry the heavy box to her door. He smelled of whisky. I thanked him.

"That's quite all right. Nice kid, that Lombard girl, huh?"

"Mhm," I uttered.

"Well, so long. And a merry Christmas to you." He locked the door; the house lights went out again. I stood near the festively decorated Christmas tree and suddenly I felt lighthearted. I looked up into the multitude of white flakes. Flakes fell onto my face, lightly, gently, and I imagined them to be tender kisses, Lillian's kisses.

Slowly I made my way back to the station. And again and again I lifted my face to the snowflakes.

For fully a quarter of an hour Professor Mohn made an analysis of Professor Hoche's euthanasia philosophy and Delacorte's concentrated application of it.

Once in a while there would be an interruption from Minski that showed his deep distress over these revelations. When finally Professor Mohn paused, Paradin asked him whether that was all he could say. Mohn implied that there was more, but he was silent. Then Paradin, reading from a series of papers, showed that they had a great deal of factual data of Delacorte's methods of mass murder. It was a catalogue of horrors, the least of which was sterilization. Other methods involved chemicals to weaken the system, scientific starvation quite apart from the usual process of gas chambers. Mohn was asked whether these gassings were eliminated when the public learned of them.

"Yes," he replied, "Temporarily."

A questionnaire had been sent out by the director of a Saxonian mental hospital to the parents of mentally unfit children. Would they agree to a kindly program which would "release the child from life." To the astonishment of the director well over half of the parents gave a positive reply. A smaller number were uncertain and the rest were opposed to the program.

Minski, surprisingly confused to my thinking, began to ask philosophical questions. How was it possible that both Professor Mohn and Delacorte had had the same training in the rationale of euthanasia and yet he had had the courage to resist? Mohn's reply was inconclusive. Paradin made some trivial observations. The noises of street traffic interrupted our conference, and my thoughts reverted to Lillian.

Tiny flakes dropped into the burned-out, roofless church. Candles which had been lit were almost immediately extinguished by the wind. Now only two spotlights illuminated the devastated altar, its crudely hewn crucifix and the gaunt figure of the minister. The nave, still rank with the odor of burned wood, with its annealed stone and metal, lay in darkness. At this midnight mass the church was filled to capacity. Lillian in a much-worn fur coat and I in a dyed navy blue U.S. Army coat stood close together holding hands. Our breaths, mingling with the snowflakes, took visible form on this very cold night.

On the morning of December 24, twelve hours after I had left the box stuffed with groceries at Lillian's door, she had come to the MP station. My shift had ended at eight A.M. I was asleep in my room in the villa at the Richard-Strauss Allee since I had volunteered to work a double shift for Paradin and our third interpreter, the former banker Eugen Reck. Both men had been invited to visit Reck's sister for Christmas Eve. Lillian spoke with Paradin. She regretted having been so brusque with me, she said, and that she would have liked to invite me for dinner that night. Paradin, whom I had told about Lillian, made no mention of his own invitation and promised to inform me. When he did he brushed aside my objections and insisted on working the two shifts for me.

Punctually at eight P.M. on this Christmas Eve of 1947 I arrived at Lillian's door. My dyed uniform pressed, in a new shirt, new tie and a new pair of shoes—Tiny's Christmas present.

Lillian was in an evening gown which was neither new nor fashionable, but she looked absolutely beautiful. Her small basement apartment was very warm: the American officers living upstairs kept the steam heat at full pressure. They had guests. We heard shouting, laughter, girls screeching, glasses splintering, and loud, hammering jazz.

Lillian had furnished the apartment comfortably with her few remaining antique pieces: dark chests, cabinets, carved chairs, a round table, now nicely set up. Candles flickered in silver candelabras.

"There're still candles from the time of air raids, the only things that were left over in enormous amounts," Lillian explained. We were sitting opposite each other, eating the excellent dinner she had prepared from the cans and packages which had been in the box.

After dinner Lillian opened a bottle of whisky. We had a few drinks, switched on a radio. The AFN broadcast dance music and we danced a little in the flickering light of the candles. Then we sat opposite each other, looking at each other, hardly speaking.

"I'd like to go to a midnight mass," Lillian finally said, somewhat embarrassed. "The last time I went, I can't even remember when that was. It must be all of ten years now."

"With me it's even longer," I said, finishing my drink.

"Are you Catholic?" Lillian asked.

"Protestant. But I'm not practicing. What about you?"

"I don't know what I am. I was baptized in the Catholic faith, but . . ."

"I understand."

"Do you?" she asked.

I nodded.

"Would you give me another drink, too?"

I did. "What do we drink to?"

We toasted Tiny, then I added Lillian.

"You will go with me to a midnight mass?"

"If you insist."

"You don't want to go?"

"Well, yes, surely . . . if you feel like going."

"Yes, I do," Lillian said. "Do you know a church we could go to? I don't know any."

"Yes, I know one." So we walked through unlit, war-ravaged streets, through the whirling snow to the burned-out church where the Reverend Matern held his services.

The mass had already begun; we had to stand in the rear. Matern read a long, moving letter from a man to his still unborn child. It is curious how this has remained in my memory. The congregation sang and Lillian, who had tightly gripped my hand during the service, looked at me. We left, walking through streets where hardly a house still stood, while snow blanketed the ruins, a subtle shroud. We came to a small bridge spanning railroad tracks. As we stopped and kissed, a locomotive passed, enveloping us in its smoke.

That's when we heard a man's voice call for help in broken German. It took us a while to find him. He was kneeling beside a woman. They both looked very poor. Bulgarian, I guessed.

"Help, please," he said.

"What's wrong?"

"Woman . . . have baby . . . go to hospital, understand? No car come . . . live out there in camp . . ."

The woman groaned.

"I'll stay here," Lillian said, kneeling beside the young woman. "See if you can find a telephone, Richie." For the first time she had used the familiar German *"du."*

I ran until I found a house where the residents, annoyed at being awakened from sleep, permitted me to use the telephone. I called Tiny at the MP station, gave him the address and waited for him outside. Tiny knew his way around Frankfurt. Within fifteen minutes he arrived. We picked up Lillian and the young couple and Tiny, carefully avoiding potholes, drove us to the hospital where she was immediately admitted.

We stayed with the nervous young husband for a while longer.

"Camp no good," he said. "Many people. Cold. Dirty, understand?"

"Yes," Tiny answered.

Lillian asked his name.

"Zarko Vlasek," he answered.

"And your wife's?"

"Olga," he said, surprised. "Why?"

"I just wanted to know," Lillian said, pulling a few bills from her coat pocket and pressing them on him. He tried to kiss her hand.

"Good night," he said. "I wish you happiness. A good life."

"That's what I wish you, too," Lillian said. "You, your wife and the child. Good night."

"Good night," Tiny said, pushing a pack of cigarettes in the man's pocket.

Lillian and I sat in the back of the jeep. She was fast asleep on my shoulder when we reached the Stresemannstrasse. Carefully I pulled the keys from her coat pocket, and together with Tiny I carried her to her apartment. She murmured in her sleep, but I could not understand anything. We took off her fur coat and shoes, placed her on her bed and covered her. On tiptoes we left the apartment.

Driving back to the MP station Tiny drove at top speed. The jeep bounced and slid across the road and Tiny sang as loud as he could, *"Stan'* still, Jordan . . ."

"The dangers of the analytical method we are using here to shed some light on Delacorte's life, before and while he committed his crimes, are obvious," Walter Paradin said. "I always try to find a perspective, try to understand, but I must add one word of caution. We have tried to analyze Delacorte extensively. If we continue, Delacorte the man and his deeds will become obliterated; we will be left with basic characteristics common to all men, neither good nor bad, merely human. One must not forget one's original aim, the reason for analysis. So that that will not be forgotten I must show you something."

Paradin pressed a button. Part of the wooden paneling slid aside, showing a small movie screen. Paradin limped to a shelf on the opposite side where he opened a small door. Behind it stood a 16-millimeter movie projector. He switched it on and said, "Delacorte often had a cameraman accompany him on his trips. Several films were found when he was arrested at the end of the war. This film here consists of several strips which were spliced together. You must see it."

The motor began to hum; Paradin switched off the overhead light as the first frames began to appear. They showed Delacorte in field-gray SS uniform and white coat, laughing, slapping his thighs, surrounded by comrades. They were standing in a yard enclosed by a high wall. A seemingly endless line of emaciated figures in striped, long shirts tottered past them. The camera showed close-ups of apprehensive faces and Delacorte again and again—laughing, slapping a riding cap against his boots, ordering, selecting. Delacorte at a parade; Delacorte playing piano; Delacorte with a German shepherd.

The cameraman must have had a strong nervous system—better than mine at any rate. For he had filmed the selection of victims, the transportation in buses, the arrival at the camps, the undressings, the march into the "showers" and, through observation windows, what took place when the gas began to flow.

I could endure it only a few minutes. Then I rose, found my way to the door and just managed to reach a bathroom, where I was violently sick.

I washed myself then went out into the corridor and opened a window for fresh air. I felt faint. Above the roofs enclosing an inner courtyard I saw a piece of dark, cloudy sky; I tried desperately not to think of the horrifying pictures I had just seen. I remembered another film I had once seen with Lillian a long time ago.

Heidi, a Swiss film and a masterpiece. Dated as a children's classic, yet it had been skillfully modernized without destroying the *fin de siècle* glow. Even today I can recall some of the touching, enchanting scenes.

Lillian and I met almost daily after that Christmas Eve—if only briefly. Paradin was ill with influenza and I was substituting for him at the station.

When we left the movie theater Lillian took my hand and we walked in silence.

"Sometime I'd like to write a movie like that," I said finally. "Something so perfect, so beautiful . . ."

"You will write a wonderful movie, Richie!" Lillian said.

I remember precisely that she said that. And the time did come when I wrote a script for a movie which won many awards. A good movie—a film with which I was to seal my fate . . .

We came to the Friedensbrücke.

Lillian said, "I want you to stay with me tonight."

People hurried past us, bumped into us. We were oblivious.

"I've fallen in love with you, Richie," Lillian said. "Come, come now, quickly . . ."

That night I stayed with her. We embraced each other violently again and again. We had not had anything to drink, yet we both were in the grip of a delicious intoxication.

Our hands, our lips clung to each other's, our bodies made for each other, thrill followed thrill. As Lillian reached climax each time, her face showed an exquisite torment, a grimace which at first startled me. Lying closely together, we smoked, we talked softly until our passion, seemingly insatiable, mounted again, was briefly satisfied, then flared anew. Finally, exhausted, we fell asleep in the closest possible embrace of two bodies.

When I returned to Paradin's office the overhead light was on again, the paneling hiding the movie screen closed. Minski and Mohn looked very pale. When he saw me Minski said, "Richie, I'm sorry I yelled at you. You're right. And the rabbi, the wise man, is wrong. One cannot close one's eyes and ears and pretend not to know what's going on. That's what everybody in this country has done and what is the result? Hatred and suffering. And it will happen again if we don't sort out the cursed past. It will come back to haunt us, I don't doubt that. Delacorte is a good example. But we must do it for our children if not only for ourselves. I understand that now. I've already told Dr. Paradin that I'll cooperate with him."

"Thank you, Herr Minski," Paradin said.

Boris's hand wiped away the words.

"My wife," he said. "When I think that Professor Mohn said my Rachel was most probably ill in the camp. To think that Delacorte might have seen her . . . But you can count on me, Dr. Paradin. I'm ashamed and I apologize for my behavior. I'm a cowardly Jew."

"That's nonsense," Paradin said sharply. "You're not at all cowardly! You're as courageous as anyone else. Just smarter. Sometimes that can be a disadvantage. You've realized that. Now don't worry, Herr Minski. From now on you, your employees, your club will be under continuous surveillance."

"Oy vey!"

"Not the way you think. We're not going to interfere with your business. We're going to investigate anyone who might possibly take exception to your show and inform the police. I really don't think that will be the case. . . ."

"I don't think so either," Minski interrupted, grinning. "At least not for a week." To me he said, "God must be on our side, Richie! Vanessa is not able to perform and Corabelle and the boa, Annamaria, are harmless. They can't be stopped from performing. And who knows what will be in another week . . ."

I was to remember that sentence, too.

"But thank you for protection." Minski, sitting, bowed to Paradin, who nodded and turned to me.

"I guess you'll want to fly back to Treuwall?"

"Yes," I answered. "As quickly as possible."

"You're free to leave anytime, Richie. But do you realize the risks you're taking?"

"I'm aware of them."

"We can keep an eye on you in Treuwall, too. Eilers and Lansing are reliable. I've worked with them on another case. But how much can we protect you?"

"I have to return to Lillian," I said.

"Yes," Minski agreed, "you must go to Lillian, Richie. I see that now. Stay until she's well again. I'll manage somehow while you're gone. But where you're going the whole mess is only about to start! And you'll be right in the middle of it!" Minski's voice rose; he talked faster. "It's not only Delacorte there! Just as his unscrupulousness helped him in his successful career during the war,

258

he was able to embark on a postwar career in the north, where he'd gone not without good reasons, because there he knew a great many people and knew about them."

I seemed to hear Lillian's voice, "He knows something. So many people are afraid of him—politicians, the police, his medical staff . . . He could kill me in the town and get away with it. . . ."

Paradin said, "I think we can be certain of several things. Those three men, Delacorte's closest associates, were murdered to prevent them from telling tales out of school. I'm positive that they were killed on orders and by specialists of the 'Spider.' "

"What's the Spider?" Minski asked.

"The most far-reaching and powerful Nazi underground movement. Almost everywhere it has bases, men who donate money, agents, hideouts, planes, ships, transmitters, clinics. This organization encircles the globe just like a spider's web. Originally its purpose was to help war criminals to leave Germany. Then came Austria, Italy, and finally it was active in all of Europe. That's when the Spider began to dispense its own kind of justice. Those who constituted a danger—by talking, for instance—were eliminated."

"And you believe the Spider was responsible for the poisonous liquor . . ." Minski began.

"No," Paradin resumed. "No, I don't. There was no reason to kill Delacorte. He had dropped from sight and he kept silent. I think that the attempt on his life was arranged by people who could no longer endure his blackmail . . . by honorable citizens of Treuwall and environs. Only after the murder attempt had failed and things began to happen did the Spider intervene. It is not certain if Dr. Hess was the organization's first victim. His death might possibly be charged to the account of Treuwall's unsuccessful conspirators. Ericksen surely was a victim of the movement; Geyer was a member, I'm certain. And it is that organization which is trying to intimidate you, Herr

Minski. As you can see we have groups who, presumably, will come to blows once we have Delacorte. This is where I shall need your help, yours, Herr Minski, and yours, Richie. Everything and anything that might happen to you is of interest to us even if you think it of little importance. All right?"

Minski and I again agreed to help. Boris added, "I'll do anything to clean up that nasty mess up there."

"You're right, Herr Minski, it is a nasty mess. What we don't know is how extensive it might turn out to be." He pushed back his glasses. "Let's forget for the moment all those who had protected and helped Delacorte following his escape. Doctors, lawyers, civil servants . . . all those who believed that the past ought to be finished and done with. Surely there must have been many who helped him to a new start. What do you think, Professor?"

Mohn answered, "To rise to a position such as Delacorte had held he probably had the help of people in various departments. Legal administration. Civil service. Public Health Service . . . and that as high as the Federal Health Department."

Paradin nodded. "Right. Another thing to consider is that since his escape Delacorte has been in the Federal criminal search files! Complete with description and photograph: Wanted for murder. When we catch up with him—hopefully—it won't be because our police has been so efficient or because someone informed on him. Now do you see that we're only at the start of a very messy and tricky affair?"

And Lillian was embroiled in it.

In January 1948 I vacated my room in the Richard-Strauss-Allee villa and moved into Lillian's basement apartment. I no longer volunteered for night shifts, or I wouldn't have seen much of Lillian, who was now working as a secretary in a law office.

I wrote during the day when I was off at night and at

night when I was on duty. The typewriter Tiny had appropriated from the Nazi official's residence was constantly on the move between Stresemann and Baselerstrasse. I had started work on my second book even before the first had been published.

On those days when I was off duty I took Lillian to her office before I began to write. Lillian always came to the MP station after she had finished work and we walked home together, hand in hand, through bombed-out streets where *Trümmerfrauen* worked, women who cleared away the rubble. At night I read to Lillian what I had written that day. Frequently she had inspirations or she did not like something—I could tell by her large, dark, expressive eyes. I reworked the passages that she had disapproved. Even today, so many years later, I look back on those hours as among my happiest.

Stan' Still, Jordan had been published in September 1947.

Even today I can't quite explain the book's success. Perhaps its contemporary character, but probably it had just been my good fortune among young German authors to have had a book published right after the war when no books could be issued without the military government's license. *Stan' Still, Jordan* became a bestseller, a word then still unknown in Germany. Within two years more than 100,000 copies had been sold. The book was translated into eleven languages and dramatized for radio. It made a good deal of money for me—some of it, after the monetary reform, even in Deutsche marks, which retained their value. Nevertheless Lillian and I continued to work.

We had not heard anything of Lillian's husband's fate. We were almost convinced that he was no longer alive. Had he been alive Lillian would have asked him for a divorce. We had no choice but to wait—until May 19, 1950.

From returning POWs I heard that my brother was interned in a Russian camp and was not permitted to write. Since we had never been on good terms this left me indifferent.

I met Boris Minski in 1948 when Lillian and I frequently dropped into his bar, GI Joe, after work. Minski had already installed a jukebox with forty-five-rpm records which always played the latest hits. I never knew where he managed to obtain the records, or, for that matter, the alcohol. He always had a good selection of domestic and imported wines and liquors. ("From friends," Minski said.)

He seemed to like me immediately but remained polite and formal with Lillian. Once, I asked him about it.

"You like venomous women, don't you, Richie?" We still used the formal *"Sie"* although we were on a first-name basis. "Beautiful, exciting women, like Lillian."

"Correct. It's always the same type. But what do you mean venomous?"

"The type. All women of that type are venomous. I don't really know if venomous is the right word. I call them that. I heard there are orchids, the most beautiful ones, that are poisonous too. If you understand what I mean . . ."

A few weeks later he took me aside and whispered, "I think I was wrong. She isn't one of the poisonous ones. She's okay."

When we were sitting at our favorite table, whisky before us, Minski went to the jukebox and threw in a coin. Lights came on, a record was lowered to the turntable and the vocalist began to sing:

"When I hear that serenade in blue . . ."

I looked up. Minski pointed to Lillian, who smiled.

"From you?" I asked.

She nodded and placed her hand in mine.

"But how . . ."

"Tiny," she said. "I'd asked him to get the record for

me. That was the song I heard when I came to your station, that first time."

"Our song," I said. "Cheers, Lillian."

"Cheers, Richie, I'm very, very happy with you."

"Fifty pfennigs," I said severely.

Contritely, she handed me the money. It was a game we played. We had often told each other how happy we were until one day Lillian had declared, "I can't hear this insipid word any more. Whoever says it pays fifty pfennigs penalty!"

After then we paid—very often.

We looked at each other, sipped our drinks, and listened to our song. Minski stood by the jukebox; he smiled, yet as always his dark, luminous eyes remained serious. In a glow I raised Lillian's hand and kissed it. Then I searched my pockets for coins, and silently I placed them before Lillian.

The record came to an end.

"Forever more," Lillian said softly and raised her glass again.

Forever more . . .

The plane which was to take me back to Hanover left at six-thirty P.M. Before leaving for the airport Minski took me in a taxi to my apartment in the Humperdinck-strasse. Hurriedly I packed a suitcase and carrier. Minski helped me. We hardly spoke. I think I've already mentioned that I am superstitious, as are all those who are not able to believe in anything. When I left my books, my pipes, my small Utrillo, my records in this peaceful apartment I had this strange feeling: Questionable, very questionable if I'm coming back here again.

Minski accompanied me to the airport.

"You'll still have to look over Corabelle."

"Vanessa is going to do that. I telephoned her and told her about everything," Minski said.

There was still time until the plane was to leave. We

went to the restaurant. I ordered a double whisky and thought, tired, yet wide awake, that I would probably drink quite a few more before the day was over. Boris, who never drank alcohol, ordered juice. Suddenly Vanessa stood before us—in a bottle-green suit, mink coat, a mink beret on her blond hair. She was very beautiful and very elated. Before we could say anything she embraced and kissed us.

"Well!" Minski muttered. "You meshugge too?"

"What's the matter, Vanessa?" I asked.

"What's wrong with Corabelle?" Minski asked. "And who is minding the store?" Vanessa opened her alligator bag and pulled out a folded paper. She opened it. I saw a black-rimmed, printed announcement of a death.

"Oh, God, I'm so happy . . ." Vanessa stammered. Her breasts heaved with excitement under the green suit. "There!" She handed me the paper.

I read, *"Le coeur bien gros je vous announce que ma mère chèrie Aglaja Mitsotakis, née Chyranos . . ."*

"Panos's mother?" I looked up.

"Yes." Vanessa nodded. "She is dead. After a short illness. Terrible for Panos. But he sends me a letter. Oh, God, I'm so excited. This came with the afternoon mail. I thought I must show this to Richie before he leaves. I came as quickly as I could. I . . . I need a drink. I'll have a whisky, too, please! I'm so lucky," Vanessa continued. "Am I not? I almost didn't believe he would . . . and now he wrote."

"He didn't write," Boris said. "He sent you a printed announcement."

"Yes, but he sent it. He wouldn't have done that if he didn't think of me, right? He wouldn't have had my address any more. And at a time like that! He thought of me! He loved his mother so very much. Now he's all alone in Paris. Do you think I ought to catch a plane and go there?"

"You're crazy!"

"Why? I can't work just now anyway. Just for a couple of days. I just want to tell him . . ."

"Vanessa!" Boris held his head. "Vanessa, pull yourself together! You can't—because of an announcement—and even if he does think of you, that's one more reason why you shouldn't! Besides, you're not allowed to go to France—had you forgotten that? You were deported!"

"Then . . . what should I do?"

"Write to him. Console him. Then you'll see if he answers. And then . . ."

"Of course he'll write again!"

"Well, I don't see that naturally follows."

Through a loudspeaker a woman's voice announced the boarding of flight 134 to Hanover, my flight.

"Boris, you know him! Would he have sent me this if he didn't want to have anything to do with me?"

"He didn't want to—for such a long time."

"But now his mother died. He is all alone. No one can stand that."

"Stand what?" I asked.

"To be completely alone," Vanessa said. She drank a little of her whisky. "What do you think, Richie?"

"I think you're probably right," I agreed, feeling pity for her.

"There you are, Boris!" Vanessa slapped Minski's shoulder so hard he flinched.

"But Boris has a point. You must be cautious. Write him. Wait how he reacts. You should be spared another disappointment."

Vanessa looked at me with her big blue eyes.

"I'll write today. Express!"

"Don't make a mountain out of a molehill." Minski's voice was long-suffering. "You're always exaggerating."

"Who is 'you'?" I asked.

"Never mind," Minski said, "I've told you I'm sorry, and I was wrong and the rabbi, too."

Vanessa didn't understand that; she kissed me once

more. Now there were tears in her eyes. "Boris told me everything when he called me. Richie, now I can understand you . . . with Lillian . . . really . . . if there is anything I can do for you . . . for both of you. You've always done so much for me."

"Love! A force of heaven!" Minski groaned, rolling his eyes.

"I'll do anything to help you! Anything." Vanessa held my hand. That night none of us knew how soon she was to be able to help me.

"That's very nice of you, Vanessa."

"I didn't really mean all I said about Lillian," she murmured. She looked at me, eyes flickering. "Of course I meant it. But that was——"

"Before you received the letter," I said. "Come on, let's have another drink."

"It was . . . I love you too, Richie. It was . . . jealousy, nothing else."

"Oy, surprise!" Minski exclaimed.

"I'm not going to say another word against Lillian," Vanessa promised. "Not one word. But watch yourself, Richie. I . . . I have such an uneasy feeling . . ."

You too? I thought.

". . . that something is going to happen to you up there if you're not very careful."

"I'll be careful," I promised. "And I'm not going to stay long. I'll be back in a few days."

"Yes." Vanessa said. "You and Lillian, right?"

"Yes."

Through the loudspeaker I heard my name. I was asked to board the plane. I rose.

"I'll take care of the bill," Minski said. "We'll stay here. It's better Vanessa cries here than out there among all those people."

"I'm not going to cry!" Vanessa cried, tears already wetting her cheeks.

"Of course not," Minski agreed. He gave me his hand.

"And call me as soon as you're in Treuwall so I'll know where you're staying."

"Okay, Boris."

"Good old Richie," said Minski and jabbed my side.

"You stupid ass," I said and jabbed back.

I embraced Vanessa. Her wet cheek touched mine. She kissed me once more. Then she made the sign of the cross before my face and said, *"Shalom."*

Shalom. Peace.

Little did I know that this day, this evening, these few hours were to be my last peaceful ones.

We were flying above a thick blanket of clouds below a clear, star-studded sky. It was a restful, calm flight and I thought that I would go to see Lillian on my arrival in Treuwall before I would find a hotel, and soon I was engrossed in memories of yesteryear.

In the early fall of 1948 my second novel, *No One Is an Island,* was published. It brought me even more recognition and success than *Stan' Still, Jordan.*

Now my pattern of living began to change. Tiny's skillful intrigues succeeded in obtaining for me the first-floor apartment in Lillian's villa for our use. The second floor was still occupied by American officers. We moved from the basement apartment, bought new furniture, had a telephone installed. Tiny brought dresses, cosmetics, stockings for Lillian, clothes, shoes for me from the PX— something not exactly legal. I had the money to pay for those things, but without Tiny we would never have been able to obtain them.

In the spring of 1949, when it was evident that my second book was a success, I resigned my position at the MP station. Paradin and Reck had already left. Paradin had received his citizenship papers and was now a prosecuting attorney. Reck, who had given up all hope of ever starting up his bank, was manipulating blocked mark holdings and ended up with a fortune. The expression

267

"blocked marks" at that time meant the financial resources of foreigners in Germany which their owners could disburse only by special permission. Otherwise such expenditure would prejudice the stability of the currency. Before 1951 such marks could only be sold abroad surreptitiously. One hundred blocked marks as a rule brought from $8 to $10, a low price.

Tiny was still waiting for permission to marry Ellen Herbst. Mickey, her daughter, was speaking English as well as German. Tiny often came to visit us. The new interpreters were worth nothing, he said, the job was very routine, and he was taking voice lessons from a German concert singer.

"Just for the hell of it," Tiny explained. "The man says I have a good voice. Boy, I've got a hundred voices! He says I'm going to be a great singer. Boy, just imagine. Tony Caruso! But one has to do something before the army turns one into a moron. So, what do I do? I work my shifts and sing *do re mi fa so!*"

I had no financial problems, I was happy with Lillian, we had no worries—and yet I did not feel good. I felt depressed by the general development of the world. Wars, revolutions, unrest were the order of the day. The cold war had become acute, the blockade of Berlin had necessitated the gigantic American airlift, the differences between Russians and Americans increased daily. And in 1949—four years after the war—there were again right-wing political parties in the German Federal Republic.

I had become a well-known and popular author, enriching my publisher and myself. I spent freely but was never quite certain where my money had gone. Yet we were not living in such grand style.

Now I had more time to write. Strangely, leisure didn't seem to agree with me. I wrote laboriously, made little progress. My third novel, so far still without a title, was overdue. Yet, I worked every day, often discarding what I had written. It was inadequate—simply trivial.

I put on an act for Lillian. I said that I wanted to finish half of the manuscript and then I would read it to her. This was contrary to my usual practice of reading portions, but she accepted this.

When writing my other two books I had followed a definite plan—this time I had none. At night I had always known I would continue the next morning. Now I rarely knew. I also put off my publisher, promising him half the novel and the other half soon thereafter. An understanding man, he also knew he could not afford to add to my confusion by pressing me.

I was—God knows why—very apprehensive. It couldn't have been only the political developments—at least not at that time. Rather than that it was fear. I had written two successful books. Could I write a third? Yes, it was probably the constant fear of failure; the recurring thought: Are you really a writer? Or did you just write down what millions of others had on the tips of their tongues and for which one did not have to have the skills of an author?

Then came April 14, 1949, an unforgettable date. My publisher telephoned me in the afternoon. He was elated. The movie rights to *No One Is an Island* had been bought by a French company. Naturally, I was happy too. Lillian was beside herself with joy. My self-confidence was partly restored. Lillian skipped and danced around the room. It was obvious that I would not write any more today.

"Come to bed," Lillian said. "Let's love one another and have a drink."

We had no whisky in the apartment and I left to buy some.

"I'll make myself pretty for you," Lillian called after me. She undressed as soon as I had left, and had put on perfume, makeup, some black lingerie when the doorbell rang.

Lillian, in her excitement assuming that I had forgotten my keys, hurried to the door in her high heels and opened it. She drew back with a startled cry. Outside stood a tall, emaciated man with brown hair, dark eyes, narrow nose and a prominent lower jaw. The man wore a quilted Russian uniform jacket, Russian uniform trousers, Russian boots, and held a fur cap in his hand. Slung over his shoulder was a knapsack. For a moment he was surprised; then he began to grin and gazed interestedly at Lillian, who was now trying to cover her near-nudity with a drape.

"Who are you?" Lillian stammered, startled.

Just as I opened the downstairs door, two bottles of whisky under my arm, I heard his answer loud and clear.

"I am Werner Mark."

"I've had it up to here, this lachrymose national masochism, the continual self-recriminations that we Germans were the biggest swines ever in this world!"

"Same here!"

"Shut your big mouth!"

"Shut yours!"

"At least there's one good thing about this meeting: Finally we really get to know the Nazis in our town!"

"Allow me to answer your insult, sir. You are a Communist!"

"Red swine!"

"Brown swine!"

"Somebody kick in this Ulbricht-fanatic's teeth!"

"Silence. Order."

"Just try it, you bastards! All you need now are the jack boots and everything is again the way it used to be!"

"May I ask you, ladies and gentlemen . . ."

"Only twenty years ago you were scared stiff!"

"Ladies and gentlemen, ladies and gentlemen, please allow me to continue . . ."

But they did not allow the speaker to continue, this man with the deep, resonant voice, whose declaration that he had had enough of this lachrymose national masochism apparently reflected the sentiments of a good part of his audience.

"Pretty soon *you'll* be scared stiff! They forgot to gas you!"

"Next time we won't forget anyone!"

A cutting voice: "I ask you to immediately desist from such noise. This is not a meeting of National Socialists!"

Roaring laughter. Many thought that comical.

The reverberations of the laughter caused a long row of glasses to jingle. The glasses were lined up on two glass shelves underneath the many bottles behind the bar. The bar was situated at the far end of the foyer of the Hotel Kaiserhof in Treuwall. The roaring noise came from the so-called banquet hall. I had no idea where that was.

The bartender placed another glass before me. It was my second double whisky in this bar. I had lost count of the drinks I had had that day. Although I had had a lot to drink, I felt no effect, as was always the case when I was excited or overly tired. Tonight I was both. Besides that I felt cold. The car heater had broken down on my drive from Hanover to Treuwall. The heath had been icily cold and I had frozen. There was always something going wrong with those expensive, showy supercars. I had already owned two of them. Now I had had enough. I decided to buy an ordinary, useful car—very soon.

But I thought, sipping my drink, I know I won't do that. Good intentions. They never came to anything. I had intended to buy a smaller car for the last ten years. I had also intended to live less expensively, to smoke less, to drink less, to whore around less, to believe in something. It just never seemed to work. There was a lot wrong with me, that was obvious. As always I began to feel better as soon as I told myself that there really was a lot wrong with me. I didn't have to do any more.

For instance I knew perfectly well why I always bought those thirty-five-thousand-mark de luxe cars. Inferiority complex. Guilt. Blah blah blah. All perfectly obvious. So there. But I didn't want to come down with the flu. Perhaps I had caught it from Vanessa.

So I told the bartender, "The same again. And have another drink yourself. What are you drinking?"

"Cognac. Thank you, Herr Mark."

The noise from the banquet hall was as raucous as before.

"Doesn't anybody here realize that we're going to be used again?"

The cutting voice again. "As coordinator of this meeting I *order* you to be quiet. Equal rights for all! The Herr Doctor will speak now. You will have your chance later. We're living in a democracy!"

"Yes, unfortunately!"

To judge by the applause, many seemed to regret that.

"Herr Doctor, please . . ."

Again the sonorous voice of the trained speaker, "I spoke of war atrocities which we Germans are alleged to have committed. Allow me to explain: We have never participated in atrocities. I, myself, was . . ."

"No kidding!"

". . . a soldier for four years and was deeply shocked when, perforce, I witnessed Jews being herded together by Polish civilians. Yet, twenty years later we Germans are still being blamed for everything. We are still being defamed. No other people would be treated as shamefully as we are being treated!"

Thunderous applause interspersed with shrill whistling.

The bar, in contrast to the impersonal hotel, was comfortable. It was separated from the foyer by a trellis thickly covered with creepers growing from innumerable brass flowerpots, and open only on one side, the entrance. The wide long bar had low chairs on the same level with the bartender because of the sunken floor behind the bar. Many small bulbs glittering starlike from a metallic ceiling gave only scant light. Behind the bar stood a stereo radio and tape recorder and many cassettes.

In the foyer men were working at the reception desk. Two women stood talking in the cloakroom. A few bus-boys were hanging around aimlessly. A girl straightened out her newsstand. The light in the foyer was very bright. The employees appeared not to hear the noise from the banquet hall. They continued with their work, talked in undertones, telephoned, calm, indifferent expressions on their faces.

The large square in front of the hotel had been jammed full with cars when I had driven my mud-spatttered car to the hotel garage. At the hotel entrance a placard had caught my eye.

NEW NATIONALISM——A DANGER
FOR DEMOCRACY?

After my long drive I had been too cold to be in-terested in reading more. I had taken the elevator up to a clean, quiet room, 311, its window facing a small court-yard. I had taken a warm bath, changed into my own clothes and hung up my brother's suit on a coat hanger. I had some food brought to my room.

Inspector Eilers had wanted to talk to me about the murder of Dr. Hess and discuss my experiences with Ericksen and Geyer. He was very busy but would come to the hotel at 10 P.M. I felt miserable, I could not seem to get warm, and so I decided that the bar was as good a place as any to wait. I had taken some tablets, too many, but I felt feverish and I did not want to fall sick, not now.

"What does that mean, we didn't commit any war atrocities? What about the Auschwitz trial?" A boyish-sounding voice.

The marvelous doctor. "If you please . . . the wit-nesses all came from the east!"

The boy did not give up. "Well, where else should they have come from?"

"You don't understand me! In fact I think it a matter of the greatest urgency for the federal office of statistics to finally ascertain how many Jews actually have perished. Six million . . . that's Communist propaganda!"

A girl's voice. "Then it makes a difference to you whether six million were murdered or perhaps only one or three?"

"I am very serious, young lady, when I answer to this. Yes, it makes a difference. A very decided difference whether we have to pay for one or six million Jews!"

The bartender filled the glass before me, raised his and said, "Thank you. Your health, Herr Mark."

"And yours, Pierre."

It is a routine with me to ask a bartender his name, gossip a little, establish an amiable relationship. Most bartenders are friendly, and because of their local knowledge they can be most useful.

I think Pierre liked me immediately. He was as tall as I but heavier. Almost bald with only a little black hair at the temples. I guessed it was dyed. A large gray face and permanently tired eyes. I know about bartenders and bars. Pierre worked hard, harder than some of the guys in our Strip. But they were much younger. We couldn't have employed an older man. The work in a nightclub is too demanding.

Pierre—his real name was Max Kramleder—spoke with a southern accent—I thought Bavarian. He had worked many years in various cities of Germany as well as in Paris and Rome; as is generally true of these traveled bartenders, they end up in a hotel such as this one. Not a bad hotel—the largest of the town—but then it was not a large town.

The stereo played soft music. Pierre was polishing glasses at the other end of the bar. He spoke only when I talked to him.

I was his only guest. He had told me that business was poor. This was the off-season and since people were apprehensive of an imminent economic crisis, they drank less or inexpensively and preferably at home. Perhaps business would improve after the meeting in the banquet hall had come to an end, he said. I was growing increasingly tired but I had to wait for Inspector Eilers. He had been in the hospital when I had arrived.

"An officer is constantly on guard outside Frau Lombard's room," he had told me. He chain-smoked and he too looked exhausted. The day had been as long and strenuous for him as it had been for me. "Our police physician and his assistant are taking care of her. She is off the critical list. A few more days . . ."

"May I . . . may I see her?"

"Of course," Eilers agreed.

Lillian had been asleep. I had stayed a few moments at her bedside, then wrote a note to tell where I was staying, to telephone me at any time and to expect my visit the next morning. I added she need no longer be afraid and that I loved her. I had placed the note on Lillian's bedside table and then returned to the hotel.

In the banquet hall television was now under attack.

"We have no anti-Semitism, ladies and gentlemen! We strongly reject anti-Semitism! I put it this way. Every Jew who is a good German citizen is welcome here. But what does our television do? Continuously we are being shown plays dealing with our recent past. In them the Jews are always portrayed as magnanimous. Those who are beneath contempt are always Germans. Such concepts, ladies and gentlemen, only serve to arouse new anti-Semitism!"

This speaker has a new approach, I thought.

"What kind of gathering is that in there, Pierre?" I asked. "NPD?"

"It's a meeting called by our Adult Education Department."

"You're kidding!"

"Well, it was intended to be different, you know."

"How?"

Pierre came from the other end of the bar after I had signaled him to give me another drink. While he filled the glass he explained. The local NPD had felt itself slandered by an article in the local Treuwall newspaper and had demanded a chance to refute the charges. The Adult Education Department had arranged for the meeting. The banquet hall's capacity was three hundred persons. It was immediately sold out. "There are at least four hundred people in there now. Police and security people are there in case of trouble. But nothing is going to happen. They're all agreed anyway."

"Who?"

"The speakers."

"The one who is on about the television . . ."

"That's Doctor Römer. Do you know him?"

"Only the paper he publishes." Dr. Herbert Römer's radical right-wing publication had, by a succession of high officials, been repeatedly declared damaging to the opinion of Germany held in foreign countries because it was violently reactionary. I knew that Dr. Römer was touring the country and giving lectures. Now I heard him for the first time.

"Who are the other speakers, Pierre? I haven't heard anyone oppose his views . . . apart from those in the audience."

Pierre grinned. "The only ones who agreed to come were two representatives of the federal diet. One is a member of the Christian Democrats, the other a Social Democrat."

"But I don't hear them."

"Oh yes," Pierre said. "I know their voices. You'll hear them. Sometimes they agree with Römer, sometimes they protest . . . not too much though. They're from around here, Hanover and Bremen. If they disagree with Römer, they lose votes. They think."

276

"Is that correct, you think?"

Pierre looked at me sadly. "You know, it reminds me of my youth. When I was an apprentice in Munich we had little money. I used to box a bit. Met a lot of people, journalists, writers, actors, people who were educated. We used to go to the old Circus Krone where they held political meetings. Hitler spoke there too. We used to go for the fun of it. Jeered and applauded. Just like those over there. And then? Some had to leave the country. Some were beaten and arrested by the Nazis. The rest of us—to the battlefronts. Some died, some missing, some crippled. Some survived the prison camps as I did. But my wife and children died in our little house in Giesing in an air raid. Those who returned struggled to make something of their lives. Some are well off, some not so good, some very well indeed."

"Yes, I can hear that!"

"Oh, no," Pierre disagreed. "Those who are in the hall over there, those who are shouting hurrah, they are not the satisfied, the successful."

"Who then?"

"The dissatisfied. Nonachievers. Hysterical women. Angry youths. All evening I've been remembering the Circus Krone and what happened afterwards. . . ." He turned abruptly, his face grave. He placed another tape on the stereo and we listened to the music. I drew my glass closer to me and poured some soda into the whisky. I was beginning to feel better; at long last I felt warm. I heard the music and the yelling from the banquet hall.

"We've had enough of being exposed to the world's contempt. German history encompasses heights and depths. But always there is talk only about the last thirty years. We're not the best but we're also not the worst. We are nationalists, yes. But nationalism merely means political loyalty and devotion to one's own people! Enough of those payments to foreign nations at the bidding of other foreigners! Those payments are not in German nor in European interests! Enough of the falsified picture of our recent history; of the immorality of contemporary literature, stage and screen; of the immorality of intellectuals who reduce the German woman to the level of a prostitute and drag all national, moral and decent values into the mud! There has to be an end to this soiling of our own nests! When. . ."

"Richard Mark?"

"Yes?" I turned and faced a tall, elegant man in a blue coat. Hat and gloves in his hand, ash-blond hair meticulously combed. His glasses flashed briefly in reflected light; a thick dueling scar resembled a thick black rope. Neatly trimmed mustache. Pale blue eyes, a wide forehead. A truly imposing figure.

"Professor Kamploh . . ."

"Or Delacorte, if you prefer!" He bowed slightly. "I just arrived in Treuwall. I heard that you were staying here and I hurried to shake your hand!" Before I could stop him he had seized my hand. A brief, firm handshake.

"But . . . why?"

"You've discovered my true identity," he said, forcefully though kindly. "You have reported me to the police. Now I am going to be arrested. I want to thank you for that. You cannot possibly know that you have rendered me a great service," the euthanasia mass-murderer Professor Dr. Delacorte said. "I shall be forever in your debt. You have saved the life of the woman I love, dear friend. And you are also saving mine. Now I am going to straighten out a few things here."

THIRD MOVEMENT

Adagio molto e cantabile

MY BROTHER SAID, "I've read the manuscript."

"And?"

"Do you really want to know?"

"Of course, or I wouldn't have given it to you."

"Okay," my brother said. "What you've written there is drivel. But you know that yourself."

"I know," I said. "But I wanted to confirm it."

We were talking on a sultry afternoon in May 1949. Lillian, at my request, had left two weeks earlier to stay with friends in the Taunus. She had seen that I was not making any progress with my manuscript, and her constant, growing concern had increased my irritability.

I was in a terrible state, drank too much, could not sleep, could not write. What disturbed me was the hostility between Lillian and Werner ever since their first meeting. Lillian insisted that Werner was mean and nasty. He said she was untruthful, vicious and influenced me against him.

I should mention that Werner's manner toward me for the first months had been very obsequious. Despite Lillian's furious protests I had given him the basement apartment, arranged for new clothes and shoes for him. Although he took his meals with us, he rarely visited us in our apartment. Usually Lillian would withdraw or there would be loud and heated quarrels. During those months of tension and squabbles we all drank too much. My brother was the cause of Lillian's and my first arguments since we had met.

"Throw him out!" Lillian had demanded repeatedly, breathless, her face flushed. Her rejection of Werner seemed almost theatrical to me. "He uses you! He will come between us with his lies, his hatred of me!"

"Nonsense!"

"It isn't nonsense. I hate him too. He knows that. Why did you allow him to live here?"

"He has no place to go. And, after all, he is my brother!" I said, exasperated. I seemed to have forgotten that Werner had been my greatest adversary since our childhood. An unexpected feeling of solidarity now bound me to him. I remembered my mother's maxims. One must help one's relatives. I recalled that he had come to my rescue when I had needed help. I made it quite clear to Lillian: her constant attacks would only serve to strengthen my newfound feeling toward my brother.

"You'll see how it'll end," Lillian had once said, bitterly.

My publisher had phoned to express his doubts that I would have a manuscript to deliver by the end of June.

If only I had confirmed his suspicions! But my obstinacy and vanity had prevented that. I shouted at him: provided he did not call me any more, I would meet the deadline. He had apologized, coldly. I had thrown down the receiver, then with hatred had stared at my typewriter. I drank and I wrote nothing.

Not a day passed by when I was not high by midday, completely drunk by evening. Then, feeling euphoric, I would make notes which I either could not decipher next morning or which proved to be nonsensical scribbles. Sitting before my typewriter I would suffer through another day until the evening when, once again, I would be filled with ingenious ideas.

After Lillian had left I called my brother and we drank together. The miseries of war and prison seemed to have left no scar. His readjustment to his former way of life had been remarkably swift. He talked about Russia, of his experiences, of ideas for new books. He had been tried by a denazification board, sentenced and prohibited from working for a period of four years. Though well aware of the justice of his punishment, that realization did not ease his burden. His publishers had either died, lost their businesses or were prevented from publishing. Newly licensed publishers were afraid to employ my brother even under an assumed name.

"They're so scared," Werner said. "It'll be ten years before they'll dare publish one of my books. Cheers, Richie!"

In May, during another evening of drinking, feeling particularly close to my brother, I had showed him the manuscript, *The Great Cold*, which I could not seem to finish. Werner read it promptly and had as prompt an opinion, which he gave while we were in my study. There we awaited the first clap of thunder that would mean the relief of a storm on this unbearably hot day. On the table between us lay the manuscript and a large tape recorder, one of Tiny's gifts.

"When did you last record something?" my brother asked, again filling his glass.

"Don't know. Quite a while ago." I pressed the switch.

". . . is the Soviet Union prepared to sign a nonaggression pact with the United States of America to safeguard peace of the world? And, finally is Stalin prepared to meet with President Truman to discuss these matters?"

Lightning was followed by resounding thunder, day was night, rain came with such roaring force I had to turn up volume on the tape recorder. What was left of daylight now had a greenish hue. Lightning and thunder were continual. A most impressive downpour.

"At last," my brother said, stepping to the open window. Rain splashed him.

". . . INS reported President Truman's readiness to meet with Stalin, provided the meeting would take place in America . . ."

"Boy, you must have been drunk!" my brother said. "Amazing you could still talk."

"Tass reported today that Stalin's health would not permit an extended trip but that Moscow or any city in Poland or Czechoslovakia would be acceptable."

"Can you explain whatever this nonsense is supposed to mean?" Werner asked.

"No," I answered. But I could have explained how I had felt when I spoke those words into the microphone. With revulsion and desperation I had realized the swift change the world had undergone; the open hostility of Allies and friends of yesterday. Tiny's song had not stood still for one single second; what we had hoped for was in vain; what we tried to do now would prove meaningless, ridiculous—especially writing books. But now I lacked the strength to explain these angry and sad thoughts to Werner.

"I listened to the news at eleven P.M.," my voice said. "INS reported that the USA insists on a meeting in America. Stalin's offer had been rejected." A pause. Then, "So that's that. And one would like to overeat in order to vomit more."

"Nothing more," I said. "I remember now." I switched off the tape recorder.

"So that was February 17," Werner said. "You know what you are?"

"Yes," I answered moodily.

"That's good," he said. "That makes it easier for me to help you."

"Help me?"

"Yes," he said. "Help you and myself."

"How?"

My brother held his glass out to me and grinned while I refilled it. He spoke directly into my face. "You are allowed to write but you can't. I can write but am not permitted to. You get the idea?"

I stared, shocked.

"It's very simple," he said. "You can pour in a bit more Scotch."

I did not move. He took the bottle from my hand and filled his glass to the brim. Very matter-of-factly he asked, "What's your deadline?"

"Eight weeks."

"That's not much time to write a book," he said. "But I think I can do it. I'm well rested. Can you keep Lillian away that long?"

I nodded. I didn't mean to but I was drunk and indecisive.

"You can tape whatever ideas you might have. So that I have something to go by. You said you have some good ideas when you're drunk."

"I do, really," I heard myself say, defiantly. Eight weeks, I thought. Could he do it? I know I won't. I would be saved. But this is fraud. I felt both admiration and hatred as I said, "It's out of the question. Forget it."

"Ah, shut up," my brother said softly. "No one will know. Not even Lillian. As soon as you've told me the kind of book it is supposed to be . . ."

"An anti-Nazi book. That's one book you won't be able to write!"

"There isn't a book I can't write," Werner said, grinning.

The storm had abated. It had brought a most welcome coolness. It grew lighter.

"No one will know. Don't be afraid. I'll take fifty per cent of all the income. My name must never be mentioned. Now have some more to drink and talk a bit about the book, Richie."

"Never," I said, "will I agree to that."

Eight weeks later I delivered *The Great Cold*, a typescript of five hundred and eighty pages to my publisher. He brought it out at the end of October. By Christmas fifty thousand copies had been sold. Two years later the figure was a quarter of a million. My greatest success. Werner had written the book from the first sentence to the last. He was already working on my next.

"You know there is a God," Lillian said to me one night. "During those bad days, I prayed every day that you would be able to write again, that God would help you, help us. And He did help us—now I believe in Him. And you must too. Will you promise me that, Richie?"

"Yes," I said, "I promise."

From the basement apartment I heard the rattling of the typewriter I had bought for my brother. He always worked at night and slept during the day. I had told Lillian that he was typing my handwritten manuscript.

"This self-vilification must come to an end!"

I had slid off my chair and looked at the elegantly dressed man who had just thanked me for having denounced him to the police. Victor Delacorte still gripped my hand, still looked directly into my eyes.

The voice of the speaker rose again, persuasive, forceful. "Three million German civilians were victims of Allied air raids! Did they die easier than the Jews?"

"That is disgraceful," Delacorte said, his face showing disgust. "Who is that oaf making the speech, dear friend?"

Before I could answer he turned to Pierre, beaming, "Ah, Pierre! Haven't seen you in some time! How are you? Would you give me an Armagnac, please?"

I turned. Pierre looked pale and nervous. He was staring at Delacorte.

"Pierre! Aren't you going to give me a drink?"

284

"Yes . . . of course . . . right away, Professor," Pierre stammered. With unsteady hands he filled a brandy snifter.

Delacorte took the glass, swirled the Armagnac, sniffed it appreciatively, raised it to us before he finally drank.

"Ah, that is good," he commented. "Now, Pierre, would you be so kind as to call the police and ask them to send someone over here?"

"There are policemen . . ." Pierre swallowed hard. "There are some at the meeting over there."

"Well, then, would you ask one of them to come?"

Pierre coughed helplessly. He came out from behind the bar and hurried toward the banquet hall.

"How do you know that I denounced you?" I asked Delacorte.

"Didn't you?"

"Yes."

"You see," he said. "Pure deduction. Dr. Hess called me this morning at my hotel in Munich and told me what had happened." His face grew hard. "Poor Lillian . . . those blackguards almost . . . The poisoned Armagnac was meant for me, of course. But now I'm going to put an end to this spooky business. I've already waited much too long."

"Dr. Hess is dead," I said.

Delacorte nodded. "I know, I know." When he became aware of my steady gaze he added, "Terrible. Those criminals."

"Criminals? Who?"

"Well, those who murdered him."

"How do you know he was murdered?"

"Frau Taler, my housekeeper, told me. I called her as soon as I had arrived in Treuwall," Delacorte explained, smiling. "I called my home first, of course, but there was no answer. The policemen who are waiting for me there did not answer. Very clever." He laughed heartily, self-satisfied. "Had I gone home I would have been arrested

285

and who knows when I would have been able to see you. And I had to see you."

"You did?" I felt that I was close to losing my reason.

"Frau Taler told me that you were staying in the Kaiserhof. To anticipate your question—she had been told by a detective. Talkative gentlemen. They told her quite a lot. And she told me."

I was wondering whether, indeed, Frau Taler had informed him or if, perhaps, it had been a detective, such as Geyer?

"She also mentioned you and your brother. Lillian has told me terrible things about him. A most dreadful marriage. But you, you were Lillian's first love," he said, smiling. "I do believe you're blushing!"

I felt myself reddening—with rage. But I could not utter a word.

"Lillian has often spoken to me about you," he continued. "Yes, I know a lot about you. I know that she wrote your telephone numbers on the back of my photograph, the one in the locket. For a while I was actually jealous—you can imagine—but then . . ."

"Yes?"

"Then I realized that for Lillian you were a sort of talisman. I hope I haven't hurt your feelings? That was not my intention! Yes, a mascot. Lillian clings to you as she clings to her past . . . those wild, wonderful years after the war . . . her youth, isn't that so? I can understand that. I, too, have my memories. I'm jealous, very jealous, I admit! But strangely, not on your account. But there are others, other men, I have proof." He leaned closer to me. "Listen carefully: Lillian telephoned you last night. Don't contradict me, I know. Frau Taler told me. You've saved Lillian's life. I shall never forget that. My love for her is very deep. I'll be arrested now but I'll be in jail for only a brief period." His manner of speaking reminded me of a general, a victor of a battle. He spoke urgently, volubly about his feelings for Lillian, the need to protect her . . .

"You will protect her for me, won't you? May I rely on you?"

Was this naïveté? No. Here was power. The power he had once wielded and had lost. He meant what he said. He was not in the least interested in my feelings. I had to admire his nerve.

"You can rely on me," I said.

He gripped my hand and shook it. "Thank you, Herr Mark."

A nightmare. Yes, that's what it was. What had happened to Pierre? Where were those accursed policemen?

Almost automatically I asked, "How did you know that you were to be arrested?"

"The car radio, dear friend. The Criminal Police is always asking citizens' help." He laughed. "And then one wants to help and then one is not even picked up!" Abruptly he said, "You love Beethoven. The Ninth."

"How do you—" I was nonplussed.

"Frau Taler again. And the detectives. That you'd noticed the line missing in the fourth movement. Then you do love the Ninth?"

"I . . ." Dammit, I did love the Ninth!

"Then I was right. And I'm going to make you a present of the score."

"I could never accept . . ."

"Please! Of course you can! After all you have done for me. And will be doing in the future."

"What does that mean?"

"Well, Lillian . . . you've promised—" He broke off. From the banquet hall the audience began to pour into the main foyer. Hurrying ahead of them were Pierre and two police officers. No, they were not hurrying. They were being pushed ahead, shoved ahead. The policemen appeared uncertain, perhaps, I thought, frightened. The crowd was unruly.

"Finally," Delacorte said and finished his drink. I saw athletic, stern-faced young guards in blackshirts, black corduroy shorts, white knee socks trying to contain the crowd, shouting. A hotel porter hastily reached for a telephone. The policemen and Pierre were being pushed into the bar. Behind them I could see flushed, excited, hate-distorted faces, shouting.

"Hands off the professor!"

"Just try it, you swine, and we'll take you apart!"

"Shut your mouth! We're not in America!"

"Why don't you arrest him then, you bums!"

I stepped back. I have always lacked the tendency to be a hero. Pierre, next to me, cursed softly. "Goddamn mess! When I spoke to the officers someone overheard me and, of course, they all had to come!"

Delacorte stepped close to the policemen, who seemed extremely uneasy.

"Professor Kamploh," one of them began, "in the name of the law—" and got no further. Someone pushed him and he stumbled against Delacorte. The man had had enough. He yelled, "Get back, right now!" when someone kicked at his leg. He went down. Immediately three, four men jumped on him; others tried to help him. The guards suddenly swung into action. I saw billies, knuckle dusters, fists in violent use. Screams, shouts, curses. A large woman with an oversized handbag was laying on, hitting anyone within reach quite impersonally, yelling, "You're going to arrest our good professor, are you!"

"Silence!" Delacorte roared.

For some seconds the fighting stopped. A slight, sharp-featured man had worked his way to Delacorte's side. As soon as I heard his sonorous voice I know who he was. "Professor, I am going to give this affair full publicity on your behalf!"

"Who are you?" Delacorte asked.

"Römer. Dr. Herbert Römer. Editor of—"

"Oh. I know. Very nice of you, Doctor."

"Not at all." The editor suddenly assumed an exaggerated posture and clicked his heels. "My paper is at your disposal!"

A murmur arose in the crowd.

"Thank you, Doctor," Delacorte repeated. The thought that he had anticipated just such a situation and was now using it crossed my mind. Delacorte raised his voice to appeal to the crowd. "Please, dear friends! An arrest warrant has been issued for me. These officers are only doing their duty!"

"Arrest warrant!" Someone repeated it in an angry shout, and the fighting erupted again.

"Why? What did you do?"

"Some Jewish swine in Frankfurt—"

"Frankfurt?"

"Frankfurt was always full of Jews."

"This isn't Frankfurt. This is Treuwall. Professor, we're coming to get you out!"

"Not another step!" The policeman had come to his feet again. The woman's large handbag caught him across his neck. He fell against his colleague, almost upsetting him.

A smoke bomb exploded, partly covering the small bar with a white fog. Moments later a second bomb went off. It shattered glasses and shelved bottles behind the bar. Heads down, everyone was desperately protecting his face from flying glass splinters. Pierre shouted something.

Delacorte had covered most of his face with a handkerchief, something I quickly did too. He seized my arm.

"Get out of here! They'll kill us!"

I'll never know how, in that fog-filled room, he managed to find his way out while dragging me along. He obviously knew the interior of that hotel well. Quickly we were in a room where he bolted the door. His face was pale; I realized that he was fleeing. I forgot my fear and blindly followed him through corridors and the service quarter to a truck alley. Cars were parked there. Delacorte headed toward one of them. He suddenly seemed to remember me. He was older than I but stronger—at least at that moment. He practically threw me into his car. Then he was off with a roaring start, managing a turn on two noisily protesting wheels. Driving as one possessed, he passed red lights, narrowly avoiding collisions, the car vibrating under the pressure of speeds of 100 kilometers.

"They're not going to get me, the swine," Delacorte hissed through clenched teeth.

The near hits of other cars and pedestrians should have made a wreck of me. But, curiously, my thoughts were on two pistols in my hotel room that I had taken from the police detectives who had shot each other. One, I recalled, still had four bullets in it. If only I had that with me now, I thought, I could stop this madman.

"Delacorte!" I yelled.

He did not answer. The speedometer needle indicated 105.

"Yes . . . yes . . . gently . . . oh, that's wonderful . . . yes . . ."

That was Lillian's voice, low, throaty, breathless. I caught my breath. I had returned from a trip two days earlier than expected. It was almost midnight, April 28, 1950. I had quietly opened the door, carried my suitcase, quietly entered our apartment so as not to awaken Lillian. The light had been burning in my brother's apartment. He usually worked at night. Our apartment had been dark too, but through the half-closed door of Lillian's bedroom the light of a bedside lamp shone into the hall. I set down my suitcase and looked into the bedroom.

My brother was kneeling before Lillian, who was completely nude. Her body writhed, her hands in my brother's hair, her own spread wildly over the pillow. She moaned, her face distorted. "Now . . ."

I turned and went back to the entrance door. I picked up my suitcase.

"Who in God's name . . ." That was Lillian's voice.

290

"Who is there?" My brother's voice.

I slammed the door shut behind me. As though drunk I staggered down the stairs, thinking that I could not live after the scene I had witnessed. I was going to kill myself. I was going to go to the river. I went to the Frankfurter Hof instead. The doorman greeted me. I had become quite well-known after another successful book. That, as well as the previous one, had been written by my brother Werner.

By six o'clock the next morning he had located me.

"Let me come up, Richie, I must talk to you!"

"Go away! I'll call the police if you don't."

"I've already done that," he said, his voice flat.

"But why?"

"Two hours ago. Lillian . . ."

"What's the matter with Lillian?"

"I left her alone to look for you. I called her—she didn't answer. I raced home—she . . . she had slashed her wrists."

Startled, I sat bolt upright in bed.

"Dead?"

"Critical. She's already in the hospital. Let me come up, Richie! I must talk with you, I must! Let me come up!"

My prison guard, Officer Stalling, has joined the NPD. This morning, as usual, he sat and talked to me while I was cleaning my cell.

President Lübke, in a speech made before officers, had declared, "The German soldier might conceivably have to fight against his own people."

That quote had been his deciding factor.

"If my son has to join the army," Stalling had told me, "he might have to shoot at his own cousins. Two of them are already serving in the Volksarmee in the east! A government where the president says something like that is bad. Why? Because it's not nationally oriented. Why aren't we allowed to be national? No one forbids the Swedes or British or French or Americans or Australians to act in their national interest? Look at the German Democratic Republic! Nationalism there is perfectly acceptable! Hitler and the Nazis were the worst criminals, that's what our politicians say again and again, right? The Communists fought Hitler and the Nazis. Today? Today we're patented democrats while the East Germans are antidemocratic, totalitarian and radical—why, *because* they're Communists. What is that supposed to mean? My relatives are good, decent people. They were never Nazis or Communists! Do you know what Adenauer said as early as 1949? I just read it yesterday. Those who would again make Berlin the capital of Germany would ideologically create a new Prussia! You know he doesn't even consider the people in the east to be German! Reunification—they've never intended that. Just political talk. To shoot at them, yes, that's another matter, according to Lübke. The gentleman has no relatives there, I guess. The NPD is the only party to realize that we're one country, one people, not two who might have to shoot each other. Who's there to prevent that from happening? The NPD is the last hope for all the decent, little people. Don't you agree?"

> Alas, 'tis true I have gone here and there,
> And made myself a motley to the view,
> Gored mine own thoughts, sold cheap what is most
>   dear,
> Made old offenses of affections new.

This portion of one of Shakespeare's sonnets—I had borrowed his works from the prison library—aptly describes my behavior. For indeed, after I had surprised Lillian and my brother, I betrayed myself, played the fool, sold cheaply what is most dear, namely, my self-respect.

That night, when Lillian had tried to kill herself, I naturally relented and asked him to come up to my hotel room. Werner was pale, extremely nervous, pacing up and down.

"She won't die," he assured me. "The doctors promised me. She's lost a great amount of blood, but she'll live, Richie!"

I asked, "Do you love Lillian?"

He answered, "Yes, I do."

"How long has this been going on?"

"About six months . . . a little longer. I know this has been a great shock to you, Richie. I can imagine how you must feel. What we've done is unforgivable but—" he stopped abruptly.

"Yes?" I prompted. I was curious what he would say now.

"But we did fight it! We tried, but it was stronger . . ."

"You said that beautifully!"

"Don't be so flippant! I'm serious!"

"So am I. I'm so touched I'll puke any moment."

He stopped before me, breathing heavily.

"Can you really appreciate what it means to live under one roof with a woman you desire, who desires you, each glance, each word gives evidence of that? Do you think that is easy to live with?"

"Terrible," I said. "Must have been terrible. I really should have stepped aside."

"Stop jeering! I'm your brother! I—"

"This is precisely the moment to remind me that you are my brother."

"What I mean is, the fact that you are makes it doubly difficult to bear, for me and for Lillian. Lillian repeatedly told you of her dislike for me, didn't she?"

"True, she did."

"That was self-defense! But you were blind, Richie, blind as a bat! The first time I saw her, do you remember the afternoon?"

"Perfectly."

"From that moment on there was that spark, a hate-love relationship, madness . . . I can't find words to describe it. The first time we were together she behaved like a mad woman—it was crazy. Richie . . . we were weak . . . we couldn't help ourselves. . . ."

"I am going to throw up after all."

"You make things very easy for yourself," my brother complained.

"That's right," I laughed sardonically. "I make it easy for myself. And you betrayed me. Whenever I was not at home."

"That's right." Infuriated now, he vented his defensive anger in a rapid confession. "Even when you were at home. We met secretly—in small hotels, at friends' of mine, in the country . . ."

"And she had time for me too," I said. "A very vivacious lady. Why don't you marry her?"

"What did you say?" He came to a sudden stop by the window, hung with heavy drapes. The first rays of the morning sun filtered through them, slightly parted, dimming the still-lit electric bulb.

"I said you should marry Lillian if your love is so overpowering. In just another month the time is up and her husband can officially be declared dead."

"Are you serious?"

"Yes."

"Do you realize that then you'll never see us again? Not Lillian, not me?"

"Yes, I do, dearest brother. Did you think that the three of us would live together happily? You'd better get out of here!"

"Being cynical . . ."

"Get out! I don't know if I am as strong as you are but unless you get out right now I shall try to kick your teeth in, you dirty bastard, you lousy son-of-a-bitch. Get out! Now!"

"You'll regret having spoken to me this way."

I seized an ashtray from the bedside table and hurled it at my brother. It missed Werner's head by a fraction, crashed against the wall and broke. Werner was breathing noisily.

"Will you leave now or shall I try it?"

"Try it," he snarled, showing his teeth.

I tried.

He beat me until, bleeding and almost unconscious, I lay slumped on the floor near the bed. He stood over me, his voice oozing with self-pity.

"I've warned you, Richie. What I've done hurts me as much as it hurts you. I don't mean the beating, I mean . . ."

"Just get out of here, you bastard!"

"But I can't leave you in this . . ."

I rolled over and kicked at him with the little strength I had left. "I'll stay in the hotel until I've found an apartment."

"But your home . . ."

"I'll never set foot in it again," I screamed. "It's Lillian's house. I'll have my things picked up. And if you don't leave now I'll have the hotel staff throw you out!"

Leaving he said, "If you only knew how sorry I am for you."

"You dirty swine," I called after him. After he had closed the door I dropped back onto the floor. A wide strip of sunlight now shone through the opening of the drapes, falling diagonally on my battered body. All I thought was, she won't die. The doctors promised Werner.

During the following two weeks I heard neither from Lillian nor Werner. I continued to live in the Frankfurter Hof. Toward the end of the second week Lillian called several times from the hospital. Each time I hung up as soon as I recognized her voice. Whenever I was not there she left word for me to call her immediately upon my return, it was of the greatest urgency.

I never called.

I drank every night—with Tiny in Minski's G.I. Joe. Both were very sympathetic and tried to console me. Minski reminded me that he always had thought Lillian "venomous" and told me a Russian proverb, "A chicken is no bird and a woman is not human."

"And your wife?"

"There are very good and very bad chickens," Minski answered.

Tiny advised me to fight for Lillian. "She loves only you. I know both of you! He's bewitched her, confused her. Say one word and I'll beat him to a pulp for you!"

"No," I refused. "That's foolish."

"I know she loves you. I've watched you," Tiny insisted. "She loves you."

"Yes," I said, "that's why she's been sleeping with my brother for the past six months."

"Let's have another drink," Tiny said.

That's how these talks always ended. Minski and Tiny meant well, but they couldn't help me.

Early one afternoon my publisher, a heavy-set, dark-complexioned man, came to see me at my hotel. I was still on my drinking spree and he had a drink with me at a table in the almost-deserted bar.

He told me that the American publisher who had bought the rights to *No One Is an Island* wanted me to rewrite or tone down two passages dealing with racial discrimination, incidents which had occurred in the Southern states of America.

As usual, time was pressing.

"I'm sure you'll be able to take care of this matter right here in the hotel in a few hours," he said. I promised that I would and took a bottle of whisky to my room. I had a copy of the book and a portable typewriter. I wrote the passages perhaps a dozen times. Each was worse than the last. I had written this book, not Werner, and yet two years later I could not write a single, decent sentence. I was also very drunk. It was a heroic battle among myself, the typewriter and the bottle. The bottle won.

About four o'clock in the morning I ordered a taxi, took the book, went to my brother's apartment and rang the bell furiously. As he opened the door he looked at me as though I were a ghost, laughed foolishly and then admitted me. My brother had different ways of laughing. I knew all the variations; this was a frightened laugh.

I noticed that the rooms were in disorder and dirty.

"How much longer is Lillian going to be in the hospital?" I asked.

"She's not in the hospital any more."

"What?"

"Hasn't been for the past four days," Werner said with a nervous laugh.

"Where is she?"

"Gone."

"What does that mean, gone?"

"It means what it means. She returned only to pick up her things, clothes and such. Withdrew money from your account. Said that she was going on a trip. I never saw her after that. Said she had written to you but you had refused to accept the letter."

"That's correct."

"The letter is over there," my brother said, indicating a table in the living room with the soiled dishes of a meal he had prepared himself. "She left it here. Just in case you might come here at some time, she said."

I tore open the envelope.

My Dear One.
So I am to continue living. How I don't know as yet. I am leaving Frankfurt. I must leave here. You cannot forgive what I have done. And you don't have to forgive me. I am bad and wicked and worth nothing.
I'm sorry, Richie. Truly! But apparently

no one can be any different than one is. I wish
you all the best and happiness. The time I spent
with you was wonderful. I don't know why I
am the way I am. If there is a God he'll know
why he has made me the way I am.

She had really made things easy for herself.

But then, perhaps, no God exists. I wish
there were. A permanent wish. That Christmas
when we found the woman about to give birth
to her child, when our love began, I fervently
hoped that a God existed. And when you began
to write again I believed that there was. Now I
don't know any more. All I know is that I love
you, Richie. Only you. And that I shall always
love only you. You can laugh at me, curse me,
wish me death when you read this, and you can
think of me what you will, do whatever you
want, call me whatever you want, but it is true.
I don't have to write this, this crazy absurdity
which, nevertheless, is true: I shall always love
only you.

Lillian

I dropped the paper.
"Hysterical whore," I said.
"That's right," my brother said.
"Shut up!" I shouted.
"But . . ."
"That's not for you to say."
"But you're saying it."
"That's different," I said, loudly and drunkenly.
"She left me . . ."
"She left us both," I said. My brother looked at me for
some moments before a smile came to his lips again, not
an apprehensive smile but one of gloating triumph.

"So here we are alone," he said.

"Yes," I agreed.

"Welcome home, Richie."

"I suppose you think you have me in your pocket now, eh?"

"Well, haven't I?" he asked. "Now that Lillian is gone you'll see how nicely we'll now be able to work. We'll forget Lillian. A family has to stick together. What is it that brought you here? The American translation?"

"How do you . . ."

"Those incidents in the South? I thought that those passages might have to be changed somewhat."

I nodded.

"When are you supposed to deliver it?"

"Tomorrow at the latest. That is, today."

"Did you try to rewrite it?" he asked, smiling.

I nodded again.

"And couldn't?" He was beaming now.

I shook my head, threw him the book, sat down at the untidy table and seized my head in my hands.

"I'm just going downstairs for a moment," Werner said. "I have the two passages there."

"Why . . ."

"As soon as I'd read the book I typed a second version. It seemed obvious that we would need it." He said *we*. "By the way, the passage about de Gaulle will have to be changed for the French translation. You'll see. I've already prepared that too." Walking to the door he said, "Man, am I glad that we're together again. A woman isn't going to alienate *us*."

I was silent. All I could think of at that moment was how fortunate it was that Werner had already finished those passages. I was very tired, very drunk, very relieved, glad to be back in my old apartment. When my brother returned from the basement I had fallen asleep, my head resting on the table. Later I awakened—alone. The lights were burning. Two rewritten passages were on the table, neatly typed. From Lillian's bedroom came the sounds of Werner's snoring. I went to my bedroom, dropped onto the bed and felt very contented.

Yes, it is true. I had gone here and there, played the fool, sold cheap what is most dear, made old offenses of affections new.

What poetry, what a great poet Shakespeare had been. What a blackguard, what a cowardly weakling I was.

The illuminated red speedometer needle quivered at 105 kilometers. The horn blared almost incessantly. Delacorte, hunched over the wheel, did not utter a word. I was holding on to the dashboard but was still thrown about whenever Delacorte braked sharply before taking a curve at high speed. I was apprehensive, my eyes still burned from the smoke of the bomb, I felt sick, yet I considered ways of bringing this madman to a stop. If only he would slow down a little!

I had no idea where we were. We had raced through wide roads, through narrow heavily traveled streets, Delacorte completely ignoring traffic lights. I considered throwing myself from the car but decided against that. Suddenly I saw him step on the brake. At the same time I bent down and slipped off my left shoe (I am left-handed). The car rolled toward the brightly illuminated facade of a large, outmoded building. Now he stepped on the clutch. Immediately I straightened up, the shoe in my hand—when I saw a white sign with the black inscription:

POLICE HEADQUARTERS

Delacorte said, "I think I've lost them. Quickly now before something happens."

The car stopped. He jumped out, taking long strides toward the entrance of the building. My shoe back on my foot, I hurried after him. The policeman on guard beamed when he recognized Delacorte.

"Herr Professor!"

"Good evening," Delacorte said nervously. He automatically shook the hand the policeman held out to him.

From the ensuing conversation I understood that Delacorte had saved the man's wife. Professor of neurology and psychiatry, I reflected.

"And how is your wife now, Herr Groll?"

"Just fine, Herr Professor!" The man swallowed hard, obviously touched that Delacorte had even remembered his name.

"I'm glad. Please remember me to her, Herr Groll. Now, would you please tell me where the Criminal Police headquarters is? I would really like to be arrested now."

Late one night one week after I had returned to the house in the Stresemannstrasse, Lillian telephoned me. Her speech was slurred, she sounded drunk. In the background I heard voices talking, laughing, and dance music.

"Forgive me, Richie," she said. "I'm sorry. Send your brother away. He is an evil man. I'm bad too. But I love you, Richie. Send him away and tell me to come back to you."

"No."

"Please. Just one try. Please."

"It's your house. If you want to come, come. But then I'll leave."

"It's not my house any more, Richie. I've sold it. The people will get in touch with you. You'll have to pay rent to them. I don't want the house any more. I want you. I want you back."

"Do you have company?"

"Yes. Friends. Awful people. Let me come to you."

"No." I felt adamant.

"Not under any circumstances?"

"No. I've had enough of you, Lillian."

"I don't believe that," she said. "I won't come if you don't want me to. But you haven't had enough of me and

I haven't of you. We'll never have enough of each other. I don't think that makes for happiness."

"I agree."

"It's a curse."

"Drunken nonsense."

"No, it's not. You'll see. We . . . we shall never be able to let one another go until one of us dies."

"Farewell, Lillian," I said and hung up. For the remainder of the night I was unable to sleep. She called again the following night and the one thereafter. I had my telephone changed to an unlisted number. This took ten days, during which Lillian called fifteen more times. Each time she sounded drunk and our conversations were repetitions of our first one.

Once I had an unlisted number Lillian's letters began to arrive. Within a year I must have received at least fifty—all of which I returned unopened. Her return address differed: Hamburg, Düsseldorf, Berlin, Rome, Paris, Athens, New York, Belgrade, Los Angeles, Munich.

My brother and I moved into a lovely villa in the August-Siebert-Strasse near the Grüneburgpark. We each had our own apartment, our own affairs. I knew many girls then but threw them out after a brief period, or they left me because of my unpleasant behavior. My brother did not have as many affairs; he was working too hard.

In the fall of 1957 the new book by Richard Mark, actually written by Werner, was released. My publisher sent me on a lecture tour through the Federal Republic. I read from the book every other evening in a different city. By now this unusual state of affairs had become a habit. It rarely disturbed me. Officially my books, published at almost regular intervals of eighteen months, were acclaimed by the critics.

Every seat in the hall in Hamburg was occupied. I had just ascended the platform when I saw Lillian in the center of the first row directly in front of me. She was smartly dressed, heavily made-up, her lustrous black hair upswept.

Her large, beautiful black eyes gazed at me steadily. It was the worst reading I ever gave. Perspiration dripped down my back, soaking my shirt. I fluffed my lines. I had to clear my throat repeatedly. Whenever I raised my eyes I met Lillian's glance.

After the reading I fled outside, rudely brushing aside people holding out copies of my book for my autograph. A taxi started by. I raised my hand. The car stopped, I jumped inside. The taxi moved forward.

"Hello, Richie," Lillian said, and flinging her arms around my neck, she pressed her lips on mine. With sudden desire I returned her kiss, feeling her teeth bite into my lips. I tasted blood, warm and bitter.

She stroked me and as I slipped my hand under her suit jacket I discovered that she wore no brassiere.

"Where are we going?" I asked.

"To my place," Lillian whispered, kissing me again.

She lived in a new house in the Adolfstrasse in an expensively furnished apartment.

"Is this yours?" I asked looking around while she brought glasses and champagne from the kitchen.

"Yes." She handed me the bottle. "Open this, please."

I opened it and noticed the many vases with red roses and orchids in the room.

"Who's your friend?" I asked.

"A rich man," she answered. "Lives in Cologne. But he's always in Hamburg on business. Every week. Then he lives here. He's always traveling. All over the world. Almost always he takes me along. As his secretary, you know."

"I understand." I said. "Your letters came from many parts of the world."

"Yes," she said. "From those trips." She still looked as beautiful as always. Only her voice had changed, more brittle now, throaty from too much smoking and with an

303

occasional sharp inflection. "From those trips," I repeated, while I wondered how I had changed.

"A girl has to live, Richie," Lillian said.

"Of course," I said. "What happened to the money from the sale of your house?"

"I had some bad luck."

"Bad luck?"

"I met a young man. In Munich. He resembled you. No, he was better-looking. But essentially he was of your type. I had had an unhappy love affair. So had he. He said. So we set up a cozy little home." She had developed a somewhat vulgar manner of speech. Her smile was frequently cynical.

"He invested my money. Told me that he knew what he was doing. He did too. He managed to disappear with it and my jewelry. Left the country. I've no idea where he is. The jewelry I have now is from Thomas. The moneybags from Cologne. Married. Two children. Loves me madly. He sent me those flowers. Lovely, aren't they?"

"Get undressed," I said.

"Wouldn't you like a drink first? His champagne is excellent."

"I feel as if I were a pimp."

"A terrible feeling?"

"Marvelous feeling. Get undressed."

She went into the bathroom and I poured out two glasses of champagne. When she returned she was nude and as beautiful as I remembered her. With outstretched arms and a smile she approached me on high-heeled slippers. Her arms around my neck, she snuggled against me, pressing close, kissing me. I stroked her abundant black hair now falling loosely about her shoulders. Then I grabbed her hair, pulled her head back and hit her in her face with my left fist.

She cried with pain, staggered backward, and fell over an armchair. I ripped an extension cord from a lamp. With both ends firmly in my hand, quite mad at the moment, I began to lash her. She writhed on the carpet, moaned, but did not cry out. Finally she lay motionless. Red, bloody welts covered her back. I gulped both glasses of the champagne I had poured, seized the bottle and emptied it over Lillian, cursing her in the vilest terms. She did not stir. I flung the electric cord from me and started from the room. But at the entrance I turned, then hurried back. I kneeled alongside her, stroking and caressing her, asking her forgiveness. She rose without a word, went to her room and, on her blood-smeared back, lay on her bed in a lascivious posture. It was no time for me to undress. We embraced fiercely, clinging wildly to each other, convulsed in each other.

Afterward, drunk with champagne, we fell asleep, our bodies entwined. Lillian awakened me the next morning for breakfast. A beautiful day, sunlight flooding the room. Lillian's face was swollen, one eye almost closed from my punch, her body bruised. My lips had swollen from her bites, making eating difficult. After breakfast I dressed. Lillian was still sitting at the table, staring out of the window, when I came back to the room. I tried to say good-by but found no words. I just stood there for a long while until, finally, she placed her hand on mine and nodded. That was all. I walked toward the door firmly resolved never to see her again. At the door I stopped, turned and said, "Let's marry, Lillian. Right away. Let's get married and never part again."

The large, brightly lit room held several desks, and office equipment. The air reeked with cigarette smoke. Slim, brown-haired Inspector Eilers looked worn and pale, while an angry expression lit his eyes. He chainsmoked. Both Eilers and the blond Inspector Lansing had taken off their jackets. They were sitting behind their desks in shirtsleeves, their ties loosened, their topmost shirt buttons undone. Delacorte, splendidly attired, and I were seated before them.

We were awaiting the arrival of officers of justice called by Eilers. Delacorte had demanded immediate imprisonment in the town's jail. He felt that police custody involved greater risks than jail. As I gathered from the conversation, the jail was next to the district court but some distance from police headquarters.

Lansing, typing with two fingers, had completed the necessary forms for Delacorte's arrest and transfer to the jail and handed them to Eilers, who signed them. The inspector grimaced as he perused the papers.

"So you are completely innocent, Herr Professor."

Delacorte crossed his legs.

"You can't imagine that that could be true, can you? Not that I care what you think," he added arrogantly.

As soon as we had arrived he had made a statement affirming his innocence of all charges. Indeed, he presented himself as a "resistance fighter" who had saved thousands of people from death under the infamous T4 action by sabotaging its execution wherever and whenever possible. Now, he insisted, he was going to prove this.

"The witnesses who gave evidence against you . . ." Eilers, struggling with fatigue and rage, began, but Delacorte interrupted abruptly.

"Those witnesses had to give that evidence. Do you think that at that time I could have sabotaged openly? The witnesses gave evidence that was subjectively correct yet objectively false."

"Then you have never participated in selections?"

"I have. Frequently. I was forced to so as not to become suspect. But I have also prevented countless selections."

"You have never worked in concentration camps?"

"Never!"

"We have witnesses to your operations and X-ray treatments!"

"Those witnesses must be mistaken. Or they are lying intentionally. I was present at the . . . hm . . . treatments and operations in order to render *negative* reports. After all, the experiments were discontinued, weren't they? Owing to me."

"Documents prove otherwise."

"At that time many documents were falsified. By me too! I had to protect myself. I played a very hazardous game then."

"The letters you wrote to your wife?"

"I knew my mail was being censored. Accordingly I wrote my letters."

"The films which have been found?"

"I had had them made for the same reason," Delacorte continued, imperturbable. "You cannot imagine how dangerously I lived then. Threatened daily by death."

"Really."

"Yes, really. I had a deadly enemy. Professor Albricht."

"The man who fell out of the window of the Frankfurt courthouse."

"The same. A most ambitious man. Wanted to get rid of me."

"How convenient that he is dead," Eilers commented, his tone embittered.

The doctor merely shrugged his shoulders. "I'm not interested in your views, Inspector. Others are going to judge me now. Fortunately they will not be as resentful as you."

"Herr Paradin—"

"Is not going to be my judge! Only my prosecutor," Delacorte broke in.

"You're not worried about the judges, are you?" Eilers asked, reddening with rage.

"No, I'm not," Delacorte answered softly. "I have proof. I, too, have witnesses who will confirm the truth of my statements that Albricht had denounced me, that he called me an opponent of the regime, that . . ."

"You were an opponent of the regime?" Eilers asked slowly.

"Certainly. Inspector, you don't look well. Is there something wrong?"

"I feel sick," Eilers answered. "Not only since you entered this room. I've been feeling sick for years in this town."

"Me too," Lansing declared. "Although I must say that this talk with you has considerably increased this feeling."

"You will have to answer for this impertinence."

"I'm convinced of that," the young inspector said, grinning. "But I had to say it or I would have choked. So we'll have to prepare ourselves to hear from you that the man whom you so valiantly fought, Professor Albricht, was the guilty party—and not you."

"That is the truth. Of course you will not believe me," Delacorte went on. "That is precisely the reason why I dropped from sight after the war. Because no one would have believed me. Now I'm here. Very good. Now I'm going to talk. Then things will look quite different . . . not only in Treuwall, you'll see. It became quite impossible to live here. One couldn't breathe in this den of corruption and iniquity! You just cannot imagine, Herr Mark, how some of the gentlemen in the public eye have changed during the past twenty years."

"Those gentlemen who helped and protected you twenty years ago," Eilers commented, a disgusted expression on his face.

"Why did they? Because I knew all about them! Then they were still meek and mild. Today—but that's going to change, you can rely on that. I am not going to be liquidated by some rogues who think I'm too powerful and dangerous. When I begin to talk there is going to be a scandal which will shake the foundations of the Federal Republic! Also I trust that you will take better security measures to protect me. Up to now you have been not particularly efficient, gentlemen."

Eilers rose. For a moment I thought he was going to punch Delacorte. He glared at him, red with rage.

"Or are you of a different opinion?" Delacorte asked amiably. "What kind of policemen were those in the Kaiserhof Hotel? Did you arrest the man who threw the smoke bombs? Or the men? Did you arrest anyone at all?"

"Quite a number of people," Eilers answered. "As soon as we were notified by the hotel manager we sent two riot-squad cars. I'm sorry you had to wait so long, Herr Mark. I was just about to telephone you when the call came in."

"And the culprits waited until the squad cars arrived, naturally." Delacorte sneered. It obviously amused him to provoke Eilers. "Thank you, Inspector, now I'm reassured." He glanced at me. "And I'm sure Herr Mark is too, as far as his safety is concerned."

"Pretty soon you'll change your tone," Eilers said evenly, sadly.

"We'll see, we'll see. You don't seem very well, Inspector. Exhausted? Troubles? I can assure you that I will create more problems for you. Just to show you that I am serious about cleaning up Treuwall, let me ask you this. Where is Inspector Fegesack?"

"That's none of your—how do you know him?"

"Where is he?"

Lansing stepped closer. "At the Autobahn Helmstedt-Hanover. There has been some trouble . . ."

"Ah, yes. The shooting. Ericksen and Geyer. Your officers, eh?"

"How do you—"

"A little bird told me. Gentlemen, it is probably too late by now, but I would advise you to at least try to catch Fegesack, provided he is still in Europe . . . and in a country which extradites political criminals."

"Political criminals?"

"Inspector Fegesack's true name is Waldemar Böttger and he was SS Obersturmbannführer in the concentration camp Oranienburg."

Eilers stared at Delacorte, who was calmly lighting a cigarette.

"Up to today he has never been found. His photograph and description have been in the criminal search files since 1946." Delacorte turned to me. "Fegesack was in my house when you arrived there this morning, wasn't he, my friend?"

"Yes . . ."

"I expect he saw you taking my photo."

"How . . ."

"Or he wouldn't have fled. Now. Did he grin when he saw you taking it?"

"He grinned, yes . . ."

"Same old Böttger. Can't help it, you know." Delacorte exhaled a cloud of smoke. "People grin. People smile. Different smiles for different occasions." I thought of my brother. Delacorte was right.

Eilers had taken a heavy book from a shelf and had leafed through it. Now he said, "That's right. Here is his photograph, his description. Special peculiarities: spasmodic grinning." Eilers placed the open book on a desk and stared at Delacorte. Lansing hurriedly left the room. "Was this Böttger already in Treuwall when you arrived in 1946?"

"An unnecessary question," Delacorte answered. "Of course he was here. That's why I came here too. He was not the only one of that type who arrived here. There were quite a few more. But really, Inspector, I don't want to name them all now. That's one game you'll have to play according to my rules. And there I have some definite ideas, you know."

In the summer of 1952 my publisher had sent me on an extended trip, during which I visited Cairo for the first time. In the harbor of Piraeus, near Athens, was the ocean-going yacht of a famous German deep-sea diver and explorer. He knew my name, my books, and invited

what *you've* done! It never will make any difference to me whatever you might do!"

"That's why you beat me."

"Forgive me."

"I deserved it. And more. Richie, if we were to marry now, would you throw out your brother and admit publicly who had written your recent books, and that you won't ever publish another book because you can't write any more?"

"I will."

"Well, that's what you say now. But it's not true. You wouldn't do it. Being a woman I know and I am more honest than you. I wouldn't have answered as quickly had you asked me, 'Will you betray me with another man if we get married now? Will you never ever leave me? Can I trust you as I did?'" She shook her head. "Both of us have done things that cannot be undone. And we will continue—because we can't help ourselves. It seems to me as if we have only now come to realize what we truly are. At least I have. I don't like what I've discovered. But I can't change that. I'm not sure if you like yourself, Richie."

"Not much."

"Then why haven't you changed your life? It didn't necessarily have to be connected with me, did it? We were like children. Now we're adults. Whenever one thinks of the other one becomes sentimental and wishes everything could be again as it once was. But that's impossible, Richie! Our love is the longing for a paradise from which we've long been expelled." She gently stroked my hair. "That's why we can't live together. The present is stronger than we are. Soon, very soon, we would part again—adversaries—and for always. I don't want that. I don't ever want to lose you, never! That is why I have to let you go."

"Lillian, you're really out of your mind."

"Surely. But believe me, Richie, that is how it would

be, is bound to be. I see that in your heart you are beginning to realize that too."

Of course I didn't believe what she was telling me but . . .

"This way whenever and wherever we meet we'll be able to lose ourselves in the past as if time had stood still, as if the past were the present, and we'll always cherish our love, Richie." She raised a hand. "But just for a little while. And that only if we recall the wonderful days we've shared and not what else we know about each other and of ourselves. That is possible. Something that can last a lifetime. But not if we live together permanently. I don't want to lose you, I want to love you, for a lifetime. With longing, with desire, with expectations. And with contemplation. That's what our love is: reminiscences. Memories. An escape into our youth. Way, way back. If you like you could call it a special kind of regression."

"You're too goddamn clever," I said.

"Perhaps. I wish I wasn't. Perhaps if we both were a little less complicated we could find a way. Saying this is not easy for me but . . ."

"But you'd rather continue to whore around than live with me," I said cruelly.

"And you," she countered, "you prefer your life of duplicity, Richie, darling."

"That's not true!"

"Isn't it? Then call your publisher now and tell him the truth. Go on! Then I'll call my friend to tell him we're through. So, go on!"

Quickly I went to the telephone and gave the operator the Frankfurt number. Lillian at the table watched me intently. My publisher answered. White spheres and stars whirled before my eyes. To steady myself I had to hold on to the chest upon which the telephone stood. I replaced the receiver.

I turned slowly.

Lillian stood before me.

She embraced me, kissed me very gently and said softly, "I love you for that too. But now you know, don't you? You do see, don't you?"

I nodded.

"We missed the right moment, Richie," Lillian said. "We love each other. We shall always love each other. We shall each go our own way. Alone. Whenever we meet it will be a gala occasion. For a little while. But there may be one thousand of them! You know there is a certain type who demand that every day be a holiday."

"Yes. Damn neurotics."

"And what are we, Richie?" Lillian asked. "The whore and the fraud. And both of them so sensitive . . . longing desperately for their lost paradise . . . neurotics with a pronounced regressive urge."

"Was your friend who took off with your money a student of medicine?" I asked, spitefully.

"Yes," she answered, smiling. "I knew that you would come to that. He taught me a great deal. The truth about myself, for instance. Now go, Richie. Go, but always return. You understand now that you cannot ever stay, don't you?"

I said nothing.

I left.

And our relationship had remained thus: filled with restlessness and tension, passion and longing, never harmonious, never for long.

Now we had met again on the yacht of the Greek millionaire. Lillian came to my cabin the first night and our tormenting passion engulfed us once again. I thought it strange that Lillian did not seem concerned that we might be surprised, and I was relieved when she told me more about her wealthy Greek.

"He wants to marry me," Lillian explained. "He absolutely wants to marry me." She was lying on my bed.

"And you? Don't you want to marry him?"

"I don't know if I could stand it," she replied. "He's so terribly depressed."

"Crazy?"

"One could probably call it that. He doesn't speak for days. He stares into space. He says he despises people and that there is only one creature he loves."

"Who's that?"

"Aphrodite," Lillian said, laughing hysterically. "Aphrodite, his little duck. Her initial is on every sheet, towel, napkin, cup and knife—everything on board this ship. *A* for Aphrodite, goddess of love and beauty . . ."

"Where's that duck?"

"He is very distressed that he cannot take the duck wherever he goes." Lillian suddenly spoke in an affected manner. "Aphrodite lives on the Riviera, on Cap Ferrat. The climate there is better for it than in Athens or anywhere else they've tried. In Cap Ferrat he has a villa where the duck has its pool and where a veterinarian and two servants attend it. Damaskinos regularly calls Cap Ferrat. Now at sea, he often receives radio telegrams."

"Why?"

"When he cannot be with her he has to know how Aphrodite is," Lillian said and laughed again. The quality of her laugh made me feel uneasy. "On our last trip, right after he had made love to me, he got up and sent a cable to Cap Ferrat. He'd thought of a new tasty dish for Aphrodite."

"While he was—?"

"Presumably. If he'd thought of it before he'd have cabled first, wouldn't he?" With sudden reckless abandon she embraced me, pressing her head to my chest. "Richie," she murmured, "oh, Richie, why did this have to happen to us? Come to me," she whispered. "Come, he always takes potent sleeping pills."

Two days later on Aphrodite's birthday Damaskinos sent a cable to Cap Ferrat. At night he was giving a gala banquet when he suddenly began to weep and returned to his cabin. That night Lillian again visited me. "I don't think you'll be able to live like that," I told her.

"Well, I can at least try," she answered.

I left the ship in Genoa. Damaskinos was taking Lillian to Cap Ferrat to meet Aphrodite. He hoped that the little duck would like Lillian. So much depended on that, he told me. He invited me to come along, but I wanted to return to Germany. My brother had finished another novel and I had to deliver it to my publisher as if I had written it.

When we parted I gave Lillian my unlisted telephone number and told her to call me if she should need me. This cruise had sealed the conviction that she had been right. We were bound to one another. For us there would always be the joy of meeting, our insatiable passion, the acceptance of parting.

Two weeks later I read in a society gossip column that Lillian Lombard, constant companion of the Greek shipowner Zacharias Damaskinos, had attempted to kill herself by swallowing excessive amounts of barbiturates and was at present in a hospital in Nice.

I finally located the hospital, called and reached Lillian. Her voice sounded weak; I could hardly hear her. Our conversation was brief.

"Aphrodite . . ."

"What?"

"The duck didn't like me, wouldn't let me touch her. It was dreadful. Damaskinos was in a terrible rage. I tried to run away. He had me watched. That's when, that's when I did it."

"And now?"

"Oh, now he's very reasonable. He can't afford a scandal. He gave me a lot of money and the address of friends who own a plantation near Rio. I'm to go there and recuperate. He's also given me jewelry, and, as I said, much money. The perfect poule de luxe, my love."

"Lillian . . ."

"I can't talk any more. Good luck, Richie. I'll write you from Rio. *Ciao*."

I saved the postcard of the Copacabana she sent from Rio. "Richie, darling, Rio is wonderful."

The pharmacist Jakowski, accused of the murder of one hundred and twenty-four inmates of the Auschwitz concentration camp, serving a life sentence, at present awaiting the result of his appeal and, as I am, a prisoner in the Rindsgasse, was serving the rations.

"Thank you for the newspapers," he had said. "I have torn out the report on the Berlin NPD so that Officer Stalling will not become upset by it."

The report he had referred to concerned the chairman of the Berlin chapter. He had been discovered to be an agent of the state security service of the East German zone in addition to using the title of doctor fraudulently and having once been convicted of indecent assault. His successor had been thrown out of the Nazi party in 1937 when it was proved that he had been in jail on three different occasions for theft. In 1963 he was rumored to have been involved in legal proceedings for pandering. Since 1959 he had employed a total of twenty-three "housekeepers," some of whom had since become well-known prostitutes.

Jakowski had removed these reports, since Officer Stalling, in his desperate search to save family, children and fatherland, had retreated to the supposedly secure refuge of the NPD. For dedication to the "protection of the honor and dignity of the German woman" was one of the party's programs.

"He must not suffer because of this slanderous campaign—if we can help it. Right, Herr Mark?"

I was waiting, sitting on a bench outside Inspector Eilers's office. Delacorte, escorted by five armed officers and accompanied by Eilers and Lansing, had been transferred to the prison. Paradin had been informed and was expected to arrive this morning. Since Delacorte had been arrested in Treuwall and because of disclosures promised by him, Paradin apparently intended to conduct the investigation right here.

Inquiries concerning Inspector Fegesack's whereabouts had so far been without result.

"Then you'll probably have to forget about him," Delacorte had said. And to me: "I'll say good-by for the moment. And you will look after Lillian, won't you?"

"I will."

"Thank you. I'm told that all I own has been sequestered for the moment, but Inspector Eilers knows that I made you a present of the Beethoven score. You'll receive it as soon as possible."

Beethoven's Ninth had completely slipped my mind until he mentioned it. Eilers had asked me to wait for him. He wanted to talk to me about my brother.

So I sat on the bench outside his office, sharing it with a rather pretty woman in her thirties. Her eyes were red and swollen from crying.

"Excuse me," she said. "You are Herr Richard Mark, aren't you?"

"Yes."

Her coat was open and I saw that she was pregnant.

"I'm Frau Ericksen. You were there when Geyer . . . when it happened, Herr Mark, weren't you?"

"Yes."

"And you're certain, quite certain, that Geyer killed my husband?"

I nodded.

"And Geyer? He was shot in his legs?"

"Yes."

"But both of them disappeared." Frau Ericksen placed her hands on her body as if to protect her unborn child. Tears flowed from her red, swollen eyes. "Why? Why hide a dead man? I can't understand it. Geyer and my husband were friends. If I were quite sure, absolutely sure that Paul is dead I'd rather be dead too."

"But your child . . ." I began.

"I know. I must think of the child. And so far it is not absolutely sure that Paul is dead, is it, Herr Mark? You could have been mistaken. You could have thought that he was dead, but you could be mistaken. Isn't it possible?"

I could not stand her imploring look. I averted my eyes.

"As long as he hasn't been found there is that chance. You can say what you want. Not that I don't trust you, but you could have been wrong. You're not a doctor. You just saw blood, a lot of blood, right? And you thought that . . . it's perfectly understandable . . . but you can't be sure! Can you, Herr Mark?"

I was too tired, too cowardly to rob this poor woman of her last hope. Someone else would have to do that. I said, "Of course I can't be that certain."

She took my hand and pressed it, and smiled. "Thank you! Naturally you can't be sure! My husband's alive— wounded surely—but he's alive. They've hidden him somewhere. I told that to the inspector too. He says he will be found. They're searching for him now. I'm going to wait here until the inspector is notified that Paul has been found."

"But that might take days," I said. "You ought to think of your child. You must be exhausted."

"The inspector said I could lie down and rest on the couch in a room downstairs. But I'm all right. I'll wait here as long as I can. Now that you admitted that you could possibly have been mistaken, that Paul is alive, I'm feeling much better."

I realized how irresponsible I had just been, how much greater the shock to the poor woman once they found her husband, her dead husband. But my irresponsibility had made her happy. I recalled what Minski had once said:

"It's almost as easy to make people happy as it is to make them unhappy."

In 1955 the German Federal Republic became a member of NATO. Once again we had an army. It took part without restraint in the NATO air maneuvers over Germany. The maneuvers left the generals with a profound realization: "An atomic war has no victors." As a capricious consequence of this knowledge, East and West increased their preparations for an atomic war during the following years.

In 1955 I frequently had to go to Berlin, where my novel *Black* was to become a movie. *Black,* which, inevitably, had been written by my brother, depicted the life and experiences of an American Negro soldier in Germany. My producer had engaged an American director of excellent repute and a considerable international cast.

I was to write the script. Since I could not even do that, I had gone to Berlin to meet the producer and director. I was, therefore, able to explain to my brother their concept of the film. The script he wrote was enthusiastically accepted by all concerned.

In Berlin I always stayed at the Hotel Kempinski. One morning I received a call from the desk that a lady was asking for me. There was a hesitant pause before the word "lady."

"What's her name?" I asked, knowing who she was before he could answer.

I was shocked when I saw Lillian in the foyer. Her dress was outmoded and did not fit properly; with her run-down shoes, her hair carelessly combed, she made a dismal and despairing impression. Under the curious stares of the hotel clerks we walked to the almost empty, dimly lit bar. She asked for cognac.

"Isn't it a little early for cognac?"

"I start early these days."

"That's how you look, too."

"So what? Richie, I'm broke. Broke and pregnant."

She spoke brusquely. I could see she was close to tears.

"I've behaved like a tramp during the last few months. Rio wasn't so . . . so wonderful, you know. There was a scandal. Because the man was a senator the whole thing was blown up and I had to leave the country. In Germany I met a few men, but I have no luck with men." The bartender brought her cognac, she emptied it and said, "The same again.

"The jewelry and money I had went—two men took care of that. And I had promised myself that that wasn't going to happen again. It happened twice. Here in Berlin I met a Belgian." The second cognac was brought. This time she drank it slowly. "He was a nice guy. Extremely handsome. You know that I always fall for those good-looking ones. You were the only exception. You were and are the only exception. You know that, don't you?"

"Yes."

"All other men are swine. Including your accursed brother. How is he?"

"Fine."

"I hope he drops dead. Be on your guard against him, Richie."

"Why should I be?"

"I don't know really. I have this feeling. Please, promise me you'll be careful."

"All right, I promise."

"Could I have another drink?"

"You'll be drunk."

"I want to be."

I asked the bartender to bring two cognacs.

"Doubles," Lillian said.

"Doubles, yes, madam. Right away."

"Shit-Belgian," Lillian said. "He said he'd marry me. Bachelor. I made inquiries. Rich. Owns textile mills. It's time I was married, isn't it? Well, he came to Berlin regularly on business. Great love affair. He talked about marriage and having children and all that. Didn't watch out.

I said nothing. I thought if I became pregnant he'd hurry things up. He did too. Once I was certain, I told him that I was pregnant. I haven't seen him since."

"He disappeared?"

"No. He still comes to Berlin. I have a small apartment here that he bought for me. But it is in his name. His lawyer wrote me that I have to leave it by the fifteenth. And if I were to say that the child is his he would report me for blackmailing him. I don't stand a chance, Richie, or do I?"

"I don't think so."

"Then I'll have to have an abortion. There's still a little time. I know a doctor in Switzerland who's done it for me once before. But I have no money."

"How much do you need?"

"At least three thousand, I guess."

I took out my checkbook and wrote a check for ten thousand marks.

"You're crazy!" Lillian gasped.

"Had you forgotten?"

She stared at the check.

"Never."

"Never what?"

"We shall never be able not to love each other. Never."

The bartender brought the drinks. Lillian seemed slightly drunk. I had to get her out of there. She made it easy for me.

"Shall we go to my place?" she asked.

"Now?"

"Yes, now. And you don't have to be careful. Isn't that marvelous?"

"I'll take you home," I said. "But I have an appointment. I can't come up to your apartment."

"Of course you can."

"No, really, it's impossible."

She smiled at me and at that moment she looked a whore.

"Wanna bet?"

I didn't bet. She would have won.

It was completely dark.

"Lights!" Eilers voice commanded.

Three strong spotlights illuminated the nine men in the police lineup. All of them were dressed in blue suits and raincoats, about six feet tall, broad-shouldered with brown hair and eyes, high foreheads, narrow noses, full lips and of my brother's age, in their late forties. My brother stood under card number four.

I was sitting between Eilers and Lansing. Before us sat an older woman and a pimple-faced adolescent.

After a little while Eilers asked, "Well?"

The woman turned toward him.

"I'm sorry," she said, "I don't recognize him. They all look alike."

"How about you?" Eilers asked the young man.

"Same here," he said. "I can't be sure."

"But this morning when our detectives talked to you you remembered having seen this man. And when we showed him to you, you identified him, independently of each other." He was referring to Werner.

The pimply youth murmured rebelliously, "But then you showed us the man alone, not with eight others!"

"Quite right," the woman agreed.

It was almost midnight. Eilers, chain-smoking, exhausted and embittered, could hardly speak. "Now look here. Are you saying that you do not recognize the man whom you identified this morning?"

"That's right," the youth said belligerently.

"Take your time. You must recognize him!"

"No." After a quick glance at the nine men the woman said, "No, I don't. At first I thought it was number three. But now I'm not sure at all."

"I thought it was number eight. But I couldn't swear to that."

The woman said, "You tricked us this morning. You

shouldn't have shown us this man alone but in a proper lineup. We would have told you then that we couldn't identify him. You have no right to force us to make an identification. I've asked my lawyer. We've come here voluntarily, to please you, and in the middle of the night, too."

"Because you have to let the man go, whoever he is, if we don't recognize him and there is no other charge against him," the youth chimed in.

"Have you consulted your lawyer too?" Lansing inquired.

"Anybody knows that," the young man said, insolently.

"Then you refuse to make an identification."

"Yes," both answered simultaneously.

Lansing dismissed the men in the lineup, the spotlights went out, the regular lighting came on.

"Meanwhile you've heard that Professor Kamploh is a wanted war criminal?" Eilers asked, barely civil.

"Yes."

"How did you hear that?"

"Everybody in the neighborhood is talking about it."

"On the radio," the youth answered.

"Did anyone suggest that you ought not to identify this man in connection with that case? Did anyone threaten you or make any promises?"

"That's enough!" the woman cried. She rose and I saw that in addition to being old she was also very fat. "My lawyer, Dr. Tarron, is going to contact you. I'm not going to put up with this!" She left abruptly, her companion following her, moving lazily, insolently.

We watched them leave the room. Eilers extinguished his cigarette by stepping on it. Lansing cursed.

"Oh, stop it," Eilers told him.

Before the lineup, in Eilers's office, I had once again recounted my experiences in the hospital with Dr. Hess and on the autobahn with Ericksen and Geyer to a stenographer. In the morning I was to sign the typed statement. Outside Eilers's office I had noticed Frau Ericksen again. She had fallen asleep on the bench.

Eilers yawned expansively.

"Your brother will be released. We can't charge him with anything now, since we cannot prove he was in Treuwall yesterday morning."

"Why did you ask these people to come back again?" I asked.

"Your brother demanded a lineup. That's his right. What took place this morning really wasn't very correct . . . but our officers were pressed for time," Eilers added.

"I'm certain those two recognized him," I said.

"Of course."

"They're afraid. They don't want to become involved," Lansing said.

"Half the town is afraid now that Delacorte is in jail and no one knows who will be his next victim."

"And there is nothing you can do about those two lying?"

"Nothing. Your brother is clever," Eilers said, bitter. "Delacorte is clever. Geyer is clever. They all are."

"Not all of them," Lansing said. "Hess. He wasn't clever enough."

"True. Hess was stupid. But this attendant who was no attendant, he was clever. And those who are standing behind them. And they have money and power." Eilers stared into space. "Fegesack," he said. "He was clever too." He rose. "I'm going to get some shut-eye. If anything happens I'm in the room downstairs. I've had it. Good night, Herr Mark."

"Good night, Inspector."

"Lansing, will you look after Frau Ericksen? See that she sleeps on the couch. Get her a blanket."

"Will do."

"And tomorrow I can tell her that her husband is dead," Eilers murmured, shuffling to the door. "Perhaps the day after tomorrow if they find him by then."

"Perhaps it will be another week," Lansing said.

"Perhaps," Eilers said. "Goddam, what a mess I've made of my life. Why wasn't I a prominent Nazi? Or a German hero? Why weren't you? We were stupid asses. Imagine the positions we'd hold today!"

"Perhaps behind bars, look at Delacorte," Lansing pointed out.

"I might not mind sitting behind bars with that knowledge and power," Eilers countered. "You and I, Lansing, we have a flaw in our character. We hate the Nazis too much. That's not normal. Normal people don't feel that way today any more. We ought to have our heads examined."

"Yeah, by Delacorte." Lansing grinned.

"I'm serious," Eilers said, tight-lipped. "You've a trauma owning to your father's fate."

"And you?"

"The Nazis locked me up for three years. Others have had worse experiences and are today mellowed and wise. Not I! But one can really go to pieces if one feels too strongly that way. Often, even my wife has had enough. I'm sending a man to your hotel now to pick up those pistols, Herr Mark," he said, his voice normal again. His hand brushed across his eyes; he nodded to me, opened the door. There he collided with my brother, who apologized; Eilers said nothing, just left.

"Hello, Richie," Werner said. He was still wearing his furlined raincoat. "We can leave if you're ready to go, can't we? You are finished here, aren't you?"

"Yes," Lansing said.

"Where are you staying?"

"Hotel Kaiserhof."

"Then let's go," he said merrily. "I'm dead tired. Nice hotel? Surely. I'll stay there too."

We found a taxi to take us to the hotel.

Werner engaged the room adjoining mine. The hotel foyer was very cold. Windows, doors stood open. There was still a pervading odor of smoke bombs. Hotel staff were busily cleaning up.

Pierre, the bartender, was on his haunches behind the bar picking up pieces of broken glasses and bottles which were lying in a lake of alcohol. Here the smell of alcohol was stronger than that of the smoke bombs. One could almost become drunk just breathing. As soon as he saw me he cried, "At long last we've had some action around here, Herr Mark! I haven't had such a turnover in years! The insurance will pay for it. A fast profit for me." He rose with difficulty and pulled out a bottle of Scotch from under the bar. "You'll permit me? This is on the house."

"But after all that has happened to you?"

"That's exactly why! The insurance will pay for everything. I can easily cheat on a few bottles. I gave a few bottles to the hotel clerks too. No one can possibly say how many bottles were really broken. I shall consider it an insult if you don't accept the Scotch!"

"God forbid!" I said and took the bottle. Then I introduced my brother.

"Happy to meet you," Pierre said. "Ice and soda? I'll send it up to your room. It's impossible to drink here right now, I'm afraid."

Just then the clerk from the reception desk called, "Herr Mark!" When both of us turned he added quickly, "Herr Werner Mark!"

Werner went to the desk where a tall, thin man in a black leather coat stood. He spoke to Werner briefly, who nodded and returned to me. Suddenly he seemed as upset and fearful as he had this morning.

"What's the matter?" I asked.

"I have to go somewhere," he said hurriedly. "Won't take long, I hope."

"Listen, it's past midnight. What does the man want?"

"I have something to talk over with him."

"Now?"

"Yes, now." He went on quickly. "Wait for me. Have

328

a drink but leave something for me too." His laugh seemed forced. "You have my suitcase. Would you put it in my room please. Here's my key. Don't fall asleep. There's something I have to tell you."

Before I could say anything he returned to the man in the leather coat. Both hurriedly left the hotel.

"Isn't your brother feeling well?" Pierre asked.

"Why do you ask?"

"He looked quite ill, don't you think?"

I was silent.

"Probably the light in here," he said quickly. "I'll see to your drinks in a moment.

A few minutes after I had taken Werner's suitcase to his room Pierre brought the tray with Scotch, ice, soda.

"Have a drink with me," I said and brought a glass from the bathroom. After Pierre left, I poured myself another drink, dropped into a comfortable chair, slipped off my shoes. Having been overly tired I was suddenly wide-awake. The ice clinked in my glass. The desk announced a police officer who was to fetch something. He came up and carefully wrapped Geyer's and Ericksen's pistols in handkerchiefs before placing them into two paper bags. He politely refused the drink I offered him, saying "Never on duty," and left.

I telephoned the hospital. When I asked for Frau Lombard, a detective answered. Yes, she had read my note, she was awaiting my visit and yes, she was feeling fine.

I telephoned Minski at the Strip, told him where I was staying, gave him the number of my telephone.

"Everything all right there?"

"Fine. We're full up."

"How's Vanessa?"

"She's with Corabelle. They're still rehearsing with the snake. I'm sure she'll be okay. Vanessa is going to write Panos later on. We also have two detectives here. They're working at the bar. Just in case. What's new with you?"

"Delacorte's in jail."

I told him briefly what had happened.

"Richie," Minski then said, "when I listen to you talk and think of us, of our future, I have this very ominous feeling."

"I feel it too."

"Well, so long then, Richie."

I sat quietly then, refilling my glass from time to time, listening to the wind, dozing. About one o'clock I began to wonder where my brother had gone. By two I was quite drunk and my brother still had not returned. He came just before three, entering without knocking, his face deathly pale, his lips a narrow slit. He threw his coat on the couch, fixed himself a strong drink, gulped it, poured another, then dropped into a chair, looking at me speculatively.

"Richie, my boy," he said putting his feet on the table, "this was a long day's journey into night. And the journey has not yet ended. In fact, it's only starting."

"What do you mean?" I felt that somehow it would be better if I was less fuddled, so I quickly drank a Scotch, neat. It had always had a sobering effect on me.

"Well," Werner said, "so Delacorte's in jail. They caught him."

"How do you know that his name is Delacorte?"

"I was gone for some time, wasn't I? I had an interesting conversation."

"With the man in the leather coat?"

"With him and others. Well, Richie, my boy, I'm sorry but this means work for you. Quite a lot of work and difficult too."

"I don't understand."

"Have another drink. You'll need it. I need it, too. I've never been in a situation as bad as this. And only you can help me. And you will. You'll pull me out of this hole into which I've fallen, by getting Delacorte out."

"Out of what?"

"Out of jail, you idiot. He has to be out of there, the

quicker the better. And the only man who can pull that off is you."

"I'm going to telephone for a doctor for you," I said.

"I don't need one, dearest brother. I'm perfectly healthy and sane. You will do exactly what I tell you now. It isn't easy and not without danger. But you can do it. You will do it. If you don't, you yourself will go to jail. For fraud. Repeated fraud. You might get four years for that." Just then the telephone began to ring.

Minski, at his old-fashioned desk in the Strip, had finished writing the note which was to go with the beautiful dark brown mink he had bought for Rachel for their twenty-fifth wedding anniversary. He intended to visit the Hornstein Sanatorium and spend the day, November 24, 1966, with his wife. She often had expressed the wish for a mink coat, a wish Minski had ignored for some time.

"What does Rachel need a mink for—out there?" He had frequently asked me. "Give me one good reason and I'll buy it for her right now."

I couldn't give him a good reason. It had been Vanessa who gave him the excuse that he wanted.

"There aren't and there shouldn't be reasons for everything, Boris. You love Rachel. You have enough money. She'd like a mink. So give her a coat not for any reason but just out of love."

Minski had kissed her forehead.

"Good girl! One should always ask a woman. And soon we'll have our twenty-fifth wedding anniversary!"

Now Rachel's wish was going to be fulfilled. Satisfied, he glanced at the expensive coat on the shabby leather couch. He looked at Vanessa, wearing a black, off-the-shoulder cocktail dress, sitting at my desk, absorbed in composing a letter to Panos, a French dictionary beside her. Minski smiled, his eyes remaining serious as always. She intended to write only a brief letter—now she was filling the fifth sheet of blue airmail paper.

Minski's eyes narrowed as he looked through the one-way mirror into the club. Corabelle, closely resembling Vanessa, tall, blonde, blue-eyed, was dancing with Petra Schalke. The lesbian held the scantily clad girl close, a hungry expression on her hard face.

Corabelle was good-natured but not too bright. Whenever Vanessa was unable to work and Corabelle took over, Petra Schalke amused herself with the girl. Vanessa hoped that she would fall in love with Corabelle, but this hope proved to be in vain. As soon as Vanessa appeared again, Petra Schalke once again pursued her.

Corabelle's act with the python borrowed from a colleague had proceeded smoothly. Yet, performing a series of extremely lascivious poses in the nude, she had been somewhat nervous. Corabelle had been happy to return the snake to a suitcase in Vanessa's dressing room.

Minski looked into the dimly lit corner where Petra Schalke's friend, Tonio Prinz, sat. The bleached-blond dress designer with the dark-rimmed glasses, gold bracelets on his wrists, was sitting close to two young men, one blond, the other brown-haired. They couldn't have been twenty-one, but Minski had permitted them to enter. They were over eighteen and looked quite grown-up. They seemed to be new friends of the blond designer.

Tonio Prinz did most of the talking. The youths hardly spoke; they nodded, drank, allowed Tonio to touch and fondle them.

The brown-haired boy rose and headed for the toilets. Minski glanced at his watch: it was half-past two. Tonio Prinz placed his arm around the blond youth's shoulder. He placed one hand on the boy's knee. The blond boy did not move. Tonio's hand moved slowly higher as he talked. His hand met something long, firm and smooth. He seized it. The something in his hand felt cold and moved suddenly. Immediately thereafter a hissing sound came from underneath the table.

Tonio looked down. What he saw terrified him. He screamed, jumped up, swayed, fainted. His companion had also leaped to his feet. Petra Schalke and Corabelle screamed.

"For God's sake," Minski shouted, horrified. "What did that fag do now?" He hurried through the door into the bar. Vanessa ran into the corridor and pulled a lever. Bright light flooded the bar.

"The snake!" Petra Schalke screamed, fleeing in the direction of the dressing rooms. A bartender would not let her pass. A second bartender turned up. Now everyone was yelling and shouting. Corabelle had seized the python which was moving threateningly.

"Don't! Let me do it! You don't know how to do it!" she cried as the bartenders moved to help her.

Minski and Petra Schalke were kneeling beside the motionless dress designer. Minski rolled him over onto his back and slapped his face. He opened his eyes and color returned to his face. The blond youth was halfway to the dressing rooms when one of the bartender detectives noticed him.

"Hold it!" he yelled.

The boy ran; the detective followed. He caught up with him before the boy reached the dressing rooms and struck his neck with the edge of his hand. The boy crashed to the floor and groaned.

"Where is the other one?" Minski yelled.

"Yes, where is Detlev?" Tonio complained before he caught sight of the snake near him. Then he fainted again.

"Let him alone," the second detective said quickly. "He'll be all right. Was there another boy?"

"Yes," Minski answered. "Brown-haired. He just left a moment ago. I thought he had to take a leak."

The second officer ran toward the corridor. He returned shortly. "Through the window of number seven," he explained. "Door's open; so is the window. He took off."

"Number seven, that's my room," Vanessa cried.

"Then I know how the snake came out here," Minski said, furious. "Door open, window open. Cold draft. Remembered it was warmer in here. Goddamn mess. There he is again."

He looked at Tonio, who moved, groaned.

The detective who had struck the blond boy asked Tonio, "How long have you known the two boys?"

"Since today . . . they came to my salon."

"What are their names?"

"Detlev and Klaus."

"What else?"

"I don't know," the designer moaned, sitting up, staring at the python which had become calm under Corabelle's gentle hands. "Oh, God, I feel so sick. I beg of you, Manny, give me something to drink, quickly!"

Petra Schalke poured out a glass of champagne and handed it to him. As he drank, part of the champagne spilled over his midnight-blue tuxedo.

The first detective bent over and seized the blond youth by his lapels.

"What's your name, sonny?" he asked.

The boy clenched his teeth.

The officer shook him and pushed him roughly against the hat-check counter. The boy screamed.

"Watch it!"

There was fear in his voice.

"*What* did you say?" the detective said very softly. He looked at his colleague. They found what they expected to find underneath the hat-check counter. A metal box that ticked. (Later on we learned that it had been a small but efficient time bomb, set for 4 A.M.)

"If this explodes here there's not going to be much left of your club," the first officer said as he seized the box and ran out into the yard.

"Did you bring that in here?" the second man asked.

The boy was silent.

"Does anyone else live in this building?"

"No, there are only offices—but yes, there is a janitor!"

The other detective returned, ran to the telephone in our office and began to dial.

"I asked you: Did you bring this box in here?"

The youth remained silent.

"I'm dying," Tonio announced. "I'm dying, Manny. God help me, I'm dying."

Petra Schalke stroked him gently. Corabelle stroked the snake.

"If anyone had been here during the explosion he would probably have died, wouldn't he?" Vanessa asked.

"Very probably," the detective answered. To the blond youth he was holding he said, "You'll live to regret this, sonny."

Minski said, "And I was going to leave the mink coat here. Twenty-five thousand marks. And not yet insured."

The second detective said to the boy, "If you don't admit right now that you brought in this box you're going to be sorry."

The boy said, "That swine took off and let me hold the bag. That swine, that goddamn bastard."

"Your friend?"

"I'm not saying anything."

"We'll find out anyway. You might as well tell me."

"I won't." He straightened up. His face hardened.

"All right," the officer said and relaxed his grip on him—for a moment.

The boy tried to run. That was what the officer had expected. He seized his shoulder, turned him around and punched his face. The boy howled.

Tonio Prinz, still on the floor, also howled. "Manny, Manny, that's terrible, Manny."

The boy held his face.

The detective said, "You tried to escape. These people here are witnesses to that. Now, have you had enough or do I have to stop another try?"

The detective telephoning in our office was asking for the bomb squad and reinforcements. The youth suddenly slumped against the wall. "What's your name, sonny?"

Sobbing the boy answered, "Hans Eilers."

"Eilers? Is your father . . ."

The youth's face was contorted with hate. "Yes," he said, "My father is inspector in Treuwall."

". . . He said he was Inspector Eilers's son," Minski said breathlessly. He had talked for almost ten minutes without stopping. My brother had poured himself a couple of drinks. He was watching me thoughtfully.

"From Treuwall," Minski said, "Eilers. Do you know him?"

"Yes."

"Is he really with the police?"

"Yes."

"But how do you explain that?"

"I don't," I said. "I can't explain it."

My brother grinned—not a frightened grin. He stretched lazily, "You don't have to guard your answers so carefully, dear brother. Your friend is shouting so loudly I can hear every word. Besides, I know all about it."

"You do?"

"Certainly. Did you think the man in the leather coat came to pick me up to show me around Treuwall? I've found out a few things."

"Who's there with you?" Minski asked.

"My brother."

"Tell him to hang up," Werner demanded. "I have to talk to you."

"Listen, Boris, I have to hang up. My brother . . ."

"Something wrong?"

"Hm," I said.

"You can't talk?"

"No."

"God, what a mess. If you were here—they took the boy away. He's only eighteen. Listen, Richie, I'm afraid."

"So am I."

"Come on now," Werner said.

I spoke hurriedly. "I'll call you tomorrow. Perhaps I can come and we'll talk things over. I have an idea."

"That's enough now," my brother said, sharply.

"Good night, Boris," I said, and hung up.

I stared at Werner, who grinned and raised his glass to me. "*Santé*, mon petit frère!"

"You knew that . . ."

He nodded.

"A warning. At the right moment. So that you'll see that they mean business. Of course it was supposed to go off. These bottle babies made a mess of it. You were supposed to hear of it tomorrow morning. Well, you have your warning now. Imagine if Minski had stayed overnight. Or anyone else."

"Murder is amusing to your friends, eh?"

"I'm afraid so," Werner said. "And now we'll talk about you. You're going to get Delacorte out of jail or you'll end up there yourself."

"Right," I said. "But if I go you'll go too."

"I don't care," he replied. "I'm caught in an inescapable situation. I'm finished now. That's why I'm in the stronger position than you since I have no choice. Clear?"

"No. Who's blackmailing you? What's the reason?"

"I'll explain later. Do you agree that you must do what I ask of you or else I'll see that you go to jail . . . immediately?"

"I understand."

"You know that I can do that."

"I know that," I said, and poured myself another drink.

Actually I had always known that at some time or other Werner might blackmail me. He had taken his time. Now he was trying to collect.

337

Looking back, the whole story really began with Tiny in 1953. He had married Ellen, the blonde German girl, had become a regular army man living in army quarters outside Frankfurt. In 1953 he was already a well-known baritone who sang at shows and parties still "just for the hell of it," as he expressed it. By chance the director of the Berlin opera house heard him and offered to help him sing professionally. It was the start of Tiny's impressive career. His discovery and the circumstances leading up to it were the beginning of *Black*, my novel, the book my brother wrote about the experiences of a Negro soldier in Germany. It was made into a movie in 1956.

Tiny by then had enjoyed great success as Rigoletto, Yago, Papageno at the Städtische Oper, Berlin. He had bought a war-damaged house in the Grunewald. *Black* won great honors at the annual Berlin film festival for cast, technical staff and the script writer—Richard Mark.

I accepted the award and the twenty-thousand-mark prize from the Minister of the Interior, Schröder. One year later I accepted the Federal Literature Award for "meritorious services to humanity and furthering international understanding." The award was endowed with forty thousand marks. I accepted it in Darmstadt.

"Yes, you defrauded the state twice, Richie, my boy. Naturally I can prove that I have written all your recent books—and the script. I still have the manuscripts in my handwriting. Yes, I'm certain, you'd go to jail."

"Both of us," I said. For the past few hours I had had the feeling that the floor underneath me vibrated, swayed, that it might suddenly rise up, slip from under me, turn upside down, that I would fall into a void, forever falling.

"Both of us," my brother agreed. "In my case add another fifteen years to life."

"What did you do?" I asked.

"When Berlin was sealed off, isolated, I came into contact with a resistance group of press corps members. A few of the reporters had access to the shelters of the party bigwigs. There was a conspiracy to liquidate the leaders. When I had sufficient proof I informed security. Twenty-three men were hanged. Telephone wire was used for that execution. By order of the Führer. Security ordered me to make my report in writing—to make sure of me. The report did not fall into Russian but into German hands. Have you ever heard of the Spider organization?"

"Yes."

"The Spider has that report I made in 1945. The Spider has many such incriminating reports involving many people. Whenever it thinks it necessary it uses them. In my case, and pertaining to Delacorte, it thought it important enough."

Werner refilled our glasses.

"Not much ice left," he remarked casually. It was almost 3:30 A.M. It had begun to rain again. "You will understand that I have no desire to go to jail for even a short period of time—let alone for life. My explicit report of 1945 would be sufficient for any court."

"Since when have you been blackmailed?"

"For about the past six months," he drank. "You see, Delacorte was becoming grandiose, impossible to tolerate. Some people joined together and tried to do away with him. Unfortunately, the effort misfired. It would have saved us a lot of grief. Now Delacorte will presumably try to persuade his enemies to get him out of jail by demonstrating that otherwise he will tell all he knows about them. He already took care of Fegesack. To demonstrate that he can deliver. Well, Richie, my friend, you will find that you'll have many willing helpers. You and I and the Spider."

"Just a moment," I said. "What was your original assignment?"

"To prepare Delacorte's kidnaping. I was eminently suited for it. I knew Lillian. It was well known. I was to meet her, pursue her, be seen with her. Being seen in Treuwall was reasonable then and would cover up any business I had here."

"Your love for Lillian was an act, then?"

"Certainly."

"Really?"

"Word of honor." He laughed. "You talked to her—in the hospital. Did *she* believe that I wanted to marry her again?"

"She thinks you're lying, that there are other reasons for your newly discovered love."

"Smart girl."

"Then you were in Treuwall yesterday."

"Of course."

"And those two witnesses who saw you and then couldn't identify you?"

"They were intimidated." He shrugged his shoulders. "Those gentlemen employ very effective methods. I hope that you'll never find out personally."

"I'm experiencing them now."

"You're lucky that *I'm* talking to you. They wouldn't talk so much. They would *do* something. They've done a lot during the past few hours, haven't they? And that's only a beginning."

"What did you do in Treuwall?"

"Nothing. Everything went wrong."

"What were you supposed to do then?"

"They had found out that poisoned Armagnac had been sent to Delacorte."

"Who sent it?"

"They didn't tell me that. I assume it was a joint venture. They think so too."

"Who's 'they'?"

"Several men—not always the same—I don't know their names. They blackmailed me. Showed me my hand-written reports." He spoke seriously, nervously. I believed everything he said. Not for a moment did I think that he might be lying. "The Spider wants Delacorte out of Germany. He has resolutely refused to leave. Citing the poisoned Armagnac as an example, I was to impress on Delacorte the danger of his position."

"Then perhaps the Spider did send the liquor?"

"That's what I thought at first. But they wouldn't have made any mistakes. They would have known that Delacorte was going to leave earlier for the medical convention. Also that Lillian was returning sooner. But nothing worked out. Delacorte was no longer there; the liquor hadn't arrived yet; neither had Lillian."

"Why did you have a suitcase and your clothes in our car?"

"I've had those with me for some time. Since working on Delacorte. And in case the police ask questions, I could always say that I was on my may to Eckernförde."

My brother owned a cottage there. He often went there to write.

"You can imagine how I felt when your . . . your stripper called that night to tell me that Lillian had poisoned herself."

"It was obvious when you arrived at the hospital," I said. "It still is."

"But now it has nothing to do with Lillian any more. It's hell, Richie. I wouldn't blackmail my brother if I knew any other way out. Don't grin so idiotically, man! Or go ahead and grin. In any case you've got to do what I demand of you. I can't. The police are suspicious. I'm sure I'm being watched. You're clean. You'll be the last person they'll suspect. Paradin is your friend. It will be easy for you to get Delacorte out."

"And how am I supposed to do that?"

"You will be instructed."

"And that's all? I'm just to get him out of jail?"

"That's all."

"But you say they want him out of Germany?"

"Once he's out of jail I take over."

"And I'm in the clear?"

"Right. The moment Delacorte is hidden in a safe place, you'll receive the manuscripts of your novels from me. I'm not going to get my statement until Delacorte is in . . . in a safe place."

"And who guarantees that you tell me the truth? That you will give me the manuscripts when you say you will?"

"Just think for a moment. If I don't you would probably inform the police at a time when Delacorte is still in Germany. I'd be digging my own grave. Besides, the Spider insists that you'll be given the manuscripts. Too dangerous not to give them to you."

It made sense. Nevertheless I said, "You guarantee it then?"

"I guarantee nothing. There's always the possibility of something going wrong. I promise. I can only guarantee what happens if you don't help me. Listen, if I have to tell those guys tomorrow that you refuse to go along, then you and your friend Minski won't live to see another week. I hope you believe me, especially in view of what happened to Ericksen and that idiot, Dr. Hess."

There was no reason not to believe him. "Who stabbed Hess? The attendant who wasn't one?"

"Presumably."

"Why?"

"I heard Hess wanted to quit after you'd escaped him." He looked at me searchingly. "Now, what do you say?"

"If I'm caught—"

"You won't be."

"Suppose something goes wrong? After all your mission in Treuwall was foiled too. Then what?"

"Then you're out of luck," he answered impatiently. "If you don't go along with it now you're finished right now." He repeated, "So what do you say?"

I picked up my drink, sipped at it slowly, thinking all the while.

Under no circumstances must I be a party to any plan

which would enable Delacorte, a mass murderer, to escape.

Nothing must happen to Lillian, Minski, Vanessa or me.

Could I confide in Minski? He was smart; he might devise a plan. But I can't talk to him now. Werner demands my decision now.

The immediate step must be this: pretend that I accept Werner's demand to help Delacorte escape from prison. Having done my part, Werner will then turn over his manuscripts to me. Then I shall have to find some way to prevent Delacorte's escape and thus create the impression that my brother had failed. The Spider had to be convinced of that. Werner's incriminating statement would then be exposed; he would be tried and, according to him, probably convicted for fifteen years to life.

At the moment it was only wishful thinking, but I would find a way once I had time to think—and provided I had some luck.

"Well?" Werner asked.

To be convincing I must not agree too hastily.

"That's impossible, Werner! I . . . I just can't do that!"

"Then you'll go to jail."

I jumped up. I paced the floor, I cajoled, I begged, I threatened to inform the police of both his and my wrongdoings.

He went to the telephone, dialed, only to have me knock the receiver from his hand at the last moment.

We drank.

We argued.

He rose, about to leave. "All right. You won't help. You'll see soon enough what'll happen next." I forced myself to wait until he had opened the door before saying—

"Wait!"

He turned. His forehead was beaded with perspiration. So was mine. It dripped, ran into my eyes, stung.

"Yes?"

I said, "I'll do it."

I hoped that I had been convincing. I searched his face but it was smooth, as expressionless as a mask.

"Naturally you are going to try to betray me," he said. "You can shake your head all you want; of course, you'll try. I would too. You merely agreed to win time. Time to think. Time to consult with Minski. Save yourself the trouble. There's no way out. Not for you, not for me, not for Minski if you should decide to confide in him."

I was silent.

"Naturally they want to make sure of you. Just in case. For the period when Delacorte is out of prison but not yet out of Germany—the time when I'm required to perform my part of the bargain."

"Make sure of me? What do you mean?"

"You are to buy a small tape recorder."

"I have one."

"Good. You will buy tapes on which you will record everything that has happened, is happening, everything you have done, are going to do. Everything, you understand? You will hand the tapes over to me at regular intervals. If you try to trick me, if you don't do it properly, I'll inform the police. Don't forget, I can't get more than life—something I'm resigned to, more or less. This is really only a last attempt. Clear so far?"

I nodded.

"A man is going to contact you. You will do whatever he says. From now on he is your boss. From now on you will lead a double life. You work for this man but you continue to live as if he didn't exist. You have a reason for being here: Lillian. You have a reason to go to Frankfurt: your club. This is extremely important. Your friendship with Paradin and your connections with the police are very useful. Take good care of them."

"What are you going to do?"

"I don't know as yet. I shall receive my orders also

within the next few hours. We're in the same boat, Richie, as always the inseparable brothers." He grinned, a grin of uncertainty and apprehension.

"And it came to pass when they were in the field, that Cain rose up against Abel his brother and slew him. . . ."
Where is the field? Where shall I find it?

Just now prison officer Stalling came to my cell. "Adenauer is dead!" he cried. Today is April 19, 1967. Stalling told me that Adenauer will be given the most impressive state funeral since Bismarck. One of our greatest statesmen, he gave our hated and despised, war-ravaged, wretched country a new prosperity, made it a respected member of the nations of the free world.

"And you're quite sure that it is cold enough in the winter at Lake Maggiore to wear a mink coat?" Rachel Minski asked uncertainly. "It would be terrible if I couldn't wear it now that I have one."

"You can wear it, Rachel," Minski said. "Besides, the wealthy people go to St. Moritz for the winter. If you like we could go there too."

"Are there many people at St. Moritz?"

"Well, yes," Minski said, uneasily.

"Then I'll be afraid to . . ."

"The professor will be there, too!"

Rachel nodded, reassured. "Yes, if he is there I'll be all right."

"You see." Minski smiled his sad smile whenever he looked at Rachel; other times he appeared troubled. Always he tried to give Rachel the impression that he was happy.

They walked slowly through the park of the Hornstein Sanatorium. This park had been ablaze with the colors of a bright summer when he had first come here in 1948.

Eighteen years ago.

Rachel had partially regained her mental health although she was still unable to live away from "her" Professor Mohn. She was vivacious, cheerful; she dressed fashionably. But never having regained her normal weight, she looked years older than forty-eight. She walked carefully at her husband's side below leafless trees, over wet, rotting leaves, along narrow paths, snow-covered and frozen in places. A cold east wind blew on this clear morning under a gray sky. Blackbirds circled above Hornstein, screeching.

Rachel's fine, white hair had been set and given a blue rinse. The hairdresser came regularly to the sanatorium. She wore a little makeup on this, her wedding anniversary.

"My mink coat," she said, gently stroking the soft fur.

"A very beautiful coat," Minski said.

"It was probably terribly expensive," Rachel said.

"Hm," Minski mumbled.

Rachel had given him a present too: a cushion. She had spent hours embroidering Minski's favorite butterfly, *Vanessa atalanta*, in petit point, copied from an illustration of a book Professor Mohn had lent her. Minski had been moved to tears.

"Boris, when are we leaving Germany?"

"Soon," Minski smiled at Rachel, thinking worriedly of the events of the past two days. "As soon as Professor Mohn retires we'll go to Switzerland."

"I think we ought to go soon," Rachel said.

Minski nodded. He recalled the time bomb.

"I've never been in Switzerland, Boris."

"You'll like it there. It's beautiful, Rachel. And you're going to put on some weight. Change of climate."

"I'm eating as much as I can, Boris, but it doesn't seem to make any difference. I'm still skinny."

"Here, yes," he replied. "But in Switzerland——"

"Buon giorno. Come sta?" Rachel asked.

"What's that?" Minski asked.

"Grazie, non c'é male! E te?"

"What does that mean?"

" 'How are you?' " Rachel interpreted, beaming. " 'Fine, thank you. And you?' I'm learning Italian. Every day. Professor Mohn gave me books. I'm preparing myself for Lake Maggiore. I've already learned a lot. I'll be able to talk to people there. What are you going to do?"

"They speak German there, too."

"Many speak French. I know how to speak French. Now I'll learn Italian. Would you like to hear some more?"

Minski nodded, surprised and happy.

"Guido va nel gabinetto da bagno e prende una doccia fredda."

"Rachel, that's enough! It's scary! You know that much?"

"I know more!" Rachel said, proudly. "Much more. Let's go to Switzerland, Boris. I want to go to the Lago Maggiore."

"And just imagine, Richie, she's already learning Italian. She's happy. She's looking forward to leaving here. Of course, I was very careful not to show how worried I've been." He nervously paced through the office of the Strip, grimaced and breathed noisily as always when he was upset. "It's so peaceful in that sanatorium, Richie, so quiet—a paradise. And here we are in this awful mess. I'm curious to see what'll happen next."

You'll know soon enough, I reflected sadly.

"Such peace, such quiet . . . when I walked through the garden with my Rachel I—God forgive me—I wished for a second that I were meshuggana too. They're happier than we are, Richie, believe me. Naturally, the professor's influence cannot be denied. He had dinner with us. A lovely, festive dinner. He's a wonderful man, Richie. He and Rachel conversed in Italian. I didn't understand one word. He says her pronunciation is excellent. Well, she always had a talent for languages, even in Kamenets-

Podolski. And now we're in this mess. We'll have to be especially careful now."

Again and again Minski stopped before the old leather couch on which he had placed Rachel's petit point butterfly cushion and straightened it. It was almost four o'clock in the afternoon. When it was quiet we could hear the detectives walk around and talk to each other. Four nice young men were guarding the Strip around the clock. They had also been of great help to me with the reporters.

I had arrived at 3 P.M. when a half-dozen newspapermen and a pretty girl who had been waiting outside the club surprised me before I could disappear through the rear entrance. The press had heard of the aborted time-bomb attack on the Strip on Frankfurt police radio. Police headquarters there had also informed the press that night of the arrest of the wanted war criminal Delacorte who, under the name Kamploh, had previously been director of the hospital in Treuwall. My name had not been mentioned, but the first reporter who arrived in Treuwall, upon questioning the hotel staff at the Kaiserhof, had soon found out my part in the affair.

I had been unable to avoid the journalists and photographers of newspapers, magazines, television and newsreels. Although I refused to answer their questions, they photographed me, Paradin and his colleagues when they arrived at the hotel, and my brother; they followed me to the hospital when I visited Lillian; they followed me later to the airport at Hanover when I flew to Frankfurt. The midday papers already showed those pictures and reported the story which, meanwhile, had been reported by every radio station.

The reporters who had quickly surrounded me outside the Strip also took pictures. The connection between euthanasia—mass murder and the strip-tease milieu was just what they needed. I was pulled here and there by the reporters, who grabbed at my sleeves; they shouted and yelled offers for an exclusive interview. I yelled just as loud for them to go to the devil and, yelling, mouth wide open, fist raised in a threatening gesture, they photographed me. I seized one man's camera and threw it to the ground. Had the detectives watching the club not come to my aid I would have become embroiled in a fist-fight. They pulled me into the club. The reporters stayed. Some of them left to find Vanessa, of whom there were large pictures in the club. I had called Vanessa immediately.

"Let them come, Richie!" she had said. "I've been waiting for just such an opportunity! I'll tell them an interesting story—I, Britt Rending!"

"And why do you want to tell them that story?"

"I hope it'll finish off my dear father, naturally."

"And Panos? You just wrote to him. Do you want him to read about your work in the Strip? It would be better if you just gave the reporters a few photographs."

"Oh!" Her voice had sounded high and shocked. "I never thought of that. Darn, what a situation. It could have been the opportunity . . ."

"Well, not all good things come in one package. Then you'll throw those guys out, eh?"

"Of course, Richie. I, I want to thank you . . ."

"It's too bad," I had said. "Suppose it had happened two days earlier?"

"Human beings have little luck," Vanessa had replied.

Minski had entered the club without being recognized by the reporters outside. I had listened to him talk about his visit with Rachel until he had exhausted the subject. Now, I thought, he will be responsive to my problem.

Automatically the ventilator switched on and Minski yelled above the noise, "Now, what's up? You said you didn't think that anything else would happen here."

"That's right," I yelled back. For the fiftieth time I resolved to buy a new ventilator.

"Nothing will happen if—"

"If?"

A minute later the ventilator had switched off. The ugly, shabby little office was suddenly quiet.

"You won't like what I have to tell you, Boris."

Minski looked at me, serious.

"More trouble," he said, resignedly. "Great. I should have known. So, what is it?"

The telephone began to ring.

I jumped.

"Your nerves are really shot, aren't they?" Minski said as he picked up the receiver. "Vanessa," he said, "yes, dear, what is it?"

He listened, praised her for throwing out the reporters. I sat behind my old desk, the palms of my hands moist. The ringing telephone had vividly, frighteningly brought back the memory of the one which had rung this morning in the hospital in Treuwall. Carrying a large bouquet of red roses, I had gone to visit Lillian. Opposite her room, in a small nurses' lounge adjacent to the service elevator in which Dr. Hess and the huge attendant had taken me to the mortuary, sat a gray-haired, portly, pipe-smoking detective guarding Lillian's door. His name was Ring, he told me; two hours ago he had relieved his colleague of the night watch.

"How is Frau Lombard?"

"Our doctor is very satisfied with her progress. He examined her an hour ago. But, if possible, she should not become excited. We have told her that Professor Kamploh has been arrested—for political reasons, his Nazi past. Nothing about euthanasia, nothing about Delacorte. The doctor asks you not to mention it to her either."

"All right. How did she take the news of Kamploh's arrest?"

"Remarkably well. She seemed strangely relieved. Isn't that peculiar? After all, he was her lover for two years. Oh, excuse me. How tactless of me. I didn't think that you—"

"Forget it. You have to understand—Frau Lombard

was afraid of Kamploh; she thought he wanted to poison her and she was going to leave him."

He gave me an odd look.

"Of course," he agreed, "one has to remember that. Besides, who of us knows how a woman might react, right?"

I didn't like his answer.

"What do you mean?"

"Just what I said. We men will never . . ." he began, when the telephone began to ring. He answered, then handed me the receiver. "It's for you. Your partner from Frankfurt. Herr Minski."

He went to the door to continue watching Lillian's door. I stood near the window of the small room. It was raining steadily, a cold, thin rain. Low dark clouds. I saw meadows, fields, the dense forest at the rear of the hospital.

Apprehensively I said, "This is Mark." It seemed improbable to me that Minski would call me here.

It wasn't Minski.

I heard a voice I had heard once before but I couldn't remember where. "When I talk to you now you will address me as Boris once every so often or we're through before we've begun. Understand?"

"Hello, Boris," I said, reflecting that their idea to call me here was ingenious. It would have been too dangerous to call at the hotel. It also demonstrated that I was under constant surveillance.

"Your brother instructed you to follow our orders, has he not?"

"Yes, he told me that."

"I assume you don't know where the Black Gate is?"

"No."

"That is a prehistoric cairn in the heath. South of the town. Very desolate. The country is very flat, easy to observe. A road leads past it. Buy yourself a map. Leave the car on the road. Walk to the cairn. Understood?"

"Yes."

"Yes, *Boris*, goddamn it!"

"Yes, Boris."

"Be there tonight at nine. You will come alone and, of course, without any weapons."

"Yes, Boris."

"You're being watched at all times. Don't try any funny business. Don't discuss this with anyone. You've been warned. There won't be another warning. Understand?"

"Every word, Boris."

"Apropos Boris, you're going to see Boris in Frankfurt today, aren't you?"

"I don't know yet."

"Don't talk nonsense. Of course you know. We've taken it into consideration that you're going to confide in him. He's also being watched. So go ahead, talk to him, confide in him. As smart as he is—this time he won't be able to find a way out." I had to admire the man's nerve. He was taking his time, perfectly unconcerned. I know that guy—I know that voice. If only I could remember where I had heard it once before.

"Take the same plane you took yesterday. Lufthansa. At thirteen-thirty hours. Then you can also take the same plane back at eighteen-thirty from Frankfurt. From the airport you leave directly for the Black Gate."

"Then what do I do?"

"You'll see. Remember all that is at stake. For you, your Lillian and your friend Minski."

I didn't answer.

"Did you understand me?"

"Yes, Boris."

"Fine. Until nine then. Be on time. And say so long properly to me."

"So long, Boris."

The connection ended. I replaced the receiver.

"Your friend had a lot to tell you, didn't he?" the portly detective asked, amiably.

"Yes," I answered.

"About the time bomb last night?"

"That's right. About the time bomb."

His smile was friendly.

"You could go to Frau Lombard now," Detective Ring suggested, removing the wrapper and handing me the roses. "I'll call a nurse and ask her to bring a vase."

"It was all nonsense. Stupid nonsense."

"I don't understand."

"What I once said to you. That we cannot live together. That we cannot be happy together," Lillian explained. She was still very pale, but her face had lost the yellowish-white color; her eyes were again dark and shiny. Her hair was combed, her lips showed a trace of lipstick. A sure sign that she was feeling better. I had prayed to God to protect her. Now, looking at her, I thanked him, gratefully, piously. Sickening how religious I can be at certain times.

"Of course it was nonsense," I agreed. "Now you can forget it. It's all over now."

"Is it? Really? Can you forget all I've done to you?"

I nodded.

"That I married Werner?"

"We both know why you did," I said. "Besides, it didn't work out."

"Is he still here, Richie?" And when I nodded she went on, "I don't want to see him." Her voice rose, her eyes grew even larger. "I don't want to see him under any circumstances! Not here, not anywhere, never!"

"Lillian," I said, placatingly, surprised and reassured by this sudden outburst. "You don't have to see him. You don't have to see anyone you don't want to see. That includes Kamploh."

"Kamploh," she repeated tonelessly. A long silence. I heard the rain falling on the window panes and thought of the ordeal before me tonight in the heath, at nine o'clock. I was frightened but managed to conceal my fear. "Kamploh," she repeated again. "I was a war criminal's mistress. That's what he was, wasn't he?"

"It seems that way," I answered vaguely. "That's why he was arrested."

"He won't go free, will he?"

"I'm sure he won't."

"I'm afraid of him after what he did."

"What do you mean?"

"The Armagnac."

"Ah, yes. It's not that certain that he did that, you know. It could be that someone else tried to poison *him.*"

"Who?"

"I've no idea who. One of the many people who hated him because he blackmailed them. You said yourself that he exerted power over many people. Perhaps several of them had joined together and—"

"I don't believe that, Richie."

"The police seem to think so."

The door opened.

Detective Ring was followed by a nurse, who placed the roses, now in a vase, on a small table near the bed. She was friendly and admired the flowers.

"Yes," Lillian said, touching my hand, "they are beautiful."

The nurse and the officer left.

"How much longer will you have to stay here?" I asked.

"A few days, the doctor said. Just to make sure. Not much longer. Will I still have to be guarded?"

"I should think so."

"I wonder why?"

Yes, why? Delacorte was in jail. What reason could Paradin have to leave the detective here? I decided to ask him.

"Do you object to a guard?"

"No, I feel safer this way. I'm just wondering what the police are thinking."

"The situation is probably still confusing even though Kamploh is in jail. They'll want to protect you after all that has happened."

"When I leave here, will they still watch me?"

"I don't think so." But I did think so.

"A few more days here. Then what'll I do, Richie?"

What would be in a few more days? Perhaps in a few more days I would be behind bars. Perhaps I would be dead, yet I said easily, "Then you'll come to me—after you've picked up your things from the villa."

"Come to you in Frankfurt?"

I nodded.

"Richie, is anything wrong? You look troubled. Is there something that bothers you?"

"No." I said. "On the contrary, I'm thinking how happy I am that we'll be together again. A sentimental thought."

"Dear Richie," she said. "I'll be a good wife to you. I swear I'll be a good wife to you." She grasped my hand and placed it on her breast.

Waves of fear engulfed me again and again whenever the thought of that telephone conversation came to mind. I thought of my old nurse when I was a child.

Think of something beautiful, she had always advised.

Quickly, eagerly I said, "You know, we're not going to stay in Frankfurt. We're leaving Germany."

"Soon?"

"Yes, soon."

"Where do you intend to go?"

"Switzerland. Lake Maggiore. Minski is going, too. We've planned this for quite some time. We have enough money, don't worry. We'll live a good life in Switzerland."

"At Lake Maggiore?"

"Yes. Don't you want to go there?"

"I want to go wherever you want to go, Richie," Lillian said. "How lovely. Lake Maggiore. When do you think it will be?"

"Soon. Next year. Perhaps next summer. It depends a

bit on the political developments here. But in the fall at the latest. Before January 1968. Because of the tax situation."

I was amazed how easily those words came. Who could say now if I would ever reach Switzerland? Or that my plan—which so far was merely a confusion of distorted thoughts—would succeed? And *if* I could free Delacorte —was it not reasonable to expect that my brother would not return the manuscripts until he was sure that Delacorte had actually left the country? Wasn't that sufficient reason to compel me to inform Paradin and the police *at once?* Even if I could prevent the escape and trick Werner somehow, the consequence would still be a trial. A trial at which my guilt would be forgiven magnanimously and only my brother punished? Or rather both of us? Even if I were to receive only a light sentence wouldn't the Spider then take revenge on me?

Such thoughts kept me in turmoil, relieved occasionally by a momentary unconcern. I felt the excitement and desperation, mingled with hope, that a gambler feels, fearful of losing, expectant of winning.

"I would love to be in Switzerland." Lillian's voice held longing. "With you. In the warm sun, near the water. Far, far away from all this here."

"We will be there soon," I assured her, thinking of the Black Gate. "Very soon. Just believe in me, Lillian."

And it was at this time that Boris Minski was describing the new life they would lead at Lake Maggiore to his wife Rachel in the garden of the Hornstein Sanatorium.

I had left my car in the hotel garage for a checkup, gone to the hospital and returned to the hotel by taxi. I bought a map of Treuwall in the hotel lobby. One of the clerks informed me that Paradin had left a message for me to call him, room 412.

As soon as he heard my voice he asked me to come up.

"But I'm going to Frankfurt."

"That's just why. It will only take a moment."

"All right. I'll be there in a second."

I asked the clerk: "Is my brother in?"

He looked at the key board.

"No, he's out, Herr Mark."

"Did he leave a message?"

"No, I'm sorry, no message."

The map of Treuwall I had bought I stuffed into one of the inside pockets of my coat before going to Paradin.

His suite, a confusion of folders and official papers, was thick with cigarette smoke. Eilers and a young man with blond, unruly hair rose from their chairs while Paradin, limping, came toward me to shake my hand.

"So nice of you to come so soon, Richie. How is Frau Lombard?"

"Fine, thank you," I answered somewhat irritated by the presence of the two other men. Eilers's face was ashen, fatigued, with black circles under his eyes. The ashtray before him was filled to overflowing. His handshake was feeble in contrast to the blond man's.

"Olsen," he introduced himself. The young man had a pleasant, open face with intelligent gray eyes.

"Hermann Olsen is one of the men with whom I have worked several times before. Take a good look at him, Richie. From now on he is going to keep an eye on you."

"I'm going to be your shadow," Olsen said, winking at me.

"Glad to meet you."

"From now on you'll notice me frequently." He turned toward Paradin. "Do you still need me here, chief?"

"No, thank you, you can leave now."

Olsen raised one hand in a gesture of leave-taking to all of us and left.

"So you're taking a plane to Frankfurt, Richie?" Paradin asked.

"Yes," I answered. "I have to talk to Minski about the club. He's worried."

"Well, that's understandable," Eilers commented, tonelessly.

"Are you taking the car to Hanover?" Paradin asked.

"Yes."

"Then would you mind taking Eilers with you? He also has to go to Frankfurt."

"Yes, of course."

"Thank you," Eilers said, his head bent low.

"Oh, yes, of course your son—" I began and broke off quickly. "I'm so sorry. Please forgive me."

"It's all right." He said. The large man seemed close to tears.

"We can leave whenever you're ready," I said.

"I have lots of time now," Eilers said so softly I could hardly hear what he said.

"What does that mean?"

"It means that the chief of police has relieved Eilers of his duties for the present. It would have been better if you had asked for special leave," he said to Eilers. "You've been overworked as it was and now that your son is in jail and your wife left you . . ."

"Your wife left you?" I asked, shocked.

Eilers averted his head.

"Yes," Paradin continued, "he has had a very hard time of it, poor fellow. That's why I asked you to take him to Hanover, to Frankfurt. I know that you have your own problems, but I don't want Eilers to be alone during the next few hours. He likes you. I have to remain here. Perhaps you could look after him a little, Richie?"

"Certainly," I said, feeling keenly that I was contemptible, a traitor trusted by his friends.

Jochen, Prison Officer Stalling's eighteen-year-old son, commented on his father's decision to join the NPD. "My old man is getting stupider and stupider. It's incredible. Now he's actually joined this shit party."

His friend replied, "One really must be ashamed to have such a father."

"I am ashamed," Jochen had answered. "The stupid ass. Well, I let him know what I think of him. He never says anything more about my behavior in school. He doesn't want to upset my mother by arguing with me, he says! Of course it's only his guilty conscience.

"If I had any money I'd have left home long ago. I've had it with my old man and my mother. She's always sick, always in bed, always complaining. I stay out of the way as much as I can, but having parents like that sure is a drag!"

His friend repeated Jochen's views at his next argument with his parents. They promptly called Officer Stalling, who told me that both had come to no conclusion on how to deal with such impudent louts as their sons. Stalling had begged Jochen's friend's parents not to inform his ill wife about their son's vicious talk.

Hans Eilers was well-matched with Jochen in his attitude toward his father. He had despised him from his childhood days. Now he also hated him.

"My old man? That decrepit old fool! He makes me sick with his eternal anti-Nazi prattle. I just can't stand listening to it any longer. I'd rather he croaked today than tomorrow. Mother would get a pretty good pension. Not a fortune but we could live on it until I'm able to make some money. We have the house. And there is quite a substantial life insurance policy. He's a shit-bag, my old man! That antifascist freak!"

Inspector Eilers, fifty-one years old in 1967, had lost his family and his closest associates during the Third Reich. His father, uncle and friends were executed in 1943 as members of a resistance group. Two brothers died at the eastern front; sister and mother victims of air raids on

Hamburg; a cousin executed for "undermining and impairing military discipline."

Eilers, who had been fighting at the eastern front as a soldier in 1942, was arrested shortly after his father. Although his membership in the resistance group could not be proved—he had never been involved—he was dishonorably discharged from the army and sentenced to fifteen years imprisonment at hard labor. He was confined in the Hamburg-Wandsbeck penitentiary until 1945. The prisoners there were forced to remain in their cells during air raids. Some screamed with fright when bombs exploded, some became insane, others were injured or killed by the concussion of exploding bombs, many died when the jail was hit. Eilers survived but had to spend a year in a mental institution, where doctors treated his shattered nerves.

In 1947 he married Carla Zantow, a nurse working in the sanatorium situated near Lüneburg. Carla's parents had left her a beautiful house in Treuwall. Eilers loved the heath; he no longer wanted to return to Hamburg. He joined the criminal police in Treuwall. His wife bore him a son in 1948. Four years later Eilers was promoted to inspector. At this time he was already aware of the many important Nazis living openly in Treuwall, secure from prosecution. He made it his mission to rid the town of "those Nazis who are setting the trend," yet his efforts were unsuccessful.

Eilers was a good officer, respected by his superiors— one reason why his embittered and persistent talk about the "old and the new brown pestilence" was usually tolerated. After all, the poor fellow had had a rough time of it. . . .

In the town he had the reputation of a crank, though one who could be pitied. His social life dwindled; he didn't mind. His family was enough, though his wife suffered from her husband's self-imposed isolation. Since he had acquired the reputation of an argumentative eccentric, his wife, too, was generally avoided by Treuwall's citizens. His son, for the first year in school, also suffered.

"All the boys in school say you're a Communist, Daddy. What's a Communist?"

"I can't explain that to you. You're still too little. Besides, I'm not a Communist."

"But their parents say so too!"

Eilers brought up the subject during the following PTA meeting. The parents were indignant and disavowed little Hans's assertion. As a consequence Hans was beaten unmercifully by his schoolmates because he had told on them "so he'll remember."

Hans remembered. He never again told at home whatever he heard in school and elsewhere about his father the complainer, the Red, the slanderer, the kook—who, after all, had once been in a "funny farm"—the fool, the mudslinger, the blackguard, the poor old fellow. When Hans was nine he said with firm conviction, "So what if he is my father. My father is an asshole!"

From then on he was left alone, even pitied, an attitude he enjoyed.

Meanwhile, Carla realized that she no longer loved her husband. She knew that he was right in what he said. She knew that he and his family and his friends had suffered during the Third Reich. But she could no longer bear to listen to it. She simply could not! Yet she had to.

Eilers, at last, had found a man who shared his point of view: Inspector Lansing who had been transferred to Treuwall from Hanover. Lansing hated Nazis even more than Eilers.

"And yet the Poles murdered his father. He said so himself. It's a disgrace, that's what it is!" was the general opinion in Treuwall.

Lansing did not care. He knew what was being said. He had no family, he was alone. He often came to visit at Eilers's invitation, not his wife's.

Eilers's son, afraid of his father, vented his rage on his

mother. He was insolent, became a poor student and, to prove that he was no sissy in spite of such a father, became the leader of a group of boys always scheming new mischief.

Eilers repeatedly was called to school because of his son's misdeeds. Repeatedly he was forced to apologize, make good the damage his son had caused.

"What kind of a son can a man like that have, after all?" many in Treuwall asked. His wife heard the gossip. She was deeply grieved.

"That poor woman," everyone said and continued to gossip.

Lansing and Eilers often talked through the night, their subject politics. Lansing brought books to Hans on the Third Reich, telling him urgently of its injustices, the crimes it had committed, crimes of which Lansing's father, too, was guilty. But Hans already saw Lansing's father in the glorified light of a grand hero who had died a martyr's death.

When he was fourteen Hans was eager to enter a boarding school. There were three in the vicinity of Treuwall, in the heath, but his father refused. Hans painted swastikas on the walls of the school, was caught—because he intended to be caught. Eilers was asked to either remove the boy from school (in which case the entire unpleasant incident would be hushed up) or have his son prosecuted. Hans was thereupon sent to the boarding school, away from his hated home. His mother, distressed, reproached her husband for driving her son away.

Hans became a model student, liked by teachers and his contemporaries at the boarding school. He managed always to contrive a new excuse not to have to go home on holidays and vacations.

When Eilers mentioned it to the director of the school, he told him, "Dear Herr Eilers, perhaps you ought to ask yourself the possible cause for your son's attitude? After all there must be a reason for not wanting to go home."

Eilers remained silent—conscious of guilt for the first time.

The showdown came during the night of November 23, 1966, after Eilers had been informed of his son's arrest in Frankfurt.

"That's impossible!" Carla cried. "How could he have done that? How could he have left the school?"

"I don't know. In any case, he's in jail. That's a fine son we have," Eilers said, his eyes red with fatigue and showing suppressed rage. "A murderer . . . within a hair's breadth."

"And who made him like that?" Carla suddenly exploded, expressing the accumulated bitterness of many years. "You! You with your constant anti-Nazi talk with which you also destroyed our marriage."

"Carla!"

"Yes, you did! Do you think I've kept my mouth shut all these years because I shared your point of view? You drove my son away! He couldn't stand it at home, that's why he wanted to go to a boarding school! I'm all alone, too, and it's all your fault, yours! Yours! Yours!"

"Have you lost your mind? How you speak to me. We've arrested one of the greatest Nazi criminals today and you—"

"Nazi criminals!" she imitated him, her hair disheveled, her face distorted with hate. "That's all you're interested in! I'll tell you something! It wasn't that man you arrested today who made Hans what he is! It was you! You're a madman," she shrieked.

Eilers slapped her face. She fell back. Then she said, "That's it. I'm going to get a divorce."

"Yes, yes," he said.

"I'm serious!"

"Yes, yes," he repeated. "I have to go back to headquarters now. And tomorrow I'll go to Frankfurt to see what I can do to help that no-good son of mine. I'm sorry I slapped you but you provoked me." He looked at her. She averted her head. He left.

He telephoned an hour later. There was no answer. When Eilers returned home the house was deserted, the rooms in disorder, closets open, some clothing strewn around. In the kitchen he found a note.

> *I'm going to stay with my sister in Hamburg until the divorce is final. Don't bother to contact me. I shall never return to you.*
>
> *Carla*

"I telephoned her there this morning," Eilers said on the plane taking us to Frankfurt. He had talked and smoked incessantly on our drive from Treuwall to Hanover, then in the plane. He looked haggard, exhausted. I knew so much of Eilers's life but could not help him. Neither could he help me. It would have been diverting had I now unburdened my heart.

"She said she was seeing a lawyer today. What can I do now, Herr Mark?"

"Nothing, I'm very much afraid."

Minski was chewing his lower lip, shaking his head persistently. I was sitting on the old leather couch, looking at him. I had told him everything. He had listened without interrupting once.

"No," he finally said. "No, Richie, you cannot do this thing." His voice was friendly but very decided. "Even if your brother blackmails you ten times over you cannot do what he demands of you."

"But then he'll go to the police—"

"And you go to jail. Yes. Or you'll help a man, who has murdered thousands, to escape. Two different things entirely. You know I'm not a moralist but this is impossible for any decent person to do."

"It's easy for you to talk," I said. "You're not in danger. You don't have to face the prospect of going to jail. It's all new and unfamiliar to you. Up to now you didn't even know that my brother had written my books."

"Of course, I've known," Minski replied. "Do you think I'm completely stupid? A writer who doesn't write a single book since his brother began to write again and becomes my partner in managing a bar. What do you take me for?"

"Well, if you knew, then why didn't you ever mention it?"

"Because I like you, Richie." Minski's mouth smiled while his eyes remained sad and serious as always. "Because I didn't want to embarrass you. Perhaps you hadn't noticed. I'm a man with a tender heart, deep-felt emotions. That's why I tell you you cannot help in Delacorte's escape. I would never be able to talk to you again if you did."

I went to the shelf and poured myself a stiff drink. I drank and paced the floor in the office.

"Then what do you advise me to do?"

"First of all, don't talk so loud. And don't be mad at me. *I* didn't do anything to you."

"I'm sorry."

"And sit down. Your running around makes me nervous."

I sat down.

"Now, go on."

"I hope you didn't believe those fairy tales your brother told you."

"Of course not," I murmured.

"Well then?"

"What do you mean, well then? I asked you what you thought I should do. It's not that simple!"

"Isn't it? You go to the police, or to your friend Paradin, and you explain how you came to defraud the state, that your brother's blackmailing you and what he demands of you. Any court would grant you extenuating circumstances. That's the solution. Don't drink so much."

"That's some goddamn solution!" I yelled.

"Go ahead and yell," Minski said angrily. "I may as well ask the gentlemen of the police in the bar to come in here. Why don't you like the solution?"

"Because I could tell them that but I have absolutely no proof! Without my brother I can't even substantiate my claim that he had written my books! He has the manuscripts, and he'd never show them! He'd say that I wanted revenge for something or other, that I want to ruin him, that I . . . that I lost my mind!" I emptied my glass, rose, refilled it, drank.

"Don't drink so—"

"Blackmail? He'd just deny it. The Spider would—for the moment at least—refrain from taking any action against him. Now, how do you like that?"

Minski was silent.

"I asked you a question!"

"I'm thinking. There's something in what you said."

"There sure is."

"Just the same," Minski said. "That doctor was killed. Those two detectives disappeared. You yourself saw one kill the other. I received threatening phone calls. That time bomb in the club . . ."

"It only proves that there are people who are very interested in Delacorte, something Paradin has known for twenty years. Also that they're angry at me and you, since we're partners, for informing on him. But who are those people? Members of the Spider who are blackmailing my brother to blackmail me?"

"Hm." Boris looked dejected.

"That's the trap, you see? Only after I have worked with them, have helped Delacorte to escape, will I know who they are. I know you're right but I have to go along with them, pretend to go along with them or I'll never escape this devilish circle."

Boris was silent for a long while. Finally he said, "I'm afraid you're right. They really thought this out

366

thoroughly. Since they permit you to discuss this with me they must be damn sure of themselves. Naturally they're counting on you to try and prevent Delacorte from leaving Germany. Your brother confirmed that they've taken that into consideration. What I don't understand is why they're not afraid of me."

"Why of you?"

"I'm sure they must have considered the fact that I might be up in arms at what you've told me, that, in spite of our friendship, I might go to the police. I'm a Jew. I was in a concentration camp. So was my wife. That I don't love Nazis must be a simple deduction. Still they let you talk to me." Minski sighed heavily. "They've also got me, somehow, I just don't know how yet." He shrugged his shoulders. "All right. I'll agree with you. You're right. You will have to go along with them for the present. But Richie, we will have to watch so that Delacorte doesn't give us the slip! Imagine, if he escapes we'll both be criminals, but real ones."

"You're smart, Boris. I won't make a move without you. We'll stay in touch. . . ."

"If we're not forcefully separated."

"How could they do that?"

"I could be bumped off for instance."

"Good God, Boris, you have police protection!"

"Yeah," he grinned sadly.

"Now don't exaggerate! Sure, we need a good portion of luck. I wasn't born yesterday. I'll fix them, you'll see! Then I'll go to the police and confess my sordid story. And . . ."

The telephone rang.

Minski answered. I could see he was frightened.

"Professor! Did something happen to Rachel?"

I jumped up.

He gestured for me to be quiet.

His usually pale face became even paler.

"Yes," he said, "yes . . . no . . . no . . . yes . . . you're

sure she's not injured? You give me your word? Of course
I'm upset! . . . Yes, I believe you, yes . . . I'm all right
now, yes, thank you, Professor. Thank you . . . thank
you . . ." He dropped the receiver onto the phone and
looked at me.

"What's the matter, Boris?"

"Those swine," he said, breathing heavily. "Those accursed, dirty swine."

"Who? What happened? So tell me!"

"Now I know why they're so sure of me."

"Boris! Will you please tell me what happened!"

"That was Professor Mohn. He told me that they found
my Rachel half an hour ago. In the garden. Unconscious.
She'd been knocked out."

"What?"

"She can't remember anything except that someone hit
her over the head from behind."

"In the garden?"

"That's what I said! She'd wanted to take a little walk
in her new mink coat and when she was walking—"

"But who could have done that?"

"The professor says anyone could have done it. Any
visitor coming to the sanatorium could easily have reached
the garden through the big park. It could have been a
patient. Nothing is easier than to arrange an assault in an
institution such as Hornstein, the professor said."

Not only in a mental institution was it easily possible,
I thought, but even in a general hospital. I could attest
to that.

"It could also have been a member of the staff, but the
professor doesn't think that's likely. He knows his people.
But he ordered an investigation and notified the police.
But the chances of finding out who it was . . ." Minski
shrugged his shoulders. "They're not very good."

"Was your wife seriously hurt?"

"No, thank God. A flesh wound. She lost some blood.
Shock, naturally. And she'd been lying on that freezing

ground for at least a half-hour. But the professor is personally looking after her. In a few days she can get up. But then what is going to happen to her if I don't play along?" Minski groaned. "I'm caught just as you are, Richie."

"More so," I said.

"Yes, more so. If I don't play along they'll kill my Rachel, no police in the world can help me there. That was their foolproof idea. If I'd had a bit more time to think I'd have come to it that that was what it had to be." He stared at me, forlorn. "And the rabbi, the wise man, he was right after all. We should never have involved ourselves in this business. Never! But we did. Now we have to pay."

The NPD elections results now being in gave me an opportunity to check on Minski's predictions about the party's strength. I remembered the map he had marked with such emphasis and found that he had been fantastically accurate. They had made their best showing where the Nazis had once been most numerous.

Officer Stalling was obviously delighted with the results. I needed his help just then for the important chore of cutting the nails on my left hand as I am left-handed. His help made me a captive audience. He expressed concern over the brittleness of my nails. A lack of calcium, he thought; something to report to the doctor on his next visit to the jail. Then he went on, quoting NPD political predictions, and comments on economics. He was particularly happy at having joined that party at an early date, a boast frequently made in former years by Nazis.

"Herr Richard Mark, please come to the information desk." A girl's voice reverberated through the airport building. I had just arrived from Frankfurt carrying a blue linen bag which contained my small but efficient tape recorder and ten cassettes I had brought from the

Strip. The cassettes contained jazz I had recorded for use at the club. Now I would use them for my reports for Werner instead of buying new tapes.

Dectective Olsen went to a newsstand while I hurried to the information desk staffed by three girls and a man. They were busy talking, telephoning.

"I'm Richard Mark," I began when the man in a blue uniform held out a telephone receiver to me.

"Call for you, Herr Mark."

I took the receiver. People pushed past me, talked to the stewardesses, telephones rang.

"Mark," I said.

Immediately I recognized the voice I had heard this morning in the hospital, the voice I had heard before then but could not remember where. "Had a good trip? Very good. Herr Minski all right? Excellent. It is now seven-thirty. You have sufficient time to keep your date at the Black Gate."

A stout woman next to me was arguing with a stewardess.

"But the poodle is well-behaved!"

"I'm sorry, madam, animals are not permitted in the cabin. I can only repeat what you have already been told at the ticket office."

"My dog? Travel in the freight compartment? Never!"

"There is no other way, madam."

"But how am I going to take Putzi to Vienna?"

"It won't be so easy for me to keep that date," I said.

"Why not?"

"I'm not alone."

"Oh, you mean the man who is accompanying you. He won't bother you. He's one of us."

I steadied myself by holding onto the edge of the counter. I suddenly felt sick and fearful. He's one of us. I'm alone and ineffectual. They are many and powerful. Did I have a chance at all? It did not seem so. It seemed as if I were caught in a net from which I could never escape.

But I won't give up! I thought, held by a sudden rage. If I'm through then at least I am going to try to take a few of them with me!

"Answer me! How am I going to take Putzi to Vienna?"

"By train, madam."

"What did you say?"

"I said the man was one of us. Did you think we're amateurs?" I looked for Olsen. He was just buying a newspaper. "He is buying *Hamburger Abendblatt*, isn't he?"

"Yes. But I don't accept that as proof. You might be here somewhere. In a telephone booth. Watching."

"All right. Ask him a question."

"What question?"

"The professor came to see you at the hotel yesterday. He wanted to form his own opinion of you. We had agreed that if he was satisfied he would make you a present. To be used as an identifying sign. He gave you a present, didn't he?"

"It's a scandal, that's what it is! If some film star wanted to transport her animal then it would be possible! But we're just ordinary people."

"We couldn't do it for a film star either. We have rules which we—"

"You just don't want to—"

"Attention please! Pan American announces the departure . . ."

"Madam, please, the gentleman is telephoning."

"So? I demand—"

"The present is unique!" The voice I still couldn't place laughed briefly. "Something is missing. Makes it even more valuable, doesn't it? Ask your traveling companion the missing words. That's what we're calling this action. If he gives you the missing words you do what he says. That's all now."

There was a click in the line, the connection was broken.

I handed the receiver back to the man in blue uniform and thanked him. The purple shade on the stout woman's face showed her rage. Two stewardesses were trying to calm her. I glanced about for the poodle but saw none. The woman had probably only come for an inquiry. Detective Olsen had opened the newspaper when I stepped close to him and asked, "Which are the missing words?"

"All mankind shall be as brothers," he answered promptly without moving a muscle. "You go first. We'll meet on the parking lot at your car. Mine is nearby."

I walked as if floating, refusing to believe what I had heard. I stepped outside in a cold wind and headed toward the parking lot. As I opened the car door Olsen stepped beside me.

"Do you know any restaurants in Hanover?" he asked me.

"No."

"Hotels?"

"The Intercontinental."

"Good. I have to call in every six hours."

"Call whom?"

"Paradin. I'll telephone him and tell him that you've had dinner at the Intercontinental and then spent some time in the bar. After all you'll return late." He handed me a package. "Sandwiches. You'll get hungry."

I took the package.

"What about you?"

"I've eaten. Can you find your way to the Black Gate?"

"Yes." I had studied the map I had bought in the hotel this morning.

"You can't drive right up to it. Leave the car on the road with the keys in the ignition. I'll drive it away."

"Why?"

"So that no one sees it. Don't worry. When you return it will be there again."

372

"What do you mean 'when I return'?"

"You'll change cars at the Black Gate. Take a little trip." He laughed briefly. "I'll be waiting for you. Then we'll drive back to Treuwall together. Everything is planned." He turned to walk to his car.

"Just a moment!"

He stopped and looked at me questioningly.

I asked, "And Paradin thinks you are one of his trust-worthy people?"

"Uh-huh."

"How long have you been working for him?"

"Three years."

"Always working against him."

"Always," he said amiably. "There's never even been a shadow of a doubt as to my loyalty."

"Just to satisfy my curiosity, why are you doing this?"

His answer was to give me food for thought. "The Czechs hanged my father. As an alleged war criminal."

The answer reminded me of Inspector Lansing's father, who had been hanged by the Poles.

Olsen added, "When I applied for the job I told them that I wanted to make amends for my father's crimes. They were all very impressed."

I remember the brutally hot day in 1956 when Werner and I were driving through the Russian zone. We were returning from Berlin where I had accepted the award and prize money for *Black*.

"Damn champagne," Werner said. "I've got a head-ache."

"So have I," I said.

We had had many drinks the previous night and not much sleep. Werner turned in his seat and extracted a bottle of beer, a thermos containing ice cubes and two glasses from a bag on the rear seat. He placed some cubes in each glass, added beer and handed one drink to me.

373

"I'll get drunk in this heat," I said.

"Not from one beer," my brother said. "Drink."

I did.

He gulped his and refilled the glass.

"One or two of these and I'll feel better. Maybe I'll be able to eat something once we've left the zone. My stomach feels awful. Well, Richie, my boy, now the time has come to say good-by."

"Good-by?"

I drove past meadows where black-and-white cattle were resting in the shade of a few trees.

"It's been fun," Werner said, wiping beer froth from his mouth, burping. "But everything comes to an end. You might as well call this our last trip together. So long, little brother, take care. I wish you luck."

I glanced at him briefly.

"Is this a joke or are you still drunk?"

"Neither. 'The Dead Have No Tears.'"

"What?"

"'The Dead Have No Tears.' Do you think that's a good title? I'm not sure. Everybody else does. What do you think?"

"What are you talking about?"

"My book." Werner again filled his glass from another bottle of beer. "That is going to be the title. Everybody is crazy about the title: publisher, editors, booksellers. Man, watch out!"

I clung to the wheel with both hands and slowed down to fifty kilometers.

"You have written a book?" I asked, my voice weak.

"That's what I just told you. I thought that this would be the best time to talk to you—after your success in Berlin and before we arrive in Frankfurt. Before you see the *Börsenblatt*." (The *Börsenblatt* is the trade paper of German publishing.)

"It will carry the first advertisement," my brother said. "They have planned a heavy advertising campaign. I don't know if that's a good thing. My publisher says yes. The new Werner Mark—after so many years. He says it's going to be a sensation. The first really objective war novel. He says that's what the public wants now."

"Who's your publisher?" I asked, concentrating on my driving. The air above the autobahn surface seemed to whirl and bubble. I took off my sunglasses. The light blinded me but I felt a little safer.

My brother named his publisher, a very famous company indeed.

"He says times have changed. Werner Mark is again socially acceptable. He's invested heavily in advertising, certain that it is going to be the event of the year. It is a good book, even if I say so myself. It took me two years to write."

"When?"

"Well, while I was writing yours. I worked very diligently. I'm in the middle of my second book now." Werner's voice was friendly; somewhat solicitous. "I'm sorry, Richie, but we couldn't go on forever, could we? And if times have changed—they must have or there wouldn't be so many publishers interested in my book."

"Are there?"

"Yes. I picked the best one—the best for me. As I was saying, if things have changed and a man is a writer he ought to write. For himself. Not secretly for someone else. It wasn't very enjoyable, you know."

The wheel in my hands seemed to vibrate and I thought the compulsive thought that the front left wheel was loose and about to come off. The thought made me break out in perspiration, dripping from my forehead over cheeks and throat onto my chest.

Werner refilled his glass with beer.

"If you like I'll drive for a couple of hours," he said. "Then you can have a drink."

"It's all right," I said. "So this is the end then."

"It is, Richie. I'm sorry but I know you understand

that now my work comes first, don't you? There's much I have to catch up on, so many lost years. The young people today don't even know my name. I've helped you a long time, I think you'll agree. I was a good brother, wasn't I?"

"You were a good brother," I agreed.

"I'm going to move out of our apartment."

"When?"

"During the next few days. My publisher has found a very nice apartment for me in Bremen."

We passed a post with a yellow sign. Another fifteen kilometers to Bitterfeld.

Following Olsen's instructions I left my car on the road which bypassed the cairn at a distance of a half-kilometer. The other side of the road was a thickly wooded forest interspersed with numerous paths.

It was quiet and very dark as I left my car and walked toward the cairn in the treeless, bushless heath. The wind had abated. Black clouds hid the sky. There was a strong odor of brackish water, peat and bog.

The Black Gate consisted of three megaliths, two of which had been set into the ground, while a third, longer than the other two, rested horizontally upon the uprights. I touched one of the stones. It felt cold and damp. Birds screeched in the distance. I waited. I strained my eyes but could discern nothing in the darkness. Accordingly I jumped when a voice directly behind me ordered, "Stand still. Don't turn around. Put your hands up."

I did as I was told.

The man behind me opened my coat, searched me for any concealed weapon. When he seemed satisfied he said, "You can take your arms down and turn around."

I turned and faced a tall young man dressed in a black leather outfit. A high forehead, thin lips. Closely set eyes in a narrow face surveyed me with curiosity.

"Punctual," he said.

"You know who I am," I said. "Who are you?"

"You can call me troopleader."

"Call you what?"

"Troopleader. My name is not important for you—get down!" he ordered. We threw ourselves down onto the damp ground of the heath. From the road we heard the engine of a car. In the restless light beams I saw the silhouette of my car. Lights were switched off. The car came to a stop behind mine. A shadowy figure alighted, went to my car, got in, drove away. Olsen.

"Where is he taking my car?"

"Away from the road. Into one of those paths in the woods. It'll be there again when you return. Follow me now." We walked about fifteen minutes until we came to a grove of trees where a jeep had been parked.

"Get in the front," the youth said. He pulled out a black cloth which he folded to form a long strip. "I must put this blindfold on. This is not a game," he warned me. "Don't try any tricks. I'm watching you."

He tied the blindfold securely. I held on to the seat as he shifted into gear. The jeep bounced, slid over stones, roots, holes. After about twenty minutes the vehicle came to a stop.

The youth removed my blindfold. We were facing an old, dilapidated antiaircraft shelter surrounded by thick woods. I saw several motorcycles and bicycles leaning against trees.

"Follow me," the young man said.

We entered a room lit by three oil lamps.

"Attention!" a voice shrilled.

Nine boys ranging in age from about sixteen to eighteen sitting at a long table jumped up and assumed an exaggerated rigid posture.

My companion also came to attention, threw up his right hand and saluted, *"Deutschland!"*

Nine arms followed suit. Nine voices shouted *"Deutschland!"*

As my eyes adjusted to the flickering light I saw dark weather-worn walls. One, facing us, was draped with two flags emblazoned with runes and stylized falcons. Above the flags Gothic lettering in white paint proclaimed

HONOR AND LOYALTY

In a corner stood several high, narrow drums painted in black, white and orange pattern to resemble flames. The youths wore pullovers, leather jackets, short coats, trousers usually worn by garage mechanics, and sturdy shoes.

"Comrades," my man addressed the boys, "this is Richard Mark. You've been told why he is here. We greet him!"

The nine at the table yelled, "Heil!"

I nodded.

"Sit down!"

The boys sat down noisily.

"Now Herr Mark will witness how effectively we deal with traitors and cowards," the troopleader announced. He yelled, "Hippel!"

A good-looking boy with wavy brown hair jumped up. He was very pale and seemed frightened.

My companion inquired sharply, "What are you, Hippel?"

"I'm a cowardly swine, troopleader."

"Louder!"

"I'm a cowardly swine!" the boy cried loudly, obviously close to tears.

"What does a cowardly swine deserve?"

"Punishment, troopleader."

"And?"

"Will you please punish me?" the brown-haired boy cried out with the strength born of desperation.

The boys' faces showed embarrassment, mingled with anxious expectancy.

"This is the cowardly swine who yesterday left our

378

comrade Hans Eilers in the lurch in Frankfurt, as you all know," the troopleader went on. I saw now that he could not be much older than eighteen himself. The boys were silent. "Trousers down, Hippel!" he ordered. "On the table."

I was witnessing a strange and inexplicable form of torture; applying boot polish to a boy's bottom, then brushing it vigorously, then adding adhesive tape in such a fashion that when it was removed the pubic hair and probably the skin would come with it.

"Now, you cowardly swine," the troopleader said. "Get up!"

The boy slid off the table. He swayed.

"Do you have anything to say?" the leader demanded.

Hippel stammered, almost crying, "Thank you for the punishment I deserved. I request an assignment which would allow me to prove that I'm no longer a cowardly swine."

"You'll be given that chance," a voice familiar to me said.

"Attention!"

The boys jumped up again.

I turned around.

Leaning on a tenth boy, a heavyset, bespectacled man in a gray suit came down the stairs which led to an upper floor of the shelter.

The boys, the troopleader greeted the new arrivals, "Deutschland."

"Deutschland." Detective Inspector Geyer, who had shot and killed his colleague, Paul Ericksen, saluted them as he descended the stairs.

The boy upon whom Geyer leaned heavily was also about eighteen years old, powerfully built, a vacuous expression on his broad face. Geyer had placed one arm around the boy's shoulder in an almost tender gesture. He held a cane in the other.

"Good evening, Herr Mark," Geyer grinned at me.

"Good evening," I replied.

"As you see I've been very lucky. The bullets didn't do any serious damage. Went clean through both legs. Had a lot of luck. And a good doctor."

"He must have been," I said. "Do you have a telephone here?"

"A telephone? Oh, I see, you recognized my voice when I called you!"

"That's right."

"Yes, well, I'm in charge of this little action. These boys here are always at our disposal. I'll explain later. No, there's no telephone here. But with the help of my good Jens here"—he tenderly stroked the boy's cheek— "and a jeep we manage. There are a few isolated farms in the heath. The people know us. Good friends. There are telephones there." He gave me a wide smile. I had broken his horn-rimmed glasses in the snow of the rest area in the Hämeler forest. Now he wore a pair of steel-rimmed glasses. His eyes behind the glasses bulged like those of a frog. "Sit down!" he commanded.

The boys sat.

"This is fun," Geyer said. "At long last something that is fun. Reminds me of the good old times when I organized the Austrian Hitler Youth from 1936 until 1938. Those boys were idealists. After the Anschluss it all became routine and uninteresting. I did it for another three years, then I'd had enough and volunteered for the front."

Remembering Eilers's remark that Ericksen and Geyer had been forty-eight and forty-nine respectively, a little quick mental arithmetic meant that Geyer must have been twenty-three or twenty-four when he volunteered. Many of his less-enthusiastic contemporaries had by then already died for Führer, Volk and Reich. I wondered if that fact had not occurred to these boys here?

"This is like old times," Geyer licked his lips. "I'm proud and happy. Boys, we've been given a great challenge. The troopleader has informed you. Is everything understood?"

"*Jawohl!*" The answer came in unison.

"Are the guards posted?"

"*Jawohl!*" The troopleader reported.

"Then you carry on here. I'll instruct Herr Mark. We'll be back." He gestured for me to follow, limped toward the stairs, still aided by Jens, and began to climb them.

At the command of the troopleader the boys broke into a song once popular with the Third Reich.

Geyer kicked open a steel door at the top of the stairs. We entered a windowless room lit by a solitary oil lamp. It contained a table strewn with papers and food, two chairs, a cot, several bottles of beer and whisky on the floor. Two machine guns stood in a corner. On the cot sat a giant of a man with thick lips, a broad nose which had once been broken, black, curly hair, a cruel expression on his face. He was grinning at me, this man who had helped Dr. Hess in taking me to the mortuary of the Treuwall hospital, this attendant who was no attendant.

"Hi," he greeted me.

"Hi," I said. "Did you kill the doctor?"

He nodded, grinning.

"Killed him," he said, "killed him. Yes, sir. With one of those knives. Zap. Very easy. Killed him quick. Killed him, hahaha." He laughed, a gurgling laugh.

"Stop it, Scherr!" Geyer said sharply. Scherr fell silent and placed his hand on his mouth in a gesture of dismay.

"Please close the door, Jens." Geyer's voice was gentle now. The boy did as he was bid.

The huge man sitting on the cot blinked his eyes and complained to Geyer, "That man, he hit me over the head!"

"And he kicked me," Geyer said, "but that was yesterday, Scherr. Now he regrets having done that, don't you, Herr Mark?" he asked me.

381

I said nothing.

"There, you see, Scherr?" Geyer said. "You must not be angry at him for that. Herr Mark is now on our side. A comrade. Do you understand?"

The giant stared glumly at me.

"All right, Herr Geyer," he mumbled and pulled at his rather colorful tie. His hands were very hairy. A powerful animal and a stupid one. Just the right combination Geyer and his people needed, I thought.

"Why did you kill the doctor?" I asked.

"Self-defense," the man answered. "After you took off he wanted to go to the police. I couldn't let him do that, could I? I held him. He got very angry. His nerves were not good. And they kept ringing for the elevator to come up. The doctor reached for one of those knives. So then I had to take one too."

"All right, Scherr. That will do. It was practically the same situation with poor Ericksen and me. He too took the first shot."

"That's one way of looking at it," I agreed, sarcastically. "By the way, where is his body? And the car?"

"You ask too many questions," Geyer said. He tenderly touched the boy's hand next to him. "You can go downstairs for a while, Jens, my boy. I don't need you for the moment."

The youth left. As he opened and closed the door I heard the marching song the boys were singing.

"Where is Ericksen?" I inquired as soon as we were alone.

"Disappeared," Geyer said. "I don't think he'll ever be found."

"His wife is expecting a child," I said.

"I know." Geyer reached for a sandwich on the table. He bit into it with gusto and continued while he chewed. "Are you hungry? Help yourself. No? Yes, it's tough for his wife. But what could I do?"

"He was your friend."

382

"You don't think I liked killing him, do you?" He used his finger to capture an elusive piece of sausage. "I'm not like that. Shooting a friend. But what choice did I have?"

"How did you clean up the rest area so completely at the Hämeler forest?"

"You really are curious, aren't you? Well, all right, I'll tell you. Two trucks. One for the car, Ericksen and me. The other had a snow blower and lots of snow. They cleaned up the tracks we left and, from the road, blew snow over the active area. Very simple. It was all planned in advance. That's where I was going to take the photograph away from you, I mean."

"And the trucks were there just in case you had to shoot Ericksen or me or both of us, eh?"

The giant of a man laughed; the sound reminded me of a sheep bleating. He seemed in an expansive mood. There was a strange glint in his eyes. But I didn't think he was drunk.

"To be prepared for eventualities is most important. And a good, resourceful organization such as the boys troop here, for instance. There are many such troops. We usually don't use them for such important missions but they will do whatever we ask them to do in an emergency. You and Scherr will work together from now on. So, you'll be friends, all right? Scherr, do you understand me?"

The huge man grinned, nodding.

"And what did you give him?" I asked.

"Something very good. Right, Scherr, you're feeling fine?"

"Fine, fine."

"We can't have Scherr feeling nervous. He has to feel good. And calm. Just like he used to be in the good old times. Always calm and in a good mood. We were often in too good a mood, weren't we, Scherr?"

"Ha-ha."

"When?" I asked. "Where?"

"In the jail at Treuwall," Geyer explained. "That's where Scherr is a jailer."

I stared at Scherr, startled. "But then the detectives must know him. I had described the fake hospital attendant to them. Didn't it occur to anyone who saw you that you could have been that man?"

Scherr was seized with uncontrollable laughter.

Geyer answered for him. "They thought of that. And questioned him. But Scherr had a cast-iron alibi for the time in question. Naturally, we took care of that."

"What kind of—"

"You are really too inquisitive. An alibi, I said. The cops were satisfied. Although . . ."

"Yes?"

"It is my guess that they will trot him out just to watch your reaction. You will be amazed by the resemblance but also *very* sure that Herr Scherr is not the man who forced you into the basement of the hospital. That man was not quite so strong, not as Negroid in appearance, his hair not as tightly curled. That clear?"

I nodded.

"The Treuwall jail adjoins the county courthouse. Within the next few days you will doubtlessly be asked by Paradin to attend hearings there. That will give you a chance to take a good look around."

Scherr laughed loudly again. He was obviously under the influence of a drug.

"It is our responsibility to arrange Delacorte's escape. These boys downstairs—and more from other troops if necessary—are going to help us. Scherr already has a plan. It needs more work, naturally. At our next meeting we will begin to iron out any problems. I shall arrange meetings by telephone. I know where to reach you at any time. Clear?"

Again I nodded.

"One more thing," the bespectacled man with a penchant for youth subversion said. "We have no secrets here. It is known what you have done. It is also known what I have done. You know what Scherr has done. But not all of it. For the past few months the jail has been under investigation by the Ministry of Justice. During the past one-and-a-half years several prisoners were injured, three died after confinement in a special cell usually used for unruly prisoners. So far the investigation has not uncovered anything. The prisoners are afraid, the guards stick together. One of those guilty guards, in fact the most zealous one, was our dear Scherr here. We have proof of that, haven't we, Scherr?"

"That's right, Inspector," the huge man said, grinning, though clearly fearful.

"Just as we have proof against you, Herr Mark. You see now how it all works?"

"I certainly do."

"Help me over to the table," Geyer said to Scherr, who jumped up to help him. The former inspector pushed aside groceries and papers and unrolled a map. "Look. This here is the courthouse and this the jail. Now Scherr will explain his plan to us."

The jailer, conscious of his importance in this venture, began to talk—slowly and awkwardly. As was frequently true of dull-witted men, he was cunning and intuitively shrewd. Essentially his plan was a scheme involving four keys.

On a clear, cold November day in 1956 I walked about Frankfurt, filled with memories, trying to retrace my past.

The former MP station had become a toy store, its windows displaying a variety of war toys. The rubble at the banks of the Main had been cleared. I could not find the place where I had thrown my mother's handbag containing her glasses, Werner's many war reports and a few of mine into the dirty waters of the river.

In the Stresemannstrasse where I had lived for so long with Lillian new trees had been planted, the war survivors among the houses had been restored and many new ones built. I saw unfamiliar names next to the bells on the post beside the entrance gate. Two small girls and a boy were playing there. I turned to leave. The sun blinded me and tears came to my eyes.

The church ruin where Lillian and I had attended midnight mass was no longer there. In its place stood a new, modern church, severe and ugly. I inquired for Pastor Matern and was told that he had died recently in a hospital.

I found the narrow bridge across the railroad tracks where Lillian and I had kissed for the first time that Christmas Eve in 1947. I waited for a train to pass underneath the bridge. Its engine smoke would envelop me as it had before, but no train came.

I searched in vain for the place where we had come upon the Yugoslavian DP and his pregnant wife. Every part of it was new. I decided to go home.

Ten days after Werner and I had returned from Berlin he had moved to Bremen. I knew his address, but we had neither telephoned nor written to each other. Werner's book had been published and acclaimed by the critics. Back in the city once more I passed bookstores, their windows displaying copies of *The Dead Have No Tears,* some also featuring a picture of Werner. "Fifty thousand copies sold during the first six weeks," some signs proclaimed; others: "The book of the year." The critics' praise and effective advertising would sell another fifty thousand by Christmas, I reflected. This fall no book by Richard Mark had been published.

I walked to Minski's G.I. Joe but found it still closed. I tried the door. It was locked.

My feet suddenly hurt, I felt cold and thought that I shouldn't have walked so long, so far. I hailed a cruising taxi and gave the driver my address. An Italian sports car was parked in front of my house. In the last rays of the setting sun I saw Lillian sitting behind its wheel, smoking.

As I placed a hand on her shoulder she did not start but slowly looked up at me.

"Hello, Richie."

"Hello," I said. "Have you been waiting long?"

"Very long," she answered. "But it doesn't matter. Where have you been, Richie?"

"Out for a walk."

"I must speak with you. That's why I came to Frankfurt. I must tell you myself. Explain. So that you'll understand."

"Understand what?"

"Why I am going to marry your brother," she answered.

"You're going to do what?"

"Marry your brother," she answered calmly.

The air vibrated with the noise of a plane zooming above us. I looked up at the sky, bright and silvery and blood red where the sun was setting in the west.

"Couldn't we go inside?" Lillian asked.

"Oh, sure," I replied. "Of course. Yes. Excuse me," I helped her out of the sports car. She was dressed in a smartly styled, white wool trench coat. I opened the gate and walked ahead of her across a carpet of colorful leaves. Inside it was dark. We entered my apartment on the ground floor. I was about to draw the drapes and switch on the light when Lillian said, "Don't."

"Aren't you going to take off your coat?"

"I feel chilly."

It was warm in the apartment; the heating was switched on.

"Would you like a drink?"

"No, thank you."

She sat down on the wide couch in front of the fireplace, her legs pulled close to her body, and nervously lit another cigarette. I threw my coat across a chair and sat down beside her.

"I could start a fire," I offered.

"No, don't," Lillian said. "You haven't been here for three months. No one could reach you for three months and one week."

"That's right," I said.

One day after my brother had moved out I had begun to travel—Madrid, Nice, Rome, Cairo, Dakar, Capri. I did not remain in any one place for long. I drank. I frequented bars, I went to shows, to bullfights, staying up nights, sleeping days. At that time I became aware of a new development: claustrophobia. That morbid fear forced me to avoid crowds, suffer torment in airplanes, leave a restaurant in the middle of a meal. I was never really to lose that fear again. Those three months after my brother had left me are vague in my memory. I did not care about anything or anybody. That included Lillian.

She had learned my first address, the Castellana Hilton in Madrid, from my publisher. From then on each hotel gave her my next address. She had telephoned me, had written letters, sent telegrams. I threw them away unopened since I knew they all asked me to return home or let Lillian come to me. But I had no desire to see her or hear what new disaster had befallen her.

"There's another woman behind all this," she had insisted during one telephone conversation.

"No, there is not."

"Then what's the matter with you?"

"Ask my brother," I had answered, and given her his new address. From that day on I received no more letters, telegrams or calls.

My trip became an alcoholic nightmare. Finally I resorted to Benzedrine and other drugs. I don't remember the women I slept with, the cities I visited. I have no recollection what I did and knew only later by hotel bills and plane tickets where I had been. On Capri I suffered my first heart attack—I came to my senses. I returned to Frankfurt.

An ash dropped from Lillian's cigarette onto her coat. She did not notice it. "Of course you must have realized that something pretty drastic had happened to me when I pursued you so insistently."

"I did."

"But you didn't care."

"Something pretty drastic had just happened to me, too, as you knew."

She nodded.

"Fate," she said. "It must have been fate that it happened to both of us at about the same time."

"Sure," I said. "Of course it was fate. Everything that happens to us is fate. We are something very special, two chosen ones."

I rose and walked to the window which looked out over a dismal garden, then stopped before a small Utrillo painting. I studied it, my back toward Lillian.

"You know that I was Herfeld's mistress."

I knew. Herfeld, a very wealthy man, a steel magnate of the Ruhr.

"Herfeld wanted to divorce his wife and marry me."

Utrillo had been a drunkard just as I was now. But he had been a great artist, a man who had suffered, who had undergone treatment in many clinics and mental institutions until, after an especially long stay in a hospital, he had stopped drinking. According to many experts, that ended the expression of his great talent.

"Are you listening to me at all?"

"Of course, Lillian."

It was becoming darker in the room.

"I'm going to be thirty. I can't go on this way, can I?"

"No. What happened?"

"His wife instituted divorce proceedings before he had a chance—and had named me as the corespondent."

"That so?" I said, surprised, and turned around.

"It doesn't occur very often. But when it does the guilty party can be sent to prison. It happened just when you were going on your trip. That's what I wanted to tell you but you didn't let me."

"No."

"Well, I saw a few lawyers after Herfeld's wife found out. There was a terrible scandal—I shall never be able to go back to Düsseldorf. That's why I wrote you and telephoned but you never wrote to me. You didn't even listen to me."

"I'm sorry," I said, thinking how strange, this time, this one time I was not there ready to help her she could not forgive me. How absolutely sure she must have always been of me. But I said nothing, knowing that she would have denied that opinion of her anyway.

"All you gave me was your brother's address," she continued. "And he helped me." Lillian's voice had a metallic quality.

"How did he help you?"

"He found me another lawyer who explained that I had been slandered, that I had never destroyed Herfeld's marriage, that indeed I was about to marry Werner. That was his condition, Richie. He told me that he would help me if I agreed to marry him. He loved me from the very beginning, when we first met, he says. Now, he says, he is in a position to marry me. Now he has the financial freedom—you understand what he means. After all, I had no idea that you had split up. Only when his book became such a success . . ."

"Yes," I said, "yes, of course."

"I'm telling you the truth. We promised to tell each other the truth, always, didn't we? Werner said he was well aware that I was not in love with him. Perhaps I would learn to love him. He . . . he is most generous. I have every personal freedom as long as I marry him and do not leave him. He knows I am here with you. He practically sent me. He thought it would be better if I spoke to you personally."

"I bet."

"You're cynical and bitter," she said. "But if you had been there . . ."

"Yes?"

"All this wouldn't have happened."

"Naturally not," I replied. "Then we would have married. You and I. Something we never intended or wanted to do. Then you would have married me, now that I'm finished, with absolutely no prospects . . ."

"You're despicable."

"So are you," I said. "That's why we love one another. Go on, Lillian. So the trick worked."

She extinguished her cigarette. Meanwhile it had become so dark I could see her only in silhouette.

"Herfeld realized that his wife held all the cards. It was somewhat difficult to withdraw the complaint but Herfeld is very influential. He stays with his wife. I am going to marry Werner. December fifth. In Bremen."

"Congratulations," I said. "That car outside, is that Herfeld's gift or already Werner's?"

"Herfeld's. Was it necessary to mention that?"

"Yes," I answered. "Werner is good in bed, eh?"

"Great," she replied promptly.

"And now he makes a lot of money and will make even more in the future."

"That's right."

"While my future looks dismal." I could not help thinking that she enjoyed this scene.

"Very dismal, Richie."

"A woman needs security," I continued. "A man she can rely on. In bed. And financially. Not a drunkard who doesn't come running when his mistress whistles."

"You swine," she said. "You bastard. You know that I shall always love you and that this marriage is going to be a farce!" She jumped up, quickly pulling off her coat. She slipped off her essential clothing and dropped back onto the couch. "Come to me, Richie, let me prove that it is going to be a farce."

Three steps brought me to her.

We clung to each other. Without words we merged, again and again, until finally Lillian slipped away from me. Motionless, I remained on the couch, exhausted, my heart and temples pounding. I heard steps, a door closed, and another. Steps across the pebbled path, a car door opened, the engine started.

She had left without saying good-by.

In December 1956 she married my brother in Bremen. Reading the notice in the newspaper I found myself thinking how much I loved Lillian and how much she loved me. I felt quite calm.

Just before midnight I was back in my hotel in Treuwall. The troopleader, after again blindfolding me, had driven me back to the Black Gate. At the roadside I found my car, keys in the ignition. Driving back I noticed the lights of another car following me. My shadow Olsen, presumably.

The foyer was deserted. Pierre was just closing the bar but agreed to bring me whisky, ice and soda. After he had left my room I tore open the envelope of a letter which the desk clerk had handed me. I recognized Lillian's handwriting. The note was brief. "With longing and love— Lillian." A most welcome note.

I fixed myself a large drink, took off my jacket and shoes and began to record the first of ten tapes for my brother. "Thursday, November 24, 1966. My name is Richard Mark. I'm recording in the Hotel Kaiserhof, Treuwall. This is the first installment of the story concerning the crime I am going to commit. . . ."

The ancient safe in our office in the Strip holds a remarkable item. A typescript of almost nine hundred pages. Almost indecipherable with its corrections, signs, numbers excised, and substituted sentences and words; twenty-two beginnings of about thirty pages each of the same novel. These useless, ineffective pages constituted one year's soul-searching work. That was 1956–1957, a year filled with absymal distress, a nightmare of desolation and abortive writing. There had been no communication from Lillian or my brother. I neglected and lost most of my friends. My weight was down. I drank mostly at Minski's G.I. Joe, awakened frequently in a strange bed, a strange girl by my side, without any recollection of the past hours.

Had I not had any funds I might have been spared some of that misery. As it was the books Werner had written for me continued to be successful and very profitable. I moved into a comfortable, smaller apartment in a quiet house near the Park Luisa.

In December 1957 the rumor reached me that my publisher had written me off as a burned-out author, a man with a writer's block, a not uncommon occurrence. He was most sympathetic, reassured and comforted me, but the fact remained that he obviously did not count on me any longer.

In the fall of 1957 I completely lost my self-respect. It became routine for me to go to Minski's bar every afternoon. My claustrophobia was plaguing me strongly at that time and I left when the first customers began to arrive. I selected Doris Day records from the jukebox which held pleasant memories of my life with Lillian. One day, drunker than usual, I hurled my heavy whisky glass at the music box. It broke. Minski said nothing. He brought me another drink, nodding his head knowingly. I wrote out several checks before I had one legible enough for Minski to cash. I went home. During the following three days I did not leave my apartment but tried my utmost to write.

I had just realized that even the twenty-second effort was as useless as the previous ones when the doorbell rang. It was a very nervous, embarrassed Minski who sadly surveyed the disorder of my apartment.

"Richie, I cannot stand by and watch you killing yourself." His long-lashed black eyes seemed moist.

"I'm not killing myself."

"No, no, of course not. Another year of this and you'll be watching daisies grow from below."

"So what? Who cares?" I said belligerently, yet filled with self-pity.

"I do," Boris replied.

"You? Why the hell should you?"

"Because I like you. Don't ask me why. I don't know. Now, how much money have you left? Or don't you know?"

"Seventy, ninety thousand, I guess. Why?"

"I have a proposition for you."

"Such as?"

"I didn't come here as a good samaritan. I want to enlarge my bar, you know, make a nice club of it. I'm looking for a partner. What about it, you want to become my partner?"

"Do I want to—?"

"Is that so shameful? Why are you looking at me like that? Hey! What is this?"

I said, "Has it come to that so soon? That people feel sorry for me?"

"No one feels sorry for you. You're sorry for yourself," Minski said sternly. "Very sorry. So, what is it? I don't have much time. If you don't want to . . ."

"Why are you making me that offer? Pity, that's why!" I said, tight-lipped.

"I told you, because I like you. Besides, it is not good nowadays for a Jew to own a nightclub, a big one. I'd like an Aryan partner! It's been my dream for quite some time now. You're a handsome, smart Aryan, I could really flaunt you and—"

"You know what, Minski? They can all kiss my ass! I'll quit writing! I'll accept your offer."

"Finally!" Minski said. "Tonight I'll show you the

plans for the club, we'll start remodeling in the new year and take care of the legal aspects and all that. There's one condition."

"Yes?"

"That you don't write another line," Minski said. "You'll pack some clothes and tomorrow you'll go to Bavaria, somewhere where there's snow and you'll recuperate there. I don't want a ghost in the business once the hard work begins."

I went to Garmish-Partenkirchen. I slept, I skied, I relaxed in the sun and recovered. Tanned and rested I returned to Frankfurt the beginning of January 1958. The first night I spent in my apartment the telephone rang. I picked up the receiver.

"Richie, at long last!" said Lillian's voice.

"Here is your score," State Prosecutor Paradin said. "Lansing doesn't need it any longer. I see no reason to hold it here."

He handed me the leather-bound Beethoven Symphony. Disgust with myself rose in my throat and made me swallow hard.

"Please sit down, Richie. I'd like to discuss something with you."

I sat on a high-backed, carved chair before a carved, ornate desk. Paradin had been assigned a large, pleasant room on the fourth floor of the county court building overlooking new houses, baroque buildings and churches of Treuwall. A cold, pale, sun shone this morning.

The slight, white-haired man, dressed as usual in a dark suit, was limping to and fro.

"Have you seen Tiny yet?"

"No. Has he arrived?"

"He has already been here, identified Delacorte and signed his statement."

"Where is he staying?"

"At your hotel. He arrived last night. You hadn't returned by then. He asked me to tell you to meet him in the hotel bar at twelve. He'd like to have lunch with you."

Paradin pushed back his gold-rimmed glasses, which promptly slipped down again.

"Perhaps I'm crazy," he continued meditatively, "but I have a peculiar feeling as far as Delacorte is concerned. I think he counts on being spirited out of jail." He looked at me. I met his eyes calmly, but tightly gripped the score which had almost slid off my lap.

"From jail?" I asked, feigning amazement.

"Not only that. But out of Germany too. I feel it."

"What makes you suspect that?"

"His behavior. He affects this air of superiority. His answers are insolent and provoking. His defense: documentary evidence against him is falsified, mostly by himself since he was, after all, a resistance fighter. You have probably heard that already at the police station, haven't you?"

I nodded.

"I think he is killing time. At first he was going to inform on all kinds of people. Now he drags it out. Why? Probably waiting for me to make a mistake. Which I won't. I think he is stalling until his friends are ready to move. What do you think of my theory?" The question had no special intonation. I had to pull myself together. Paradin trusted me. This was a discussion among friends. Among friends . . .

"The experiences you've had with Delacorte's friends would naturally make you cautious and suspicious."

"That too," he said. "But I think my theory holds some truth."

"But who would help him escape?" I asked. "Those men who are afraid of him? If that is technically possible, which I doubt . . ."

"We'll come to that presently. Basically, I think only the Spider has the people, the organization to bring off a feat like that. The situation has probably changed somewhat so that both groups now have the same interest. The Spider presumably has wanted Delacorte out of Germany since the trouble began. Those who are afraid of him will want that also. Now more than ever I'm convinced that the good doctor has let them know: 'If you don't get me out of here quickly I'm going to sing!' And do you know who is basically responsible for my theory?"

"Who?"

"You, Richie."

"I?"

"Yes," he answered, smiling amiably. "Because as far as you are concerned there is obviously a lot that doesn't make sense."

I managed to meet Paradin's eyes and smiled.

"Really?"

"I mean the whole thing is an utter and complete sham."

"What is?"

"The act Delacorte put on for you. Comes to the hotel to thank you. For what? That you denounced him?"

"That I saved his Lillian's life."

"Oh, come on now. He even asked you to look after her, didn't he? He who is even jealous of men who have nothing to do with Lillian, who is well aware of how long you've known her."

"He said that Lillian told him I was more or less a sentimental memory, nothing else."

"And she carried *your* telephone number in her locket. When she was about to die she called *you*. Sentimental memory. That man is no fool! I'm prepared to believe that she told him stories like that but never that he *believed* them."

"But what reason . . ."

"There is a reason." Paradin remained adamant. "A very good reason. I know it sounds crazy but when I see that antique score I could almost swear that he had a reason for giving it to you." How uncomfortably close he

397

was to the truth! "Delacorte doesn't do anything rash. He is a master of deliberation, of planning and restraint! If I only knew a little more, something specific. The only thing I'm sure of is that he loves Lillian. Which doesn't help much."

I remembered something.

"Why are you still having Lillian guarded?"

"Why am I having you guarded, Richie?" he asked. "Because I don't want anything to happen to either of you."

"I see."

"By the way, are you satisfied with Olsen?"

"Very."

"Nice man, isn't he?"

"Very nice."

"How was your dinner in the 'Intercontinental'?"

"Excellent."

"That is another thing that worries me, Richie. But we'll find out eventually why you—I don't know why I'm so sure—have been chosen to play such a key role in this. I can't even guess what part. But everything points to that. But you must admit that Delacorte's behavior was more than just strange."

"Yes," I agreed, looking directly at Paradin. "Yes, you're quite right."

"Olsen will watch out for you. But that might not be enough. You must be very careful, Richie. Promise me that you will inform me at once of anything unusual."

"I will."

"Something should be happening soon."

"Why?"

"Because I've arranged for some changes to be made," Paradin answered. "Which brings us back to your question if it is technically possible to help someone escape from prison."

"So you've changed something in the jail," I said,

thinking that now I should affect a calm but curious manner.

Paradin went on. "I spent three hours there yesterday. I investigated everything thoroughly. Inside and outside."

"And?"

He raised his shoulders. "They run a tight ship. Especially now they're under investigation."

"What investigation?"

"Well, a little while ago there were some charges of prisoners being beaten and that several died as a result of beatings. Some guards were suspended. Those on duty now are probably all right." If you only knew, I thought. "I think an escape is unlikely. But I did discover one weak point."

I said nothing.

"There is a left and a right wing, you see. Delacorte is in the left one. At night two guards are on duty. Each has four keys to enable him to patrol inside and outside. That's too dangerous. If one of them should be outside at any one time and he is robbed, four keys are gone—and a prisoner could quite easily be taken out."

"I see," I said. It was exactly what Scherr had explained to Geyer and me.

"From now on one guard remains inside, the other patrols outside. So the guard outside only has one key for the gate in the wall. The others stay inside. Simple, isn't it? I think it is now foolproof."

"I think so too," I said.

"That is why I have this premonition that something is going to happen to you, that you'll become involved in it when those people cannot make any progress. You call me immediately, Richie!"

"Of course." I must inform Geyer of the change right away, I thought.

My apologies, Paradin, but that was the only thought in my head at that time. Except for thinking how incredibly lucky I really was!

I had dinner with Tiny in the hotel.

Many reporters had returned. It was noisy in the dining room. I had not seen Werner at the hotel again. Fleetingly I wondered where he might be?

"I'd like to see Lillian," Tiny said. "But I must fly back to Berlin tonight."

"We could go to the hospital this afternoon," I said, "if that's all right with you."

He nodded. Tiny was an imposing figure, meticulously dressed in a blue pinstripe suit, but he was no longer the old Tiny who had always been ready for a joke, happy and content. He was not even the same Tiny I had seen three months ago in Berlin. Now he looked tired, troubled, preoccupied.

"What's wrong, Tiny?" I asked him.

"Does it show?"

"Yes."

He cut his meat, taking his time, while I thought that this man, born of poor parents in Alabama, was now a famous opera star, a gifted man, a wealthy man—but not a happy man.

"There was this boy I grew up with. We were in the army together until I became an MP soldier." He lowered his knife and fork and said softly, "He became a major. He was killed a month ago in Vietnam. He had no relatives, that's why I was notified."

"I'm so sorry, Tiny," I said lamely.

"So am I," said Tiny. "In the official letter it said he was killed during an attack against a Vietcong stronghold. But I also received a letter from one of his friends. Do you know how he died? He had requested artillery support for his unit. He got it too. They hit their own people. Thirty-six men were killed before they noticed their mistake. Richie, I'm afraid of that war. I'm afraid that it might be the start of a third world war. Not only because I'm depressed over my friend's death. You know that I meet many people of all nationalities. I've just sung in

Moscow. The topic of conversation is the same there, too, Richie. The Russians are just as upset over that shit-war we're waging in Vietnam as are those millions of Americans. Our idiotic specialists with their insane ideas of escalation, deescalation, a limited, controlled war! The way things are going only a miracle can prevent an out-and-out confrontation with the Chinese. A war between China and the U.S.A. is not going to be limited to those two countries now, is it?"

"Do you really believe that?"

"Many intelligent militarists and politicians believe that today, even if they don't say so," Tiny sighed. "My God, Richie, when we met twenty years ago we thought a new era had begun. No more war. Do you remember?"

"Very clearly."

"Is there anything wrong with you? You look so—any problems?"

"No, everything is fine. Must be the lighting here—more suitable for a morgue than a dining room."

"Well, then, Richie, cheers," Tiny said as he raised his wineglass to me. "To the third world war."

"That it won't take place," I added, also raising my glass.

"It will," Tiny said pensively. "Try to be happy with Lillian."

"We're going to stay together now," I said, "and we're going to leave Germany." As if by repeatedly mentioning it my wish would come true, I added, "We're going to Switzerland."

"Why is that?"

"I want to live in peace, in security."

"Security!" Tiny sounded woeful. "The next time there will be no security. For no one and nowhere. Security. That doesn't exist any more. That's why I'm staying in Berlin. It will make no difference at all. This is good wine. Shall we have another bottle, Richie?"

401

"A good idea," I answered. "Remember how you put on a falsetto voice when you talked about a bottle?"

"Yes, years ago," Tiny said.

The Marienkirche in Treuwall has a massive tower with a patina-green roof. Originally a Gothic hall church, in the latter half of the fourteenth century it had been enlarged by aisles and chapels. It thus became almost as wide as it was long.

Its sixteenth-century organ of baroque appearance, and fifteenth-century altar carvings and paintings are counted among the most splendid art treasures of the period. The vestry holds a reliquary of gold-plated silver depicting a Gothic church. There are two fonts, Gothic candlesticks and ornately carved choir stalls. It was dark in the aisles. Few people were in the church. Fading daylight filtered through the pointed, soaring stained-glass windows.

"You're sure you've understood everything?" I asked the troopleader sitting next to me. At my request Olsen had contacted Geyer, who in turn had set up this meeting.

"Perfectly," he replied. "We shall find out when Scherr is patrolling outside. Until then we cannot plan any details. You've done your job well. My comrade will be pleased."

"I'd like to get all this over with," I said, thinking that now it was just beginning.

"We do too." The troopleader lowered his head onto his folded hands resting on the back of the bench before him. A man and woman passed, then he straightened up. "You'll hear from us. Wait ten minutes before you leave." He rose and left.

When I finally left the Marienkirche I passed a woman in the nave leaning forward, her face raised to the altar, weeping, her lips moving soundlessly. Frau Ericksen. Her husband had been dead more than two days, I thought, wondering what they had really done with his body.

"Richie, at long last!" It was Lillian's voice I heard through the telephone that evening of January 1958. "I've been calling you for three days."

"I've been away."

"Can I come to see you?"

"Where are you? "

"Here in Frankfurt. In a hotel."

"Alone?"

"Yes."

"Where's Werner?"

"In Hollywood. He's been there a month and will stay for another. His last novel is going to be made into a movie. He's writing the script."

"And he didn't take you along?"

"No."

"Why not?"

"Our marriage was no good." She laughed hoarsely. "We decided to separate for some time and then try again. If it doesn't work out, then we'll get a divorce."

"Who's at fault?"

"Both of us," Lillian said. "I married him because he demanded it. He only demanded it to hurt you. He hates you."

"You don't say!"

Irony had always been wasted on Lillian.

"Werner only wanted to take me away from you. That's why he insisted on our marriage. Now I know. Oh, Richie, why weren't you there to help me that time?"

"It is too bad, isn't it?"

"Don't be cynical. I only came to Frankfurt because . . ." After a brief pause she went on, "because I couldn't stand it any longer. . . . I must see you—let me come to you, Richie."

"You must be crazy. You must think you can do anything with me!"

"Can't I?" she said softly.

I threw down the receiver.

Half an hour later the doorbell rang. It rang for almost fifteen minutes before I opened the door. Lillian wore a chinchilla coat, her blue-black hair brushed high and her make-up heavy.

"I don't want you here," I said sternly.

She stepped into the foyer.

"Did you hear? I don't want you here! If you don't get out of here right now . . ."

"Yes?" she asked, opened her coat and smiled languidly. "What happens then? Are you going to beat me then, as you did once before, do you still remember?"

I stared at her and did not answer.

"What a splendid opportunity to revenge yourself on your brother," she continued. I opened the entrance door.

"Get out!" I said harshly, turning to face her.

She lifted her pleated skirt. Only stockings and a tiny garter belt. Smiling lazily, she looked a whore, a born whore. I closed the door.

When I awakened the following morning—my head ached from too many drinks—Lillian had already left. A note on the bedside table said, "As long as we live . . ."

Cursing loudly I suddenly, furiously, punched with both fists at the pillow, still redolent with Lillian's perfume.

"I'm so glad that you two are together again," Tiny said. We were having a drink in the hotel bar before going to drive Tiny to the airport for his return trip to Berlin.

This afternoon we had visited Lillian in the hospital. Tiny had given her a small record player and several records by Doris Day. Lillian had been very moved by Tiny's thoughtfulness. We had listened to the records and reminisced. Tiny's German was now fluent and almost without accent.

"I often think of the MP station," Tiny had said. "The first time Lillian came there she wore a blue dress and a ribbon in her hair. She came on a bike. I remember it very well. Richie was working on his first book then. Now he is a famous author."

"Who no longer writes!"

"You will, now that Lillian is with you again." He turned to Lillian. "How much longer do you have to stay in the hospital?"

"Just a few more days."

"Then go to Switzerland just as you planned. Quickly. These are uncertain times."

The doctors had asked me not to tell Lillian the entire truth about Delacorte. But she had inquired fearfully about Werner as soon as we had arrived. I had told her that he had gone to Bremen but that he was going to return. Paradin still needed him.

In the crowded bar, I asked, "What is it, Tiny? Still that fear of another war?"

"I guess so. Well, forget my fear. Perhaps I'm wrong. I hope so. Let's have another drink. Pierre, the same again!"

I glanced at Olsen, who was reading a paper at a nearby table. A page boy carrying a sign bearing my name went slowly through the bar. Answering my question, he told me that I was wanted on the telephone. The phone booth was hot. I heard Vanessa's breathless voice, "Richie! Richie! I'm so excited I can't tell you—Oh, God, Richie . . ."

"Vanessa! Calm down!"

"You're the first one to know. I haven't even called Boris yet."

"Where are you?"

"At home. I'm not working yet. And five minutes ago the telegram arrived. From Paris! From Panos! He has some business at the university in Frankfurt and he wants to see me—next week. He's arriving Tuesday, six o'clock in the evening. Oh God, Richie! Panos is coming!"

"That's great," I said. "I'm very happy for you."

"I knew it! I always knew Panos and I would one day . . . I'm so happy."

405

Several times I repeated how glad I was for Vanessa while she repeated herself. I felt apprehensive.

As I returned to Tiny a young couple I had seen before in the hotel stopped me. Could I introduce them to Homer Barlow? They wanted his autograph. Tiny, amiable as ever, signed his name with a flourish on a wine list Pierre brought. As they left, Tiny remarked, "So young, so much in love, so innocent."

"So happy," I added.

"Yes," Tiny agreed. "I hope nothing will separate them from the little moment of happiness left for them. That is left for all of us."

Tiny's plane had gone on time.

I was about to get into my car on the airport parking lot when Olsen, my faithful shadow, came toward me.

"Right after Gifhorn, on the right side of the road, you will see a farmhouse. From there you are to drive at sixty kilometers while counting to sixty at the same time. Then stop and wait."

"Wait for whom?"

"For the chief, he wants to talk to you." With that he turned and walked back to his car. I climbed into mine, and while I was starting the engine I recalled what Lillian had once said, "Apparently no one can be what one is not. I don't know why I am the way I am. If there is a God he must know why he made me like this. . . ."

Bent over the wheel of my car, Olsen's headlight in my rear mirror, I reflected that if there was a God he had made Olsen the traitor that he was. Everything was traceable to God. Olsen a traitor, his father a war criminal hanged by the Czechs—Olsen's excuse for his treachery. Unless, of course, he was lying. Blame it all on God, who has His own inexplicable reason for the world's confusion. Olsen, the trusted officer, as a traitor made it easy for me to be one. Still, I thought, this sort of reasoning is weak, decadent.

I drove through deserted villages. There was Gifhorn. There was the farmhouse. I slowed down to sixty kilometers and began to count. Olsen's headlight were no longer visible in my rearview mirror.

58 . . . 59 . . . 60.

I stopped and lit a cigarette.

Almost immediately I heard steps. In the weak, red glow of the rear lights I recognized the strong youth whom Geyer had called Jens. He supported Geyer. Both wore dark leather coats. I opened the door on the passenger side. Geyer slid onto the seat. He smelled of perfume.

"Follow us in the jeep," he instructed Jens, and to me, "Start driving. Steady sixty kilometers."

I drove.

"You've done that beautifully," Geyer continued. "Finding out about those new duty arrangements."

"Good evening," I said.

"Good evening," he replied, surprised.

"How are your legs?"

"Two, three days and I'll only need the cane. My compliments, you've really done that splendidly. You know I'm beginning to feel young again. Now, working with those boys, just like the good old times in Vienna before the Anschluss! How do you like Jens?"

He did not wait for an answer but went on, "A wonderful boy. Never met a better one. Loyal and honest . . . and . . ."

He cleared his throat. "We have been in contact with Scherr. The new duty schedule has been made known. Accordingly Scherr will be on day duty the day after tomorrow. Monday he will be on night duty but that is too early for us. We still have to complete arrangements."

"What do you mean? Too early for us? How much longer are you going to wait?"

"We must complete preparations," Geyer said doggedly. "We know what we're doing. You had better prepare yourself for a lot of work too."

"Such as?"

"Don't be so curious. You'll find out soon enough." He grunted. "A week from Thursday Scherr is on the night shift. He relieves his colleague at nine-thirty for the outside patrol. The night from the first to the second of December."

The road showed a wide, long curve. Suddenly the road was brightly lit. I stepped on the brake and, in my rearview mirror, noticed the headlights of the car behind me, presumably Jens's jeep, flashing in quick succession. A warning. I came out of the curve. Bright lights from a car on the other side of the road were focused on two men in white coats standing in the center of the road. I recognized white police hats, gun belts and pistols. One policeman held up a white, red-edged dipper motioning to stop.

"Damn!" Geyer cursed.

My heart beat furiously. That's it, I thought. Finished. Suppose I made a run for it? The policemen would have enough time to jump clear.

The accelerator roared. The car shot forward. Then Geyer reached forward and switched off the ignition. The car rolled to a stop directly in front of the two police officers.

FOURTH MOVEMENT

Presto

MY BROTHER SAID, "You look pathetic, Richie. That expression of fear and a guilty conscience! You must pull yourself together."

The morning following Tiny's return to Berlin I had seen Werner again in the hotel foyer. He had returned from Bremen and was on his way to see Paradin. I had locked myself into my room and had taped another segment of my recent experiences.

"You don't look so great yourself," I said to Werner.

"I know it. Paradin remarked on that too," he replied. "He doesn't like me. He likes you. But it seems he doesn't trust either of us. I hear something is going to be done to change that in your case?"

"Yes," I agreed, thinking of my nighttime drive with Inspector Geyer.

"What about the tape recordings?"

"I've already started."

"Let's hear."

I locked the door and played back the first tape. He listened briefly, then made a gesture of annoyance. I switched it off.

"What's the matter?"

"This is absolutely worthless," he said, angrily. "These tapes are meant to prevent you from going to Paradin and blowing the whistle on us. We need more detail. And not only of what is happening now. Talk about your past. The books I wrote for you. Why I wrote them. My bosses need a detailed confession."

"All right. I'll give full particulars to the extent that you can write a book about them," I said. That amused Werner.

"By the way, why did you bring so many tapes?" he inquired.

"They were in the bag and I left them in there."

"Your subconscious must have been at work," he remarked, grinning. "The need to confess. Do confess, Richie. Confess. Can this bag be locked?"

"Yes."

"I'd like you to give me each tape as you complete it. And record only on two tracks. Four would take too long. To leave partially completed tapes lying around here is too risky."

I did as I was instructed. Had those tapes not been stolen from me when I fled Cairo as recorded at the beginning of this account, the Associated Press Service would have had their scoop and I would have been in Buenos Aires, a free man, instead of writing this report in prison. My plan had failed miserably. Whoever has those tapes today has an advantage—but not for much longer. This report I am writing now for Paradin will ensure that.

They should have killed me as I fled. They should have made sure that I could not write or talk again. But then they had really tried to kill me, not merely faked it, as they were about to do in Treuwall. That attempt on my life was scheduled to take place at 10:42 A.M. on November 26. Inspector Geyer had impressed upon me the necessity of being punctual the night we were stopped by those two policemen.

As my car rolled to a halt, one stood in front of it, the other approached me. I had wound down the window thinking that this surely was the end. Caught and finished. Why had Geyer switched off the ignition? We might have slipped through, I thought confusedly.

"Evening," the policeman said. A narrow face. Gold teeth flashed.

"Evening comrade," Geyer said. "You did well. Punctual."

"You were on time too!"

The policeman looked at me with curiosity.

"He wanted to drive on, did he?"

"Yes," Geyer chuckled. "A real wild one, he is. No, really, that was excellent," he said to me, giving me a pat on the back. "It was, of course, the worst possible thing you could have done under normal circumstances. But with me in the car, and it was an impulsive reaction—we really should be very pleased with you." To the policeman he said, "You'd better take off those coats double-quick and get out of here."

"Okay. So long."

The men took off their white coats as they returned to their car. Both wore civilian clothes and boots.

"We can go on now," Geyer said and laughed, amused.

"Very funny," I said, starting the car.

"A necessary test. We must know how you react, right?" He inhaled deeply. "You know I feel twenty years younger."

I saw car lights appear in my rearview mirror—presumably Jens.

"You seem to have a hell of a lot of helpers," I said.

"Oh, yes," Geyer said. "More than we need. Don't worry. It's going to be a piece of cake. You keep your head. Then nothing can go wrong."

"If Paradin doesn't trick us," I said and told Geyer of the state prosecutor's suspicions.

"Do you think he suspects you?" Geyer finally asked.

411

"I'm not sure. It is possible. After all Delacorte's behavior was pretty unusual."

Geyer laughed. "It was meant to be. We did want to direct some attention to you. Paradin is smart. Now we have to weaken his suspicion of you."

"How are you going to do that?"

"Well, he expects something to happen to you. Something will." Geyer opened the window. He inhaled deeply. "The air in the heath is really wonderful."

"What is going to happen to me? What are you planning?"

"A murder," Geyer said, bemused. "Murder is very convincing."

Treuwall is built on five hills. The district and county courthouses as well as the prison are built on one of them. In medieval times the courthouse had been a city hall. Gothic gates and gables, numerous heraldic figures, coats of arms, an arched, open arcade once used for legal proceedings—as I was told. The prison is a building of the nineteenth century. Outside the courthouses stands a well dating from the sixteenth century, picturesque with its bronze figures and gargoyles. The cobblestoned road is narrow here and slopes steeply. The traffic, accordingly, is always dense at this point. Facing the courthouses stands a beautiful, old gabled house, the city library, rich in rare books and medieval manuscripts.

This Saturday was a clear, cold day with a pale sun. I passed the well and at exactly 10:42 reached the sidewalk outside the courthouse. An engine roared. A gray Peugeot, its license plates encrusted with dirt, shot toward me. I took three more steps and had thrown myself down when three bursts of a machine gun came from the car moving quickly downhill. I had been expecting the fusillade but felt very frightened when I heard the bullets strike the wall behind me. Pieces of brick and stone fell on me. Men shouted, horns blared, women screamed hysterically. From one corner of my eye I saw a furniture moving van pull out of a side street and block almost the entire road. A pursuit of the Peugeot was impossible.

Half an hour later I was sitting opposite Paradin.

A physician had examined me and had found no injuries, merely a mild case of shock. I nervously folded and unfolded my hands, trembled frequently, hoping that that would be sufficiently convincing.

In addition to Paradin and myself my shadow Olsen and Inspector Lansing were in the comfortably furnished office of the state prosecutor. Other officers were questioning several excited citizens of Treuwall, witnesses to the attempted assassination. Several bullets had been dug from the façade, photographs had been made, the police had questioned me thoroughly.

Olsen's statement was as vague as mine. He had been about to cross the street after me when the Peugeot drove by. Two men had been in the car, he thought. He had not been able to see into the car, the sun had blinded him. The license plates had been unrecognizable.

"I'm sure that those guys had been waiting for Herr Mark." Olsen spoke heatedly, as if the attempt had been made on his life.

"Don't upset yourself, Olsen," Paradin said.

"Well, after all, this is the first time since I've been working for you that something like this has happened to me! I wanted to fire at the car, hit a tire, but I was unable to do even that—too many people. Damn bad luck. I'm really very sorry."

"All right," Paradin said. "Any questions, Lansing?"

"Yes, one," the inspector answered. He turned to me. "When did you throw yourself down? I mean, why did you?"

"I saw a gun being pointed through the open window of the car. That's when I hit the ground." Geyer had told me the exact moment when I was to drop because immediately after that the troopleader was to fire. I had not seen who had been driving the car.

"Did you see the assassin?"

"No."

"You demonstrated great presence of mind, Herr Mark."

"Would you rather I had reacted slower?" I asked, annoyed and irritated.

"Excuse me," Lansing said gently. "You're still upset, I see. No more questions."

"Then would you leave me with Herr Mark, please," Paradin said. "He told me that he had something of importance to tell me. Stay close by, Olsen."

"Yes, Chief." The young man rose. "I'm really very sorry," he said.

"For heaven's sake," I admonished him sternly. "After all it's not your fault."

Lansing and Olsen left.

"Well?" Paradin's glasses had slipped down his nose but this time he did not push them back. He was watching me intently above them. "What is it you have to tell me, Richie?"

I had surreptitiously glanced at my watch. Paradin was to receive a call at ten minutes past eleven. It meant that I had to stall for three minutes.

"I feel nauseated. Could I have a glass of water, please?"

I was given the water and I sipped it slowly.

"Well, Richie?"

"Yes, well, I received a telephone call this morning. In the hotel."

"From whom?"

"I have no idea. He didn't give his name."

"You didn't recognize the voice?"

"No." It had been the troopleader's.

"The man's voice said that by denouncing Delacorte I

414

had committed a serious crime. I deserved to die. I could escape that fate if I were to—"

The telephone rang.

Eleven-ten, exactly. These guys were reliable.

Paradin picked up the receiver. Almost immediately thereafter his eyes narrowed to slits. He pushed back his glasses and handed me the receiver while he reached for another which he held to his ear.

"Yes?" I asked.

The troopleader's voice. "Well, did we promise you too much? So you went to the courthouse anyway. Told everything, eh? No need for you to answer. We know. And it doesn't matter. One thing, Mark. We didn't intend hitting you this morning. We could have shot you, but we merely wanted to reinforce our warning. The warning you've already told Paradin about."

"I've said nothing!" I affected a strangled tone, swallowing hard.

"But you will. Paradin is listening in now. If you care to live a while longer you better get set. Next time we shoot to kill. Herr Paradin, meanwhile, may as well make out his will. So long."

Paradin and I replaced the receivers.

"Now, what did that man say this morning?" Paradin began. He was still watching me intently. I felt ill at ease.

"That was the same man who had called me at the hotel this morning!" I said.

"Yes?"

"He said that I deserved to die for—"

"Yes, you already told me that. Go on." I didn't like the sound of Paradin's voice.

"And he said: 'You can make amends.' "

"He used those words?"

"That's right." He really had.

Paradin laughed.

"I don't think it is so funny," I said, furious.

"I'm sorry."

415

"You haven't been shot at just now! But just wait! You're on their list too. You especially. Wait until it's your turn! You won't laugh then!"

"Don't worry about me. I'm used to such calls—during the past twenty years. Naturally, it was a frightening experience for you. All right. You can make amends. How?"

"He didn't say. He told me to be prepared. That there was a task for me. If I was prepared to accept that—and not tell you that I had been contacted." I threw back my head. "You see, I'm doing exactly what the man demanded of me. Now we see the first results. But you prophesied something like that," I added casually. I hoped it sounded casual.

"You mean I prophesied that something was going to happen now that I changed the duty roster at the prison?"

I nodded, sipped more water. For some obscure reason drops of sweat suddenly came out on my forehead.

"And promptly something occurred," Paradin said pensively and nodded. "Very promptly." He looked at me steadily. "One could almost say too promptly."

Now I had to show anger. I jumped up.

"What do you mean by that? I'm the one who pointed out Delacorte to you—and now you're suspicious of me? That's incredible! That's—"

"Sit down," Paradin said, very softly. The expression in his eyes made me comply. "And don't shout. There's no need for that."

Quite a long silence ensued. It was broken by a knock on the door.

"Come in!" Paradin called.

Scherr the prison guard entered, a file in his hand. Since I had been prepared for just such a casual confrontation with Scherr I did not lose my composure but watched him, wide-eyed, following Geyer's suggestion.

Scherr, who did not even glance at me, delivered his file and left.

"What's the matter, Richie? You look as if you'd seen a ghost."

"That man . . ."

"A guard at the prison. Half Negro."

"Yes, precisely."

"Was he the man who attacked you?"

I shook my head.

"You're sure he wasn't the man?"

"I'm quite certain," I answered. "My man was not that tall, not so broad. And his hair was not so curly. He had a narrow face. No, no, he wasn't the same man. I was just surprised. Apparently I'm still quite shaky."

"Yes, yes," Paradin said. Another long silence ensued.

"Richie," Paradin said, finally, "I am your friend. At the moment I think your best friend."

"You are suspicious of me," I said stubbornly. "Why?"

"Because many of the circumstances surrounding you are very strange indeed. We already discussed that once. Richie, we've been friends for a long time; before it is too late: is there nothing you have to tell me?"

"Tell you?"

"Is something bothering you? Are you being black-mailed?"

"What gives you that idea?"

"Are you being blackmailed?"

"Of course not. Threatened yes, but you know that."

"I don't mean that."

"Then I don't understand what you mean."

He came close to me and looked directly into my eyes.

"This is one great theatrical performance," Paradin said. "I don't know the part you're playing. I'm afraid it might not be a pleasant one. Richie, is there anything in your past for which you could be blackmailed?"

"No."

"You're sure?"

"I'm sure."

"And you won't give me an explanation for Delacorte's strange behavior toward you?"

"Won't? I can't."

Geyer's plan was a good one, I thought. Delacorte's visit in the hotel bar. The show of gratitude. Making me a present of Beethoven's Ninth. All this to concentrate attention on me. It bound me to Geyer while the plan could unfold. Geyer and I had discussed it in detail the night I had driven Tiny to the airport. If there were any last minute changes Olsen would serve as go-between. Until the actual start of the attempt to free Delacorte I was to remain isolated and inactive—under suspicion by Paradin and the police. Not a bad plan, I thought with grudging admiration. Meanwhile, my brother, no, all of them could make their arrangements without any trouble.

"I like you, Richie," Paradin sighed. "I'm sorry that you . . . that you're in such an unpleasant situation. I could still help you if you decide now to tell me everything."

"I've told you everything," I growled wrathfully.

"Too bad," Paradin remarked, shrugging his shoulders. "You realize, of course, that later I will not be in a position to help you."

"I don't know what you're talking about," I said heatedly.

"No, of course not," Paradin said. His narrow face suddenly expressed fatigue and disgust. He moved away and stood motionless, with bent head, slight and vulnerable.

"If I get another phone call, if those people want me to do something I shall inform you immediately," I declared defiantly.

"Yes," Paradin said, turning his back toward me, "yes, naturally, Richie. You'll report it to me. I can depend on you, I know that. Now I know it for sure."

Embittered, I thought: Geyer and his friends have thought up a splendid idea. I felt anger and admiration, bewilderment and fear as I realized fully that I was the bait.

Saturday morning twenty-five pink carnations had been delivered to Vanessa. An FTD order from Paris. The Frankfurt florist had enclosed a note, *"Très cordialement, Panos."*

This bouquet in her arms, Vanessa danced through her apartment, laughing and crying. She had called Minski and breathlessly told him about the flowers Panos had sent. Minski had told her that he was happy for her. ("But of course I knew that she would create problems for us—which she promptly did!" he had told me when we met again.) Vanessa had tried to telephone me in Treuwall but I had already left the hotel. I was on my way to the courthouse where the attempt on my life was faked.

Vanessa rarely drank during the day but on this day she decided to open a small bottle of champagne. Two glasses had helped restore her equanimity somewhat. The doorbell rang. Still in her robe and without makeup she opened the door. At the door stood a very attractive brunette, green eyes giving her features a feline look. Yvonne Rending, second wife of Vanessa's father, had changed very little since Vanessa had seen her last. She seemed upset, yet eager for reconciliation.

"Hello, Britt," she said. "Sorry to surprise you like this. May I come in?"

Taken unawares, Vanessa mumbled, "Yes, please come in. Excuse me, I'm not dressed yet. What happened? Something wrong with father?"

"Yes. A nervous breakdown. Admitted to a Hamburg clinic yesterday." Yvonne Rending slipped off her ocelot coat. Vanessa noticed that her stepmother was very pale under her skillfully applied makeup. Yvonne sat on a couch, crossed her shapely legs. She extracted a cigarette from a gold case and lit it with shaking fingers.

419

"Breakdown?" Vanessa repeated, surprised that she felt concern.

"He hasn't been well for some time. It shouldn't be difficult for you to guess why. You knew exactly what you wanted." Yvonne exhaled cigarette smoke. "Now you've succeeded."

"How did it happen?" Vanessa asked reluctantly.

"Reporters," her stepmother answered. "They would not let him alone. They followed him to his office. They waited for him outside our villa. They photographed us constantly. They were the same reporters who had come to see you."

"I threw them all out."

"We did that too. But they kept coming back. They telephoned. They begged, they threatened. Yesterday one of them told your father that he had sufficient photos to write a shocking story even if we—and you too—didn't say one word. The reporter worked for a magazine. An hour later your father . . ." Yvonne brushed tears from her eyes. "Britt, the man said he had pictures of you—from the club! If this story is published we are finished."

"I've waited a long time for that," Vanessa said.

"I beg you, think of your father. The excitement will surely kill him. Britt, he is your father. I know you hate me and my son, but your father . . ."

"I hate him too."

"But he is no longer the man you remember. He's very ill . . . only a shadow of his former self! Don't you think that your occupation has not been talked about in Hamburg? That your father does not try to put an end to that? That he ignores it?"

Vanessa looked at her beautiful stepmother. She had dreamed of this hour; the thought of revenge had sustained her so many years. Now that the moment had arrived she felt insecure and frightened. She glanced at the pink carnations. Panos was coming Tuesday.

Panic gripped her. "When is this story to be published?"

"I have no idea. Soon, probably in a week or so."

"Is there any way to prevent them from coming out with this story?" Vanessa demanded abruptly. Her features showed her nervousness.

Yvonne stared at her in utter stupefaction. "I . . . do you *want* to stop this story?"

"Yes."

Yvonne jumped up, hurried to Vanessa and tried to embrace her. Vanessa pushed her away. She tossed her hair back.

"Don't touch me! I'm not doing it for you! I'm doing it for myself! Tell me! I'm sure you've already seen your lawyer . . ."

"Yes."

"Well, what did he say?"

"He says if the man who employs you protests against your photographs being published . . ."

"Minski. He can do that?"

"My lawyer says that, according to the new law, you have sold or rented your body to—?"

"Minski."

"Yes. Well. Minski's approval is necessary to publish your picture in magazines, movies, or whatever. Please, Britt, you must call him. You can have my jewelry, my furs, whatever you want. I'll give up my inheritance—but call this Minski. If he protests they can't publish your photographs; then they have no story. But you must hurry . . ."

"Shut up," Vanessa said hoarsely.

Panos. He must not see me in a magazine. I can no longer perform. That had never occurred to me, she thought. Oh, God, I hope Minski will understand . . .

Vanessa went quickly to the telephone next to the vase with pink carnations.

Ill with flu, I had been confined to the infirmary for seven days. Now, still a little weak, I am once again in

421

my cell. Officer Stalling helped me make my bed. Once again I was a captive audience.

A meeting of the NPD for the express purpose of electing a new executive board had been scheduled for May 10 in Nuremberg. Thielen, chairman of the NPD, had left the party and founded the Nationale Volkspartei (NVP). About twenty-five hundred members had arrived in Nuremberg from all parts of the Federal Republic. The exhibition halls had been rented to the NPD for the meeting. Suddenly the city council decided to cancel the contract. A court injunction to open the fairground was ignored, whereupon a four-thousand-mark fine was imposed. Adolf von Thadden was forced to dismiss the twenty-five hundred angry members who had been waiting in the hot sun. The meeting could not be held. What a disgrace after the recent progress the party had made!

Officer Stalling is very angry because many newspapers have taken the incident at Nuremberg as renewed evidence of the disintegration and end of the NPD.

"The city council disregards the law and that's supposed to mean that our party is falling apart?" Officer Stalling asked, bitter. "No, Herr Mark, if you knot the corners of the sheet like so"—he deftly slips them over the mattress—"then the sheet will stay smooth." While I admire his efficiency he continues. "But I'm not upset. Luckily I ran into an old friend this morning. His name is Grieben; he used to be my superior when I first started here. He must be going on seventy now. Also an NPD member. Comes from Berlin originally. He's been through all this before, you know, I mean those years before 1933. He said to me, 'Man, why are you so depressed?' and I said, 'Well you know,' and he said, 'Don't make me laugh. The Nazi party was supposedly falling apart too, up to 1933 that is. There were half a dozen splinter parties. Then there was Röhm, he was a queer in the Nazi party, right? And when his letters were published everybody was yelling that's the end of the party. There were other scandals and the SA mutinied—two months later Hitler became chancellor and there was no more talk about the party being finished.' Grieben said, 'You just wait, it's going to be the same with this party. We're only just beginning. Someone will whistle the right tune and everybody will then fall in step.'

"Well, we've finished your bed all right, Herr Mark. Easier for two than for one. I'm always glad for a chance to talk to you. You're always so understanding. Well, even if our party falls apart a hundred times we'll be victorious in the end just as once before. That seems obvious now after what Grieben told me this morning. Don't you think so?"

"Perfectly obvious, Herr Stalling," I agreed. Then before I returned to my writing I quickly scanned the newspaper. Minister of Justice Heinemann has declared that 6,179 of about 74,000 accused of Nazi crimes have been tried and sentenced since May 1945. That is less than ten per cent.

"Now that she's received those flowers that girl is completely meshuggana. I ask her what are carnations? Just a little courtesy, I tell her. No, she says, it's more, much more. And right away there are tears in her eyes again. Flowers! What they do to a woman! It's incredible."

Minski brushed nervously across his forehead. The bags underneath his eyes were purple from lack of sleep. After a busy night in the Strip he had had only time to shower and change before flying to Hanover. Now we were sitting there in the airport restaurant having breakfast, as was Olsen at a nearby table. Boris had to return to Frankfurt soon. During last night's telephone conversation we decided that here were several things that had best be discussed vis-à-vis.

"I can't come to Frankfurt," I had said, "I have to stay here. You come here, I'll be expecting you."

"All right, Richie."

Followed by Olsen I had left Treuwall while it was still dark. Dawn came slowly on this Sunday morning. From time to time the sun broke briefly through scurrying clouds.

Minski ordered more coffee.

Olsen seemed to be reading his paper. There were many men in the restaurant this morning similarly occupied. I felt as apprehensive as I often had during the war—spending a quiet, uneventful night, knowing that an assault would come at dawn. Waiting was straining my every nerve. Waiting for Thursday night, the night of the planned escape. This was only Sunday.

"Well, Vanessa is so sure that Panos still loves her. So sure that she promised her stepmother that she will no longer perform in our club—but I already told you that on the phone. Thank you." The waiter had brought Minski's coffee. "I don't understand women. Half the night she cried and carried on. That we have to release her from her contract. Immediately. She'll pay any penalty. But she won't perform the candle act any more." Minski snorted in an effort to conceal his feelings. "I guess it's reasonable enough. That's why I didn't have the heart to say no to her."

"You said yes?"

Boris sighed deeply and nodded. "I said yes. I also called my lawyer and sent a telegram to the magazine. They're not going to publish Vanessa's photographs. She's minus that problem. And we're minus Vanessa."

Preoccupied with my thoughts I said, "You'll go to Paris and find a new act. You always have."

"Yes, probably," Minski said glumly.

"What about Corabelle?"

"We can use that act and her snake Annamaria, but what are those acts compared to the candle act? Richie, I feel as if I had lost my own daughter."

"It really is too bad. But if Panos really wants Vanessa now she cannot perform in the club any more."

"That's why I said yes. She hugged me and kissed me, and I'm to kiss you for her and God knows what else but we're without Vanessa now, Richie." I smelled the faint fragrance of lavender as he bent toward me slightly and said gravely, "Everything is falling apart, Richie. I feel it. Everything we've built up—I can see it. And I feel we're in danger. That's how it was in Kamenets-Podolski, months before the Germans came. Everybody said, 'It won't be so bad,' but I knew that it would be bad, very bad, Richie. And it was. And there was nothing I could do about it. Nothing."

"Just like now," I said softly.

"There's something we can do. Must do. Or we'll be destroyed," Minski said. "But I don't want to discuss that here. Let's take a drive somewhere. I could use some fresh air."

We left the restaurant, followed by Olsen. Several men left at the same time. Perhaps they, too, were following us. While I was driving to the zoo, I told Minski about the most recent developments. His face was very serious. He sighed deeply several times.

We walked along the path between the enclosures for wild boar and deer but saw not a single animal. Couples, children with scooters, children playing ball, laughing, running, and Olsen following us at a discreet distance. We could not be overheard.

Minski said, "I have this uneasy feeling. We're in a terrible situation."

"How is Rachel?" I asked.

"Better. But she caught a bad cold lying in that garden for so long. Now the police are out there keeping an eye on things. Everybody is keeping an eye on Rachel. As much as possible. At the moment I'm more worried about you. I've come to the conclusion that they're deliberately maneuvering you into a spot that will automatically make you the prime suspect after the escape."

The bait. I was not only the bait but also the scapegoat.

"Now listen and try to keep calm. It looks pretty bad for all of us, but for you even worse. One reason, Richie, you had better prepare yourself that it might all go wrong."

"Yes," I said, "I've thought of that too."

"Then you'll have to disappear."

"Where to?"

Minski stopped, took off his hat and thoughtfully scratched his head.

"We have to think, calmly and reasonably. They're counting on us to become rattled. If we're smart enough we might just outsmart them. If we run into some bad luck—it can happen to anybody—then you and Lillian will have to leave Germany . . . that is if you want to take her along."

"I won't do anything without Lillian!" I said emphatically.

"I believe you even if you don't shout," Minski said, suspiciously glancing at passersby. "Richie, you know that if you get caught you'll go to prison for many years."

"Your position is not so great either," I said.

"I'm not directly involved. They'd have to prove that I knew what was going on. You didn't tell me anything."

"That goes without saying," I said.

"So, we get back to you. To be prepared for any event it is essential that you have false passports. You and Lillian."

He was right. He was always right.

"Where can I obtain false passports?"

"I can get them for you. I know someone in Frankfurt. He changes expired passports into current ones. For that I need photographs. I brought a camera with me. We'll take a few pictures in your car. Or on the autobahn if we can lose your watchdog for a moment. I'll leave the camera with you. You will have to take a couple of pictures of Lillian. Today. Then you will also have to tell her the truth. Do you think you can do that?"

I swallowed hard and nodded.

"Can you trust Lillian?"

Again I nodded.

"If you can't, that will be the end of everything. You know that. That's what worries me the most. We know how trustworthy she has been in the past."

"It's different now."

"Is it? How?"

"Because she really wants to be with me now. I know it. If I'm wrong about Lillian I'd just as soon go to prison. Then I don't care one way or another!"

"Empty talk," Minski said pointedly.

"I'm sorry, I just can't stand you doubting her."

"Richie," Boris mumbled, "you're a poor bastard. I won't say any more. Either both of you'll get through or both of you won't or—"

"Or I will get caught and Lillian will get away!" I was furious. "That's what you were going to say, weren't you?"

A man and a woman looked at me with curiosity as we passed them.

"I'm sorry," I said. "Go on, Boris. My nerves are really shot."

"That's just what we need," he said simply. "All right. Lillian can be trusted. So you photograph her. Send me the film tonight. Express. You can send it from the station. They are open late. The man needs three days to fix the passports. Visa for Egypt and another country, I think, where you would be safe from extradition. Just to give you a choice."

"Argentina?"

"Argentina is fine. You'll also need international vaccination certificates. My man will get those for you also. What are you thinking?"

"Nothing special," I lied. But I had been wondering if I could trust Lillian. I had come to the decision that from now on I would.

427

This was the first afternoon that Lillian had been permitted to leave her bed for a few hours. Her clothes had been brought from Delacorte's villa. She wore a suit of shimmering fabric. I pulled out the camera Minski had given me and photographed Lillian, pretending that I wanted a few snaps as a souvenir of her stay in the hospital. The camera was compact, expensive and relatively easy to use. Just to be sure I took four pictures, listening for footsteps. A detective was still watching Lillian's room from the nurses' lounge opposite. After I had packed away the camera Lillian said matter-of-factly, "Then you think that we might have to leave the country?"

I stared at her in utter stupefaction.

"Put on a record," she said. "We can talk then without having to worry about being overheard."

"What is it you want to tell me?"

"Several things," she answered.

I selected a record. A moment later Barbra Streisand's voice filled the room—rather loudly.

Lillian looked at me, her face grave. "At least you're considering the possibility that we might have to escape if you're going to obtain false passports for us."

"False passports—?"

"Richie! Now don't let's play games. It wastes time. You only took those photos because you need them for a counterfeit passport."

"What gives you that idea?"

"Paradin was here."

"Again?"

Lillian had been questioned repeatedly by Paradin and men of his staff. I had presumed that they had concluded their questioning.

"Yes, again. He came alone to talk to me about you."

"What about?"

"He wanted to know if I could think of any reason why you would help free Kamploh from jail," Lillian Lombard said.

Having read once more what I have written, shocked, astonished, I realize that Lillian, my love, the most important person in this book, is the only one left without a biography. Yet there is a simple explanation for that. I am to this day ignorant of her origin, her childhood, her parents, the events which shaped her character and life. I never asked for and she never volunteered any information. I wondered if I had intuitively avoided inquiring about Lillian's past and, if I had, why? Was there anything I knew concerning her that I have not already mentioned in this, my story?

I think only this: her marriage to Werner had been dissolved in the fall of 1958. She was adjudged the guilty party. That same fall she came to me in Frankfurt, declared that Werner was a devil, that I was the only man she loved—and then had me take her, several hours later, to the train bound for Rome. A count had invited her to stay with him.

There was a year in Rome before the affair with the count ended, a whole week with me in Frankfurt, and then a quick exit to London and another lover. This time she was abroad for a year and a half before returning to Frankfurt in the manner of one who had never left. Fool that I was, I broke off my relations with a woman I held dear to be with Lillian, only with Lillian—for a month. Then, in the Strip, she made the acquaintance of a wealthy Spaniard who took off with her to Spain.

During the last two years I heard only very rarely from her. She had not written as was usual with her, only telephoned two or three times. That is why I knew nothing of Delacorte's existence.

"Haven't you a light for my cigarette, Richie?" Lillian asked.

I struck a match and held it out to her. She inhaled and said, "Paradin also told me that Kamploh is Delacorte and who he really is."

I jumped. The match had burned my finger. I dropped it and stepped on it. Lillian's face was composed, her voice calm. "I didn't know, Richie. I swear that I had no idea. Paradin believed me. Do you think Paradin believed me?"

"I don't know what he believes. But I believe you, Lillian!"

"I know that." She smiled.

"It must have been terrible for you to find out that—"

"Yes, quite terrible." She nodded. "But Paradin broke it to me gently. He was very considerate. Then he talked about you. I think he worries about you."

"He what?"

"He likes you very much. And he is very suspicious of you."

I remember that at this point Lillian seemed insensitive. Could she really control herself to that extent? Was she so coldblooded, so unfeeling?

This woman had lived for years with a mass murderer. How had she responded when she had been told?

"Quite terrible . . ." That's what she had said.

"Lillian," I began, "I know you must feel very upset since Paradin came to see you. I can understand that. By the way, when did he come here?"

"This morning. I have had sufficient time to cry and calm down again, Richie. I shall never see Kamploh again, only as a witness in court, if it becomes necessary. He will follow me into my dreams and that will be terrible for me. I shall no doubt think of him and that will be terrible. But I will get over all that."

It seemed to me that she had said that rather quickly, a skilled actress delivering her lines. But then, I thought, as usual looking for excuses for Lillian, perhaps it was merely self-preservation, self-defense.

"Kamploh, he belongs to my past. You, you are here. I want to live with you. Only you are important to me."

Something was wrong here. "Tell me, Richie, Paradin has reason to suspect you, hasn't he?"

Now was as good a time as any to explain myself to Lillian. If she were to betray me—no, she had called me when she was dying. She loved me. Yes, I had to trust her now.

"Yes, Paradin is right to be suspicious," I said. I rose, turned the record over and waited until the music resumed before I told Lillian what had happened. I spoke quickly and to the point. Lillian smoked and listened in silence. Once in a while she nodded as if she had pictured it that way. When I asked her, she replied, "I've had much time to think about everything since I've been here. It had to be something like that."

"But can you understand me? How I became involved in all this?"

"Yes, I can understand it," she assured me. "Paradin has also had time to think. He has come to similar conclusions. He thinks that you're being blackmailed by someone."

"Did he say by whom? With what?"

"No. I asked him but he said he didn't know. He said it was merely an assumption. He wanted to know my opinion. I told him that I was very upset—because of Kamploh—and that he was imagining things as far as you were concerned. He was very polite and apologized for upsetting me. Then he warned me what to expect if you were indeed to take part in an attempt to free Kamploh and I knew of it and kept silent. At that time I knew nothing so I could swear to that. He gave up then. Not that he is satisfied or that he believes me."

"And what are you going to do?" I asked, my voice hoarse. "Now that you know everything?"

"Silly boy. I shall do everything you might want me to do. I hope that it will all come to a good end, but if it doesn't, I shall stay with you, go with you wherever you go, Richie."

"Are you aware of what that might mean? Perhaps we'll have to flee: weeks, months, hunted, being afraid, in hiding—will you be able to stand that?"

"There is nothing I cannot stand if you're with me," Lillian said. She took my head between her hands and kissed me. With her enormously large eyes she looked at me, serious. "What else could I do now without you? Can you tell me that?"

"You could live in peace. Without me," I said.

"Now there is no peace without you," she said. A rather lofty sentiment, I thought. But at the moment it contented me. Well, in some situations triteness might be forgivable.

Again we kissed and the sweetness of her caress gave me new courage, new resolution, renewed hope.

I opened my eyes and looked toward the door.

Olsen stood there, an insolent expression on his face.

"How dare you come in here without knocking?" I snapped.

"I did knock. You didn't hear it. I'm sorry, madam." He bowed to Lillian.

"What are you doing up here anyway?" I demanded abruptly.

"I'm relieving my colleague. He just stepped out for some coffee. There's a telephone call for you, Herr Mark. I hope you'll excuse the intrusion." He smiled at Lillian. She nodded nervously.

"Who?" I asked.

He only grinned.

As soon as I had picked up the receiver in the nurses' lounge I heard Geyer's voice.

"So, confessed everything?"

"I didn't—"

"Save it." He sounded dangerous. "This morning you spent hours with your friend Minski. Paradin spent hours with your Lillian. Now you're playing records in her room so you cannot be overheard. Look, Mark, whatever you

432

planned with your friends—if it interferes with our plans you're in for it. Not only you. Frau Lombard is not going to get away with a little poison the next time. That clear?"

"Yes."

"Yes, *Boris*."

"Yes, Boris."

I heard him laugh. "And should you conceive of an extravagant idea to betray us and, if that fails, to flee— alone or with your beloved—you'll be in for the surprise of your life. You can rely on that!"

I was silent.

"Now return to your hotel," Geyer continued. "Go to your room. Your brother has something to tell you." The connection was interrupted. I hung up. Little did I know that, indeed, I was in for the surprise of my life.

Werner, pale and haggard, smoked nervously as always when he was agitated. He was sitting on a chair in my hotel room. The electric light was burning.

"I'm to explain the plan to you," Werner said. He suddenly crushed out his half-smoked cigarette.

"Are you afraid?" I asked.

"Yes, Aren't you?" I kept quiet. "Only idiots wouldn't be afraid in a situation like this," Werner said, lighting another cigarette. I wondered, was this fear genuine? I was almost inclined to believe it.

"Now: Delacorte is going to be sprung Thursday night."

"Yes. Scherr. The keys. Geyer, the troopleader and his boys. What do I have to do?"

"There's a good boy," Werner said. "Always obedient. Lillian is going to be discharged from the hospital on Tuesday."

"How do you know that?"

"You didn't know? Paradin is through with her. She hasn't even been told? They really do have their people everywhere! It's reassuring though to know how many friends one has."

Yes, I'm sure it is to you, I thought.

"After Lillian has been discharged you are to help her with packing her clothes and so on in the villa. Then both of you are to leave Treuwall and go to Frankfurt. Paradin doesn't trust you. That is why you must be in Frankfurt at the time of the escape. Let them keep you under surveillance there. They're sure to do that anyway. They'll concentrate on you instead of the prison and me."

"Doesn't Paradin suspect you?"

"He does suspect me. Very much so! There's so much that speaks against me that he cannot imagine that I'm up to something else. You're a puzzle to him. You've noticed that, haven't you?"

I nodded.

"All right, then you'll take Lillian to your apartment. Thursday night you'll be in the Strip. At nine-thirty A.M. the prison guards change over."

"I know."

"At ten P.M., provided everything goes smoothly, Delacorte will be outside. I'm going to be notified by telephone and—"

"Where? Where are you going to be?"

"In Bremen. In my apartment. I, too, have to be out of Treuwall. After all, I'm also under surveillance. Only after Delacorte has been freed do I leave Bremen. That's when my work begins. Now, as soon as I'm notified I shall call the man in Frankfurt who will bring you the manuscripts. Five novels and a script. Right?"

"Correct."

"That's quite a big package. My man will bring it to the Strip."

"But that could attract attention."

"No, it won't. He is coming in a delivery van. Champagne. A late delivery. The manuscripts will be in a box. You can check them immediately for authenticity and completeness."

"Suppose they're not?"

"They will be."

"Quite. But if they're not?"

"You can raise the alarm. Call Paradin and so on. You can call him if you haven't received your delivery by ten-thirty. But you'd do that in any case, wouldn't you?"

"Yes, I would."

Werner rose and began to pace the room. Cigarette ash dropped. He didn't notice.

"What happens if I inform Paradin even after I receive the manuscripts?"

He stopped abruptly. A grin contorted his lips.

"If you do that, little brother," Werner said, "you're not going to live long. Not much longer at all. Lillian would be first. And that very quickly. I'm going to make this very clear to you since that possibility has already been taken into consideration. After all you have observed up to now, I trust you believe me?"

"Yes," I said.

Still I had to do it, I thought. In spite of everything and in any case I must do it. I had to make it appear as if Werner alone were at fault when the entire action failed. I already had an idea how that could be done.

"How's Lillian?" my brother asked.

"Fine."

"Does she still say she doesn't want to see me under any circumstances?"

"Yes."

"Bad, bad Werner," he grimaced. He scratched his chin. "If I only knew why she's so afraid of me."

"Afraid?"

"Yes, afraid," he insisted. "Think about it. It's the only explanation. She's afraid of me. But why?"

Soon after that he left. I took out the tape recorder, thinking that with a bit of luck nothing dreadful would happen, not to Lillian and me, Minski and Rachel. If my plan failed, then there was only the last resort of escape.

I had mailed the film from Minski's camera before I had returned to the hotel. The film was on its way to Frankfurt.

I suddenly felt inexplicably optimistic. Since I could think of no concrete reason for my sudden confidence, I ascribed it to the fact that I had just seen Werner very much afraid.

I recorded my recent experience in great detail as Werner had instructed me to do. After about two hours of taping I carefully locked away the tape recorder in its bag, which in turn I locked in a suitcase. I slipped the key into my pocket and left my room. I wanted to eat something. As I left the elevator someone called my name. It was Pierre the bartender, who was gesturing to me from his bar. I went to him. There were several people in the bar; soft music filled the intimately lit room.

Pierre was beaming. "Herr Mark, there's something I want to show you."

"Look over there," Pierre said to me. We were standing at the entrance to the large dining room. At a table at the far end I saw Chief Inspector Eilers and a blonde woman about forty years old, his wife. They were obviously too happy to be with each other to notice us.

"They're back together again," Pierre said, beaming. He must have noticed the question in my eyes, because he began to explain.

"You know when I finish working here, Herr Mark, I usually go to another bar. Meet a lot of my friends there for some talk and a drink. Just to unwind, you understand. Just lately I've found Chief Inspector Eilers there and pretty drunk. I took him home a couple of times. He sort of fell apart—only smoked and drank, wouldn't shave, wouldn't go out except at night to this bar. As you know people didn't like him because of his political views. But after his wife left him and his son got into trouble everyone began to feel sorry for him. One night he said to me that it was all his fault. That business of hating and hunting down Nazis made him disliked. He realized that he'd have to be like everyone else or leave a country he liked. Well, to make it short, he promised me he'd keep his mouth shut. All he really wanted was his wife to come back to him. But he was afraid to ask her; well, I did it for him. You can see the result. Like it should be—two happy people."

"Everything is all right," I said. "And Eilers is not going to say any more against the Nazis."

"That's right. He's an intelligent man. He was just wrongheaded about his business. Now he's seen the light— just the way you and I realized somewhere along the way that it just doesn't make any sense any more. One ends up looking ridiculous or unhappy. It's much too late for that sort of thing anyway; times have changed and those things are not important now."

"It's not important that there are Nazis here?"

"But no, Herr Mark," Pierre admonished me. "That's not what I mean. I mean it's not important because one cannot do anything to change the facts." He smiled, happy but fatigued. "Didn't I do a good job? Two happy people."

"Three," I corrected him. "You forgot yourself."

"Right, three." He nodded. "When they have finished eating they promised to come and have a drink in the bar. It would be nice if you would come, too, Herr Mark."

"I'd like to."

"We'll celebrate a little."

"The happy end."

I could not find any sleep that night, and so I completed another tape. I was still recording when morning dawned.

She had intended to run to him, embrace him, kiss him, but now that he was walking toward her she found it impossible to move. As though paralyzed, she stood motionless, her blue eyes open wide, her blond hair falling loosely about her shoulders. She was wearing a leopard coat over a sand-colored wool dress, a small alligator bag in her hand. Panos Mitsotakis, in a gray suit and blue raincoat, looked thinner than a year ago when Vanessa had last seen him. The expression in his black eyes was one of great embarrassment. Vanessa's trembling lips formed a smile. Then he also smiled. Now he stood before her. She flung her arms around him and buried her head on his chest.

He stroked her hair, called her name and then they looked at each other, unable to speak. Vanessa felt close to tears. She laughed instead, a hysterical, uneven laugh. His laugh was forced, nervous. She took his hand and together they picked up his suitcase; in silence they walked to her car. Vanessa drove. Panos cleared his throat, straightened his tie, brushed back his thick black hair. Finally Vanessa asked, "Excited?"

"Yes," Panos answered.

"So am I. You can't be as excited as I am. Have you eaten?"

"No."

"Wonderful. I've prepared dinner for us."

"You shouldn't have done that. A restaurant—"

"Restaurant! Out of the question! I have a small apartment, Panos, I think you'll like it." Vanessa had recovered her equanimity. She glanced at him briefly. "You look good."

"Britt! Watch it! That bus!"

"In fact, you look great," Vanessa went on. "Better than a year ago. How are things at the Sorbonne?" Traffic was heavy. Vanessa had to concentrate on her driving. "Are you still living in our hotel?"

"No."

"But you did get my letter?"

"Yes, of course. They, they forward my mail."

"I'm so glad, Panos. So happy that you finally came. I've missed you so!"

He was embarrassed. "You'll have to forgive me, Britt."

"But I have forgiven . . ."

"That's not what I mean. I was . . . I have . . . it is . . . I have to explain. There's so much to explain."

"Later," Vanessa said, her eyes dancing. "Later you can explain, Panos. We have a lot of time."

He was silent.

In Vanessa's small, modern apartment she offered Panos a martini while she busied herself with the dinner. Finally she appeared, curtsied, holding her hands out to him, *"Monsieur est servi!"*

She led him into the pink-and-white dining room. On a small table in a silver ice bucket stood a magnum of champagne. It was excellent wine and Panos praised the dinner.

Vanessa was radiant.

He ate about half his dinner before he put down his knife and fork.

"What is it?" Vanessa asked, alarmed. "Don't you feel good?"

He shook his head.

"Then what is it? Don't you like the food?"

"Yes, it is delicious but I—"

"Yes?"

"I shouldn't have come here. I should have told you at the airport. I had intended to do that. It was a mistake to come here with you. It makes everything twice as difficult."

"Makes what difficult?"

He did not answer.

"Panos!"

He gulped a glass of champagne.

"It's all a misunderstanding," he said, hoarse. "A terrible mistake. I . . . it wasn't my fault, Britt, or yes, maybe it was. I came to explain to you . . ."

"Explain what?"

"Britt, that letter, my mother's obituary notice . . ."

439

"What about it? Tell me!"

"It was sent to you in error. You shouldn't have received it at all."

"Then why did you send it to me?"

"I didn't send it."

"Well, who did then?"

"Georgette." Panos looked at Vanessa, his eyes troubled and unsteady.

"Who is Georgette?"

"My wife," Panos answered.

At about that time Lillian and I arrived at my apartment in Frankfurt. About thirty meters down the road the car I first noticed following us on the autobahn had parked. While it was still light I had seen the two men inside it but had not recognized them. Olsen apparently was not on duty. I felt reassured that Paradin had used new men to watch us. Reliable officers, not traitors like Olsen. Paradin after all couldn't be surrounded only by traitors.

The day before we left Treuwall I had gone once more to Paradin's office at his request.

"Frau Lombard is going to be discharged from the hospital tomorrow," he told me. "I expect she will want to leave here right away."

"Yes. I promised that I would take her to Frankfurt for the time being. If you don't mind."

"Why should I mind?"

"Well, perhaps you still need her."

"I have talked to her often and extensively. I spoke to her even on Sunday," Paradin said.

"I know," I said.

He stopped before me and looked straight into my eyes. I met his gaze openly, calmly. A useful trick I had perfected.

"Richie," Paradin said, "this is your last opportunity to make a clean breast of everything. This now is the lull before the storm. It won't be much longer before something happens—and then it will be too late. Then I won't be able to help you. Well?"

"Well, what?"

"Why don't you confide in me? I promise you that I shall do everything in my power to protect and help you no matter what you've done. I promise, Richie!"

"There is nothing to tell you."

"Richie, we've known each other a long time. I . . . I like you. Be sensible. Come over to my side."

"I'm not on the other! I'm just as sorry as you are that our friendly relationship has been marred, but there is nothing that I can do. You're forgetting that it was I who set you on Delacorte's trail."

"I'm not forgetting that," he said softly. "That's one fact I keep remembering. It could be cited as an exonerating circumstance should you be accused of complicity in an attempt to liberate Delacorte."

"You still believe that is going to happen?"

"I'm convinced of that now more than ever."

Vehemently I said, "I've had enough of this! Can you prove that I have done anything wrong, even a trifle?"

"No. Unfortunately."

"Then I demand to be left in peace! Another thing! I've also had enough of this snooper of yours, this Olsen! I don't want to be watched forever more! I have just had it!"

"You will have to leave it to me to decide how much longer you need to be guarded."

Now I knew what I wanted to know.

"Then I'm free to go now?"

"You can go," Paradin said contemptuously, turning his back to me.

I left, thinking that Paradin was feeling exactly as Geyer and his principals had intended he should.

The remaining part of that Monday I spent in the hotel. I completed taping my detailed confession for Werner.

441

That night I gave him the last four of the ten tapes, also the tape recorder and the blue bag. He spot-checked the tapes and seemed satisfied.

"So, you're leaving tomorrow. With Lillian. Lucky you. I'm just curious to know what you've thought up to trip me up at the very last moment."

"If you don't have the manuscripts in the Strip at ten-thirty on Thursday you'll find out very quickly."

"You know what I really mean," he said, laughing. "You've thought up something. But it won't work, Richie."

"If you leave me alone, I'll leave you alone," I said curtly.

"You'd be smart to do that, little brother. You're no match for those guys. Or for me for that matter. If you'd keep quiet—that would save you. But, of course, I can't tell you what to do."

He was still laughing as I was leaving—an uneasy laugh, I thought.

"Give my humblest regards to Lillian," he called after me.

I went down to the bar for a last drink with Pierre, who seemed sorry to see me leave.

"I'll think of you often, Herr Mark. I bought one of your books today. Already started to read it too. Great!"

"Which book?"

"*Black*," he said promptly. "You won an award for it, didn't you? And also for the film? I saw the movie when it came out. Great, really, just great!"

I slept soundly that night. The following morning, after packing, paying my bill and distributing tips I left the hotel.

I picked up Lillian at the hospital. The detective who had guarded her there accompanied us to the villa in the Waldpromenade. He had the keys which had been found on Lillian the night she had been admitted to the hospital. It was cold in the villa. I helped Lillian pack several large suitcases. The detective, a short man, stood nearby, helped

442

her but spoke very little. Watching Lillian choose from her many clothes and pack them very carefully made me nervous, and I tried to start a conversation with the taciturn detective. Soon I learned that he had been a friend of Paul Ericksen's.

"How is Frau Ericksen?"

"She'll pull through this somehow."

"There still no sign of her husband?"

"Not the least. What's more I don't think we'll ever find him," the officer said. "My sister and I are looking after his wife now."

My car was heavily loaded when we finally left. The trunk barely closed; there were more suitcases in the back seats. Lillian fell asleep for a while and awakened just as we arrived in Kassel. It had grown dark meanwhile. As we had not eaten since breakfast, we stopped for a while to have sandwiches and coffee packed for us in the hotel. We felt better after that and then drove on.

As we passed the next rest area I noticed another car pull out and follow us at a safe distance. Nearing Frankfurt I thought I recognized Olsen's car—twice. He had known that we were driving to Frankfurt and could easily have calculated the time we would arrive. All he needed to do was wait at the exit of the autobahn. Now, as I was unloading Lillian's luggage from my car, I did not see Olsen's car. The other one, carrying the two detectives, was parked down the road. It was a very windy night in Frankfurt but not cold. I had emptied the car except for two carefully packed suitcases which I locked into the car. One was mine, the other belonged to Lillian. The suitcases we would take if we had to flee.

Lillian decided not to unpack that night. She talked very little, but whenever our eyes met she smiled. She seemed happy.

"I have to go to the club," I told her. "What are you going to do?"

"Take a bath," she answered. "And go to bed. When will you be back, Richie?"

"Late. Probably very late." There was much Minski and I had to discuss. "I'll leave you the keys. Lock yourself in, but don't leave the key in the lock so I can come in. Don't open the door for anyone. Don't answer the phone. I'll let it ring three times, hang up and ring again."

Lillian nodded, yawning.

"You'd better go to bed right away," I said.

"Tomorrow—the day after tomorrow is Thursday. Do you think we shall—?"

"No."

"But you're not quite sure?"

"No."

"Don't make such a face, Richie. Are you afraid?"

"A little, sure."

"I'm not. Now that we're together—for the first time in years really, we're truly together, aren't we, Richie?—now I'm not at all afraid. Are you sure you're going to get these passports?"

"I'm positive."

"Then whatever is going to happen, let it happen. I don't care. As long as we're together. Richie, kiss me."

I kissed her soft, warm, exciting lips. My very being was overwhelmed with tenderness as she pressed close to me.

"Tell me that you love me," she whispered.

"I love you."

"And I love you," she whispered. "I love you, I love you, I love you."

I locked the door from the outside. As I got into my car one of the men left the car parked down the road and the other followed me. As I came to the end of the road I recognized Olsen's car. He was sitting at the wheel. Stopped at the next traffic light, I could see both cars in my rearview mirror.

"Your wife——?" Vanessa asked.

"Yes," Panos, obviously unhappy. "It was a terrible mistake. I really didn't want to hurt you, Britt. When I found out that Georgette had sent you the notice it was already too late." Panos spoke French now and very quickly. "I only found that out when I received your letter. I had flown to Athens for my mother's funeral. Georgette had the notices printed and had compiled a list of addresses she had taken from my old address books. She had shown me the list and had asked me if these were the names to whom she ought to send notices. I was so upset at the time—I loved my mother very much. . . ."

"How did your wife find my address? After all, you always returned my letters." Vanessa's voice was calm now.

"That's true, but at that time, during those first few weeks, I meant to write you. I was very unhappy after you left me. I couldn't write, I hated you for leaving me, and I longed for you at the same time. I know it's crazy . . ."

"It's not that crazy," Vanessa said softly. She poured herself a glass of champagne. "Would you like some more too?"

"No, thanks."

"Too bad," Vanessa said. "Too bad about the wasted dinner. At least the champagne is not going to be wasted too." She emptied her glass and refilled it. "So that was your wife's handwriting. How long have you been married?"

"Since May."

"Six months?"

"Yes. I . . . I couldn't stand being alone any more. I met Georgette during the winter. She studied at the Sorbonne. Her father is a doctor."

"Where are you living now?"

"Georgette had a small apartment at the Quai d'Orléans

445

on the Ile Saint-Louis—opposite the Cité and Notre-Dame."

"Very good neighborhood." Vanessa looked searchingly at him. "You're not driving a taxi any more, are you?"

Panos blushed.

"Georgette inherited the apartment from an aunt who died. She's not wealthy if that's what you mean."

"Not poor either."

"No, not poor either. Her father's a successful MD. He sends her a check every month. But I'm not living off her! I earn money. I tutor students in physics, math and chemistry. I have many students. I earn quite a bit of money, Britt."

"I'm glad for you," Vanessa said. "Why did you send me those carnations?"

"I . . . I wanted to do something. I was sorry . . . and Georgette was sorry too when she found out what had happened. She's not jealous."

"That she needn't be."

"She asks you to forgive her."

"For what?" Vanessa asked, sipping champagne.

"Well, we have . . . she . . . we must have hurt you, upset you. My God, you must have thought that I—"

"Yes, I did indeed." Vanessa smiled. "But now I know better."

"You're taking it very well," he said.

"If you only knew. Is it true that you have something to do at the university here? Or did you come just because of me?"

"No, that's true. I've been asked to give a lecture here. Some professors read a paper I wrote about some work I've been doing. They were very impressed. A great honor for me . . ." Panos, relieved that Vanessa was not making a scene, talked quickly, switching from French to German. She doesn't cry. She doesn't scream. She's quite a girl. And I'm a decent guy. I didn't avoid this meeting with her.

"The university also paid for my flight and a room in a hotel here. Perhaps I ought to call and let them know that I've arrived. Could I use your phone a minute, Britt?"

"Of course," Vanessa said. "And you'd better call for a taxi to take you there, too. You must be tired. You'll need to rest for your lecture tomorrow."

There was surprise in his eyes.

"You want me to leave? Now?"

"Yes," she said. "That's what I want. It would be nice of you, Panos. It was not your fault. I can understand. It was nice of you to come here and explain, but now I think I'd like you to leave. The telephone is in the living room. A telephone book too."

He made his calls, then put on his coat in the small foyer before coming back to Vanessa, who was still sitting at the dinner table.

"Farewell, Britt," Panos said, holding out his hand to her.

She grasped it weakly.

"So long, Panos," she said without looking at him. "Good luck to you. And to your wife. I'll keep my fingers crossed for your lecture tomorrow."

He kissed her hair, gently brushed over it and walked to the door. It closed behind him. Vanessa did not move for some time. Finally she rose and began to clear the table. A dish slipped from her hands and broke, its contents splattering. Vanessa began to laugh hysterically.

"Well," Minski said, "and that's that."

We were in our office in the Strip where Boris had just told me the story he had heard from Vanessa an hour ago. Now, dressed in an elegant, black, décolleté dress, she was sitting in the mirrored room with Petra Schalke. The masculine lesbian was aglow with happiness that Vanessa permitted her to touch and fondle her. Vanessa was intoxicated but not obviously so. I wouldn't have suspected it if Boris had not told me. Tonio Prinz was missing. Perhaps he was still unnerved by his experience with the snake.

Through the one-way mirror we could watch the statuesque, blonde Corabelle perform her act with the python: a nude girl becoming increasingly aroused by the slow sensuous movements of an extraordinarily affectionate snake. It was an excellent act but not as superb as Vanessa's candle act.

"And she laughed about that?" I asked Minski.

"Hysterical, of course," Boris explained. "Had a lot of alcohol, too."

"Poor thing."

"Poor thing, my foot," Minski said, vehement. "I ask you, what did she expect? Spent only a day and a night with the bum. Okay, must have been a great night. But then she doesn't hear from him for a year. Then comes the obituary notice. What's an obituary notice? Any normal person can count it off on his fingers that something is not quite kosher!"

"But Vanessa is not a normal person," I said patiently. "We know what she's been through. Always alone. Deserted. Always bad luck with men. Hating her father. And then comes this one man with whom she knew happiness. You must admit a girl like Vanessa performing here is just as unreasonable to expect as what she now expects from Panos."

"With just a little sense she—"

"Sense doesn't even enter into it. Other women would have reacted differently. More logically, reasonably. Vanessa is still a child—she always will be. If you didn't know that yourself why did you always treat her as if she were our child? Why did you release her from her contract? Be honest, Boris. You too thought it possible that Panos would come back to Vanessa!"

"Possible . . ." he muttered. "If I had been Vanessa—" He broke off. "All right, Richie. You're right. What do

448

we know of women? Nothing. Nothing at all. It's terrible for her. She didn't deserve——"

"What is she going to do now?"

"She didn't say. But when I see how she behaves with Petra Schalke . . ."

"She's drunk."

"That's not all. Something different. She's been hurt badly. Something's snapped tonight. What am I going to do with this?" He indicated the antique Beethoven score. I had found it on the rear seat of my car. Somehow it had escaped me when I had unloaded the car.

"Put it in the safe," I answered. "It's valuable and I don't want to leave it in the apartment, especially since I have no idea how long I shall be there. Apropos——"

"Yes. I talked to the man. He'll have the passports tomorrow. Says they're first-rate. Cost a fortune. But then you get what you pay for. But even with those passports it won't be easy for you to get away."

"Why not?"

"Because borders and airports will surely have been alerted by Paradin just in case. Then perhaps you'll have to leave in a great hurry and no suitable plane or train leaves just then. You'll have to rent a car. More complications." Minski had opened the safe and placed the Ninth inside.

I was watching Corabelle's performance. The girl was an excellent acrobat, I thought appreciatively. Petra Schalke's hand had all but disappeared down Vanessa's low-cut neckline, her face enraptured. Minski was observing it too.

"Vanessa ripped up all the posters in her room. She gave me this." He raised the piece of paper upon which Panos, in Greek letters, had once written:

MAN HAS LITTLE LUCK

"She said she'd had enough of men," Minski declared

mournfully. "That Schalke woman won after all. In the end it's always just a question of patience."

"Vanessa is really going to . . ."

"Yes. That's what she said. She also said she had a surprise for us." He scratched his head. "We're to wait for her."

Vanessa came a half-hour later.

"I don't have much time," she declared.

Corabelle's act had come to an end. People were drinking and dancing. Petra Schalke was sitting alone at a table, smiling, an expression of triumph on her face.

"I can't let Petra wait long," Vanessa's voice was hoarse. "Got a drink for a girl? Whisky."

I poured a drink for her. She gulped it, then held out the glass for a refill.

"I need a lot of this, you know, boys."

"Don't do it, Vanessa," Minski said. "You don't have to do it. Go and have a good sleep. It will pass."

"What will?"

"Your grief about Panos."

"Who is Panos?" Vanessa asked pointedly. "I'm going on a trip, Boris. Next month. We've already discussed everything. We're going on Petra's beautiful, wonderful yacht. It's going to be a beautiful, wonderful trip. I must get back to Petra. You know, she's really quite nice. Really. Stupid prejudices I had as far as lesbians were concerned. Very stupid." She swayed. "Can't let her wait. So I had better come to the point right away. Boris, you'll have to forgive me."

"For what?"

"Yesterday, when that man was here, I listened at your door."

Minski grew pale. My hands became moist.

"Which man?"

"Come on," Vanessa said. "Don't let's play games. The

man who's bringing counterfeit passports for Richie and Lillian."

"Really, Vanessa . . ." I began but Minski gestured for me to be quiet.

"You're not angry that I listened? I only did it because I worried about you and Richie. You're so involved in this business."

"It was nice of you to listen," Boris said. "Shows how devoted you're to us. I'm really sorry you're leaving us. Couldn't you——?"

"No," Vanessa answered, quickly. "Now listen. I heard the man say that Lillian and Richie were still running risks because of the border controls and so on. Even if they went by car. Right?"

"Yes, and?" Minski was very calm.

"Richie," Vanessa again filled her glass, "you know how I feel about you. But I'm not jealous any more. I want you to be happy with Lillian. And safe. So: Petra was so surprised and overwhelmed by happiness that she asked me if I had a wish, any wish, that she could fulfill. I told her. She was touched by the modesty of my request."

"What request?" Boris asked.

"Petra owns a plane, right?" Vanessa sipped her drink. "A Bonanza. Big enough for six people. Modern. And a pilot."

"Yes, and?"

"Well, I asked if I could have the plane and the pilot. Not as a present, but just as a toy. I told her I loved to fly and I would love to show off the plane as if it belonged to me. Petra was delighted. She calls me her sweet little child." Vanessa laughed. "She said police and customs at the airport know her pilot. His name is Wohl. And a call is sufficient for him to be ready for take off in an hour. From now on the plane is at my disposal and of that of any of my friends if I wish it. I already have Wohl's telephone number. All my friends need are valid passports. Petra instructed him immediately. Somehow I think the pilot is glad to have something to do. If you let me know, Richie, then you and Lillian can be away in an hour. Comfortably and safely. Am I good to you or not?"

"You're marvelous," I said.

She came to me and kissed me on my lips.

"Aren't I though?" she said. "I am the most marvelous girl in all this world. Petra says so too. . . ." She reached for her mink stole. "Have to get back to her. So long, boys."

She left quickly.

"What's up?" Minski's voice was shaky. He glanced at me. "What are you thinking?"

"You know that night Lillian called here, that night everything began, Petra Schalke was in Vanessa's dressing room. Then I had a peculiar feeling that she would play a very important part in my life. Strange, isn't it?"

"Very strange," Minski said. "God forbid that all feelings turn out to be true. I have some, too, you know."

It was almost 4 A.M. when I returned to my apartment. Lillian was awake and I told her of the counterfeit passports and Vanessa's Bonanza. Lillian was very excited about it all.

While I showered I thought about the detectives guarding us. This time it was a different car and different officers who were parked down the road. Relief men no doubt. I had not seen Olsen's car.

That night was the first time in two years that Lillian and I embraced one another. It was as if we were together for the very first time. We were swept away in a wave of tenderness and passion and fell asleep only when dawn came, arm in arm, body to body. That was Wednesday, November 30.

We spent most of that day at home and only went out to eat. From the restaurant I called Vanessa. I was in luck. She was at home. She told me that to make the pilot's acquaintance she had already completed a sightseeing trip with him over Frankfurt that morning. It had been fun, the pilot was a nice guy and she was going for another flight tomorrow morning.

"By the way, I'm going to move to Petra's tomorrow." She gave me her new friend's address and telephone number.

That night I again went to the Strip. Vanessa and Petra Schalke were not there. I returned home early. We had another night of the sweet contrasts of love—of passion, of tenderness. For the first time in years I felt happy. I had received the counterfeit passports from Minski, with valid visas for Egypt and Argentina, and international vaccination certificates. Lillian's passport was in the name of Angela Dirksen, mine, Peter Horneck.

Thursday, quiet, uneventful, was mild but wintry-gray. Lillian and I went for a walk. We left the house by the rear door, which led into a garden separated from the Park Luisa by a small gate. Though always locked, each tenant had his key. The park was large and poorly lit at night. It seemed inconceivable to me that this side of the house was not under surveillance. I had come to that conclusion after going several times through the same exit without ever meeting or seeing a person in the park or at the Forsthausstrasse which adjoined it. I was to find out later just how well the villa was being watched—but by then it was too late to be of use.

Just as a test Lillian and I again left the house by this rear exit. Our apparently unobserved exit was reassuring. From a telephone booth in the Forsthausstrasse I called Vanessa.

"You know, it could be that I might need the plane tonight—rather late. Friends of mine might want to fly to Switzerland. Zurich, probably. They aren't sure of the time yet or if they're going to leave at all, for that matter. But if you could ask your pilot—what's his name?"

"Wohl."

"If you would ask him to be at the airport at nine P.M."

"Okay, Richie. How many passengers will there be or don't you know that yet?"

"Two. A man and a woman."

"He won't ask any questions. As long as their passports are okay . . ."

"They are. Now, if until midnight—or better one A.M.—no one arrives he can go home again. Do you think that's too much to ask?"

"I don't think so. He told me only today that his life consists of waiting. He is a philosopher. He doesn't mind."

"Then I can rely on it?"

"Definitely."

"And how is everything with you?"

"Great, Richie, just wonderful."

I left the telephone booth.

"Well?" Lillian asked, her arm firmly in mine.

"The plane will be at our disposal from nine o'clock on," I answered.

About eight o'clock that night I left Lillian to go to the club. She was to call me from the telephone booth in the Forsthausstrasse the moment she became aware of anything unusual. The telephones in the club were not tapped. One of the detectives guarding the club and working at the bar had told Boris that the police had tried to tap them. They had been unable to do so since the house, being old, still had the original cables, which could not be tapped. I gave Lillian keys for the doors and the gates and left by the front entrance. As I drove away I saw a different car follow me; a different officer stayed behind. Naturally they worked in shifts. Surely Olsen was relieved also. I did not see him.

The Strip was almost empty at this early hour. Minski and I were sitting in our office, waiting. At 9:30 I said, "Now they're starting."

At 9:20 December 1, 1966, after the lights in his cell

had gone out the prisoner Delacorte, using his canteen, a hairnet and pajamas created the impression of someone lying underneath the rumpled blanket of his cot. Delacorte was dressed in civilian clothes but without a tie or shoelaces. His cell, number 19, was situated on the ground floor in the left wing of the old prison.

Everything I am now reporting I was told later by Delacorte.

Patiently the prisoner waited until Scherr opened his door four minutes later. The man did not speak. Scherr, on duty inside the prison, was in the possession of three keys. In stockinged feet, carrying his shoes, Delacorte slipped through the door which Scherr locked soundlessly. The hall was sparsely lit. Both men hurried toward an iron door which Scherr opened, and then locked behind him.

With his third key he opened another iron door, one that led into the prison yard. Scherr hissed, "Wait in the shadows!" Delacorte slipped past him into the open.

Scherr locked the door from inside, passed through the iron gate they had gone through a few seconds earlier and hurried to the glass-enclosed turret on the second floor of the center building. He arrived there exactly at nine-thirty. Under the watchful eyes of the sergeant on duty he turned in his three keys, receiving one from the guard with whom he was now switching his tour of duty. That single key opened the door in the high wall enclosing the prison yards. Extending from this wall was another which enclosed the entire building and, opposite the main entrance, a massive gateway for trucks, alongside of which was a small guardroom.

In a heavy overcoat Scherr made his way to the main entrance where a colleague unlocked the door for him. Outside, he patrolled the area, saw that the officer in the guardroom was dozing, hurried to the gate in the wall enclosing the left wing and opened it. He stepped through it quickly into the yard and whistled softly. Delacorte appeared by his side. Together they passed through the gate, and waited in the shadows.

Promptly, according to plan, a sudden tumult broke out on the road outside the prison. The elderly guard, infuriated by the noise made by some ten youths embroiled in a fight, dashed from his room, cursing and swinging a nightstick. At the same time Scherr and Delacorte quickly crossed the well-lit yard and passed through the gate. To their left was the guard still berating the youths, to their right a small delivery truck of the Hand Laundry Oscar Hippel. The two men ran toward it. Scherr, arriving there first, flung open its doors. Delacorte jumped in, Scherr followed. The driver was the brown-haired youth who, for his cowardice in the Strip, had been punished so barbarically by the thin-lipped troopleader. A second youth in the back of the truck locked the doors as soon as the two men were inside. The truck had disappeared before the elderly prison guard had chased the noisy, fighting youths down the road far enough away from his prison. Cursing, he returned to his guardroom and picked up the receiver of the shrilling telephone. The voice of the sergeant on duty asked, "What's that ruckus out front there?"

The officer made his report.

"Did you disperse that bunch?"

"Yes, I did, sergeant!"

"Well, that's all right then."

The laundry truck came to a halt behind a hearse in a quiet street. Scherr and Delacorte, now wearing well-fitting suits, coats, and hats, alighted from the truck. The clothes they had worn remained in the truck, which immediately drove off.

The rear doors of the hearse were flung open.

"Heil!" whispered a youth inside the hearse. A second adolescent, somewhat older, sat behind the wheel. The hearse drove away. The youth who had opened the doors for Delacorte and Scherr switched on a flashlight. He spoke respectfully. "So far everything has gone well. The troopleader is waiting for you at the Black Gate. I'm to give you this." He handed over several documents, also two passports, vaccination certificates, envelopes containing German marks, Swiss francs, Egyptian pounds. Delacorte examined it all carefully.

"Excellent," he said finally.

"And here," the youth said, "are two suitcases. This one is yours." He indicated one to Delacorte. "Everything you might need. Comb, handkerchief, wallet, pen, notebook, change. If you'll put those things in your pocket please."

It was 9:46. They were on their way to the heath.

The headlights skimmed over the megaliths of the cairn. Again Delacorte and Scherr alighted.

"Good-by, boys. And thank you very much," Delacorte said.

"Heil," came the answer. The man hurried toward a spot where headlights had signaled briefly. A Mercedes. A door opened. It was the troopleader, wearing civilian clothes and a trench coat. In silence he raised a hand.

"Stop that nonsense!" Delacorte gasped. His suitcase seemed to be very heavy. "You've done a good job," he said. "Really great. Just great."

"Don't talk too soon," the troopleader said. He opened the rear door for Delacorte, who asked, "Is Werner coming to meet us?"

"No, we have to go to Bremen."

"Bremen? But . . ."

"The plan was changed," the troopleader explained.

It was seven minutes past ten.

10:28.

"Two more minutes," I said, "then I'll telephone Paradin."

457

"Take it easy," Minski murmured, wiping perspiration from his forehead. "Don't always be in such a hurry. Give the man ten minutes. God knows where he was delayed."

The telephone rang.

"Yes?"

"Richie!" Lillian's voice was breathless.

"What's up?"

"Please, come at once. The man is here with the package."

"Why is he with you? Why didn't he come here?"

"He said he could only come here. You're to come here too. He wants to give you the package. You must check it. I don't know if . . . if it's the right one."

"Where are you calling from?"

"The telephone booth. The man is here with me. We went through the park . . ."

I heard noises, then Olsen's voice.

"Evening."

"You are to take care of this?"

"You still think we are idiots, Herr Mark," Olsen complained. "Naturally your house is guarded. The rear facing the park too. My side. I take turns with a colleague. Tonight is my turn. With the help of a few skeleton keys I got in. The flatfoot outside knows nothing. That's why you must come here. I mean because of the officers in your club I can't show up there. If you leave now by the rear exit you can come here and take a look at the package. Hurry it up. I'd like to get it behind me."

It sounded reasonable, yet something seemed wrong. My apartment had a Yale lock!

"How did you get into my apartment?"

"I rang. The lady knows me. You've told her I was a detective."

True. What I hadn't told her was the kind of detective he was.

"I told her that we'd intercepted the package. That set

458

her mind at ease. Now she doesn't seem so sure she's done the right thing."

"Let me talk to her."

"Richie . . ."

"Don't be alarmed. Everything is all right. I'll explain it to you."

"But, Richie . . ."

"Later. I'll explain later. Let me talk to the man again." Olsen answered.

"Go back to the apartment," I told him. I didn't feel right about that but I had to have those manuscripts! "Go to the apartment. I'll be there as soon as I can. And listen! If anything, anything at all should happen to the lady . . ."

"Are you crazy? What do you mean happen to her? I have a job to do and the sooner that's done the better I'll like it."

"I'll see you soon," I said and hung up.

"What's up?" Minski asked, worried. I told him briefly.

"I don't like it," he said promptly.

"I don't either but what can I do?"

"Well, now you have to go there. One has to try and see the other people's situation. This way is less danger-our for them. It is important that you get your manuscripts. And that you are with Lillian. Now. Is there anything you want me to do?"

I glanced at my watch.

"It's just ten-thirty now. If I haven't called you by eleven o'clock—no, it might take a little longer than that—if I or Lillian for that matter haven't called you by eleven-thirty to say that I have the manuscripts and Paradin has been informed, then *you* call him. Immediately, Boris! You have the number?"

"Yes."

"Just call him and tell him that you're worried—something seems wrong with me. You can also call my apartment after half-past eleven because then something did go wrong. Just tell Paradin you're afraid something has happened to me—that should do it." I rose and put on my coat. "Once Paradin hears that he'll raise the alarm. But I don't think anything will happen. They need peace and time now."

I held my hand out to Minski.

"Mazel tov," he said softly.

It was 10:38.

I left the club through our back yard, the basement of the adjoining house, its backyard and a garage. I flagged down a taxi. No one was following me. I discharged the cab, doubled back a short distance before entering the park, hurrying across the damp grass. There was the fence, the gate. I opened it, locked it behind me, hastened to the near door of the villa. It, too, was locked. After I had entered I locked that, too. I moved soundlessly, knocked at my door.

It was opened immediately by Lillian.

"Thank God that you came so quickly."

"What—"

"Nothing happened. I'm just glad you're here."

A fidgety Olsen, dressed in a dark suit and dark coat, stood in the living room. I switched off the light, went to the window looking out over the Humperdinckstrasse, parted the heavy drapes a little. On the street below a solitary man was walking up and down.

I closed the drapes and switched on the light. On the carpet was a rather large package.

"You carried that by yourself?"

"Yes. Damned heavy," Olsen said. He reached into his pocket and pulled out a pocket knife, which he handed to me. I kneeled down, cut the string of the package and ripped off the wrapping paper. The manuscripts. I recognized my brother's small, neat handwriting. The numerous corrections methodically and legibly written. Yes, these were the manuscripts!

I looked up to Lillian and smiled.

460

Then I glanced at my watch. Seven minutes past eleven o'clock.

"Satisfied?" Olsen asked.

I nodded.

"Good." He pulled a pack of cigarettes from his pocket. He offered it to Lillian, who took one, and to me.

"No, thanks," I said.

Olsen reached into his pockets, presumably for a match. I bent over the manuscripts, filled by a great sense of relief. After that everything happened very fast. When Olsen drew his hands from his pockets they held a bottle and a white piece of cloth. As I scrambled to my feet he had already poured some sickeningly sweet fluid onto the cloth, kicked my knees; and as I fell he was on me, pressing the moist cloth over my face. I fought for breath, yet inhaled more chloroform. Just before I lost consciousness, I felt the sharp pain as a needle jabbed my right thigh.

My head was splitting as I regained consciousness, my throat parched. I was still lying on the carpet. Cautiously I opened my eyes. The electric light hurt my eyes and I quickly closed them again. The room swam, out of focus, as I tried to sit up. Nausea and dizziness made thinking difficult. I tried to call Lillian, but could only squeeze out a hoarse sound. I glanced at my watch.

3:47.

I had been lying here for four hours.

Four hours.

Panic gave me strength. I staggered through the apartment. The guest room, where I had put Lillian's suitcases, was in disarray. Dresses, shoes, coats were strewn around the room. It seemed as if two suitcases were missing. Lillian was gone! Olsen! He had been alone. Had he? Perhaps after I had been knocked out other men had entered my apartment from the park. They must have knocked out Lillian too and taken her along as hostage.

461

I staggered into the bathroom, put my head under the cold water faucet. Water splashed in all directions. I turned my head and drank; I vomited, drank again. The cold water helped a little. Coffee. I staggered into the kitchen, where I put water on to boil. While the water was heating I changed my clothes. Drinking the scalding, extremely strong coffee I began to feel better, think clearer.

So they had tricked me. They had given me the manuscripts and taken Lillian. Lillian! Where was she? Where were they now? They had a head start of four hours. If Delacorte had been freed according to plan, that time was increased by two additional hours.

I had to find Lillian. That probably meant leaving Frankfurt. Leaving Germany. I had to telephone. But not from here.

I finished dressing, then opened the desk drawer where I had kept my counterfeit passport, vaccination certificate, German and American banknotes. They were still there. I had given Lillian's counterfeit passport to her. As fast as I could I stuffed the documents and money into my suitpockets and began to pack a traveling bag.

Five minutes past four o'clock.

I left the lights burning and soundlessly left the apartment. I made my way down the stairs to the rear exit. It was raining quite hard, the ground was soggy, and a cold wind was driving rain against me. With difficulty I managed to carry my traveling bag through the garden and park to the telephone booth in the Forsthausstrasse. I saw no one. I looked up the number of the airport and dialed it. A tired man's voice answered. My call was transferred and I obtained the information I had needed. Yes, the Bonanza belonging to Frau Petra Schalke had left. First stop Bremen, then Zurich. How many passengers? Two. A man and a woman.

"Could you describe them for me, please?"

"Now look here . . ."

"*Please!* What did they look like?"

"The woman was dark-haired, the man younger, blond hair . . ." I hung up.

Lillian and Olsen.

She knew that the pilot had been at the airport, waiting. She had gone with Olsen voluntarily. Why? For whom had she done that? Lillian. I groaned audibly. She had lied to and betrayed me all this time. It made no sense. She had no reason to do that! She had begged me to take her with me, not to leave her. Perhaps she had been coerced. Olsen surely must have had a pistol. Perhaps the pilot had been forced to take them, a pistol at his back.

Nonsense! But what then was the explanation?

Startled, I jumped. A police patrol car with siren wailing and blinker flashing approached the telephone booth at high speed. But it continued on its way. The siren faded.

I called the Strip.

Minski answered.

"Richie here . . ."

No answer.

"My God, Boris, can't you hear me?"

With difficulty he said, "From where . . . where are you? In Zurich?"

"Zurich, shit! I'm here in Frankfurt!"

"Oh God."

"What's the matter with you?"

"What's the matter with *me?*" he asked excitedly. I heard soft music in the background. "Why are you still here? Lillian called and told me that you were about to take off, that you were already in the plane."

"She said that?"

"Yes. So she lied. Great."

"Okay, okay! When did she call?"

"Just after midnight. I was not to worry. You would be all right, you were flying to Zurich. Something went wrong in Treuwall, they caught Geyer and a couple of others and they talked. That's why you had to leave. Olsen told you. He heard it over the police radio. Lillian said you were taking him to Zurich to give him a chance. For God's sake, Richie, what really happened?"

Briefly I explained. As I talked my hurt, indignation, anger turned into a violent rage.

"I've got to find out what happened to Lillian. So long, Boris."

"Wait!" Are you meshugge? Where are you going? Listen to me, Richie! Haven't I been like a father to you? You can't—"

"Yes, I can. And I will."

"What about Paradin?"

"What about him?"

"You'd still have a chance if—"

"Then why did you get all those documents for me?"

"Then you're not going to do anything?"

"No. Too risky."

"What do I do?"

"Wait until all the guests have left. Then you can tell the detectives in the club and the one outside that I've disappeared. Tell them I left about two and that I said I would be back. Leave it as late as you can to give me a good head start."

"Will I hear from you, Richie?"

"I'll call—no, I'll send you a telegram. If everything is all right it will say 'Arrived safely, regards, Richie.' If it isn't it will read 'Arrived safely, best regards, Richie.' Can you remember that? Regards and best regards."

"Idiot. Listen to me! Stay here and tell Paradin."

"*Never!*"

"Oh, God . . . and when . . . when will I hear from you?"

"I don't know yet. As soon as possible. 'Regards' is good, 'best regards' bad. Okay?"

"Okay, he asks! How can I help you if it says best regards? How can I?"

"I've got to go. Take care, Boris," I said, and hung up. I called a taxi service and ordered a car.

It was then 4:25.

It continued to rain.

Inside the airport building it was quiet. Many counters were closed. Several passengers were sitting or lying down on upholstered benches, sleeping. Dizzy, I sat down. I suddenly felt indifferent. Let them catch me here. So what. Lillian had betrayed me. At that I fell asleep. I awakened an hour later, surprised that I hadn't fallen off the bench. Now there was more activity in the building. I rose and dragged myself to the large information board. A Swissair plane arriving from New York at 6 A.M. was leaving again at 6:30 for Zurich.

That was my plane!

Ten minutes later I had my ticket, my traveling bag checked, and I was in the restaurant having coffee, trying to eat a roll. It was still raining. The plane landed on time. Many people left the plane in Frankfurt.

Passing through customs and passport control proved uneventful. The officers were polite. I felt very calm, unusually certain that nothing was going to happen here. No doubt an aftereffect of the drug I had been given.

In Zurich it was not raining, but it was cold and windy. As soon as we landed I made inquiries. A half-hour before I had landed in Zurich, a KLM clipper had left for Cairo; a quarter-hour following that a PAA plane had begun its flight to Rio de Janeiro and Buenos Aires.

At the KLM counter I found out that an Angela Dirksen had been booked on the Cairo plane. The receptionist could not tell me if she had traveled alone. "We were very busy. The plane was almost filled to capacity."

"When is the next plane to Cairo?" I asked.

"Tonight at eight-thirty."

But a Sabena plane left at 10:30 A.M. I booked a seat. Today I find it difficult to explain why I did what I did.

I still loved Lillian more than my life—even having accepted by now the fact that she had betrayed me.

I had this fixed idea: She was forced to betray me. She still loves me. She is in danger. She is being blackmailed. There is a dark, ominous secret in her life. I must help her. She needs me. I must go to her.

Then there was my boundless anger, bitter resentment and disappointment. I could find no explanation for Lillian's betrayal. What or who had made her do such a dastardly thing? I had to find out—even at the risk of my life.

The Egyptian customs officer in the Heliopolis airport was a typical Arabian peasant: tall and sturdily built, with almond-shaped, thickly-lashed eyes, low forehead, prominent cheekbones, a wide, thick-lipped mouth.

The officer took his time examining my baggage. Meticulously. He spoke a heavily accented English.

"Open this, please."

He rummaged around my shaving gear. Impatient passengers behind me who protested the delay were sternly admonished by him. I saw him look over my shoulder several times. I even turned to look myself but saw nothing unusual to arouse the man's interest. Many people were present; it was a busy airport. The heat was oppressive. The counterfeit passport lay before the customs official. Suddenly he lost all interest in me.

"All right, you can go."

Hurriedly, I zipped up my traveling bag and left. I had already passed through passport control. I carried my luggage to the exit. I planned to go to a hotel. Then I would begin my search for Lillian. Police, hotels, guest houses. I realized that she might not even have gone to Cairo, but I had to start somewhere.

As I reached the exit they were suddenly beside me.

"Hello," Geyer said. He walked with a cane, still limping.

"We almost missed you," the blond Olsen said. "But our friend from customs earned his money. Kept you there until we arrived." Olsen took my traveling bag with his left hand and walked very close to me. His right hand remained in the jacket pocket of his tropical suit. Something had jabbed into my side. "You know, of course, that this isn't a candy bar that's tickling your ribs?"

"Yes." I answered.

"Good. Don't walk too fast," he continued. "Turn right, over there to the parking lot. That yellow Plymouth there. No funny business now. I'm very nervous and this thing might easily go off."

I glanced about quickly. There were no people in our immediate proximity.

Suddenly Geyer stepped close and I felt something hard jab the right side of my ribs.

"Just keep walking. Nice and calm."

Perspiring freely under that brutal sun I walked on, flanked by both armed men. The dusty fronds of the palms surrounding the parking lot hung limply in the dead air.

"We made it! We made it, Herr Mark!" An overjoyed Officer Stalling entered my cell this morning to take me to the barber for a haircut. I was shaving, not yet dressed.

Today is Monday, June 5, 1967.

While I finish shaving with my battery-powered shaver which I'm permitted to use (I cannot kill myself with that), Officer Stalling warms to his subject.

"One victory after another! The party crisis has been overcome! We're now the third most powerful party in the country! That's right! In 1963 no one had heard of us. In 1965 we polled two-and-a-half percent. And, now, in Lower Saxony we polled seven percent! More than the Free Democratic Party! Now we have time to unify the party, and then the next elections will show something! And this was a socialist country! The Social Democrats lost quite a few mandates. Seven! That's the result of the grand coalition. The SPD is slipping, the Free Democratic Party is just a sad joke, what's left, Herr Mark? The Christian Union and us, the NPD. Time is on our side. Don't you agree, Herr Mark?"

"Yes, Herr Stalling," I answered. I had finished shaving and was now putting on my jacket.

"Well, then, shall we go to our Figaro? I'd like to caution you, he's a Socialist. In a bad mood today."

Olsen was behind the wheel. Geyer, a pistol on his knees, was next to me in the rear seat of the yellow Plymouth. We drove along a wide, very dusty road through level, sun-baked country. In the distance I occasionally saw clay huts, also larger buildings. Once I saw a village.

Men, women and children, dressed in rags, were working in the fields, bent low, using hand tools which had surely been made in primitive times. Emaciated water buffalo pulled harrows and ploughs.

We had left Heliopolis about thirty minutes ago. No one had spoken since then. The dreadful heat! Even the open car windows brought no relief. I had taken off my jacket. My shirt stuck to me.

"Winter harvest," Geyer suddenly remarked.

"What's that?"

"They're planting the winter harvest. The land is fertile. A long growing season. Three harvests a year here. I was here once during a sugarcane harvest." He must have been here right after the war, I thought.

"Where are you taking me?"

"You'll see."

"You had to follow us, didn't you?" Olsen said. He was driving fast.

"He's the type." Geyer smiled, playing with the pistol. "The passionate type who's apt to lose his head. And so is his brother. I saw that right away. But you didn't want to believe that. Now who was right?"

468

"Well, it's difficult to believe that someone would be that stupid," Olsen half-apologized.

"Where is my brother? Where is Frau Lombard? And Delacorte?" I asked. I felt faint.

"So many questions, tch tch." Geyer shook his head in rebuke. The thick lenses of his glasses glistened. "Just take your time. You'll find out in time. Don't lose your composure. At the moment that is the most important thing."

"Did you hear, Mark? Keep calm. Geyer doesn't like nervous people. They're likely to lose their heads. Just like Scherr did."

"What's with him?" The retarded prison attendant had completely slipped my mind.

"He's dead," Olsen replied. "He cracked up—wanted to run away, tell the police, just because the Bonanza came a couple of minutes late. After all, everybody had to wait near that little wood at the Bremen airport for us."

"Both you and Frau Lombard flew to Bremen?"

"Sure, who else? Scherr was an idiot. There was absolutely nothing to worry about. We all had excellent counterfeit passports. Frau Lombard used the one you gave her, though. The photograph was better." Olsen laughed.

"What happened to Scherr then?"

"He became very fidgety. Very noisy." Geyer raised his pistol briefly. "He wanted to run off. I didn't have a choice."

"You mean you shot him?"

"Naturally. What else could I have done?"

"We had more room in the Bonanza," Olsen remarked. "Would have been almost too crowded with Scherr in it too. We were five people. Six including the pilot. And the luggage."

"Where did you kill Scherr?" I asked.

"In the little wood. He'll be found soon. I just covered him up with a few branches and leaves. God rest his soul, he really was a nitwit. I'll never be able to understand how he got Delacorte out of jail without any problems. I always worried about that."

"The jail was his home," Olsen said. "He knew it inside out. What amazed me was how he finished off that Doctor Hess in the hospital."

"Just reflex action. The stupid bastard," Geyer said. "And we promised that he'd have a place here. Would have been ideal here for him, too."

"Where did you promise him a place?" I asked.

He ignored my question.

"Better, he's dead. Would always have been a burden. And anyway, he was a murderer. That prisoner in the jail was on his conscience, too."

Geyer was also a murderer. He had also killed twice, but I kept quiet.

Meanwhile we had reached a grove of palm trees. It suddenly grew a little cooler. Now I saw a few white villas surrounded by beautifully tended gardens. Bright-colored flowers were blooming.

We had left the main road and turned into a road leading toward a yellow, flat-roofed house with closed green shutters. A high wall surrounded the entire grounds. Olsen honked briefly when we arrived at a high wrought-iron gate. An Arab came from the small guardhouse behind the gate to open it. He waved us on. Olsen stopped on the curved driveway underneath a portico of high columns with a balcony.

"Get out," Geyer said, prodding me with his pistol. The green entrance door was opened by a young man wearing a khaki suit and shirt. "That went smoothly enough," he said in German.

"Where to?" Geyer asked.

"The drawing room." The young man indicated a door with his chin. He went ahead of us, knocked and opened the door for us. We entered a large room with Chippendale furnishings. A chandelier was brightly lighted. Chairs and couches surrounded a marble-topped table set for tea. Before the fireplace stood a tall man in a white tropical suit with meticulously parted blond hair, a mustache and a deep scar from the left corner of the mouth to the cheekbone.

"Welcome," said Dr. Delacorte.

"War! It's a war!"

Officer Stalling, for the second time this morning, excitedly entered my cell. Before the visit to the barber he had told me about the county elections. Now he had a new theme: opinions on the long-expected and well-planned war Egypt had plotted against Israel.

"Started this morning! Fighting on all fronts! Poor Israel! The Jews have to fight against everybody, it seems to me! Tanks are battling in the desert and in the Gaza Strip. Air raids! Goddamn Nasser! Ought to be strung up as a war criminal! What did the Jews do? They worked and planned and made their country prosper. Now that it is thriving he'd like to get his hands on it! I tell you, Herr Mark, if the free world doesn't help the Jews now, then America might as well shut up shop. In that case I've had enough of this free world! Everybody I've talked to agrees that this is the greatest crime in recent history. Cairo is supposed to have been bombarded! Good for them! A little while before they had been dancing in the streets, celebrating this holy war! I hope, we here all hope, that the Jews really clean out this goddamn lot there."

With that he left to spread the news throughout the jail.

War in the Near East.

The war, expected for days, weeks, had erupted. Grenades exploding, bombs falling, battles being fought, human beings dying. I had been there, where all this was now happening, just six months ago. Yes, almost six months to the day I had sat opposite Delacorte in the cool drawing room of a villa somewhere near Heliopolis. . . .

An Egyptian servant boy dressed in white had poured iced tea for us. I drank thirstily while Delacorte was sipping the refreshing drink.

"I hope you had a pleasant trip," he said. "Of course you will need some suitable clothing, Herr Peter Horneck."

"And what's your name now?" I asked pointedly.

"I'm sure that need not concern you."

"Where am I here?"

"Unfortunately I cannot tell you that."

"Can't or won't?"

"Can't. I, too, was brought here from the airport."

"By two men with guns?"

"No. By—friends," he said with a courteous inclination of the head.

"Where is Lillian? Where's my brother?"

"I don't know. I really don't know." He lifted his expressive hands in a calming gesture. "Don't upset yourself. It is much too hot to become excited. And it wouldn't make any difference. When and how you are going to leave here is not up to you or me. Other people are now deciding."

"Your friends."

"Well, yes." He cleared his throat. "You must try to understand that it would be too risky to have you at liberty right after my escape. Who knows what you might do in your perfectly understandable agitation?"

"This house belongs to the Spider organization, does it not?"

"I beg your pardon? I don't know what you're talking about."

"You know very well—ah well! I guess you don't care where Lillian is staying?" I demanded abruptly.

His face changed color. He bit his lip. I did not think he was playacting.

"I've asked you a question!" I insisted.

He rose and turned his back to me as he crossed to a window. His hands clasped, unclasped as he spoke. "On the contrary I am very much concerned. Lillian . . . Lillian was the price I had to pay for my freedom."

My hand trembled. I placed the teacup on the table. He did not turn around.

"I'll tell you about it. For a start, this is how I was freed. . . ." Briefly he informed me about the escape from the prison. "I'm not betraying any confidence if I also tell you that Lillian, your brother, Geyer, Olsen and I traveled together from Bremen to Cairo."

"I already know that."

"During the flight I had ample time to talk with Lillian and your brother. It is very simply this: Lillian has always been in love with your brother. She deceived me with Werner from the very beginning. I was suspicious of many men because she was such a skillful schemer—but she was loyal to your brother. She didn't even deceive me with you."

"I don't understand."

"I asked you to look after her in the hotel just before my arrest. I was convinced that you loved Lillian. Just as convinced as I was that Lillian did not love you. I'm sure you mean something to her—I don't know what precisely—in any case I was not jealous of you, if you can understand that. Lillian talked about you frequently, as one might talk of a good, old friend, a loyal little boy, a devoted little dog. Please, do remain seated. I don't mean to hurt you. Both of us have been deceived, if you like to put it quite bluntly. Lillian has never been able to break away from Werner. Nor has he been able to break away from her."

"They told you that?"

"In the plane. Yes." Delacorte's face was drained of

473

color. He was suffering visibly. "She despises me, she said. Now that she knows who I once was. I disgust her. She is horrified to think that I once was her lover." His hands brushed through the air as if to wipe away those thoughts. "Hysteria and idle talk, of course. You know her. I know that you love her as I do, despite everything." He coughed, turning his back to me again. "Yes. I expect you feel the same—even after what I have just told you. After what she has done to you. One does not stop loving a woman because she is a whore, does one?"

I felt ill. I held my head in both hands.

Two days ago she had been in my bed, nude, panting with lust. In Treuwall she had beseeched me to keep Werner away from her. A skillful actress—if Delacorte had told the truth.

But was it the truth?

"We must stay together. For always. I love you, Richie. You know that I have always loved only you."

No one had forced her to say that. But perhaps now she was being forced to do and say many things? There had been no need for her to lie to me, to betray me! There was some reason. I still did not know the truth, no, not yet. Lillian was not such an expert liar, not so skillful an actress, not so competent a whore. I refused to believe such evil of her.

Delacorte poured more tea for me.

"During the flight I found out the truth. And I was given a choice."

"A choice?" Again I felt slightly dizzy. I had gone through too much physically and emotionally.

Delacorte raised his shoulders.

"You see, my friend, I am offered to take charge of a neurological clinic in—well, it doesn't matter where—I would have every advantage. Almost limitless funds. Every opportunity for research. Qualified people are needed here. I will be given this position if I give up Lil-

lian. Completely. Never to see her again. That is the condition. If I don't agree to that—" he broke off.

"Yes? Then what?"

Slowly he continued, "In the plane I was told—in a way
which leaves no doubt—that, should I not agree, I would
be taken out of Egypt and delivered to the German
authorities."

"My *brother* told you that?"

"Yes. He must be a man of great influence and power."

He's also a great poker player, I thought, but you don't
know that, you poor idiot. Poor idiot? But I had not
called Werner's bluff either!

"I have proof of the ability and determination of your
brother and his friends. After all I am now a free man, a
man with the prospect of a new career."

My head ached. I was growing dizzier.

"Okay." I said. "So you gave up Lillian."

"Yes," he said. Delacorte was surely growing taller
while the room grew smaller. Was the chandelier circling?

"Don't you feel well?"

"Not very."

"It's the heat. Have some more tea." He extended the
cup to me. I drank obediently. My limbs felt heavy. I
tried to rise and could not.

"You'll feel better if you just stay seated," Delacorte
said. "Yes, I gave up Lillian. I had no choice."

"I don't believe you," I mumbled. I had difficulty in
pronouncing words clearly.

"That's unfortunate," Delacorte said. "And for once
I'm speaking the truth. But you will come to believe me,
oh, yes, you will."

My head was splitting. I sank back into my chair. Suddenly Delacorte's face was very close before me; I saw it
clearly. Everything else was blurred, swimming out of
focus. Delacorte's mouth loomed frighteningly large before me.

"I'll say good-by to you now. I don't think we shall ever meet again. At least I hope not."

"Why—good-by?"

"You were very unobservant. Understandable. Too nervous. Into each cup of tea I dropped a tiny potent pill. You will sleep now."

"I . . ."

"Don't worry. I said sleep. Not die. On the contrary. Two excellent physicians will be taking good care of you here. You have Lillian to thank for that."

"Lillian . . ."

"She insisted on it. Your brother and his friends had other plans for you. But she realized that, to avoid any problems, you had to be kept out of sight for awhile. She saved your life, you know. What a peculiar woman. She carried on like someone mad. Perhaps that's what she is. One would have thought that *you* were her lover. . . ." His face seemed like mountains, his mouth a gorge, his teeth rocky boulders. "This treatment is beneficial— especially for people with frayed nerves. Again, nothing bad is going to happen to you . . . here. Then it will all depend on you. You will be . . ."

For the second time in twenty-four hours I lost consciousness.

My memory of the following few days is partially impaired. Four or even five days seem to be missing.

I remember that whenever I awakened in my bed, the only piece of furniture in an otherwise bare room, a man in a white coat would invariably be sitting on the side of it. Gray light entered through a barred window. There was no knob at the door. A nurse, sometimes a pretty one, sometimes an unattractive one, would then bring a tray with food and a pitcher of orange juice. She would assist me in sitting up and eating. I felt very weak. Following the food I was given three pills. Ten minutes later I would sink into another deep, dreamless sleep.

"What day is today?" I once asked one of the doctors. All the staff spoke German.

"What difference does it make?" he countered.

He was right. It made no difference. By now I no longer knew where I was or what had occurred. With difficulty I remembered my name and who I was. But I was not particularly interested in anything. Sleep was a good friend; would that death would be so pleasant.

Once I was given a white powder instead of the usual pills, and the young doctor said, "Now it's about time you awakened again."

"What day is today?" I asked again.

"Wednesday," he answered.

"And the date?"

"December seventh."

"When did I get here?"

"On the second. Last Friday."

I received less and less medication until, on the eighth day, I slept, although restlessly, without a sedative. During the following three days I was examined thoroughly, pronounced weak but otherwise in good condition. Three days of good meals and walks, assisted by a nurse, in the beautifully tended garden of the villa almost brought me back to my normal self.

Returning from the garden to my room on December 11, I found that my traveling bag and coat had been returned to me. I quickly checked. Everything was there: wallet, counterfeit passport, money, flight ticket.

I sat on my bed and found myself thinking of Geyer, Olsen, Lillian, Werner. Had they all had sufficient time to disappear? I had been kept here nine days to give them that chance. But I was wrong in my assumption that that had been their plan. An hour later my door was opened and Olsen, dressed in a khaki suit, entered, smiling amiably.

"Nice to see you again," he said. "Pack your things. We're leaving."

"Where are we going?"

"Cairo."

"On whose orders?"

"Don't ask so many questions. I was told to take you there. That's what I'm going to do."

I packed. The villa appeared empty as we left. At the entrance stood the yellow Plymouth. Olsen threw my traveling bag into the rear seat. It was a dismal, humid day. Just before the airport Olsen went onto a wide road which, according to road signs, led to Cairo.

"Are you taking me to my brother?"

"I'm taking you to the Hotel Imperial," Olsen said. "You'll receive new instructions there. I am saying good-by to you today. We'll never meet again."

Ahead of us the towers of several mosques came into view. We drove through an ugly suburb of Cairo. Children in rags were playing with empty cans in the dusty road.

"You're staying in Egypt?"

"Yes. I was supposed to have been transferred here some time ago."

"By the Spider organization?"

He shrugged his shoulders.

"This was a suitable opportunity, I see," I said. "And for Geyer too. He had to get out of Germany too. Has he gone yet?"

"Yes."

"On another mission, eh? Something involving the training of boys? That old pederast!"

Olsen laughed good-naturedly.

"Well, there's a lot to do here. They need specialists. He and I, we speak French and English. Now we'll just have to learn Arabic too."

We were driving through the outer city. Olsen obviously knew his way around. He suddenly said, "Listen, Mark, I like you. Now for God's sake don't play the hero. It doesn't pay. And in your situation you have no chance

478

at all. Comply with whatever demands will be made of you."

"That depends on the demand."

"A hero. I knew it. You're going to regret it, mark my words."

We had reached the city: the railroad station, the Midan el Tahrir, the Nile Corniche, the Semiramis Bridge leading to the island of Gezireh, past Shepheards. Then Olsen pulled up in front of the Imperial Hotel.

As I am writing this I find myself thinking of the frightened foreigners, surprised by the war, unable to leave Egypt before it erupted, who are now crowding the Imperial, Hilton and other luxury hotels in Cairo. Israeli jets are thundering swiftly above Cairo's deserted streets, its people huddling in bomb shelters. This minute, this second, a war is being waged in the desert. A very strange feeling for me. . . .

A porter picked up my luggage.

"Couldn't you have got a room somewhere else?" I grumbled.

"In a large hotel you're safest," Olsen explained. "And you've got enough money on you." I got out of the car. "Be smart, Mark. Remember what I said. That's the only way you'll stay alive," he added before he drove off.

I went to the reception desk.

I said, brusquely, "My name is Horneck. Peter Horneck."

"Oh, yes, Mister Horneck." the clerk smiled. "We've been expecting you." He glanced at a plan before him. "You are in suite 907," he said, calling a bellboy.

My suite, large and comfortable, looked out on the Nile Corniche, Semiramis Bridge and the island of Gezireh. The very first thing I did in my room was to send the promised telegram to Minski. It read, "Arrived safely. Best regards, Richie." According to our agreement that would mean to him I was in trouble. I could not imagine

479

what he could possibly do to help me but I hoped that he would think of something. It was to be expected that Boris was under surveillance by Paradin, in which case the telegram would inform the public prosecutor of my whereabouts. That knowledge was not of much use to Paradin, since Germany and Egypt had broken off diplomatic relations. In any case Egypt did not extradite for such crimes as I had committed.

I had just replaced the receiver when the phone rang.

"Ah, there you are at long last." It was my brother's voice.

"That's right, here I am," I said. "And where are you?"

"In the hotel. I live here too."

"And where is——"

"In another hotel. Not over the phone. I must speak with you. Not necessarily in the hotel, either."

"Why not?"

"It's too soon after your arrival. Later on."

"But that's——"

He interrupted sharply, "Can you be in the Egyptian Museum in fifteen minutes?"

"Certainly." The museum was directly behind the hotel.

"Good. I'll be expecting you in Hall 42."

The Egyptian Museum contains outstanding examples of sculptures dating from the Old Kingdom to Roman times. Its contents make it very highly rated among the world's museums.

My brother was waiting for me on a bench set before the diorite sculpture of King Chephren that had been removed from the entrance to his tomb.

Several people were in Hall 42, which adjoined a rotunda. Elderly American couples, some English men, a German couple with their two children. I sat down next to my brother. He seemed tense.

"We won't discuss past events," he said, "only the present and what has to be done."

"All right," I agreed. I had planned to provoke Werner, hoping that he would slip some information. Apart from that I was going to stall for time. I felt physically not quite up to par. I needed more time to recuperate fully.

"My bosses wanted to do away with you right after you arrived here. Lillian was able to prevent that. It was her information about the plane available to you that saved you. The professor told you about Lillian? About Lillian and me?" His voice was more alert now.

"Yes, he did," I answered.

"And?"

"I don't believe it."

"What reasons——?"

"Many reasons."

"The professor believed it."

"You gave him no choice. I'm not he. I demand to see Lillian. I want her to tell me——when we are alone together."

"Out of the question."

I rose.

"What's the matter?" Werner inquired.

"If it's out of the question, then there is no point to this discussion," I bluffed.

"Then what are you going to do?"

I had prepared myself for just such a question. "I have friends in Cairo." I wished fervently that I had! "They saw Geyer and Olsen—I know all you have new names, but I don't know them—anyway, they watched them kidnap me. They also overheard a conversation to the effect that I was to be put on ice for a while. Nothing serious was to happen to me." I watched Werner as I spoke. He seemed unsure whether or not to believe me. "So my friends sent a telegram to my lawyer, with a prearranged message instructing him to await further instructions."

"A lawyer? By the way, my name is now Steinberg, Thomas Steinberg."

A stout, elderly man, carrying a museum catalogue sat

down on the bench next to Werner. We rose and walked slowly from statue to statue in the large hall.

"My lawyer in Frankfurt. I didn't record those tapes only for you but also for him. Up to the very last moment. I gave them to him the night I left. In his apartment. We agreed that he was to turn over those tapes to the police if he did not receive a telegram from me or my friends for a period of three days." I hoped this lie would prevent them from killing me now. Doubtlessly Lillian's influence was limited.

"You're lying," Werner stated flatly.

I shrugged my shoulders.

"All right. Suppose it is the truth . . ."

"It is the truth," I said.

". . . what do you hope to gain by that?"

"My safety. I'm sure your bosses would find it most unpleasant if those tapes were to go to the police." In my excitement I made what later proved to be a mistake. I added, "You don't have to worry though. I've sent him the telegram as soon as I arrived in the hotel. He will be waiting for another three days. Now then. What was it you wanted to tell me?"

"You must disappear. Leave Egypt."

"To go where?"

"Argentina. That was your second choice anyway. At least that's what Lillian told me. You can't stay here."

"Not that I want to. I'll go to Argentina, too. But with Lillian."

"She won't go with you."

"Let her tell me that herself."

"Why?"

"Because I don't believe you."

"After all Delacorte told you? He believed Lillian. He gave her up."

"I'm convinced that your threat to get him into German hands was a bluff. Admit it!"

He grinned. "But it worked."

"You can't do that with me. Not any more. I demand to talk to Lillian."

"She won't go with you. Never!"

"But she'll stay with you."

"That's right," he insisted. His face twitched. I could not help feeling a twinge of pity for him. He loved Lillian. I suddenly realized that.

"What are your plans now?"

"Varied. There is a lot to do. For a start, little brother, there are your tapes. In a safe place."

"They are hidden? Why?"

"Whoever owns them has a great deal of power. The tapes contain all the names of those involved in this recent business. Paradin would like to charge these men, but he has no proof against them. Nor will he ever have. Instead we are collecting more evidence against them. They will be in our hands."

"Blackmail—that's your business."

"A very profitable business. It makes today's world go round. And we're very good at it. Our organization is becoming increasingly more powerful. It is no longer concerned with saving people like the professor. It is now involved in international politics, an exciting, exhilarating game. I am being blackmailed too—but you know that. To make doubly certain that the incriminating evidence against me will be returned I had you record your tapes. I guessed—and rightly so as it turned out—that the organization would want them. Now, as soon as I have been given the incriminating documents about me I shall be an equal partner, a partner who can no longer be blackmailed, nor be given dirty work to do—only be called on for important tasks." His face was flushed now. "I am remaining here only until this business with you has been concluded, until my papers have been returned to me. I'm needed elsewhere."

"What kind of work will you do then?"

"Politics. Once I belonged to the press corps. Now I'm

going back to my old job. Propaganda. Almost unlimited funds!" He was excited now. "Planning! Preparing!"

"Planning what?"

"Something is being prepared, little brother, involving the entire world, you know that, we all know that. But this time we're in on it, my comrades and I."

"Your comrades. That includes Geyer and Olsen. Murderers and traitors."

"Today it is only important if a person is useful. Those two are—in their sphere of work. As I am in mine, I was always a good war correspondent. Novels! They make me sick. What does one do with books in today's world? No, if one can write as well as I can one must make full use of this talent! Propaganda! That's especially important in this country—at least for now. The entire Middle East will be my field of operations."

Scanning these notes I am reminded of today's news reports about the Israelis. After incredible initial victories, now they are engaged in bloody battles with Arabs unwilling to agree to peace.

Yet there is no doubt that Israelis will win this war— the Arabs miscalculated. I wonder what part the Spider organization played during the past six months.

Also in today's newspaper I read an account of a press conference in Vienna scheduled incidentally before the outbreak of the Arab-Israeli war. It was held by Simon Wiesenthal, the man responsible for Adolf Eichmann's capture. I mention this since it seems to corroborate my recent experiences.

Citing a list of names, Wiesenthal stated that Arab nations are utilizing former Nazi VIPs in their fight against Israel. He said that of the six to eight thousand German nationals living in Arab countries, several hundred are on the wanted list. Two of them, for instance, are former close associates of Eichmann's.

"The world is in upheaval," my brother said, nervously rubbing the palms of his hands together. "We're about to enter a new epoch."

"What kind of an epoch?"

He smiled, shrugged his shoulders, and I recalled that once, when everything had already been lost, he had written, "Victory is really quite close. . . ."

"What is going to happen if I won't leave for Argentina without Lillian?" I asked.

"You'll be killed," Werner said.

"In which case my lawyer will hand those tapes over to the police."

"I don't believe those tapes exist."

"You'll just have to take that chance, then."

An American couple was passing by. The man said, "Fed up. I'm telling you, I'm fed up with this goddamn stuff. I want to get out of here and have a bottle of beer—but quick!" His wife tripped angrily behind him.

"Why do you want to get rid of me at all cost?"

He wheeled around, his face contorted with hatred.

"Because you have always stood between Lillian and me—that's why!"

My heart beat furiously. So that's what it was.

"I want you out of the way! No longer available to her—under any circumstances. I want her for myself!"

"Not so loud," I admonished him. "I still demand to talk to Lillian."

"Never."

"You heard me. I expect you to tell her that and let me know where I can meet her. Don't think for a moment that you've won the game. Now are you going to ask her?"

A long silence ensued. At last he spoke haltingly, "I have an important engagement now. I won't see Lillian until late this afternoon."

"I can see her any time. I'll wait in the hotel. Well?"

Another lengthy silence.

485

"You'll hear from me," he finally said, turned and quickly walked toward the exit. I felt that I had won a first, although small, victory.

The so-called Tower of Cairo is situated on the island of Gezireh. One hundred and eighty meters tall, it has a circular bar, and, a flight above that, a restaurant which turns, completing a full circle every thirty minutes. The view is breathtaking: Cairo and its palaces, mosques, the citadels, the river with its islands and its ships, the sphinx and pyramids in the desert. Many points of interest are brightly lit at night—a splendid sight.

Lillian and I were sitting in the bar following dinner in the restaurant, during which we had talked only of trivial matters. Lillian, elegant in a black dress, was heavily madeup. She looked tired, which, strangely, made her even more beautiful. My brother had called me about six at the hotel and informed me that I was to meet Lillian at the Tower at half-past seven. He was going to take her there. He was ridiculously secretive about Lillian's hotel.

"Where are you staying?" I had asked her as we entered the tower elevator.

"Near the pyramids, in the Mena House."

I had been surprised how calm and unemotional we seemed to be. It was Lillian who spoke first.

"You know how things stand," she said. Her smile was forced, her voice spiritless. Now she was looking out through the window at the bright lights of Cairo and her smile vanished. "Delacorte told you some things—and your brother completed the story."

"Yes."

"I'm sorry, Richie."

"You don't have to be," I replied, flatly. "These things happen. I've watched them happening to you for quite a few years."

486

"I'm cursed," Lillian said.

"Don't let's have any grade B movie dialogue."

"No," she agreed. "Let's be honest with each other."

"Let's."

"But don't complain afterward. Don't be offended. You asked for it."

The waiter brought new drinks. Doubles. Armagnac for Lillian, whisky for me. We drank. When Lillian began to talk her voice was hoarse. "It would be easy for me to be dramatic, sentimental or tragic. But we have little time left. So I'll tell you bluntly: from the moment I first met your brother, from the first time we were in bed together, I have not been able to free myself from him. Not that I didn't try."

I gulped some of my whisky.

"This man and I—I find it difficult to explain—Werner would do anything for me, anything at all. He's already proven that . . ."

"And you?"

She looked at me, her eyes wide.

"I'm afraid I would do the same for him. You must be terribly disappointed—but we always promised to be honest with each other."

"You're not entirely truthful."

"What do you mean?"

"The way I understand you, you only talked about sex. Is that the most important thing in a woman's life?"

"I don't know. I hope not. But I can't help myself when Werner is near me. Never could."

"What about Werner, the man? The human being?"

"A long time ago, Richie, after the war, you were all I ever wanted and admired, before I ever knew a Werner existed."

"Something must have remained with you. . . ." I spoke hesitantly, seeking for the right words, knowing that perhaps I had a chance. "The feeling you once had for me, it is still there—or you would not have returned to me so many times, you would not have had my telephone number, or you would have called Werner and not me when you were poisoned in Treuwall . . . you would have let them kill me. We would not be sitting here. We—"

"Stop it."

"It's true, isn't it?"

Her overly large eyes were wide, her face immobile.

"It is true." I insisted.

Her eyes closed briefly, her hand trembled as she picked up her drink.

"Werner and I are brothers. You really need both of us. But the way I see things and despite all you've said—and demonstrated—bed is not always the most important thing. Not always. Not now," I said softly, placing my hand over hers. "Not right now. Is it?"

She looked at me, shook her head, her eyes were brimming with tears.

"I'm crazy," she said, "you know that, crazy. Go away, Richie, away from me as far as you can. I'll only bring you misfortune."

"I won't go away," I said firmly. "Not without you. You'll come with me . . ."

"No!"

". . . to Argentina."

"No, Richie! I won't go with you. Please don't talk about it any more! I would betray you the way I already have."

"Werner would not be there."

"Then I would leave you again—go to him—I'm cursed, really. I know it sounds ridiculous—but I can't find another word to express it. You know what I mean—I can't help myself."

"Lillian," I reminded her, "Werner has committed a crime. He will commit other crimes. He is an evil man."

"I know all that. He told me everything. Probably more than he told you. He's so sure of me—it delights him to tell me all those terrible things . . . and prove to himself that he needs only to touch me to know that I am his. I don't care what he does, what he's done, what he's going to do, how and where I am going to live with him, facing unknown dangers—it is as nothing as soon as he touches me. I'm talking very frankly. My God."

"Not pleasant," I said, "but honest, thank God." I noticed disbelief in her eyes. "Why are you staring at me like that?"

"Because you're listening to all this so calmly, that you're not furious, that you're not angry with me." She pressed her hands to her temples. "I can't bear it. I have done such despicable things all my life and especially during the last few weeks. I'm beneath contempt. And yet you still love me."

"Yes," I said. "And I always will. There are things which are constant. The physical attraction Werner holds for you, which you have for each other, will of necessity one day diminish. Then you will feel only hate, disgust and loathing for Werner. The feeling that binds us together will not die as we grow older. That is my chance. That is why I'll prevail over my brother. And that is why you will come with me to Argentina."

"Never."

"I won't press you now. Think about what I have told you. I haven't much time left, just a day or two. During those two days you'll decide—for me."

She whispered, "If I only knew . . . if I knew that I could bear to be without him. . . ."

"One can learn to forget people—if one has help," I said.

"Can one, Richie? I've had too much to drink. I can't think now. Give me time, Richie, a little more time." After a moment's pause she went on, "And if I decide to stay with him, will you accept my decision?"

"Yes."

"And you won't torture me any more by demanding the real reasons?"

"Does that torture you?"

"Very much."

"When will I hear from you?"

"I don't know yet—I don't know anything any more."

"When will you let me know?" I insisted.

"Soon," she whispered, placing one hand over her eyes, "soon . . ."

"That's enough!" Werner's voice interrupted sharply.

I looked up, Lillian started with a suppressed cry. My brother stood very close to us. His eyes were blazing.

"What do you mean by—" I began, but he interrupted me. "Shut up. You've had enough time to talk. Lillian is coming with me now. I'm taking her home."

"*I'm* taking her home," I said, rising, prepared to fight.

"Wouldn't you think that depends on Lillian?" my brother asked, placing her mink jacket around her shoulders. She shivered under his touch; tears were in her eyes as she rose. She seemed unsteady, Werner supported her.

"Good night, Richie," she whispered, turning once, nodding almost imperceptibly as she left on my brother's arm. I did not move.

I walked through the Andalusian Garden, lit by many small spotlights. The scent of many flowers pervaded the air on this warm night. A drunk, muttering to himself and unsteady on his feet, came toward me. I tried to avoid him, but he bumped into me.

"Sorry, bud . . ." he mumbled.

At that a piece of paper was pushed into my hand. He continued on his way. Holding on to the paper I walked to the Semiramis Bridge, where, glancing around to make sure I was unobserved, I read the note underneath a bridge light. It said, "Call Associated Press Service immediately. Use only public telephones. Give your right name!" It also gave the number to call.

At the hotel I looked up the APS number in a telephone book. It checked with the one on the piece of paper. From a public telephone I called APS. A woman's voice answered.

"Richard Mark here."

"Oh, yes. We've been expecting your call."

"I don't quite understand why . . ." I began.

"Mr. Mark, today you sent a telegram to Boris Minski in Frankfurt. He called your friend Homer Barlow in Berlin who called his friend, our correspondent Clark Watts in Bonn. We have been asked by him to furnish you all available help. He gave us a description of you and the hotel where you're staying. That enabled one of our men to follow you, to give you that note. Now, how can we help you? If you would tell us . . ."

"It's rather a long story," I said.

A man's voice suddenly broke in. "Just be as brief as you can, but precise."

It took me about fifteen minutes to give them the entire story.

"Damn good story," the man's voice said when I had finished. "Also one that could prove dangerous."

"If you help me I'll make you a present of it," I said.

"Your story alone isn't enough. But if we had those tapes you recorded for your brother . . ."

"I'll get them for you," I promised quickly. "It will take a little while but I'll get them for you." I had no idea how I would accomplish that. But I realized that the APS people would be interested in my safety only if they could depend on a sensational story. The tapes were essential for that. They agreed to my request to watch Lillian, Werner and me. They would endeavor to ascertain if I was being watched. I, in return, promised to deliver the tapes, sign any affidavits necessary, be photographed and sign releases.

"You want to go to Argentina, right?"

"Not alone," I said.

"Of course not. With Mrs. Lombard. But that's where you want to go?"

"Yes."

"All right. Now then. You will have to call in a few times every day. The lady who answered this call will keep you informed of any new developments. You will also have to get the tapes to us here. Everything else can be taken care of by our office in Buenos Aires. Then we can blow the whistle on that Spider organization. Is that satisfactory to you?"

"Perfectly."

"Okay. We'll do our part. You do yours and get those tapes to us."

"Naturally," I said, feeling absolutely certain that I could. My expectation was right—but my delivery was wrong.

Within seventy-two hours of the beginning of the fighting, the Israelis have occupied the Gaza Strip and taken Jerusalem. The Jordanian Army has asked for a truce. The Security Council of the United Nations has ordered Israel to cease fire immediately.

Officer Stalling commented this morning, "These Jews are simply incredible! I watched it on TV last night! They learned that from our Rommel! Blitzkrieg! Blitz victory! They learned a lot from us. As I told my wife last night. Hitler sure made a big mistake when he killed all those Jews! Who knows if we wouldn't have won the war with those six million?"

Monday morning I checked in with APS. The woman's voice again. "There's not much to report. If you, your brother or Mrs. Lombard are under surveillance it is by experts. Our people have not noticed anyone. Your brother stayed at the Mena House last night. He left there just after ten this morning." I felt a twinge of pain and jealousy. "He meets with different people. Business people. Civil servants. What about you? What about the tapes?"

"You'll have to give me more time."

"All right. Call in again."

I spent the afternoon in the hotel. Lillian called about seven o'clock. Her voice hoarse, she sounded drunk. "I can't," she told me. "Please try to understand. I can't go with you. And I cannot see you any more. I couldn't stand another night like last night. Forgive me. Please, forgive me."

"Is Werner with you now?"

"No."

"Don't lie!"

"Yes, he's here."

"Let me talk to him."

My brother's voice. "Now you've heard it. Will you give up now?"

"No."

"What do you mean 'no'?"

"Meet me at the Tower and I'll tell you."

"In the bar in a half-hour."

A taxi took me to the island of Gezireh. Werner was punctual. He had seated himself near the window where Lillian had sat the previous night.

"Now before you say anything—you were bluffing as far as the tapes and that lawyer in Frankfurt are concerned. My people have friends everywhere. For a start, you sent a telegram to Minski, not to any attorney."

"Minski is to notify him," I lied, cursing myself for having mentioned that telegram.

"Not very convincing."

"But true."

"I discussed it with my associates. They are also sure that you're lying and are prepared to take a chance on that. What else did you want to tell me before you depart for Argentina?"

"That I am going to depart but not for South America."

"But?"

"I'm going to return to Germany."

"To Germany? Voluntarily?"

"Yes," I said. "I'm going back to face Paradin and to be locked up. Then I'm going to tell him the whole story."

Werner grew pale. "You would never do that! You're not crazy. You wouldn't risk the chance of going to jail for years!"

"Lillian is going to stay with you. I don't give a damn about anything now. But it would give me a great deal of satisfaction to fix you!"

"I feel just the same about you," Werner retorted.

"Once I begin to talk, many members of your organization will be caught. In Germany and here too. You might not be extradited, but they'll get you just the same. They also have their people. And there are agents for that sort of thing too." I rose abruptly and left him.

That night I could not sleep. I was very frightened. If they really didn't believe my story about the lawyer in Frankfurt, then my time had come.

Tuesday morning I called APS again.

"Your brother and the lady are planning something," the woman's voice told me. "The lady has rented a Mercedes. She bought suitcases, clothes—it seems she is preparing for a trip. Our men followed her and your brother to Gezireh where they spent some time searching for a particular parking spot for the Mercedes. They finally decided on a narrow path in the woods off the avenue leading from the bridge to Ex-King Farouk's palace." She described the exact spot. "The woman practiced reversing the car into the path several times. One of our men overheard your brother telling her that she was to wait there for him no matter how late he might be. During his meeting with you all sorts of complications might arise."

"What was that? A meeting with me?" Fear gripped me.

"I am merely informing you of what our men have been able to find out. We can do nothing to protect you. Neither can you go to the police since you have no proof that you have been threatened. We certainly cannot help you there. We're sorry, but you'll have to rely on your own resources."

"I understand. Please go on."

"Your brother also met an Indian in a café in Cairo's old section. Our man thought that your brother and the Indian had bargained and agreed on terms. He didn't know what they agreed about. But he overheard that they were going to meet once more to discuss details."

"When?" I asked. "Where?"

"Tomorrow, Wednesday, at eleven o'clock. At the nile-post at the southernmost point of the river-island Roda. Do you know the place?"

"Yes. I'll be there."

"Do take every precaution. And do try to get those tape recordings to us. We need them, we need proof, we need you as a witness—in Argentina."

I promised again to deliver them, still not knowing how I would accomplish that. The woman's voice then discussed at length certain plans. The APS people could not accept the material from me in Egypt but would arrange to have a man aboard a plane if I would let them know in advance which plane I would be taking. That was when my Beethoven score was described and settled upon as my identification.

That night I heard my brother and his hired Indian on the island as they planned my murder.

I returned late to my hotel and was just about to go to bed when Lillian called. Her voice was clear and her manner direct.

"Richie, I'm going to go with you."

"You what?" Surprised, I dropped onto the bed.

"I'm going to stay with you. I've thought about it for days now. My decision is final. I can't stay with Werner . . . I keep thinking about what you told me in the Tower bar—about a physical attraction and growing older—I can't stay with him, I don't want to. Do you still want me, Richie?"

The trap. Another lie. Careful now, I admonished myself. What she was then saying was intended to put me off guard. All according to Werner's plan. Yes, I had to be very clever now.

"Richie!"

"Yes."

"Why don't you say something?"

"I'm . . . I'm simply overwhelmed. After what you've—"

"Forget what I said. I've changed my mind. For the last time. We'll go to Argentina together."

"When?"

"Soon. As soon as I've talked to Werner."

"He doesn't know yet?"

"No. I wanted to tell you first. I'm afraid of . . . of telling Werner, of course. But I'll talk to him tomorrow."

"Tomorrow? When?"

"I don't know yet. I'll go with you. Isn't that the most important thing?"

"Yes, naturally."

"I'll call you tomorrow. After talking to him. I love you, Richie. More than him. I know that now. Good night, dearest."

Sleep eluded me that night.

The next day was a day of feverish activity for me. In a dirty narrow street near the Ibn-Tulun-Mosque I bought a .38 Police Special with a silencer and six clips of ammunition. I booked a seat on a plane leaving Heliopolis at 4:40 A.M. for Rome and a connecting flight for Zurich. Before leaving for Argentina it was necessary for me to be at my Zurich bank to sign various documents prior to transferring my account to Buenos Aires.

I telephoned APS again, this time assuring them that I would obtain the tapes that night. I assumed, perhaps only hoped, that my brother would have the tapes with him, since he had to exchange them for the documents with which he had been blackmailed by the Spider organization. And it had to be tonight, since he had told me that the exchange of material was to take place as soon as he had settled matters with me. I knew that he and Lillian were going away tonight. But if he left Cairo without exchanging the tapes here, then he would have to take them with him. Nervous, desperate because of what I had gone through during the past few days I was occasionally confused and agitated. Logical thinking seemed difficult.

If everything went according to plan, if the hired killer were punctual and did his work satisfactorily I should be able to meet Lillian near King Farouk's palace at 1:30 A.M. I was positive that *she* would be there. I would then also have sufficient time to attend to some important details. But there might be complications. I did not want to think of them. I had finally decided on a plan, the only one open to me.

"Richie?"

"Yes, Lillian?"

"Werner is here with me in the hotel. I told him everything."

It was 5 P.M. on December 15, 1966. Again I sat on my bed, curious only about the precise language.

"Everything?"

"Yes. He took it surprisingly well." Her voice sounded choked. "He didn't yell, didn't blow up, didn't berate me. He was very calm. But I'm exhausted, Richie. I've got to sleep—I'm going to take a sedative."

"When can I see you? I'd like to—"

"Tomorrow, Richie. Please, try to understand. I need some sleep. I can't go on . . . I'm . . ."

My brother's voice, restrained, manly. "All right, little brother. I've been told. Nothing I can do now. It seems you've won."

"It would seem so," I agreed.

"Lillian needs some sleep. You'd understand if you could see her. I'll look after her now. Starting tomorrow you'll have to look after her. I'm leaving."

"Leaving?"

"I already mentioned it to you. I've got to get away."

"When?"

"Today. Late tonight. Listen, let's have dinner tonight. Who knows if we'll ever see each other again, right?"

There it was! The perfect program.

"All right," I said. "When?"

"What about nine o'clock? We'll have a drink before dinner. I've got time until midnight. Is that okay with you?"

"Sure. Let me talk to Lillian again."

"Why?"

"I've something else to tell her."

"Yes, Richie?" Now there was fear in her voice.

I said, "Thanks, Lillian. Thank you," and hung up.

It was 11 P.M. The heavy linen drapes were drawn in my suite. The lights were blazing. My brother and I were sitting in comfortable chairs, shirt collars unbuttoned, drinks in our hands. The round top of the coffee table in the main room was of a revolving type. It held a confusion of ashtrays, empty cigarette packages, glasses, several bottles of whisky and soda, an ice-bucket.

"A brother will always be a brother," Werner said, his speech slurred. "I know that now. I can't even hate you because you're taking Lillian from me. We're brothers, right? Odd brothers but brothers just the same. Not even the woman we both love will come between us, right?"

"Right."

"It does hurt, believe me. I'm really doing my damnedest to control myself. Very much so. From now on no more Lillian for me. No more Richie. A damn good reason to really booze it up for old times' sake . . ."

Everything was according to schedule. We had had wine with dinner at 10 P.M. Now we were drinking the whisky Werner had brought to my suite as a present. Six bottles of Scotch in a basket. Enough even for heavier drinkers than we were.

"Shall we call Lillian?" I asked.

"Call who?"

"Lillian. Don't you think we should call her?"

"She'll be asleep."

"Maybe not. I'd like to tell her that we're having a friendly drink here. That you've forgiven us."

"No, don't call her. I'm sure she's sleeping. Don't let's disturb her."

Disturb her as she's packing her suitcases, I thought. Dear, dear Lillian.

"All right. Let's drink to her then." And I refilled our glasses. Sometime soon he would have to slip the sedative into my drink.

"To Lillian!"

"To Lillian," he said.

"You said you were leaving. Where are you going?" I asked.

"Suez. Be there quite some time. Urgent work."

I believed him. He was so damn sure of himself. I remembered that there was an excellent road from Heliopolis through the desert to Suez. With a bit of luck on my side you'll never get there, dear brother, I thought.

I had made cautious inquiries and found out that Werner had paid his bill in the Imperial. His baggage had been taken to the main railroad station, presumably to give the impression that he was leaving by train. The real baggage was probably in the trunk of the Mercedes. Once

Werner had prepared me for his hired killer, he would leave the hotel before the assassin arrived. He would surely have an alibi.

"And what about your ace in the hole, the tapes?" I asked. "Are you taking them with you?"

"With me? I'm not crazy!"

"Well, you can't leave them here, can you?" I insisted.

"Why not? If they're in a good hiding place? Come on, let's have another drink—today is a very important day. I'm going to hand over those tapes to them tonight and they're going to give me my documents."

"Here in Cairo?"

"Here in Cairo . . . before I'm leaving town." He seemed quite intoxicated by now, while I feigned drunkenness. He obviously thought that there was no risk involved in telling me all this since I would be dead before then. "Everything has been arranged—I'm always methodical, always. . . ."

I thought it better not to press the issue of the tapes for the moment. Instead I refilled our glasses. Again we were drinking Scotch as we had on that humid, thunderous afternoon when Werner had suggested that he write my books for me; as we had in Treuwall where he had blackmailed me through the manuscripts of those books. I threw an empty whisky bottle into a wastepaper basket, broke the seal of a full one, then rose and went to the bathroom, leaving the adjoining bedroom door open. I did not switch on the bathroom light but stood behind the bathroom door opposite the mirror and flushed the toilet. Quickly my brother reached into his pocket—I saw it clearly reflected in the mirror—pulled out a box and opened three small envelopes which he took from it. He emptied the powder into the bottle I had opened a moment before. Werner put the Scotch back onto the table, reached for his drink and relaxed in his chair. I returned to the room and finished my drink. My brother's glass was half-empty.

"Refill?" I asked.

"I'll finish this first," he answered.

"Okay." I poured mine from the bottle containing the sedative. I felt Werner watching me as he lit a cigarette. His hands were steady. A very cool murderer. I bent down to put the bottle onto the table and, feigning drunkenness, I knocked it against a well-filled ashtray. Its messy contents spilled over Werner's trousers. He cursed loudly. I jumped up, apologized, and hurried to the bathroom for a towel with which I knelt before Werner, who was trying to clean off his soiled trousers.

"Wait," I said, "cold water'll clean it up in a jiffy. Here, let me." He did. "Hold the fabric taut," I instructed him. He bent forward and did as I had asked. I held the towel in my right hand and rubbed briskly. "Hold it tighter," I said. Werner bent lower, stretching the material even more.

While I was busily cleaning the ash off my brother's trousers with my right, my left hand was searching for one of the handles underneath the table which, when pulled, caused the table to revolve. I pulled a handle and, whirring silently, the table slowly turned a half circle while I instructed Werner how to hold the other trouserleg. It was very simple. He had obviously noticed nothing unusual. My left hand is even more dexterous than my right.

"Well," I said, rising, "that's that," and dropped into my chair. Since the table top had revolved, the drink holding the sedative was now directly in front of Werner. His glass was before me. I had made certain that both glasses held about the same amount of whisky.

"Cheerio," I said, raising my glass.

We drank. The sleeping powder was obviously tasteless. Without qualm but, rather, satisfied I watched my unsuspecting brother gulp down the adulterated whisky, remembering how I had drunk the poisoned tea Delacorte had offered me in the villa somewhere outside Heliopolis. Knocking over the ashtray had been done skillfully. It would have been pretty difficult if I hadn't been ambi-dextrous.

Only a few minutes later my brother's speech became slurred, his eyes heavy. Time to resume questioning him.

"Those tapes," I began. "Will your friends play back all of them before they'll give you your documents?"

"Naturally—they'll have to make sure they're bona fide . . . then I'll get my papers . . . right away . . . tonight. Have to meet them tonight . . . Don't think I ought to drink any more . . ."

"Just one last swallow," I said, raising my glass. He had to drink more! He had to have sufficient sleeping powder! "Cheers, Werner."

"To you, little brother . . ."

I was relieved when he finished his drink. He grinned at me broadly after I had emptied my glass, probably thinking that now he had succeeded.

"Suppose they trick you?" I asked "Suppose they won't return your documents?"

"They'll give them to me all right. They need me. No, I'll get the stuff all right, tonight. I'll even have time to burn it before I go to Suez . . . you know where?"

I shook my head.

He laughed scornfully. "Couldn't find out where the grip was, eh?" He moved with difficulty and extracted a strangely shaped key from his pocket.

"Look . . ." He strained to keep his eyes open. "Know what that's for?"

"No idea."

"Key to a locker in the railroad station. Surprised, eh? That's where the tapes are."

I looked at him admiringly but I was thinking, What a fool he is, how sure of himself. He continued to brag about the "good head" he had on his shoulders.

"Have to just go to the station and open the locker and—" With surprising suddenness he passed out and fell forward in his chair. The key dropped from his hand.

As I jumped up I pocketed it and then took the box of sedatives from Werner's jacket.

I undressed my brother, fetched one of my pajamas, a yellow pair, which I put on him. Werner was as tall as I. I worked hard, pulling him into my bedroom and onto my bed. I covered him. Then as I looked at him lying on his back, a feeling of triumph flooded through me: for once I would prevail over my brother. For once I would be the victor. *I, I, I!*

Hurriedly I picked up his clothing and laid it neatly on a chair. Everything was in order.

I attached the silencer to the .38 which I had had in my jacket. My watch showed five minutes to midnight.

I turned off all the lights in the apartment and went to the bathroom, prepared for a long wait.

One minute after 1 A.M. the doors of suite 907 in the Imperial opened slowly and almost soundlessly.

I heard giggling, then the beam of a flashlight reflected in the bathroom mirror. My brother's murderer had come on time.

Today I know that the Spider organization condoned my brother's intention of murdering me. I am just as certain that, had Werner lived, he would not have escaped further blackmail by that clique; they would not have surrendered his incriminating documents even in exchange for my tape recordings. There is too much that speaks against that possibility. Both Werner and I were kept under surveillance by experts more skillful than the APS personnel. They were also prepared for the possibility that my murder might not take place. My life is one of vivid memories, not many of them pleasant. I remember with particular anger the clever way in which the Spider outfit tricked me after that Indian assassin had done his work: that party in a suite on my floor, the beautiful redhead, apparently drunk, who tore my coat lapel, making identification easy for the friendly crew-cut American I met on the Semiramis Bridge and to whom I later mistakenly passed over, on the plane, those precious tapes; also the comment of the chief of the APS bureau at the Leonardo da Vinci airport. "Perfect organization. Those guys are still the best."

Monday, June 12, 1967.

Today I was permitted to receive my first visitor. Officer Stalling took me to the visitors' room. At the other end was Boris Minski, visibly aged. He stood with bent head, his face pale, the bags under his eyes prominent. Usually well groomed, his appearance now was that of a man who had given in to despair. His gray suit was unpressed, his shirt was crumpled.

He raised his head, looked at me and smiled. His eyes, as always, remained serious. "Hello, Richie!"

"Boris!"

The guard instructed us to sit, facing each other, hands on the table before us.

"I'm glad I can come and see you now," Boris said, once we were seated.

"So am I, Boris. But there's something wrong. Are you ill?"

He looked at me for some moments. Then he said, "I wasn't going to tell you, but if it's so obvious, and since you asked—Rachel is dead."

"Boris!"

"Sit down!" the guard admonished me. "I'm sorry, Herr Mark, but you must remain seated."

I sat down.

"Rachel dead? But how could that be? When? When did she die?"

"December fifth," Minski answered.

December fifth I had been sedated in that house outside Heliopolis. . . .

"But how? What did she die of?"

"Remember when she was assaulted in the garden?"

504

"Yes . . ."

"She had been lying on the cold ground for about half an hour. The head injury wasn't much. That healed very quickly. But then Rachel got a cold. They didn't tell me right away. Thought that antibiotics would take care of that, but she developed pneumonia. The day you left Frankfurt I moved out to the Hornstein Sanatorium and stayed there till the end. Closed the club for a while. The professor and the nurses tried everything. She was delirious for two days. Didn't recognize anyone, not even me. But I was with her until the end. . . ." His voice died away.

I was silent.

The prison guard looked down on his hands.

At last, seeking for words, I said, "Boris, you know how I feel about you. It is terrible—I'm so very sorry . . . I—"

"You can't find words, I know. I can't find any either. Don't let's talk about it. There's nothing anyone can do now. I buried her on the eighth."

A butterfly came to rest before Minski.

"*Agrotis pronuba*," he said automatically, staring at it. "Very tired already."

The butterfly fluttered away.

A long silence ensued.

"What did you do these last six months?" I asked, desperate to talk about something which had no connection with Rachel.

"Worked. The club keeps me busy. I found a substitute for Vanessa too—in Hamburg. Excellent girl. Not her fault business is getting worse. That's the general business climate."

Suddenly, I had forgotten my own precarious situation, seeing Minski huddled, a broken man, a shadow of the friend I knew so well.

"How is Vanessa?" I asked. "Have you heard from her?"

"Sends picture postcards, big ones, from all over the

world. Addressed to both of us. Hugs and kisses. She seems happy, Richie, very happy indeed."

Sunlight suddenly flooded through a heavily barred window of the visitors' room. The butterfly, attracted by the light, crashed against the windowpane, fell to the ground, rose again uncertainly, only to repeat the experience.

"Happy," I snorted, contemptuously. "Nonsense. Happy with that Schalke woman!"

"Believe me, she *is* happy—for the first time in her life probably, she doesn't need men any more. Whatever happened to us, Vanessa is the only one who came out of it happy. And what about you, Richie?"

"I can't complain," I replied. "I'm treated well. People are very nice to me here."

"What about your trial?"

"No date has been set as yet," I said. "Paradin is winding up things in Treuwall, and not only there. I've been very busy putting it all on paper for him."

"I know. He told me."

"The whole mess just snowballed. Might take months. Just the pretrial hearings alone. Even after I've been sentenced they'll need me as witness at other trials. So far no one is quite certain what is going to happen to me. Charges against me have not even been established as yet."

"I'm sure they're not to be sneezed at," Minski said.

"I'm sure of that, too," I agreed. "Next week I'm going to be brought face-to-face with Lillian."

"Paradin told me that, too," Minski said.

Lillian had been in detention pending investigation in Frankfurt following her extradition by Egyptian authorities in March. She had not met with any other misfortune following that night in December 1966 when I had left her bound and drugged in the barn near the racetrack on the island of Gezireh. I had been followed then. They knew

506

where to find Lillian. Yet the Spider organization had purposely ignored her. The Spider seemed content with my murdered brother. The entire affair seemed just another eternal triangle.

I wonder what kind of account Lillian has given so far. Since I know that I'm to see her I sleep poorly. I wonder how she looks, what she might say, how she might treat me. Perhaps I accused her unjustly. Perhaps my brother had not told her the entire truth in Cairo. Perhaps she had not known that Werner had arranged to have me *murdered*. Perhaps—so many mitigating possibilities which might exonerate her. So many possibilities . . .

"Oy vey," Minski said.

"What did you say?"

"The way you look. Just because you're thinking of Lillian."

I was silent.

"You know that you have every reason, every reason to hate this woman."

"Yes," I said. "I also know that I shall always love this woman. Always. Until death."

Minski mumbled something. He avoided looking at me.

"And we had plans, didn't we?" Minski shrugged his shoulders.

"We sure did," I went on. "You had prepared everything so thoroughly, calculated everything."

"Calculated," Minski repeated, his mouth forming a sad smile. "Calculated. Good God, did I miscalculate!"

The sun shone into the room, and the small butterfly continued to fly against the windowpane. It fell, stunned, yet rose again for another effort. Finally, I thought, it would fall to the windowsill and die there. Minski had said that it was already a very tired butterfly.

ABOUT THE AUTHOR

   Johannes Mario Simmel is one of Germany's best-known writers, with a long history of immensely successful novels. Simmel has been an editor on *Quick* magazine, and has written numerous filmscripts. Born in Vienna in 1924, he now lives in Germany. His best-selling novels, at the top of the list in Germany for over a year, *Love Is Just a Word* and *To the Bitter End* were published by McGraw-Hill in 1969 and 1970.

JOHN LeCARRÉ

Take a trip to the world of

ADVENTURE

National Bestsellers from Popular Library

☐	**THE HOLLOW MOUNTAINS**—Oliver B. Patton	$1.95
☐	**THE LANDLADY**—Constance Rauch	$1.75
☐	**NINE MONTHS IN THE LIFE OF AN OLD MAID** Judith Rossner	$1.50
☐	**THE BEST PEOPLE**—Helen Van Slyke	$1.75
☐	**THE CAESAR CODE**—Johannes M. Simmel	$1.95
☐	**THE HEART LISTENS**—Helen Van Slyke	$1.75
☐	**TO THE PRECIPICE**—Judith Rossner	$1.75
☐	**THE COVENANT**—Paige Mitchell	$1.95
☐	**TO KILL A MOCKINGBIRD**—Harper Lee	$1.50
☐	**COMPANIONS ALONG THE WAY**—Ruth Montgomery	$1.75
☐	**THE WORLD BOOK OF HOUSE PLANTS**—E. McDonald	$1.50
☐	**WEBSTER'S NEW WORLD DICTIONARY OF THE AMERICAN LANGUAGE**	$1.75
☐	**WEBSTER'S NEW WORLD THESAURUS**	$1.25
☐	**THE LAST CATHOLIC IN AMERICA**—J. R. Powers	$1.50
☐	**THE HOUSE PLANT ANSWER BOOK**—E. McDonald	$1.50
☐	**INTRODUCTION TO TERRARIUMS** Barbara Joan Grubman	$1.50
☐	**A BRIDGE TOO FAR**—Cornelius Ryan	$1.95
☐	**THE LONGEST DAY**—Cornelius Ryan	$1.75
☐	**THE LAST BATTLE**—Comelius Ryan	$1.95
☐	**FEAR AND LOATHING IN LAS VEGAS** Dr. H. S. Thompson	$1.75

Buy them at your local bookstore or use this handy coupon for ordering:

BOB-56

Popular Library, P.O. Box 5755, Terre Haute, Indiana 47805

Please send me the books I have checked above. I am enclosing $_____
(please add 50c to cover postage and handling). Send check or money order
—no cash or C.O.D.'s please. Orders of 5 books or more postage free.

Mr/Mrs/Miss_____

Address_____

City_____ State/Zip_____

Please allow three weeks for delivery. This offer expires 5/77.